Malpractice in Maggody

Given in memory of:

Martha Potter

Also by Joan Hess
in Large Print:

Martians in Maggody
Muletrain to Maggody
Malice in Maggody
Out on a Limb
The Goodbye Body

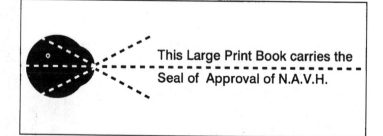

This Large Print Book carries the
Seal of Approval of N.A.V.H.

Malpractice in Maggody

An Arly Hanks Mystery

Joan Hess

Thorndike Press • Waterville, Maine

Copyright © 2006 by Joan Hess

All rights reserved.

This book is a work of fiction. Names, characters, places, and incidents either are products of the author's imagination or are used fictitiously. Any resemblance to actual events or locales or persons, living or dead, is entirely coincidental.

Published in 2006 by arrangement with Simon & Schuster, Inc.

Thorndike Press® Large Print Mystery.

The tree indicium is a trademark of Thorndike Press.

The text of this Large Print edition is unabridged.
Other aspects of the book may vary from the original edition.

Set in 16 pt. Plantin by Al Chase.

Printed in the United States on permanent paper.

Library of Congress Cataloging-in-Publication Data

Hess, Joan.
    Malpractice in Maggody : an Arly Hanks mystery / by Joan Hess.
    p. cm. — (Thorndike Press large print mystery)
    ISBN 0-7862-8368-8 (lg. print : hc : alk. paper)
    1. Hanks, Arly (Fictitious character) — Fiction.
    2. Maggody (Ark. : Imaginary place) — Fiction.
    3. Rehabilitation centers — Fiction.   4. Police — Arkansas
    — Fiction.   5. Police chiefs — Fiction.   6. Policewomen —
    Fiction.   7. Arkansas — Fiction.   8. Large type books.
    I. Title.   II. Thorndike Press large print mystery series.
    PS3558.E79785M33 2006b
    813′.54—dc22   2005034626

For my parents,
Jack and Helen Edmiston,
who encouraged me to read, create,
fantasize, explore, question, travel,
stumble, find my own way, and most
importantly, never give up.

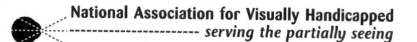
National Association for Visually Handicapped
------------------------- *serving the partially seeing*

As the Founder/CEO of NAVH, the only national health agency solely devoted to those who, although not totally blind, have an eye disease which could lead to serious visual impairment, I am pleased to recognize Thorndike Press★ as one of the leading publishers in the large print field.

Founded in 1954 in San Francisco to prepare large print textbooks for partially seeing children, NAVH became the pioneer and standard setting agency in the preparation of large type.

Today, those publishers who meet our standards carry the prestigious "Seal of Approval" indicating high quality large print. We are delighted that Thorndike Press is one of the publishers whose titles meet these standards. We are also pleased to recognize the significant contribution Thorndike Press is making in this important and growing field.

Lorraine H. Marchi, L.H.D.
Founder/CEO
NAVH

★ Thorndike Press encompasses the following imprints: Thorndike, Wheeler, Walker and Large Print Press.

Acknowledgments

I would like to express my gratitude to Don Beckman, LPC, CADC, of Ozark Guidance, a regional mental health and counseling center, and to Michael S. Goldman, MD, for their willingness to share their knowledge and expertise during what I'm sure they both felt were interminably tedious telephone calls; District County Prosecutor Terry Jones for his advice concerning legal matters; Dorothy Cannell for patiently allowing me to whine when the plot wobbled; and to an anonymous source for information about the machinations of county politics.

Caveat: There are numerous remarks contained within this masterpiece that may lead readers to believe that I am knowledgeable about herbal remedies and vitamin therapy. I am not. The information came from books and websites, and almost none of the products are regulated by the FDA for potency and purity, tested in a scientifically approved manner, or been proven to be effective. And please don't write me about whatever miraculous cure saved you from surgery (or worse). I'm happy for you.

1

❧

"So what do you reckon they're doing?" asked Estelle as she nibbled pensively on a tuna salad sandwich. She and her best friend, Ruby Bee Hanks, were sitting in the front seat of Estelle's station wagon, which was parked under a sickly persimmon tree across the road from what had been, up until three days ago, the county old folks' home. Now bulldozers and backhoes were roaring all around the shabby building, spewing clouds of dust into the bleached blue sky. Dump trucks inched in and out of the surrounding pasture like gimpy dinosaurs, while jackhammers ripped into the asphalt driveway. Stacks of lumber were piled on the scruffy lawn.

Ruby Bee reached into the picnic basket for another deviled egg. "How many times are you aimin' to ask me that? Not one soul in town has any idea what they're doing, not even Mrs. Jim Bob. You'd think, what with her being the mayor's wife, that she'd know something, but she swears she doesn't. Dahlia's fit to be tied since the patients had to be moved out and she and Kevin had to take in her granny."

"I can't say that I blame her. I can't imagine what they'll do after the new baby comes. Eileen says the twins are a handful, running around like ferrets and getting into anything that's not locked up tighter'n a tick." She put her sandwich on the dashboard and refilled her cup with iced tea from a thermos. "Want some more?"

"Take a look at that," said Ruby Bee, ignoring the offer. "That must be the limousine Lottie and Eula saw yesterday evening. Lottie said she expected the president or somebody like that to climb out. Turned out to be an ordinary-looking man."

Estelle patted her beehive of red hair to make sure no bobby pins were dangling, then said, "What say we just drive right over there and ask him what he thinks he's doing, closing down the old folks' home like that? We should tell him right to his face what a terrible thing he did."

"Hush up," Ruby Bee whispered as she leaned forward. "He's getting out of the backseat."

"You think he can hear us all the way over here? Did Lottie say he was a superhero with X-ray hearing?"

"Well, he ain't wearing tights and a cape," Ruby Bee said drily. "Those sunglasses make him look suspicious, though."

Estelle snorted. "Maybe he's wearing them on account of it being sunny. I'd be wearing mine if I hadn't lost them at that flea market at Bugscuffle last week. I took 'em off and set 'em down for five seconds while I looked at a teapot. The next thing I know, they're gone. I think that old lady with the wart on her forehead scooped 'em up. I was of a mind to grab her and —"

"I'd say he's more than six feet tall, wouldn't you? Nice silver hair, maybe in his fifties or a tad older, tanned like one of those Hollywood folks. The man that he's talking to must be the foreman."

They watched, as enthralled as children in front of a TV cartoon show, as the two men pointed at this and that, unrolled and consulted a blueprint, and then disappeared into the dust. The driver of the limo climbed out of the front seat, took off his hat, and loosened his tie. He seemed content to lean against the fender and wait.

"Well!" said Estelle. "What do you think about that?"

Ruby Bee wiped her fingers on a napkin and closed the lid of the picnic basket. "I think I'd better get back to the bar & grill and start supper. Didn't you say you have a three o'clock appointment to cut Millicent's hair?"

"We ought to do something."

"Like get ourselves arrested for trespassing? You see all those signs, don't you?"

"Just who do you think is going to arrest us? Arly's not supposed to get back to town until the next weekend." Estelle reluctantly started the engine and maneuvered until the station wagon was headed back toward the sorry excuse for a highway that curled through Maggody. "You heard from her?"

"I already told you that I haven't. Maybe you should get yourself some of that X-ray hearing, Estelle Oppers. You know perfectly well that she and that fellow from Springfield went camping up at Tablerock Lake. How's she supposed to find a telephone out there in the woods? You think there's a pay phone on every pine tree?"

"It seems to me she might have called when they went into town for supplies," Estelle countered.

"She told me she wouldn't call unless it was from an emergency room." Ruby Bee tried not to sigh as they passed the construction site. "It's only ten days, for pity's sake. I wish I knew more about the fellow, though.

She's being too secretive, if you ask me. But I'm her mother, and I can tell something serious is going on between them. What if they was to get married and she moves to Springfield?"

Estelle patted her friend's knee. "Arly's got more sense than all the Buchanons put together. She's already gone through one disastrous marriage. She won't rush into anything without thinking long and hard about it."

"Or so I'd like to think," murmured Ruby Bee, blinking back a tear.

Brother Verber, spiritual leader of the Voice of the Almighty Lord Assembly Hall's motley collection of saints and sinners (with a darn sight more falling in the latter category), was lying on the sofa in the silver trailer that served as the rectory, thinking about his upcoming Sunday sermon. A fan stirred the sour air. On the coffee table, a box of saltine crackers and a jar of peanut butter were next to the bottle of sacramental wine that he always kept nearby to inspire him. It wasn't like there was a shortage of possible topics for a sermon, he thought, but he'd just spent a couple of months working through the list of the seven deadly sins (and a few others of his own creation), and it would be nice to come up with fresh material. Something so startling that those who tended to nod off would sit up straight. Something that'd make 'em squirm.

Maybe, what with it being summer, it was time to remind the teenagers and their parents of the wickedness taking place on blankets alongside Boone Creek. The lust and depravity of supple young bodies writhing away like dogs in heat, moaning and groaning, their hands groping —

The sound of a car door slamming jerked him out of his reverie. He hastily twisted the cap on the wine bottle and shoved it under the couch as the front door opened.

"Brother Verber?" called Mrs. Jim Bob (aka Barbara Ann Buchanon Buchanon) as she marched into the living room. She stopped and looked down at him, her lips pinched. "What's the matter with you? Your face is red, and you're sweating. Are you coming down with a summer cold?"

He fished a handkerchief out of his pocket and mopped his face. "No, but I appreciate you asking so kindly. I was working on my Sunday sermon."

"You have more important work to do right now," she said as she sat down on the edge of a chair.

"Is someone hovering on the brink of

eternal damnation? Do I need to grab my Bible and go rescue this stray lamb before he falls into Satan's evil clutches?" He began to fumble for his shoes and socks.

"This is far more important. Are you aware of what's going on out at the old folks' home?"

Brother Verber blew his nose while he tried to guess what he was expected to say. "Well," he began slowly, "I know the county closed it this last weekend and told the old folks that they'd have to get out. I heard some of them were moved to a nursing home in Starley City, and a few others went back to their families. Petrol Buchanon supposedly snuck off to stay with his brother Diesel in that cave up on Cotter's Ridge."

Mrs. Jim Bob gave him an exasperated look. "That is not what I meant, Brother Verber. Have you driven by there in the last two days?"

"I don't recollect that I have. Is there some reason I should have, Sister Barbara?"

"This morning Millicent and Eula came by my house for coffee and cinnamon rolls and told me I ought to go see for myself, so I did. I couldn't believe my eyes!"

He recoiled like she'd slapped him upside the head. "You don't mean they're planning to turn it into — into one of those brothels with red flocked wallpaper and chandeliers and bleached blond hussies fitted out in tight dresses, do you? Why, every pathetic sinner in the county will be fighting to get in the doorway! Afore long, there'll be a casino with gambling, and theaters showing pornographic movies all night long. There'll be drunken louts staggering down the street, insulting the refined ladies of Maggody with foul language and lewd invitations."

"I don't believe I said anything like that," said Mrs. Jim Bob, perplexed. "I have no idea what's going on at the old folks' home, except for all manner of delivery trucks and heavy machinery coming and going. While I was watching, a van from a plumbing company arrived, and not a minute later a fancy convertible pulled up and out got a woman with an armload of carpet samples. I'm not one to judge, but she was wearing an unseemly short skirt and high-heeled shoes."

"Were the carpet samples scarlet?" asked Brother Verber as he blotted his neck.

"I couldn't see through all the dust. Are you sure you're not running a fever?"

He slipped off the couch and kneeled in front of the coffee table. "No, Sister Barbara, I was thinking of those weak-willed men in my congregation. Won't you pray with me to give them strength to resist the temptations they may face?" He clutched his hands together, closed his eyes, and began to mumble under his breath.

Mrs. Jim Bob stood up and brushed at the wrinkles in her navy skirt. It was obvious that he wasn't going to be any help, so she left and went out to her pink Cadillac. It was her only concession to vanity, but she'd repeatedly assured herself that she had a duty as the mayor's wife to own the biggest car in Maggody, as well as the finest house. There were Bibles in every bedroom and booklets of daily inspirations in every bathroom, along with little baskets of potpourri and pine-scented candles. She'd redecorated her living room so many times that she couldn't at that moment recall what color it was. As she drove home, she was thinking she might ought to buy some of those glossy magazines so she'd have some new ideas for the next time she caught Jim Bob fooling around with some floozy at the Pot O' Gold trailer park.

"I'm thinking I might as well kill myself," said Dahlia through a mouthful of chocolate cream pie. She was sitting at her mother-in-law's kitchen table, watching Eileen do the dishes. Kevin and the twins were in the living room with his pa, where a NASCAR race was blaring on TV. The twins, not yet two years old, were likely to be ripping pages out of gun magazines or gnawing on the furniture. Only that morning she'd caught Kevvie Junior chewing so fiercely on a wooden mixing spoon that he'd got a splinter in his lip. Rose Marie wasn't any better, having mangled one of her Barbie dolls till it was down to one leg and half an arm. The doctor at the clinic told her they were teething, but Dahlia figured they were going plumb crazy, same as she was.

"Why do you say that?" asked Eileen as she began to scrub a pot.

"It's my granny. We had no choice but to take her in with us. She demanded the twins' bedroom, so we moved the baby beds into ours. Now there ain't hardly enough room to get dressed. What's more, Granny snores so loudly the whole house shakes. Kevin's taken to sleeping on the porch swing. What with the twins fussing, her snoring, and me having to pee every fifteen minutes, I ain't had a decent night's sleep since I can remember. I can't nap during the day, neither, because Granny creeps into the kitchen and starts trying to cook something. Yesterday she put a pound of bacon in the skillet, turned up the heat, and then went and got herself locked in the bathroom. The grease caught fire, and it was a miracle the house didn't burn down."

Somehow Dahlia had managed to finish a piece of pie during her recitation, and was reaching for the pie plate when Eileen caught her wrist. "Dahlia, you know perfectly well what the doctor told you. You have to be real careful during this pregnancy so you don't get diabetes like the last time."

Dahlia reluctantly pulled back her hand. "I might as well die happy," she muttered. She looked down at the tent dress that covered all three hundred plus pounds of her and spotted a dribble of chocolate cream. She scooped it up with her finger and furtively snuck it into her mouth as Eileen turned away. "I don't suppose you and Pa might consider . . ."

"We are not going to have your granny move in with us, if that's what you were about to say. Won't her Social Security and Medicaid pay for that nursing home?"

"They would, but some smarmy lady from there did an evaluation and said they wouldn't take her. All I can hope is that she goes up on Cotter's Ridge to hunt for ginseng and a bear eats her. I know that ain't the Christian thing to say, but it's true."

Eileen glanced over her shoulder. "I may

have felt the same thing after Earl's pa moved in with us."

"At least he had the decency to die. My granny's probably going to be bitching and whining when the twins graduate from high school." She paused, her chins rippling as she thought. "Arly had no business going off like she did. She sure better do something when she gets back."

"If she can," said Eileen, who was thinking about what it'd be like to spend a week camping next to a lake with nothing to do but read or gaze at the water. Earl was not in the picture, having been eaten by a bear several days earlier.

Sitting at a table in the back of Roy Stiver's Antiques Store: New & Used, Jim Bob was thinking about his two pairs, tens and threes. He glanced slyly at Roy, who put down his cards and entwined his fingers over his ample belly. The sumbitch was impossible to read. Larry Joe Lambertino, on the other hand, was a mite twitchy as he stared at his cards through thick glasses. Could be on account of having three-of-a-kind or a straight, or maybe working up the guts to bluff.

Jim Bob refilled his glass with whiskey, took a gulp, and said, "How 'bout a two-dollar raise just to keep you ol' boys honest?"

"Why, Jim Bob, you know I'm as honest as the day is long," drawled Roy as he pushed his cards away and stood up. "I reckon I'd better go see a man about a horse. There's another plate of baloney sandwiches in the icebox. Help yourselves."

Larry Joe started to rise, but Jim Bob snarled, "Did you come to play cards or to stuff your face? Two dollars to stay in. You gonna hold 'em or fold 'em?"

"Oh, okay," said Larry Joe, settling back down. He unwadded some ones and tossed them into the pot. He was as tall and lanky as Roy was short and round; his height served him well when he bawled out the morons in his shop classes at the high school. It didn't help at home, though. Joyce didn't even come up to his shoulder, but she had a way of narrowing her eyes and swishing her ponytail that pretty much got her whatever she wanted.

Jim Bob spread his cards. "Read 'em and weep."

"Three jacks," Larry Joe said apologetically as he gathered up the pot.

"So, Mr. Mayor, what do you know about all this construction at the old folks' home?" asked Roy as he came out of the bathroom.

"Not a damn thing. It's county property, so they can do whatever they want with it. They sure as hell aren't wasting any time, are they? I drove out that way this morning, and from all I could tell, they could be building a pyramid to bury some asshole county commissioner."

"I parked down by the low-water bridge and walked along the edge of the pasture," volunteered Larry Joe. "Looks like they're keeping the front part of the building, and taking down the backside, along with some sheds. They've already started pouring concrete for a foundation for a good-sized addition. It also looks like they're aimin' to fence in two or three acres."

Roy reached for the whiskey bottle. "Something mighty peculiar's going on out there, mighty peculiar."

"Shut up and deal," said Jim Bob, still smarting from the last hand. He knew he might as well make the most of the afternoon, since there'd be hell to pay when he went home for supper (or dinner, as Mrs. Jim Bob insisted on calling it). If she'd stopped by the supermarket and learned that he wasn't there, she'd assume right off the bat he'd gone to comfort some lonely trucker's wife. Which he did whenever the opportunity arose. Admitting he'd been playing poker all afternoon wouldn't sit much better. At least there was a decent baseball game on later. If he was feeling generous, he'd invite her to watch it with him.

"I can't tell you what's going on out there because I don't know myself," said Sheriff Harvey Dorfer for the umpteenth time that afternoon, wishing he could rip the telephone cord out of the wall. "All I can suggest is that you call over to the county courthouse and ask them." He listened to more squawks, then said, "Yes, ma'am, I am the county sheriff. My job is to catch criminals and lock them up. The only dealings I have with the quorum court concern my budget and the possibility of building a new jail. I can assure you, ma'am, that if it happens, it won't be in your backyard. Have yourself a real nice day."

He replaced the receiver, took a swallow of tepid coffee, and bellowed, "LaBelle, get your butt in here right now!"

LaBelle, the dispatcher and receptionist, came to his office door. "I was meaning to have a word with you, Sheriff Dorfer. I'm gonna take off early today so I can go by the bakery and pick up some little cakes for my niece's baby shower."

"I thought I told you not to put any more of these damnfool calls about the old folks' home through to me." He lit a cigar and gazed at her through a billow of pungent smoke. "Was there something in my order that mystified you, LaBelle? Should I have repeated it two or three times, and then asked if you had any questions?"

"I already told you that I do not lie," LaBelle said snippily. "We are both employees of Stump County and have an obligation to serve the public."

"Put one more call through and you won't be an employee of this or any other county. However, to save you from the grief of having to lie, I'm leaving now to track down criminals fishing without a license or polluting our scenic lakes by throwing beer cans overboard."

"I told you that I have to leave right away."

"When's the baby due?"

LaBelle stiffened. "I don't rightly see that it's any of your business. What's more, I have already paid for the cakes from the bakery."

Harve was about to suggest what she could do with 'em when the telephone rang. He glared at LaBelle, then picked up the receiver.

"What?" He then held the receiver away from his ear so LaBelle could hear the snarly threats. When the voice ran down, he said, "Listen, T-Rex, I don't know what's going to happen to the old folks' home. This is the quorum court's doing, not mine. From what I heard, they met last week and voted to sell the property. Why don't you go over to the county courthouse and ask the clerk if any papers have been filed?"

LaBelle waggled her fingers and fled to the front room. After pushing a button on her phone that would automatically transfer all calls to Harve, she grabbed her purse and headed for the parking lot.

And so it went in Maggody, Arkansas (population 755 or thereabouts). For the next week, construction proceeded at a boggling rate in and around the former county old folks' home. The new addition rose almost overnight, and truckloads of immigrants appeared to pound in shingles on the roof. Exterior walls were going up as interior walls from the older section were being torn out and thrown into Dumpsters. Plumbers, electricians, carpenters, painters, and wallpaper hangers arrived early and left late. No one had spotted the limo again, but the woman in the convertible came daily. The grounds around the structure were enclosed by an eight-foot chain link fence topped with curls of barbed wire. A dozen flatbed trucks from a landscaping service delivered pallets of sod, followed by thick shrubs and good-sized trees that required special machinery to plant.

But most intriguing of all, a uniformed security guard had been assigned to prevent any unauthorized person or persons from so much as setting foot on the property. He had a clipboard in his hand, a gun strapped to his belt, and a bad-tempered German shepherd on a leash.

2

As I drove past the city limit sign into Maggody early Saturday afternoon, I could swear I heard a heavy metal door (the kind used in maximum-security prisons) slam shut behind me. There was no point in looking in the rearview mirror. When I got back to my so-called efficiency apartment above the antiques store, I dumped everything out of my duffel bag, including clothes, a can of bug spray, a deck of cards, withered wildflowers, and a couple of books I'd been meaning to read since 'long about high school. I stuffed the dirty clothes into a pillowcase and headed down the rickety wooden steps to the Suds of Fun Launderette across the road. I was moving furtively, since I knew my arrival back in Maggody would be shooting sparks along the grapevine — which happens to run right through the middle of Ruby Bee's Bar & Grill. It's a wonder the two-steppers don't end up in a pile of flailing arms and legs on the dance floor.

Cinatra Buchanon was behind the counter, swatting flies with a rolled-up tabloid. The blotches on the newsprint indicated a high rate of success. She glanced up and then, having assured herself I wasn't an armed robber with a fetish for quarters, returned to her business.

"Can you give me some change?" I asked as I pulled a couple of dollar bills from my pocket.

"Reckon so." She put down the tabloid and opened the cash register. "Back in town, are you?"

"Looks like it."

She eyed my bulging pillowcase. "You didn't take much in the way of clothes, considering you was gone for two weeks. Did you go to one of those nudist camps where everybody runs around buck-naked?"

"Just ordinary camping," I said. "Shorts, a pair of jeans, T-shirts, a bathing suit, and a sweatshirt. It can get nippy by the lake at night."

"No pajamas?" she asked slyly.

"It was the darndest thing. I took three flannel nightgowns, but somehow, beavers got in my tent and dragged them away. A few days later, I saw where they'd gnawed them into strips and used them to reinforce a dam. I wish I'd had a camera with me."

Cinatra's eyes widened. "Why, I bet you could have sold photographs to one of those newspapers like the *Weekly World*. Just imagine — beavers stealing nightgowns! I never heard of such a thing!"

We both shook our heads at the loss of this potential windfall, then she gave me a handful of quarters and I retreated to the back of the room. I managed to cram everything into two machines, and was thumbing through an ancient copy of *Field and Stream* when Ruby Bee, who happens to be my mother as well as proprietor of the aforementioned bar & grill, came marching in.

"And just when did you get back, missy?" she demanded.

"About half an hour ago."

"It didn't occur to you that I've been chewing on my nails for most of two weeks, waiting to hear about this camping trip? Were you planning to buy a postcard at the supermarket and mail it to me so I'd know you were back?"

Although the idea appealed, I said, "No, I was planning to do my laundry, stop by the PD to check the mail and messages, and then go over to the bar for a cold beer and a grilled cheese sandwich, followed by a slice of pie."

29

"So your dirty underwear is more important than your own flesh and blood? Do you know how many diapers I changed before you was finally potty-trained? How many nights I walked the floor with you while you howled like a coyote pup? How many biscuits I've made and motel rooms I've cleaned so you'd have a decent place to live? Is this how you show your gratitude?"

I could see from the corner of my eye that Cinatra was thoroughly enjoying the exchange. I lowered my voice and said, "I ought to be there in an hour, unless you're getting ready to tell me about fresh corpses stacked behind the remains of the Esso station or an invasion of little silver men with big almond-shaped eyes. In that case, I'll throw aside this magazine, collect my gun at the PD, and come out blazing."

Ruby Bee blinked. "Well, nothing that serious, but there's something real strange going on out on County 104. Everybody in town's all atwitter about it."

"If they've been twittering for two weeks they can twitter for another hour. I'll be over there as soon as I can."

She huffed at me, but when I merely picked up the magazine, she spun around and marched out with the same indignation, giving Cinatra a dirty look for good measure. Ruby Bee was short and comfortably plump, with the benign countenance of a grandmother, but there were plenty of truckers and good ol' boys who'd learned not to rile her unless they wanted to find themselves sprawled in the gravel in front of the bar & grill.

After I'd finished my laundry, I dropped it off at my apartment and walked over to the PD. The two rooms were stifling. I opened both windows and the back door before I settled down at my desk to sift through the mail. It consisted of flyers and catalogs, with only one letter from some organization that no doubt had overestimated both my salary and my charitable instincts. I hit the evil eye of the answering machine, then fast-forwarded through dozens of incoherent messages that seemed to concern the old folks' home. Sheriff Dorfer hadn't called, since I'd warned him about my vacation.

Of course I hadn't told him any details, and I had no intention of elaborating for Ruby Bee and Estelle, either. Jack Wallace was a very interesting man — tall, loose-limbed, with a slow grin and just a hint of shagginess that intrigued me. Divorced, with two children. Even when he and I had first met under less than ideal circumstances — I'd mistakenly suspected him of kidnapping one of our teenage girls at a neglected woodland retreat with the unlikely name of Camp Pearly Gates — I'd found myself nurturing adolescent fantasies unbecoming to a woman (and a chief of police, to boot) in her early thirties. On our second encounter here in Maggody, the town had been overrun by Civil War reenactors, but Jack and I managed to find time for a few games of Scrabble.

Interpret that as you prefer.

Then two weeks at the lake, in a leaky tent, eating steaks and canned beans and cornbread, sometimes talking until dawn, other times doing a lot less talking.

I had a pretty good idea how I felt about him, but I wasn't worried about it. We'd both had bad marriages, so we weren't about to scamper off to a wedding chapel in Vegas, or even to city hall to hunt up a judge. I knew Ruby Bee was in a dither, torn between the fear of me leaving Maggody and the allure of seeing me as a respectable married woman producing grandchildren on a regular basis.

As I walked across the dance floor and sat down on a stool, Ruby Bee looked as though she was restraining herself from leaping over the bar. Estelle was at the opposite end on her favorite perch, convenient to the ladies' room and situated so she could keep an eye on the booths along the wall. She could also, if she craned her neck, see who all was sneaking around the Flamingo Motel out back. Privacy's hard to come by in a town the size of Maggody; as a teenager, I'd gotten away with very little — which is why I'd gotten away as soon as I'd graduated from high school. After college, the police academy, several years in psychotically sophisticated Manhattan, and the divorce, I'd discovered that you can go home again. It's not, however, something I'd recommend to the faint of heart. Manhattan to Maggody is one helluva hop, skip, and jump.

"It's about time you got here," said Estelle, lifting her chin so she could stare down her nose at me. "You don't know what's going on, do you?"

"Not even if it's been on the front page of the *Starley City Shopper*," I said, "or on CNN, for that matter. I do know roughly what time the sun sets, how many incompetent boaters run out of gas on the lake every day, and the best remedy for chigger bites. I know that if you don't keep your food locked in the trunk of the car, the racoons will get it. I'll bet you didn't know that the damn varmints can open a jar of peanut butter."

Ruby Bee set down a mug of beer in front of me. "Estelle is referring to the county old folks' home."

"A fire?" I asked. "An epidemic? Have there been deaths out there?"

"There is no 'out there,' " Ruby Bee said, somewhat appeased by the seriousness of my reaction. "They tore it down."

"They didn't exactly tear it down." Estelle reached behind the bar and found her private stash of sherry. "Not all of it, anyway. The front part's still there, but the backside is new. And the yard is something to behold, or it was until they planted all these bushes and trees so you can't see much from behind the fence."

"Fence?" I said.

Ruby Bee grimaced. "A sight taller than Booker Tee Buchanon, and topped with barbed wire. Now there's the guard with a gun and a dog. I heard that a couple of the teenagers went over one night and darn near got their butts chewed off just for looking around. I won't mention any names, but I heard Darla Jean and Billy Dick are sitting real gingerly on the picnic tables in front of the Dairee Dee-Lishus."

I was beyond bewilderment. "And the residents?"

"They was shuffled away, most of 'em to a

nursing home in Starley City. Dahlia's granny is back at home, and nobody's real sure about Petrol. One of the old ladies got into a scuffle and fell and broke her hip. An ambulance took her to the hospital in Farberville. Mrs. Pimlico, who was the supervisor, got a job at a tattoo parlor in Branson. The aide, Vonetta, ran off with a one-legged truck driver."

I took a gulp of beer. "So what's going on out there?"

"That's what you're supposed to find out," said Estelle. "Nobody here knows anything, not even Jim Bob. I took it upon myself to call Sheriff Dorfer, but he just barked at me and banged down the phone." Her eyes narrowed as she crunched down on a pretzel. "He'd better hope folks don't recollect his behavior when election time rolls around."

"Has anybody just gone out there and asked?" I said.

Ruby Bee rolled her eyes. "Weren't you listening when I said there was a guard? He stands right at the road with a clipboard. If your name's not on it, you can't so much as turn around in the driveway. He doesn't even speak English." She took a breath and stared at me. "So that's why you need to stop sitting around on your behind and go out there to investigate. You are the chief of police, unless I missed something."

"County 104 is not in my jurisdiction," I said, shaking my head. "Whatever's going on out there is county business."

She leaned forward. "If you're planning to have supper here tonight — pot roast, fried okra, collard greens, and lemon meringue pie — you'd better go put on your uniform and your badge and find out. The same goes for breakfast tomorrow. I'm serving fresh blueberry pancakes, along with bacon, ham, fried eggs, grits, and biscuits with cream gravy. 'Course you can always get a burrito at the Dairee Dee-Lishus if you want to."

"No, she can't," chimed in Estelle. "The surly Mexican that owns it went on a month-long vacation to his niece's wedding. The teenagers still hang out on the picnic tables, but they have to buy sodas at the supermarket or bring them from home."

"This is blackmail," I said coldly.

"No," said Ruby Bee, who watches way too many crime shows on TV, "it's more like extortion. If you want to live on canned soup and baloney sandwiches, it's up to you. You can stand to lose a few pounds after all those steaks and potatoes at Tablerock Lake."

"And peanut butter sandwiches," Estelle added.

Without a word, I pushed aside my beer and left. I almost mowed down Fibber Buchanon at the door, but he had enough sense to get out of my way. Having never been a prosecutor (or watched the right shows), I didn't know if what had been presented was blackmail or extortion, but I wasn't pleased with either. And I was damn fond of fried okra, as Ruby Bee knew too well.

By the time I reached my apartment, all three hundred square feet of it, I'd calmed down. At least I hadn't been grilled about my week with Jack. I knew I would be eventually. Ruby Bee and Estelle were talented inquisitioners who would utilize their skills to leave no rock unturned, be it a pebble or the size of Gibraltar. It was the price I'd have to pay for blue plate specials and cold beer. I put on my uniform and my shiny badge that looked as though it had come from a cereal box, repinned my dark hair back into a bun, considered and then rejected the idea of lipstick, and drove out to County 104.

Once I saw the chaos of the construction site, I pulled over to plan my approach. A red brick wall was being constructed across the front, with an opening for a driveway paved with matching brick and lined with flower beds and low shrubs. Trucks and vans were parked both inside and along the edge of the county road. Workmen scampered around like agitated elves.

As promised, a guard in a uniform was standing at the foot of the driveway. A German shepherd was seated on its haunches, doing nothing more ominous than watching the mockingbirds in a tree. It was, however, a very large dog, which meant it probably had very large teeth.

I put on my best cop expression and walked across the road. "I'm Chief of Police Arly Hanks," I said, smiling politely. "And you are . . . ?"

He consulted a clipboard. *"No se le permite entrar a esta propiedad."*

I shrugged and said, "Sorry, but I don't speak Spanish. Now if you don't mind, I'll just go up there and find someone who can answer my questions."

"Tengo mis órdenes. Usted debe irse ahora."

The guard, who was hardly a rough-and-tough bandito stereotype, looked no happier than I about the situation. He was short, pudgy, and in his very early twenties. He tried not to stare at my badge, but the tiny wisp of a beard on his chin was quivering and sweat was beading on his forehead. Had it not been for the dog, I would have patted him on the shoulder and continued past him.

"I need to speak to a supervisor," I said slowly, hoping the final word might sound familiar to him.

"No puedo ayudarle. Esta es propiedad privada."

As I took a tentative step forward, the dog growled. I stepped back. Spanish classes had never been offered at the local high school, since most of the students were in dire need of English. Very few of the backwoods Buchanons are familiar with the concept of conjugating verbs, and their vocabulary, although picturesque, focuses on anatomically improbable barnyard activities. I couldn't remember any English teachers who'd stayed for a full school year; the majority of them lasted only a few weeks before disappearing.

"Por favor, señorita," he continued, looking as if he might cry. *"Mi perro está muy nervioso. Usted debe irse ahora."*

The conversation was going nowhere. I'd deciphered enough of his remarks to agree that the dog was indeed nervous, and although the guard might buckle if I shoved him aside, the dog would not. At this point, however, I was just as curious as the rest of Maggody to know what was going on behind the red brick wall. But it was not in my jurisdiction, I reminded myself sternly. I had no more right than Ruby Bee and Estelle to storm the site and demand an explanation. Sheriff Dorfer did have the right, but he either wasn't interested or wasn't telling.

"Arly!" bellowed a voice behind me.

A familiar voice, to my regret. I turned around and walked across the road to where Jim Bob had parked his pickup truck. He'd already climbed out and was leaning against the door, his arms crossed and his eyes slitted. He had some of the characteristics of the Buchanon clan — apish brow, sallow complexion to match yellow-tinged eyes, thick lips — but he was among the wilier ones. Others were easily mesmerized by inanimate objects.

"Mr. Mayor," I said without enthusiasm.

"I hope you found out what the hell's going on over there."

"Since when did I get appointed to the welcome committee? Why don't you go over and introduce yourself to the gentleman and his dog?"

Jim Bob sneered. "The spic don't speak

English, that's why. Just trot your sorry ass back over there and show him your badge."

"I've already tried that," I said as I leaned against the back fender. "Did you call Harve?"

" 'Course I did, and more than once. That smart-mouthed dispatcher keeps saying he went fishing. Heard you did, too, but not by yourself."

"How kind of you to take a personal interest in me, Jim Bob. I never would have suspected you might care what I do while I'm on vacation. I feel like I ought to give you a big ol' hug."

"Try it and you'll find yourself ripping out gizzards at a poultry-processing outfit," he said. "I don't give a rat's ass what you do on your own time, but now you'd better start earning your salary."

Believe it or not, this was one of our more amicable conversations. "You know as well as I do that this is outside my jurisdiction. What have you heard?"

"Pretty much everything, from it being a whorehouse to a federal prison for white-collar criminals. Idalupino says someone told her it was bought by a cult, one of those groups with shaved heads. Mrs. Jim Bob's second cousin Antsy Buchanon has been telling everybody it's one of those places where they cut off dead people's heads and freeze them. Roy's hoping for a spa so he can sit in a mud bath all day." He paused to scratch his head. "I told him to go find a patch of mud alongside Boone Creek. Wouldn't cost him anything, neither."

"Presuming it's none of those, what do you think?" I asked, not because he was insightful but because he'd been around the previous week and I hadn't.

"Mrs. Jim Bob and her gaggle of friends have been keeping an eye on it, and they saw some pretty fancy stuff being lugged inside. Lots of carpet, wallpaper, and porcelain bathroom fixtures, paint, tiles, gym equipment, and heavy-duty kitchen appliances. Larry Joe said they were digging a swimming pool."

"It could be a spa," I said.

"Out in the middle of nowhere? It's not like Farberville's packed with rich broads with nothing better to do than get pedicures."

"A private residence, maybe?"

He resumed scratching his head. "Mrs. Jim Bob ain't gonna like that, even if it's not actually in Maggody. Gawd, I'll probably have to put in a swimming pool, only bigger than whatever they've got, and hire some moron like Kevin to stand at the bottom of the hill to keep gawkers from trespassing. Now how in hell's name am I supposed to pay for that?"

"Try doubling the price of canned corn," I said, more interested in the limousine that was moving slowly toward us, the driver justifiably worried about ruts and potholes. The windows were tinted so darkly that anybody, from a general in full ceremonial drag to a street mime, could have been sipping champagne in the back. "Know anything about that?"

"It showed up a couple of weeks ago, and again last week."

We stayed where we were, watching as it turned into the driveway. The guard snapped to attention, but stopped short of saluting. The dog stared balefully, as if it knew who was paying for its daily ration of kibble. Once the limousine was out of sight, the guard turned back and glared at us.

Jim Bob poked my arm. "Go over there and find out who it is."

"You're the mayor," I said as I moved out of range. "You go over there and find out who it is. I'll wait right here in case I need to drag your bloodied carcass across the road and toss it on the flatbed of your truck."

"It's only a dog, fercrissake. Didn't they

teach you how to handle dogs at the police academy?"

"Short of climbing a tree, no. You got any beer?"

He opened a cooler that was conveniently located on the passenger's side of the cab. He thrust a beer at me, then opened one for himself. "You allowed to drink on duty, Miss Chief of Police?"

"You allowed to park out in front of the Airport Arms Apartments on Saturday nights and scuttle up to the second floor, Mr. Mayor?"

He chugged half his beer. "Ain't none of your damn business."

We resumed watching the activity across the road. Surveillance has never been one of my more popular pastimes, and standing in the hot sun as dust blew over us was only marginally tolerable. After a while, Jim Bob fetched another couple of beers and mutely tossed one to me. The guard was now gazing longingly at us, but I doubted he could be bribed while the boss was on the premises.

"This is ridiculous," I said at last. I lobbed the empty beer can into the back of his truck. "I'm going to go take a shower and find an air-conditioned haven. If you get invited across the road for wine and cheese, take notes so you can call me later and tell me about it."

He crumpled his beer can. "Yeah, I got better things to do than stand here like a fence post so cowbirds can shit on me."

We got into our respective vehicles and left without so much as a peck on the cheek. Hizzonor and I prefer to maintain a professional relationship — when we're not cussin' up a storm at each other, anyway.

By the time Vincent Stonebridge reached his home in Malibu, it was nearly eight. He showered and put on a thick robe, poured himself a drink, and listened to messages on his answering machine while he gazed at the last of the surfers dragging their boards along the beach. Most of the callers were women — but not patients, since cosmetic surgeons were not on call during weekends. Pity the poor ob-gyns who delivered babies seven days — and nights — a week. What kind of a social life could one lead if one were continually interrupted? Besides, none of his patients could call him at home, weekend or not. If the clinic was closed, callers were directed to make an appointment during office hours or, in a crisis, head for an emergency room. Since Vince no longer had hospital privileges in the area, he was never called in to take over a case. And if truth be known, he no longer had any patients, since he'd transferred all of them to his partners until certain sticky issues were resolved in court or by his insurance company.

He remained at the window for a few more minutes, then refreshed his drink and went into his office. After looking over the notes he'd made on the return flight and making a few additions, he picked up the telephone and punched in a familiar number.

"Randall," he said when the call was answered, "I just wanted to give you an update. You're not busy, are you?"

Randall Zumi was not busy, and rarely was so outside of his office hours. Weekends, unless he was on call, were interminable exercises in tedium. "No, Vince, just watching a video. How was your trip?"

"Tiresome, of course," said Vince, "but certainly more bearable than commercial flights. I don't know how those bovines survive standing in long lines and being frisked by pompous jerks posing as airport security. You really ought to look into a private jet, Randall."

"I can't afford to buy a jet. These days I'm squeezing the last dollop out of the toothpaste tube."

Vince hid his annoyance. "Randall, we've been over this time and again. Yes, your initial investment was substantial, as was mine, but a year from now we'll be home free. You don't have to trust me on this, my boy. You've got the figures. Once we're operating at full capacity, we'll be showing a net profit of at least three million dollars a year. Half of that will be yours. With a little creative accounting and prudent financial management, you'll be rolling in it. You've got to keep the overall picture in mind."

"The overall picture is I'm up to my neck in debt," Randall said with a sigh. "I've mortgaged my house, emptied my pension fund, sold all the stocks and bonds in my personal account, and borrowed money from my father-in-law. I have two hundred dollars in my checking account. I should never have gotten into this crazy scheme in the first place."

"Well, it's too late to back out now. If I could, I'd juggle the numbers and get you some cash, but it's risky when you're dealing with hard-nosed contractors and suppliers. Tell you what, Randall, I'll send you a personal check to tide you over."

"Thanks, but I'll get by, presuming we can start drawing salaries next month." Randall did not add that the last check he'd received from Vince had bounced so hard it had yet to fall back to earth. "Toothpaste is supposed to be nutritious."

Vince chuckled. "That's the spirit, and I can assure you that our so-called salaries will be a hell of a lot more than what you've been making at that crappy state hospital in Little Rock. You're a board-certified psychiatrist, not a janitor, although I'd be hard pressed to tell the difference from what they pay you. Private practice is the only way to go, my boy. Five years from now you'll own a fleet of jets, as well as a yacht and a Rolls with your monogram on the door."

"Sure I will, Vince."

"That's what I like to hear," boomed Vince, although inwardly he was getting fed up with these weekly pep talks. If he didn't need Randall to facilitate state licensing, he would have crushed him like the insignificant ant that he was. It was no wonder the hospital paid him less than a hundred thousand a year. Randall was short and prissy, with all the personality of stale beer. Dandruff glistened like snowflakes on his oily black hair. Although he was in his late thirties, he had the posture and deliberate caution of an arthritic octogenarian. No doubt his treatment of patients consisted of overmedicating them to keep them docile and oblivious to his incompetence. "Well, then, I'll see you Friday at noon so we can get settled in and have staff meetings the rest of the day. Everything has to be perfect when our patients arrive on Saturday."

Vince turned off the phone and went into the kitchen to find something to munch on until he took Melanie or Melody or whatever her name was out to dinner. All Randall did was whine incessantly, as though he were the only one making a sacrifice. It was hardly surprising that his wife had taken the children and fled to her parents' home. But in truth, he, Vincent W. Stonebridge, M.D., member in so-so standing in the ASAPS, master of the tummy tuck and breast augmentation, sculptor of flabby thighs, maestro of facial wrinkles and sagging chins, a veritable Michelangelo to L.A.'s richest women (and an increasing number of men), was the one who was giving up his spacious beach house, black-tie dinners, charity affairs at museums, and membership in an exclusive country club. Temporarily, at least, until the Stonebridge Foundation was running smoothly and he could escape the hellhole of a little town in the boondocks of Arkansas. He'd yet to meet any of the local citizens, but he was quite sure they all drooled.

Fistfights probably occurred over fresh roadkill. Their condiment of choice would be lard. From what he'd seen from the backseat of the limo, the storefronts were boarded up and the drab houses landscaped with clotheslines and plastic windmills. His driver had been obliged to brake on several occasions for a mangy hound asleep in the middle of the road.

With luck, he could stay within the compound, and they would be left to sniff along the fence and scratch their lice-infested heads in bewilderment. He'd been assured the fence was high enough to keep them out.

After Randall Zumi hung up, he made himself a mug of tea and flopped back on the couch. The living room was dim, but some of that could be attributed to burned-out light bulbs. There was no reason to replace them, since he was moving out on Friday. He didn't know if his wife would take immediate possession of the house, or remain with her parents. She'd mentioned that she might take the children to India to visit relatives. Since the divorce had yet to be finalized, she had full custody and there was nothing he could do to stop her. He certainly couldn't afford another court battle; he already owed his lawyer several thousand dollars. And what would he do if she suddenly sent the children for a weekend? They couldn't stay with him at the new facility, where he would be living in a small apartment with limited space. And would be on call 24/7 until profits allowed the hiring of a couple of interns.

He wasn't sure he even wanted to see his children, both of them spoiled, disrespectful, and mercenaries at heart. He had no desire whatsoever to see his wife, who was unable to so much as discuss the weather without blaming it on him. The marriage, although not arranged in the traditional manner, had been strongly encouraged by both sets of parents. Somehow or other, it had evolved into an offer he couldn't refuse. He'd been a struggling med student, and her parents had offered to pay his debts and help him set up a private practice — in exchange for the right to brag that their daughter was married to a doctor, living in the most exclusive neighborhood in Little Rock, and sending their children to the finest private schools. Unfortunately, the private practice had flopped, and his hospital salary had been inadequate to maintain the lifestyle his wife desired. She'd whined, cried, sneered, berated him, and even struck him before stalking away with the children.

Vince had made him an offer he couldn't refuse, either, but at least the money made it palatable. Randall doubted he'd be purchasing any private jets or pricey cars, but it would be nice not to have to lie awake at night trying to figure out how to juggle credit card limits to pay for his wife's and children's endless extravagances. And his admitted lack of charisma would not be a factor with the patients he'd be treating.

He was trying to remember how much cheese he had in the refrigerator when the telephone rang again. Gloomily assuming it was Vince with yet another bright idea, he answered it without enthusiasm.

"Randall? This is Brenda, Brenda Skiller. Am I calling you too late?"

"No," he said, relieved. "Is something wrong?"

"I just got off the phone with Vince. He said we're all arriving on Friday at noon, but I don't think that will allow us enough time for training. Not one of the maids or orderlies speaks English. We are going to have to walk them through every step, demonstrate precisely how things are to be done, and make sure they understand. What's more, the chef I hired has backed off because he simply doesn't approve of the dietary program I've put together. Do you know how much time I spent interviewing —"

"We'll find someone else," Randall said soothingly. "Did you tell Vince?"

Brenda sighed. "I tried to, but he was in a hurry. He doesn't appreciate how difficult it is to find a chef who understands high-fiber macrobiotics. I've spent months planning the dietary regime to best aid our patients in their recovery. I cannot allow some fry cook to come in and totally destroy the entire program out of ignorance and laziness. Even a single greasy french fry could set back their rehabilitation for weeks."

"Vince will find someone. He always does." Randall wondered why Vince had found Brenda Skiller to begin with. She had a degree in psychology, but in his opinion, she was a certifiable flake. The obscure college she'd attended lacked accreditation, due to its rather unique approach to psychology. Classes were not offered in such standard areas as developmental, behavioral, and abnormal psych, but instead in reflexology, hypnotherapy, high colonics, sensory deprivation, and other scientifically dubious fields. It was not challenging to understand why Brenda had a history of employment with institutes that were regularly closed down by the authorities because of charges of fraud, exploitation, and in a few cases, manslaughter caused by physical abuse and malnutrition. Brenda herself had never been accused of complicity, but neither had low-ranked enlisted men at internment camps.

"Then you agree with me?" she said shrilly.

Randall realized he hadn't been listening, but he knew there was no point in arguing with her over trivial issues. "Whatever you say, Brenda."

"So I'll see you Thursday at noon so we can do a final inspection and start the training regime. Everything must be spotless and functioning smoothly. I'll tackle the maids and orderlies at seven a.m. Friday, while you inventory the contents of the drug cabinets and examination rooms. Once Vince arrives, he can deal with the surgical supplies. I myself will unpack and organize the supplements."

"Thursday, at noon," Randall repeated.

"You should leave your house no later than seven-thirty, to allow time to stop for coffee or whatever." She paused, then took a breath. "Have you heard from Walter Kaiser?"

"Should I have heard from him?"

"Of course not. It's just that his telephone in Taos has been disconnected, and I thought maybe he'd contacted you."

"You're the one who hired him, Brenda. I've never even spoken to him." Randall gazed at the TV screen, which was still flickering. "If that's all . . . ?"

"I suppose so," she said. "I mean, I was just sitting here, thinking about the enormity of this project, and I couldn't keep myself from wondering if we know what we're getting into. Will the state licensing board schedule inspections, or will they send spies to investigate us? We don't know anything about the backgrounds of the staff. What if one of them is working undercover? Just because Vince swears none of them speaks English, he has no way of knowing. How did he find them?"

"Go make yourself a cup of tea. Everything will be fine." Randall hung up the phone, wishing he believed his own words. After a few minutes of brooding, he slapped together a sandwich and returned to watch John Wayne slaughter another platoon of Japanese soldiers.

Walter Kaiser made one telephone call, but it was to a pizza delivery place. He was at that moment enjoying free room and board in Amarillo, Texas, courtesy of the local constabulary.

3

Ruby Bee and Estelle had been disappointed (or even pissed, some might say) when I'd reported my failure to uncover whatever dark secrets lurked behind the red brick wall. I'd told them enough about my vacation with Jack to keep them appeased for the most part, although they continued to toss out artfully ingenuous questions in hopes of catching me off guard. The score was fairly even, and at least I was eating well.

On Monday morning I declared myself back on duty and turned on the air conditioner at the PD. After a few rumbles, it sputtered out gasps of cool, if not arctic, air. I looked over the accumulation of mail I'd left on my desk, then tossed it into the wastebasket and called the sheriff's office to let Harve know I was back.

"Why, Arly," cooed LaBelle, "I reckon you must have some stories to tell after that camping trip with your friend. How was it?"

"Fine. Is Harve there?"

"I disrecollect your friend's name, but isn't he the fellow from Springfield who was caught up with that cult at the church camp? Called themselves Moonbeams, didn't they?"

"He wasn't really involved," I said. "I'd like to speak to Harve, if you don't mind. Official business and all that."

LaBelle's voice dropped, and I could almost hear her false eyelashes fluttering. "Did you find out what's going on out there at the old folks' home? My ex-sister-in-law says she heard it's gonna be an insane asylum for criminals and perverts. I don't know how any of you will be able to sleep at night, knowing one of them could escape and come murder you in your bed. I'd be sleeping with a shotgun under my pillow."

"I'm sure you would, LaBelle," I said with a hint of exasperation in my voice. "Is Harve there or not?"

"Don't you go getting all snooty with me, Arly Hanks! Here I am trying to make polite conversation, and all you see fit to do is keep harping to speak to Sheriff Dorfer, who is a very busy man. I've a mind to hang up on you right this minute."

I bit down on my lip for a moment, then said, "If I have to drive all the way to

Farberville in order to speak to the very busy man, I'll be in a real bad mood when I get there. Now what's it going to be, LaBelle?"

I was immediately put on hold. I took a catalog out of the wastebasket, knowing LaBelle was liable to let me wait for a long time before she put me through to Harve. This particular catalog was clearly for gun lovers, or for those who were planning to barricade themselves in shacks and caves to prepare for the invasion of Darth Vader and his storm troopers. I was not quite so paranoid, and had a distaste for guns in general. Which was good, since I kept my official handgun and a box with three bullets in a locked cabinet in the back room. The city council keeps me on a miserly budget. Every once in a while I show up at a meeting to plead for a box of paperclips or a new windshield wiper blade for my police car, but the outcome's always a toss-up.

Harve came on the line eventually. "Don't tell me you're calling about the old folks' home," he began sourly.

"Well, no, but now that you brought it up," I said, "I would like to know what's going on."

"You and everybody else west of the Mississippi. All I can say is that the county commissioners decided it was costing too much to operate, so they sold it to some corporation out in California. Rumor has it some money changed hands under the table to grease the deal. It was approved after one reading, since nobody knew enough to offer any opposition."

"That's all you know? Some California corporation?"

Harve paused, most likely to light one of his cheap cigars. "To be real candid, Arly, I don't really give a damn. It's private property. So I heard you camped out at Tablerock with that fellow from Springfield. I've been trying for years to convince Mrs. Dorfer that we ought to rent a cabin up there for a few days. Was the fishing any good?"

"It's hard to say. We spent most of our time collecting specimens of bracken and liverworts. I just called to let you know that I'm back."

"There's nothing like a thick liverwurst sandwich with a hunk of yellow cheese, a slice of red onion, a juicy dill pickle, and a cold beer to liven up a ball game on TV on a Saturday afternoon. Hold on a minute — I've got something for you to look into. It's on my desk somewhere. Ya know, no matter how many times I tell LaBelle not to come in here and start straightening up my — yeah, here it is." He cleared his throat. "Albert Quivers, lives out past Belle Star on Pipple Road, reported that somebody's been stealing his catfish. He was real steamed about it, threatening to let his dogs run loose if we couldn't do anything. I've seen those dogs with my own eyes, and they're right mean ones."

I made a face at the water stain on the ceiling directly above me. "And you want me to go out there and investigate stolen catfish. Should I take my gun or a box of dog biscuits?"

"I'd take both if I was you. Just go out there in the next day or two and look around. Get what you can from Quivers, write up a report, and send it over here."

"How many catfish are we talking about, Harve — and how many dogs? Why don't you send Les or one of the other deputies out there?"

"Three, maybe four dogs, and I don't know how many catfish. It's either this one or a case of alleged embezzlement by the choir director at the Mount Zion Holy Church in Hogeye. They're so riled up over there that it might take weeks to get it sorted out. It's a mite conservative, so you'd better buy yourself some pantyhose and see if you can borrow a skirt from Mrs. Jim Bob. What's it going to be?"

"You're a colossal pain in the ass, Harve."

"So I've been told."

I hung up and rocked back in my cane-bottomed chair, wondering how long it would take to cram everything back into the duffel bag, buy a loaf of bread and a jar of peanut butter at the supermarket, and then head for the hills. Or the lake.

Kevin Buchanon was doing his best to stack up rolls of paper towels at Jim Bob's SuperSaver Buy 4 Less when Idalupino snuck up behind him and pinched his butt. All the rolls went tumbling to the floor as he whipped around. "You jest keep your hands to yourself," he sputtered, so outraged that his Adam's apple rippled as if he'd swallowed an oversized beetle. "I am a married man."

"Your wife's on the phone, shrieking like a castrated pig. She called on the pay phone up front. All I can say is you'd better not let Jim Bob catch you. He damn near bit my head off when I had to take a potty break. It's not like I had any choice, since I have a urinary tract infection. But he wouldn't even let me explain."

Kevin hurried to the pay phone and

grabbed the receiver, which was dangling almost to the floor. "Dahlia, my sweetness, what's wrong? Are you sick?"

"Yes, I'm sick to death of my granny! You know what she did, Kevvie? She decided to give the twins a bath, so she started running water in the tub. They hid, just like they always do, and by the time she'd dragged them from under the porch, there was water all over the floors, even in the living room. Now the twins are so filthy that you can't tell 'em apart, and my back is killin' me on account of having to mop up the water. Meanwhile, Granny went off to pick black-berries."

He glanced at the clock above the exit. "Gee, honeybunch, I'd come home and help, but I don't get off till five. Jim Bob's liable to blow his stack if I leave early. He's still pissed on account of I dropped a case of vinegar and the whole store stinks like a pickle factory."

"You got to do something," wailed Dahlia. "I can't go on like this."

"Did you call my ma?" he asked timidly.

"She told me to deal with it myself. I ask you, Kevvie — is that anything to say to the mother of her grandbabies? You'd have thought I was a stranger at her back door, begging for food and a place to sleep."

Kevin wasn't real surprised, since as far as he could tell, Dahlia had been calling his ma four or five times a day to complain about something. "Don't you worry," he said in his most manly voice. "When I git home, I'll hose off the twins and see to the floors. Should I bring a bucket of fried chicken from the deli?"

"You know perfectly well we can't afford it, Kevin Fitzgerald Buchanon! If you don't get a raise from Jim Bob, I don't know what we're gonna do. My granny's scrawny, but she eats like a horse. I caught her gnawing on raw potatoes this morning, and poor little Kevvie Junior and Rose Marie ain't had so much as a cookie since she moved back in with us. She steals the whole package and creeps off behind the house."

"I gotta go," Kevin said as he spotted Jim Bob glaring at the rolls of paper towels scattered all over the floor. "I'll be home shortly after five." Despite her protest, he hung up the receiver and ducked down the cereal aisle. He wasn't any happier than Dahlia about her granny moving in with them, but he didn't know what he was supposed to do about it. He couldn't drag her to the pound and have her put to sleep with all the other strays.

Mebbe, he thought, Arly would know

what to do. After all, she was the chief of police, and Dahlia's granny was clearly disturbing the peace. That was a crime, as he well knew after he'd drunk a pint jar of Raz's moonshine during a high school football game and chased two of the cheerleaders all the way to the girls' locker room. They'd barricaded themselves inside all night, or so he'd been told.

When Jim Bob got home from the supermarket late that afternoon, he found Mrs. Jim Bob seated at the dinette. She didn't seem to be doing anything, he noted warily as he opened the refrigerator and took out a beer. Her lips were tight, though, which meant she was brooding about something. He hoped it wasn't about where to put in a swimming pool. He knew damn well she wouldn't be appeased with one of those aboveground jobs, neither. Hell, she was probably thinking about landscaping the yard all the way down to the road.

"What's for supper?" he asked.

"Leftovers."

"Since you haven't bothered to fix anything for three days, that'd be leftover leftovers, wouldn't it? If you'd wanted me to bring home something from the deli, all you had to do was call." He edged toward the hall. "That's not saying I mind having left-overs. It's just getting kind of boring, having the same thing for supper every night."

She turned her beadiest stare on him. "How many times do I have to tell you, our meal in the evening is *dinner,* not supper. Common folks have supper. What's more, if you don't like what I'm serving, you can take your sorry self down to Ruby Bee's and sop up some grease with one of her so-called biscuits. I don't understand why you think I should be slaving away in a hot kitchen all day when Maggody is at risk."

"At risk of what?"

"If I knew, I'd be the first to tell you. There's something wicked going on out there at the old folks' home. When I drive by, I can feel Satan's breath on the back of my neck, and there's a stench of sulphur in the air." She sat back, her arms crossed and her face as hard as granite. "As the mayor, it's your duty to send Arly to investigate. That's what she gets paid for, isn't it?"

"She tried, same as I did, but the spic don't speak English and the dog growls like a rabid coon. She can't just shoot them. The construction looks to be pretty much fin-ished. Somebody will move in, and then we'll know. Maybe you and the ladies of the Missionary Society can drop by to welcome them and visit for a spell."

Mrs. Jim Bob didn't actually growl, but the sound was unsettling. "Are you suggesting that we walk up the driveway and knock on the devil's door?"

He headed for the living room. "Call me when supper — I mean dinner — is on the table. I can hardly wait for some more of your tuna casserole."

"Just what have you been up to these last few days?" demanded Ruby Bee as I sat down at the bar. "I am sick and tired of making you sandwiches and watching you sashay out the door without so much as a word of explanation. Does this have something to do with that man from Springfield? Are you going up there on the sly?"

"No," I said wearily as I unpinned my badge and stuck it in my pocket so all the criminals would realize that they'd have to wait for the time being. "I've spent the last three days trying to talk to a man in Belle Star. And if catfish is on the menu tonight, I'm going into Farberville for a pizza. Maybe I will, anyway, and then go to a movie."

"What were you doin' in Belle Star?" asked Estelle, who could probably hear a squirrel sneeze on Cotter's Ridge.

"Theft, but you don't want to hear the details. What's for supper? Fried chicken?"

Ruby Bee was still watching me, her eyes flickering with suspicion. "So you didn't go to Springfield?"

"I went to Belle Star," I said, "which was named after the infamous outlaw who was born in Missouri, not too far from here, in 1848. She hung out with Jesse James and the Younger Brothers, and was shot in the back and died at the age of forty. Clearly, whoever chose the name for the town couldn't spell worth a damn."

"Why do you happen to know this, Miss Zane Grey?" asked Estelle.

"I spent several hours with Albert Quivers, that's why. I also know how many catfish can thrive in a nine-acre pond, the misfortunes that befell the Pipple family and caused them to sell their property, and that Mrs. Quivers is worthless when it comes to standing guard all night because she falls asleep in the glider. Anything going on in town?"

"Not really," Ruby Bee said reluctantly. "Whatever's going on at the county old folks' home is close to being done. The only workmen out there are plumbers and electricians. The guard and his dog are still there, though."

Estelle waggled her finger. "Don't forget the plaque."

Ruby Bee frowned at the interruption, then said, "They put it up a day or two ago, but nobody knows what to make of it. It's a fancy brass thing that says 'The Stonebridge Foundation.'"

I thought about it for a moment. "Sounds like a corporate retreat or a research facility. How disappointing for Mrs. Jim Bob; I'm sure she's been praying for something scandalous so she can get her knickers in a twist. And poor Brother Verber won't get to stand on the road, thumping his Bible and preventing sinners from darkening the threshold of eternal damnation."

Estelle resumed nursing her glass of sherry, and Ruby Bee went into the kitchen to dish me up a plate of fried pork chops and summer squash. I idly watched customers straggle in for beer and pretzels. Bilious Buchanon put a quarter in the juke box and ordered a pitcher so he could literally cry in his beer. A married couple I knew from high school days glanced coldly at me before settling in a booth for their version of a romantic night on the town. I'd arrested two of their sons for public drunkenness a couple of months earlier, so I wasn't surprised when they didn't gesture for me to join them. After a while, most of the booths were occupied, as well as the stools. Conversations concerned the weather, road construction, the weather, the parking problem at the livestock barn, and the weather. The major point of controversy was whether or not it would rain any time soon. I wondered what they'd do if they woke up some morning and discovered there was no weather. Discuss it at length, I concluded.

After I'd polished off a piece of peach cobbler, I got up to leave. Before I could take more than a step, two strangers came into the bar. Since I pretty much knew everybody in Maggody (or at least their faces and parole status), I sat back down. They did not look like the sort of couple propelled by lust to rent a room at the Flamingo Motel, nor did they resemble the occasional truck driver and wife (or girlfriend) who'd stop for supper. The woman was more than six feet tall, with unevenly cropped brown hair, an angular jaw, and the broad shoulders of a football player. Her mouth was set in a frown. If she'd been carrying a briefcase, I would have pegged her for a prosecuting attorney (and if I'd been a defendant, innocent or otherwise, I would have been worried about my future). The man beside her was quite her opposite. He barely came up to her earlobes. His skin had the light brown hue of a walnut shell. He wore a short-sleeved plaid shirt, knee-length shorts, and sandals with dark socks, reminding me of a tourist at a run-down resort. Some of the customers gave him a hard stare, as though suspecting him of being "one of them thar Arab terrorists" intending to blow up a barn or two.

The pair came over to the bar and waited until Ruby Bee bustled over, wiping her hands on her apron. "We have a problem," the woman announced, her words crisp.

"We do?" said Ruby Bee, alarmed.

"My colleague and I arrived at the Stonebridge Foundation earlier today. Everything seemed to be in order, but an hour ago the power went out. Until the power is restored, we need a room in which we can continue to work. Are there any rooms available in the motel?"

Estelle leaned forward so she could get a good look at them. "The Stonebridge Foundation, you said? What exactly is going on out there?"

The woman glanced back at the rabbity man, as if warning him to stay mute. "The Stonebridge Foundation is a private enterprise. We are not at liberty to discuss it further, but I can assure you it will have no impact on any of the residents here. You do own the motel, don't you? We could find a room in Farberville, but I would prefer to remain nearby in case we can return to the foundation."

"I don't know," said Ruby Bee. "I don't rent rooms by the hour. If I did, I'd be changing sheets all night long."

The dark man shook his head vehemently. "No, madam, it's nothing like that. We just need a table, a couple of chairs, and a telephone."

Someone in a booth chortled. "Running a bookie joint, eh?"

"Or making a bomb," someone else muttered.

"Goddamn foreigners," added another. "We don't need the likes of you in Maggody."

More members of the welcoming committee jumped in.

"Raghead."

"Mooslim scum."

I decided to step in before the remarks grew any nastier. "I'm the chief of police," I said as I approached the couple. "I can let you use the back room at the PD if it's only going to be for an hour or so."

The woman assessed me as if I had a

slightly fishy odor. "You're the chief of police?"

I took my badge out of my pocket and pinned it on. "So they tell me."

"Let's accept her offer and get out of here, Brenda," the man said hurriedly. "If the electric company can't restore the power soon, we'll go to Farberville. Vincent isn't coming until tomorrow, anyway."

She nodded at me. "This is very kind of you. I hope it's not a bother."

I gestured for the two to follow me out to the parking lot and pointed. "It's that little brick building about a block from here. There's a police car out front. I'll meet you there in a minute."

By the time they parked, I was already unlocking the door of the PD. Neither looked especially impressed as they took in the faded gingham curtains, the piles of dust bunnies in the corners, the uncomfortable chair I kept to discourage visitors, and the overall shabbiness. I couldn't argue with their tacit distaste. Ruby Bee had offered to hang prints of kittens and puppies peeping out of baskets, but I'd declined. I wasn't on the FBI's most-wanted-poster mailing list, either, so the walls were unadorned with anything more than stray spittles of tobacco juice from some of Maggody's less cultivated residents. Perkin was the worst of the offenders whenever he plunked his behind in the chair and carried on about obscure issues concerning his dawgs or trespassers. Raz was also a contender, but he was keeping a low profile lately.

"I'm Arly Hanks," I said.

"Brenda Skiller," the woman responded without enthusiasm.

She elbowed the man, who gulped and said, "Randall Zumi. It's very kind of you to offer this. I hope we're not intruding."

I shrugged. "No problem, since the local troublemakers respect my office hours. Can you tell me a little bit about" — I thought for a moment — "this Stonebridge Foundation? It's not in my jurisdiction, but I'm as curious as everybody else in town. The rumors have been pretty far-fetched."

Brenda shook her head. "As you said, it's not in your jurisdiction, and it will in no way disrupt the town. That's all you need to know."

"Are you doing research on chemical weapons or something?" I asked. "Should we all be stocking up on duct tape and bottled water? We deserve some sort of explanation."

"I don't see why." Brenda went into the back room.

Randall shrugged apologetically, looking as though he wanted to dive into a corner and hide with the dust bunnies (some of which were impressive after three weeks of negligence on my part). "Let's just say we're helping people. Our success depends on the anonymity we guarantee them."

"Helping people do what?" I persisted.

"Get better."

"Better at what? Tennis? Poetry?"

"Randall," Brenda called, "bring the laptop and the folders in here. Miss Hanks, I hope you won't object if I make a few long-distance calls. I can assure you that we'll cover the cost when you submit the telephone bill. I'd use my cell phone, but there doesn't seem to be any reception because of the mountains."

I felt as though I should apologize for geological upheavals in the distant past. "You'll have to use the phone in here," I replied.

She came to the doorway. "My calls are of a private nature. If it's not too inconvenient for you, could you possibly leave us here until the power is restored? All of our phones at the foundation are cordless and require electricity. Randall, call the number. If you get the answering machine, we can return."

"Do whatever you want," I said as I

moved toward the front door. "Just turn out the lights when you leave."

"Don't we need to lock the door?" asked Randall.

I shook my head. "Don't bother. Anyone who bothers to break in here deserves whatever he can find. It won't be state-of-the-art technology, not by a long shot. If for some reason you need me, I'll be in the apartment above the antiques store. Let me write down the phone number so" — I stopped as the lights flickered and went out, leaving us in a distinctly dim room. "Hell, I guess that means the power company's digging up lines to repair your problem. If I were you, I wouldn't go back to Ruby Bee's."

Randall stepped outside with me. "I can assure you that I'm not a terrorist, Chief Hanks. My parents live in Delaware. My father's a lawyer, and my mother's a high school chemistry teacher. My family is originally from India and are Hindus, not Muslims. The only thing any of us have ever blown up is a balloon."

"I'm afraid you're going to find that this is not what you'd consider an open-minded community. Our only foreigners are a family from Mexico, and they're tolerated only because they keep to themselves. The father owns the Dairee Dee-Lishus across from the high school. Outside of Ruby Bee's and the deli at the supermarket, it's the only place in town to grab something to eat. The food's greasy, but the cherry limeades are heavenly."

He squinted at the sole traffic light, which was out. "We'll have a chef at the foundation, so that won't be a problem. I can promise you that you won't even know we're there."

"Or what you're doing," I said drily. I waited in case he wanted to say anything further, then added, "My old-fashioned phone will work if you want to call the electric co-op and try to get an idea of how long it's going to take them. If I were you, I'd go find a hotel in Farberville."

Before he could reply, Kevin Buchanon came galloping up the road, his arms flapping like a maniacal rooster. "Arly! I've been trying to get hold of you all week, but ever'time I come by, the office was empty. Did you know the electricity's out?"

"Is that what you came to ask me, Kevin?" I said.

"No," he panted, then bent over to catch his breath. "It's about my ma."

"Is she somehow responsible for this?"

He gave me a startled look. "How could she be? She ain't an electrician, for pity's sake. Why would you think such a thing?"

"Calm down," I said. "What's this about your mother?"

"I'm a doctor," Randall volunteered. "Is she in need of emergency medical care?"

Kevin straightened up. "Heck, no. I mean, she might be, but since nobody knows where she is, I don't see how you kin help, but I thank you all the same for offering." He looked at me. "This morning when Pa got up, she was gone. Her car, too. It ain't like her, unless it had something to do with Dahlia's granny. Ma ain't much happier than Dahlia about this mess. And Pa's storming around the house on account of her not being there to cook his meals. I don't reckon he's had anything but cheese sandwiches all day."

"He'll survive," I said. "Okay, Eileen left sometime before dawn, in her car. Did she take anything with her, like clothes and a suitcase?"

"Pa said that he dint think she took anything. He ain't sure, but he sez her half of the closet looks the same as always."

Randall tilted his head. "She didn't leave a note?"

"Nuthin'," Kevin said with a shrug.

"Well, that's a hopeful sign. Those planning to commit suicide almost always leave a note either begging forgiveness or casting blame on others."

Kevin gulped so loudly that he might have alarmed a possum on Cotter's Ridge. "You saying she's gone off to commit *suicide?* My ma wouldn't do that. 'Course, she's been mighty frazzled ever since Dahlia's taken to calling her all day long."

"She's an adult, Kevin," I said. "She left voluntarily, and she hasn't been gone twenty-four hours. There's nothing I can do. It sounds as though you should go home and help Dahlia." Since I knew what that problem involved, I didn't bother to elaborate for Randall's edification. Not that his initial impression of the citizens of Maggody could sink any lower.

"This is all the county judges' fault," Kevin said darkly.

I gave him a gentle nudge. "I can't do anything about that, either. Call me tomorrow if your mother hasn't come back." The stoplight came to life, and I took the green light as an omen. "Go on, Kevin."

"What about my pa? He ain't had a decent meal all day."

"Take him home with you for supper, or send him to Ruby Bee's. Better yet, tell him to fix his own damn supper. If he can drive a tractor, he can open a can of pork 'n' beans."

Kevin didn't look convinced (and I doubt I did, either), but he turned around and trudged up the road.

Brenda Skiller came out of the PD, where the lights were shining as best they could, since the town council insists that I use 40-watt bulbs — and not out of concern for the environment. "I called the foundation, and the power is back. Let's go, Randall. We'll be up half the night as it is. I brought some high-protein bars in my suitcase." She gave me a halfhearted smile. "Thank you again for your kind offer, Chief Hanks. I have a feeling we're not welcome here."

"Unfortunately, you're right," I said, "but not solely because of Randall's ethnic background. People are upset about the abrupt closure of the county old folks' home, as well as being highly suspicious that something dangerous is going on behind that fence. They're demanding an explanation from me, and I don't have one."

Ignoring me, she got into the driver's seat of a dusty black minivan. "Randall, I'm waiting for you. We haven't even started unloading all the boxes in the back. We'll be lucky if we get them unpacked and cataloged before dawn."

"Sounds like you're in for a fun night," I murmured.

"No kidding." He shook my hand, then got into the van.

I watched as they drove back up the road in the direction of County 104, which would take them to the Stonebridge Foundation. Where Brenda Skiller would unpack boxes and catalog the contents, all in order to "make people better." I imagined a ghastly scene from a B horror movie, in which Brenda sat with a shipping list while Randall put the dismembered hands in one cabinet, the feet in another, and the jars of eyeballs on a shelf. "No, Randall," she'd say impatiently, "the left hands on the left side, the right hands on the right. And do sort those eyeballs by color."

I went into the PD, turned off the lights, and returned outside. I could go to a movie in Farberville, as I'd planned, or go to my apartment and call Jack — except he'd gone to shoot a series of commercials in some redneck country inn and wouldn't be home until Friday morning. The lights were on in the back of Roy Stiver's shop; I could, if I wanted, amble over and talk to him while we sipped whiskey. He's the closest thing Maggody will ever have to a poet laureate, although he does enjoy composing ribald limericks along with the odes and sonnets. To wit:

'Twas a bleak day in June when
  Hizzoner,
Got caught with a floozy (he was on
  her).
His wife snipped off his thingie,
Stewed it up á là kingie,
And feasted on it like Miz Donner.

I haven't asked Mrs. Jim Bob to em-broider it on a pillow for me.

After standing there pondering my op-tions as the stoplight went through several rounds of red, yellow, and green, I finally thought of something that might prove en-lightening, if not entertaining. I drove over to the Dairee Dee-Lishus, where the usual suspects were perched on picnic tables, slapping at mosquitoes and drinking beer.

The beer cans vanished as I joined them. "Another wild night in Maggody, I see," I said as I sat down on a bench.

"We're not doing anything wrong," Darla Jean said sullenly. "Billy Dick thought we ought to tunnel our way into the bank, but there isn't one within twenty miles. Same problem with renting porn movies."

Billy Dick burped. "Unless that new place on County 104 turns out to be Block-buster's. Now that'd be cool."

"In your dreams," said Heather. "Wet dreams, that is."

"I need help," I said. "I want to try to get some information off the Internet."

Amberlynne smiled sweetly at me. "I'm sure Mr. Lambertino will give you the key to the computer lab at the high school. In fact, he'd probably go unlock it for you hisself if his wife would let him. I heard she still thinks you and him were a little too cozy at that church camp. My ma said Brother Verber was staring right at him during a sermon about adultery a couple of weeks back."

I raised my eyebrows. "My goodness, Amberlynne, is that a puddle of beer you're sitting in?"

"Shit!" she said as she hopped off the table. "I'm going to smell like the Dew Drop Inn. My parents will kill me."

Darla Jean looked at me. "What do you want off the Internet?"

"Something that might help us figure out what's going on at the Stonebridge Foundation, where the old folks' home used to be. I'm not very good at this sort of thing. Even if I got in the computer lab, I wouldn't know how to start."

"Come on, then," she said as she slid off the picnic table. "We can go over to my house. My parents went to some lame awards banquet in Farberville. They shouldn't be back for at least an hour. You'd better take your car."

When we got to her house, I followed her upstairs to her bedroom. It was an eclectic mess of worn stuffed animals, a dusty dollhouse in need of a redecorator, posters of male idols posing in low-slung jeans, clothes scattered on the floor, and makeup cluttering a dressing table.

She cleared a space on her bed for me, then sat down at her computer. "So what are we looking for?"

"Try 'Stonebridge Foundation,' " I suggested.

She clicked here and there on the keyboard. "Nothing. But if I try 'Stonebridge,' I get four hundred and fifteen thousand hits. Do you want golf courses, planned unit developments, restaurants, B&Bs, colleges, publishers, car dealerships . . . ?"

"All right, then," I said. "See what you can find for Randall Zumi."

"Spell it."

I didn't know how, so I offered some possibilities and added that he was a medical doctor. Eventually, Darla Jean pointed. "Here he is. It doesn't say much, though."

She got up so I could sit down in front of

the screen. Randall Zumi was employed by the Arkansas State Hospital, the primary destination for those with severe mental illnesses or those awaiting court-mandated evaluations. Randall had attended a state medical school in the East, done a residency at another, and was a board-certified psychiatrist. From the dates listed, I calculated his age to be in the thirties. There was no other personal information.

"Interesting," I murmured.

Darla Jean's eyes were wide. "So it's gonna be an insane asylum? When they show them in movies, they sure don't have swimming pools and gym equipment. It's always these long, dark corridors with steel doors and rooms where they strap people down to hook up wires to their heads. The patients all walk around with glassy eyes and talk to themselves. I'm getting scared just thinking about it."

I'd seen the same shows, and I didn't have anything to add.

4

Vincent Stonebridge was feeling quite pleased as the limo stopped at the main entrance. The facade was reminiscent of an early-twentieth-century hotel in its prime. The trees and flowerbeds looked as though they'd been there since Victoria had reigned over the fading British Empire. The porch was wide, permitting homey groupings of white wicker furniture and planters filled with cheerful blooms.

He told the driver to pull around to the back parking area and wait until someone appeared to assist with unloading the suitcases, boxes of books, cases of wine, and necessary electronic paraphernalia such as his computer, stereo equipment, and CDs that would make life in this barbarian village semi-tolerable.

After straightening his tie and running his manicured fingertips through his thick, silver hair, Vincent stepped into the reception room of the Stonebridge Foundation.

The settee and chairs, as well as the desk, were high-quality replicas of expensive European antiques. A vase of fresh flowers was centered on the oblong coffee table. The oriental rug was a muted mixture of rich colors. It was all quite impressive.

The wings on either side led to the suites and an exterior door at the end of each hall. Previously, there had been eight double rooms for the unfortunate elderly patients in each wing. Now each contained four two-room suites. He went down the left wing and opened a door. Very nice, he thought, looking at the pearl gray walls and lush carpeting. Accents in sage and cranberry enhanced the elegant brocade draperies. The bookshelf held classics bound in leather and slim volumes of poetry to elevate one's spirits. A small sofa looked inviting, as did an overstuffed chair set next to the window for those who might want to curl up and read. There were, of course, no locks on the inside of the doors, but all in all, it was as charming as some of his favorite hotels in Paris and Rome.

Vincent returned to the reception room. Due to the rush to prepare the facility, the rooms in the right wing had not yet been completely redone. Vincent's projected profits relied on the utilization of all eight suites, but that would have to wait until adequate revenues had been generated.

"There you are," said Brenda Skiller as she came through a door beyond the desk. "I expected you more than an hour ago."

"And it's lovely to see you again, Brenda," Vincent said with a slight bow. "This really came out nicely, didn't it? I must remember to send the decorator — Maribelle, I think — some flowers to show our gratitude."

Brenda frowned. "She'd prefer a check. I've been through all her bills and invoices, and she seems to have stayed on budget, with a few exceptions. The marble vanities, for example —"

"Let's not quibble over the details, my dear. Our patients are paying fifty thousand dollars a month; they would not be pleased with shoddy furnishings. A year from now we'll be adding another eight suites in a new building beyond the pool. How ironic that we'll have the most highly sought-after rehab facility in the most obscure place in the country."

"How ironic," echoed Brenda. "We still have an enormous amount of work to do before tomorrow. Randall and I came a day early to get started."

Vincent smiled. "I knew you would be an

excellent addition to our team. I need someone to help my driver move everything into my suite and office. Who's available?"

"All of the maids and orderlies are in the day room. Follow me." She spun around and marched back down a hall toward the rear of the building.

He trailed along behind her, trying not to wince as her ample derriere swished with each step. A few sessions of liposection would do wonders for her, as well as abdominoplasty, a facial restructuring to reduce her pugnacious jaw, and Botox injections to combat the deep creases defining her mouth. She would never pass for a retired swimsuit model, but in this modern era of medical miracles, she certainly could do better. He resolved to offer her a discount when the time seemed right.

The four women and four men in the day room were milling around uncomfortably. They comprised a mixture of ages and bulk, but all of them had dark eyes and brown complexions. The women wore modest gray uniforms with white bib aprons, and had been warned that jewelry and makeup were grounds for dismissal. The men were neatly groomed and dressed in white shirts and trousers. All of them had been issued sensible shoes that would not squeak as they went about their duties.

"They have about a dozen words of English among them," Brenda said. "I spent the morning demonstrating their duties to them. You realize it's illegal to hire them without verifying their immigration status and green cards, don't you?"

Vincent nodded. "And that's why I chose them, my dear. We cannot have them tattling to the tabloids. Is the arrangement I made for that apartment building across from the Farberville airport adequate?"

"I don't think so. There seems to be a significant community of Latinos in this area. I'm worried that some of these people, especially the younger ones, will find their way to bars and nightclubs where Spanish is the norm. After a few beers, who knows what they might say? A day later we'll be staked out by paparazzi perched in trees."

"Hmm," said Vincent, easily imagining her scenario. "What about the east wing rooms that haven't been remodeled? Can we keep them there?"

Brenda shook her head. "I considered that, but none of the rooms have functional plumbing. Our patients will not be happy if these people are roaming the halls in their bathrobes at all hours of the day and night. The essence of a good staff is invisibility.

I've already instructed them to keep their eyes lowered and not to speak unless spoken to first."

"Hmm," Vincent said again. It was a useful response, implying that he was mulling over options and weighing important issues.

"Randall had a suggestion," Brenda continued. "There is a motel of sorts in town. Without public transportation, these people won't have a way to get to Farberville or any of the other towns in the area. I can assure you that the local residents will not welcome them. We can use the van to shuttle them back and forth when shifts change. It will take ten minutes instead of most of an hour."

"How much?"

"I should be able to get four double rooms for two thousand a month, maybe less. It's no more than the Airport Arms, and we'll save on gas and mileage. They'll have hot plates and a grill, as we'd already planned, so they can still fix their burritos or beans or whatever. They can also walk to a local supermarket."

Since he had not thought of it himself, Vincent was loath to admit it was a better plan. However, he'd hired Brenda to deal with the petty problems, and as an effective leader, he had to delegate responsibilities. "Fine, then," he said. "You make the arrangements, while I have these men carry in my cartons and suitcases. Where's Randall?"

"In his office, unpacking books and hanging diplomas."

Vincent consulted his watch. "We will have a staff meeting in my office in one hour. I supposed we'd better include Walter Kaiser. Where is he?"

"I don't know," Brenda admitted. "I told him to be here this afternoon. He hasn't called or anything."

"Are you prepared to oversee the personalized training regimes?" he asked so coldly that the Mexicans in the room flinched. "We have four patients arriving tomorrow, one accompanied by her lawyer. This particular lawyer will provide us with many referrals in the future — *if* he's impressed. I had presumed you would handle this, Brenda. Keep in mind you are not indispensable."

Brenda's jaw quivered. "So you say, Vincent, but are you prepared to supervise the menu, arrange for the delivery of fresh fruits and vegetables, teach yoga, and provide acupuncture treatments? If the new chef quits, are you going to cook? Yes, you're

91

going to nip and tuck, but their cures have to come from within as well. This lawyer isn't going to make referrals if there's no measurable improvement."

"Well, then," Vincent said petulantly, "you'd better track Kaiser down. Make arrangements with the motel and let Randall know that we'll meet in my office at two o'clock." He gestured at the men to follow him, then stalked out of the day room.

Brenda went out into the hall. Rather than go to her office, she decided to use the phone at the reception desk so she could keep an eye on the front door. Not that she could call Walter, who could be anywhere from Alamagordo to Anchorage, although it was more likely he was in a cheap motel, sleeping off a three-day binge of drugs and booze. Maybe she'd made a mistake when she offered him the job, but she'd had no choice. Unfortunately, she'd met him a long time ago under very different circumstances. Recently he'd tracked her down and made it clear that he hadn't forgotten their first meeting — and that he wouldn't hesitate to bring it up if it was in his best interest.

"Excuse me," said a petite young woman hovering near the front door, "but I'm looking for whoever is in charge." She smiled brightly, her small white teeth neatly aligned. Her curly blond hair surrounded her face in a hazy cloud. Her blue eyes were large and wide-set, giving her the look of a fragile porcelain figurine. She was dressed neatly in a skirt and blouse, but clearly would cause testosterone to effervesce if she appeared in a skimpy bathing suit. Brenda detested her on sight.

"And you are . . . ?"

"Molly Foss, ma'am. Dr. Stonebridge hired me to be the receptionist."

Brenda sat down behind the desk. "I'm Dr. Skiller, and I'm in charge of the staff. Sit down." She waited until the woman complied, then said, "When did Dr. Stonebridge hire you?"

"Back in February, at an AMA meeting in Las Vegas. The doctor I was working for took the whole office staff as a reward. We stayed in this really nice hotel with an absolutely enormous casino and so many restaurants I didn't know —"

"I'm sure you didn't, Miss Foss. Does Dr. Stonebridge have a copy of your résumé?"

"Oh, yes, Dr. Skiller," she replied earnestly, "and he told me all about the position. I'm really excited about working here."

"Then I hope you appreciate the necessity

of never discussing our program with outsiders. Not with your friends, your parents"
— she glanced at the woman's left hand —
"or your husband. You are simply to describe it as a wellness institution. Do you
understand?"

"Yes, ma'am. I swear I won't breathe a
word, not even if I'm being tortured."

"I doubt it will come to that. You'll serve
as the receptionist and secretary. Most of
your duties will involve insurance paperwork, state licensing compliance forms, patients' private records, and so forth. You
will, by necessity, handle material that must
remain confidential. This will be your desk,
and the room directly behind me contains
the filing cabinets, office supplies, and computer. There is a panel that controls the
gate. You will be given a list of those who
have appointments. Confirm the identity of
those who request entry, and if you have any
doubts, do not buzz open the gate without
consulting me. I'll unlock the office door for
you when you arrive in the morning, and
give you the key. When you leave at five, you
will lock the door and return the key to me.
If you leave the area for any reason, you are
to lock the door and take the key with you.
Under no circumstances are you to allow
access to anyone except Dr. Stonebridge,

Dr. Zumi, and myself. The slightest violation will lead to your immediate dismissal."

Molly's face turned pale. "Wow, I promise I'll be extra careful. When do you want me to start?"

"Tomorrow morning at eight. This weekend you'll need to be here both days, but once we're functioning smoothly, you'll work until noon on Saturdays and have Sundays off. Wear a skirt or slacks, and we'll provide you with a lab coat. As long as you're already here, familiarize yourself with the facility. I'll see you in the morning."

Molly stood up, blinking uncertainly, then wandered down the hall. Brenda sighed as she picked up the receiver to call the motel — and realized she didn't remember its name. Maggody did not merit a telephone directory. She could hardly send Randall to make the arrangements, since he might be lynched on the spot, but he might recall the name.

She went down the hall. The new addition consisted of two one-story structures fronted by narrow, covered sidewalks. One side contained the day room, gym, kitchen, pantry, and employee break room; the other the doctors' offices, private residences, and the surgical suite. Between the two extensions was a swimming pool with a brick patio and wrought-iron furniture, and beyond that, a spacious garden. Patients would be encouraged to spend their free time outside, soaking up vitamin D from the sunshine while meditating or reading. Those who sulked in their suites would find themselves subjected to behavior modification.

The door to Randall's office was open. Brenda went inside and watched as he made minute adjustments to the framed diploma he was hanging behind his desk, then said, "Vincent is here."

The diploma slipped off the nail and fell to the floor. Randall stared down at it, then turned around. "You startled me. Yes, I am aware that Vincent is here. He's been shouting orders and waving his arms at those men unloading his belongings. He can be rather loud and ostentatious, you know. Perhaps that is the way one must behave in L.A. to be noticed. I seem to lack that sort of exuberance."

Brenda agreed, but she saw no reason to commiserate. "Did you happen to notice the name of the local motel?"

"Some bird . . . flamingo, I think." He picked up the diploma. "Is that all?"

"We're having a meeting at two o'clock in

his office. It'll be interesting to find out who our patients will be. Did Vince say anything about them to you?"

"No names, just a general description of their problems. Maybe he thought my line was tapped." He turned his attention to a hammer and nail.

"It's not as though we're treating Saudi princes or heads of state," Brenda murmured as she picked up objects on his desk and examined them. "Is this a photograph of your family?"

"Yes, it is."

"How charming." Brenda replaced the framed photo and picked up a crystal paperweight. "Is this a graduation present?"

Randall looked over his shoulder at her. "No, it's a paperweight. Look, Brenda, I've got a lot left to do, so if you don't mind . . ."

"We need to talk, Randall." She came up behind him and put her hand on his arm. "You and I. It's about Vincent."

"I don't want to talk about him, okay? He's my partner. I've invested every last dime I've got in this project. The only thing I'm going to focus on is making it successful. If you have a problem with Vincent, then take it up with him."

"Goodness, Randall, I don't believe I've heard you get so fired up before. You really ought to consider taking up yoga as a way to reduce stress." She left before he could respond, and continued toward Vincent's office. Boxes were stacked by the door, but the work party had been disbanded. At least temporarily, she thought as she noticed the Mexican men standing near a marble bench, smoking and laughing.

She hurried over to them. Waggling a finger, she said, "No smoking! No, no, no! And don't even think about stubbing those out on the walk!"

The men glanced at her, then pinched the ends of their cigarettes and put them in their pockets. *"Sí, señora,"* said one of them.

"And I don't want to see this again," she went on, aware that they couldn't understand the words but confident they would get the message. "Now go back and wait with the others. Go, go, go! You are not allowed to loiter out here under any circumstances." She fluttered her hand at them. "Why are you standing there? Go back to the day room!"

Smirking, they turned and walked toward the pool. Brenda was certain they were talking about her. It was not her fault, she reminded herself. It was her nature to be assertive. If she'd been meek, she'd be a waitress in a diner on a highway, but she had done what was necessary to achieve her degree. She might have caused some damage along the way, but she'd never allowed anyone to hold her back.

Vincent's office door was closed. As she slowed down, she heard not only girlish giggles and a deep chuckle, but sounds that suggested that Vincent and Molly were doing more than reviewing her résumé. She lowered her hand, continued to her own office, and went inside.

After locking the door, she slumped to the floor and began to sob.

I was doing everything I could to preserve the peace within the confines of Maggody, which meant I was sitting in the cane-bottom chair at the PD, my feet propped on the corner of the desk, watching a spider progress across the ceiling. I'd considered running a speed trap out by the remains of the Esso station, but had decided it would not be cost-effective, in that there was no traffic to speak of. Across the road, Roy was dozing in a rocking chair in front of his shop. Raz had rattled by in his pickup earlier, with his pedigreed sow Marjorie hanging her head out the passenger's side. I'd caught a flash of pink as Mrs. Jim Bob drove by, most likely heading for the rectory to harangue Brother Verber. Children screeched at each other as they rode their bicycles down the middle of the road. There was some activity at the pool hall, but nobody would get rip-roarin' drunk until evening. We might not observe the cocktail hour, but happy hour on Friday was a sacred ritual.

Lately, the water stain on the ceiling had taken to resembling a map of South America, and the spider was approaching the coastline of Brazil. I wondered if it was hoping to find its own species in the Amazon rain forest. I had just concluded it was more likely to end up in Colombia when the door opened and Dahlia thundered in.

"You got to do something!" she said shrilly.

"About the drug cartels? I wish I could, but it's up to the DEA."

This stopped her, but only for a few seconds. "No, about my granny. She's drivin' me crazy, Arly. What are you aimin' to do about it?"

"What do you suggest? I can't exactly arrest her, you know."

Dahlia flopped down on the chair across from me. "You got to make that nursing home in Starley City take her. I can have her packed up and waiting by the road in ten minutes. Go ahead and call 'em."

I waited a moment to see if the chair was going to collapse, then shook my head. "I don't have any influence with them. Have you tried the county health department? Surely they have some kind of day-care program for the elderly."

"I took her there yesterday morning, but while I was filling out some forms in the office, she took off all her clothes and climbed onto the piano. Some of the old geezers liked to have had heart attacks right there on the spot. We was out on the curb in no time flat, and it was all I could do not to just leave her sittin' there and drive off." Her brow lowered ominously. "I would have, too, but I'd already told 'em my name and address. Mebbe I should put her in a gunnysack and dump her out in the woods."

"That's against the law," I said quickly. "You don't want to deliver your baby in a prison hospital, do you?"

She mulled this over for a moment. "I reckon not. When are you gonna do something about Eileen?"

"She's not back?"

"Would I be askin' if she was?" Dahlia struggled to her feet and trudged toward the door. "Earl ain't heard from her, neither. He's mopin' around like a mangy dawg."

After she left, I did some highly intricate calculations and determined Eileen had been gone for at least thirty hours. It was premature to call in a posse or demand that Harve issue an APB, but it was worrisome. I considered calling Earl, then decided to drive over to his house and ask a few questions, some of which might be awkward.

His pickup was parked in the yard. I went up onto the porch and knocked on the screen door. When there was no response, I opened the door and called his name. I continued into the living room, and then into the kitchen, where I found him sitting at the table, dressed in grubby trousers and a torn undershirt. He had not shaved in the last two days, and his eyes were red and glazed. An empty bottle of cheap whiskey on the table did much to explain his appearance.

"Earl?" I said. "Are you okay?"

"Yeah," he muttered.

I noticed there were no dirty dishes on the counter or in the sink. "Have you had anything to eat today?"

"I don't rightly recollect."

I opened the refrigerator and took out some leftover meatloaf. I made him a thick sandwich, set it in front of him, and sat down. "Dahlia said you haven't heard from Eileen."

"Dahlia sez a lot of things. Just listening to her wears me out. I don't know how Kevin puts up with her all the time jabbering like a magpie."

"But you haven't heard from Eileen," I said.

"Nope."

"I know it's none of my business, Earl, but did you and she have an argument the night before she left?"

"She fixed supper, then went out to some fool meeting at the county extension office. Quilting, mebbe. Got home about nine, bitched at me for leaving cake crumbs on the counter, and went to bed. The next morning she was gone, slick as a whistle."

"And she didn't take anything with her?" I persisted.

He lumbered to his feet and took a bottle of whiskey from a cabinet. After a brief struggle punctuated by grunts and curses, he wrenched off the top and took a deep swig. "How in tarnation would I know? Her toothbrush is still in the bathroom, along with her bottle of mouthwash. Stuff tastes like horse piss." He dropped back in the chair and gazed moodily at the salt and pepper shakers. "Worse'n horse piss."

"Did you call her relatives?"

"Kevin did yesterday evening, and

ever'body else he could think of. Nobody's laid eyes on her."

I sat down across from him. "What about money, Earl?"

"What about it?" he said as he took another swig of whiskey.

"Did she . . . well, empty your wallet while you were asleep?"

He gave me a dark look. "Weren't but a couple of dollars in it. I reckon she could have gone to the bank. Are you saying she cleaned out the account and took off for good?"

"I'm not saying anything, Earl. I'm just worried about her, the same as you are. Why don't you call your bank and ask them about the last withdrawal, and then call me. If she has money, she'll be safer."

"That's all you have to say?" he said in a surly voice. "You ain't gonna do anything about it?" His face turned red as he thumped the tabletop with his fist. "She's got no right to run off like this! Can't you have her arrested for running off?"

I eased out of the chair and backed toward the living room. Earl was a big man, with a thick neck and strong arms from years of manual labor on his farm. He wasn't a notorious brawler, but there had been times when I'd had to drag him out of the pool hall and send him home with an acerbic lecture. At the moment, he was too befuddled to intimidate me, but I didn't want the scenario to turn any uglier.

Instead of responding, I went out to my car and drove back toward the PD. I had no idea what Eileen was up to, but I wished her well.

"Well, just what was I supposed to have said?" grumbled Ruby Bee as she filled baskets with pretzels in preparation for happy hour. "It ain't like the motel's booked up for the next six months."

Estelle leaned over and snagged one of the baskets. "I myself wouldn't sleep at night knowing that kind of people were in the next unit. Far be it from me to criticize you for wanting to make money, but don't go selling your soul to the devil for less than a million dollars — or maybe that should be pesos."

"That's the silliest talk I've heard since Berrymore Buchanon decided he was gonna run for president of the United States. Remember how he snuck around town at night planting signs in people's yards?"

"Say what you like," Estelle replied disdainfully, "but you're the one who's gonna have to put up with all manner of tacky behavior. Don't come whining to me on account of how you can't get any sleep because they're having fiestas or whatever you call 'em."

Ruby Bee went over to the window and looked out at the parking lot of the Flamingo Motel. There were two concrete block buildings, each with four rooms. She'd cut a door between numbers one and two, using one as a sitting room with a small kitchenette and the other as her bedroom. More often than not, the rest of the units were empty. Now four of them were rented for at least three months.

"They look perfectly normal to me," she said as she watched the men and women remove battered suitcases from a van. She'd prudently (or perhaps prudishly) put the men on one side and the women on the other, although there wasn't much more than thirty feet separating the buildings. And it wasn't like the Flamingo Motel had never been home to some hanky-panky.

Estelle joined her at the window. "But they're foreigners."

"So's the fellow what owns the Dairee Dee-Lishus, but him and his family are real nice. Do you recollect when their little boy played baseball on my team?"

"They don't go to church."

Ruby Bee resisted the urge to jab her friend in the arm. "Yes, they do. I told you that he said they're Catholics, so they go to Farberville on Sunday mornings."

"Catholics. Now if that don't make you nervous, nothing should."

"Estelle Oppers," said Ruby Bee, aghast, "I never knew you were a bigot. Catholics are Christians, same as us. Furthermore, just because somebody is from another country doesn't mean he's some kind of junkyard dog."

"I never said that, Ruby Bee Hanks, and I don't appreciate being called a bigot! I am just as open-minded as anybody else."

Ruby Bee narrowed her eyes. "I heard what you said — and it wasn't pretty."

"All I said was that you ought to be a mite careful with all these foreigners staying at the motel." Estelle banged down her glass on the bar and spun around. "When you're ready to apologize, you know where to find me. Have a nice day!" She stomped across the dance floor and out the door. Seconds later, her tires spun in the gravel as she drove away.

"When *I'm* ready to apologize?" muttered Ruby Bee as she snatched up the glass and washed it in the sink. "That'll be long after the cows come home, let me tell you. You can sit under a hair dryer and sip sherry all by your lonesome, Estelle Oppers. I ain't got time for bigots in this bar! Why, I've half a mind to . . ." She stopped and wrinkled her forehead, since she couldn't come up with much of anything. She dried the glass and put it on a shelf, then went into the kitchen to check on the ham and the sweet potato casserole in the oven. The pies were already done, and it was too early to start the rolls. It was tempting to go out back and welcome her guests, even though Dr. Skiller had warned her that none of them spoke English. At least they'd understand a smile and an armload of extra towels.

When she came out of the kitchen, she saw she had a customer in one of the booths. He was scruffy, with frizzy brown hair pulled back in a ponytail and stubbly cheeks. His nose dominated his face, and from what she could see of his eyes, they were small and dark. He was wearing a battered leather hat and a dirty denim jacket. He lit a cigarette, then looked up at her and said, "Can I get a hamburger and a beer?"

"Sure can," she said, wishing she wasn't alone with him. She'd been held up a couple of times over the years, and she hadn't enjoyed it one bit. Her eyes widened as he came over to the bar and sat down on a stool, but she refrained from going for the baseball bat she kept under the counter.

"Whatever you have on tap is fine," he said, "and let me have fries with the burger."

She filled a mug and set it down. "It'll take a few minutes for the food."

"I'm not in a hurry."

Ruby Bee was sorry to hear that, since she wouldn't have minded if he downed the beer and left. She moved an ashtray within his reach and retreated into the kitchen. It wasn't like he'd done anything, she reminded herself. Customers came in all the time, and some of them were strangers. It was all Estelle's fault for making those remarks earlier about the Mexicans out back, implying they were thieves and murderers just because they were foreigners. Still, it might have been comforting if someone else came by for a beer.

She fixed his plate and took it back to the barroom. He was still sitting on the stool, all innocent and smiling just a little bit. The light from the neon beer signs behind her gave him a peculiar pinkish glow, but that was hardly his fault.

"Looks good," he said as he took the plate. "This place usually so quiet?"

"Almost never, and I'll be real surprised if

folks don't come through the door any minute. My daughter usually comes by about this time, too. She's the chief of police. Sometimes she complains about having to carry a gun, but it's part of her job. She's a lot tougher than she looks, lemme tell you. She's always breaking up fights at the pool hall, and some of them ol' boys are bigger than boxcars."

He gave her a curious look, then began to eat.

Ruby Bee gave him a few minutes, then said, "Are you just passing through?"

"I plan to stay around here for a while."

"Oh, really?" She raised her eyebrows and waited, but when he didn't explain, said, "You have kinfolk here?"

"Not that I know of, but we're all part of the family of mankind, aren't we? The children of the earth goddess, the servants of the stars, the guardians of the mountain streams and gentle breezes."

"I suppose so," she said uneasily. From the way he was looking at her, she wouldn't have been surprised if he was to invite her to get nekkid and howl at the moon. "What's your line of work?"

He finished the last fry and pushed his plate aside. "I'm a personal trainer."

Ruby Bee's forehead crinkled. "Is that

like an animal trainer?"

"In a way I guess it is, although animals are probably easier to work with." He took out his wallet and put a ten-dollar bill on the bar. After Ruby Bee rang it up on the cash register and came back with change, he said, "Can you tell me how to find the Stonebridge Foundation?"

"Glad to oblige," she said, trying to keep her voice from cracking. "Take a left and go down a ways until you come to where the New Age hardware store used to be before the roof collapsed a couple of years back. It's catty-corner to what was the branch bank until it burned to the ground. These days Velveeta Buchanon parks there and sells vegetables from the back of her pickup, but she quits 'long about noon. Turn toward the low-water bridge and go about a quarter of a mile. It's right across the road from a persimmon tree. You can't miss it."

He touched the brim of his hat and left. She waited until she heard the door close before allowing herself to clutch her throat. As soon as Darla Jean had told her mother about finding the psychiatrist's name on the Internet, Millicent had wasted no time sharing the news. Now everybody in town knew the Stonebridge Foundation was a lunatic asylum. To think a patient had come into her bar & grill! Why, she could of been murdered right then and there! Arly would have come by sooner or later and found her bloodied body on the floor behind the bar. Then the sheriff and the coroner would show up, along with deputies to put up yellow tape across the front door. Her picture would be on the front page of the newspaper, and her obituary on the second page.

She was about to snatch up the phone and call Arly to tell her not to invite Estelle to the funeral when it occurred to her she was letting her imagination run wild. But she didn't have anything else to do for the next hour, so she went ahead and dialed the number.

5

※

"Would anyone care for a glass of pinot noir before we begin? It's really quite nice, and all the rage in California." Vincent was seated behind his impressive walnut desk. At the moment, its surface was clear except for a neat stack of manila folders, a gold pen, and a lamp. His walls, on the other hand, were covered with autographed photos taken of him with toothy celebrities and politicians.

"Not for me," said Brenda. "I still have a thousand details to see to before tomorrow."

Vincent gazed at her. "Shall we discuss Walter Kaiser? He is . . . well, he is not what I expected. Does he have any credentials, or did you find him at a homeless shelter?"

"He has a license and experience in his field. He may look a bit unconventional, but he has promised that by tomorrow he will present an acceptable demeanor. He is as eager as we are to make a success of our pro-

113

gram. I can promise you that you will hear no complaints about him." What she meant, of course, was that Vince would not hear any complaints if she could do anything about it. On his arrival, Walter had pulled her aside and made it clear to her that he needed the job for at least six months, as well as a substantial loan. When she'd asked if outstanding warrants were involved, he'd given her a saccharine smile. She'd seen corpses with more agreeable expressions. Several of them.

Vincent held up the bottle and glanced at Randall. "Wine?"

"No, thank you. I've treated too many people who abused alcohol because of stress. Ever since things . . . started to fall apart, I don't trust myself. I need to keep a clear head. Maybe I'll let Brenda talk me into one of her herbal concoctions."

"California poppy, passionflower, and valerian capsules will help, along with several cups of chamomile or catnip tea during the day," she said, making a note.

Vincent poured himself a glass of wine and opened the top folder. "Then let's review the case files for our patients, all of whom are arriving tomorrow. The first will be Dawn Dartmouth. She was a child actress in a sitcom. She began when she was four years old, and the show ran for seven years. During her teenage years, she had parts in several made-for-cable movies, usually playing the role of a prostitute or a runaway. Her sister died when she was fourteen. Dawn is now twenty-two. Her mother is an alcoholic with multiple failed marriages. Her father is, shall we say, missing in action. Dawn was first arrested at the age of fifteen, when she crashed her mother's car into a neighbor's garage. Her alcohol level was twice the legal limit, and she had cocaine in her possession. It was hushed up, as were many subsequent charges of a similar nature."

"A typical Hollywood brat," commented Brenda. She turned to Randall for support, but his head was bowed as he scribbled notes with a jerky hand.

"One could say that," Vincent said. "Recently Dawn was involved in an incident that could not be so easily dismissed. It seems she was romantically linked to a rock star who ditched her. She drove into his yard, shot out all the windows in the front of the house, and attacked his Ferrari with a tire iron. When the police arrived, she attempted to run over one of them with her car. She was quite drunk and high on a variety of drugs, and the gun was unlicensed.

The judge has agreed to keep the matter out of court until she completes a rehab program. Her lawyer found a place in California, but Dawn checked herself out after three days. This is her last chance. If she does not complete our program, she will go to trial."

Randall slapped down the pen. "Anger management, as well as private counseling for low self-esteem and conflicts with her mother. Tranquilizers until she's through initial withdrawal, and then mood stabilizers and an antidepressant."

"Why give her more drugs?" said Brenda. "She needs a cleansing regime and vitamin therapy. It's obvious she has nutritional deficiencies."

Vincent withheld a sigh. "In this situation, and in all the other cases I'm going to present, I believe a wide variety of therapies will be best."

"You don't dump a bucket of water on someone who's drowning," Brenda countered mulishly. "All these drugs Randall wants to give her are addictive, too."

"But not as self-destructive," said Randall.

Brenda's eyes narrowed. "So we merely exchange one addiction for another?"

Vincent held up his hand. "Enough of

this," he said as if calming down recalcitrant toddlers. "Our next patient is Alexandra Swayze."

"*Senator* Swayze?" Randall glanced up. "Isn't she running for reelection?"

"Yes, indeed. She is notoriously conservative, and an outspoken critic of anything she believes threatens old-fashioned family values. She serves on several influential committees. It is rumored that she will be offered a prestigious ambassadorship. She's sixty-one years old, widowed, and became addicted to prescription pain pills after a riding accident four years ago. In the last month, she attempted suicide twice. Her son and her political advisers insisted that she go into a rehab program, but until now she's resisted because she's afraid the press might find out."

Brenda snorted under her breath. "She advocates mandatory prayer in the schools, the abolishment of social services for low-income families, harsh punishment for unwed mothers, and lengthy prison sentences for first-time, nonviolent drug offenders. How someone can consider herself pro-family when she —"

"Her politics are not our problem," Vincent said. "Her addiction is."

"Wouldn't the press love this one,"

Brenda continued. "The hypocrisy of it is astounding. She's said publicly that addicts deserve prison, not rehabilitation. Now she's come groveling to us."

"She'll need heavy sedation at first," said Randall. "Antidepressants after she's gone through the worst of the withdrawal. We'll have to step down the drugs, and replace them. It may well take ninety days."

Brenda glared at him. "So again, more drugs. She should experience the withdrawal in order to better understand the powerful grip of addiction. Maybe then she won't be so eager to condemn addicts."

"I don't think we want her clawing the furniture," Randall shot back. "She can't go cold turkey without severe symptoms."

Vincent rapped on his desk with the pen. "If you two keep this up, we'll be here until midnight." He opened a folder. "Our next case is Toby Mann."

"The quarterback?" gasped Randall, his jaw dropping. "He was All-American in high school and won the Heisman in college. He's taken his team to the Superbowl three times."

"The same," Vincent said. He did not care for football himself, but he'd looked over the information provided by Toby Mann's agent. "He makes a million dollars a year as a player, and even more from endorsements for everything from sports equipment to disposable diapers. He was arrested last month and charged with raping a woman in his hotel room after a game. He claims it was consensual; she denies it. There have been other accusations of this kind, but each time Toby's lawyers have been able to settle the matter quietly. This time the young woman has not been obliging."

"He's a serial rapist," Brenda said flatly.

Vincent flinched. "It's a matter of interpretation, and no one except the parties who were in the hotel room knows exactly what happened. Toby has a problem with alcohol and recreational drugs, and has been taking anabolic steroids. Naturally, Toby's lawyers are reluctant to use this as a defense, since he would be suspended by the league. The trial has been postponed while Toby goes through a ninety-day psychiatric evaluation. He's under a court order, so if he leaves, he'll be found in contempt."

"I'll need a list of the steroids," said Randall. "He's certainly a candidate for anger management and behavior modification techniques."

"What? No drugs?" Brenda said in a facetiously shocked voice. "I was beginning to think you were on commission with the pharmaceutical companies."

"We can't rule out medication until we determine the level of his physical dependency."

"Shall we continue?" inserted Vincent, now visibly annoyed. "Our fourth patient's identity may amuse you. He is Dr. Shelby Dibbins, author of the best sellers *Dr. Dibbins's Diet for Longevity* and *Dr. Dibbins's Diet Dogma.* His use of the honorific is questionable, since his Ph.D. is in secondary education rather than medicine."

Brenda was not amused. "That diet is unhealthy — and dangerous. He preaches eighty percent carbohydrates, and minimal protein and fats. The human body requires a certain level of protein to function. Dibbins encourages his followers to pig out on pasta, bread, and potatoes. He should be sued for malpractice."

"I suspect I'm more familiar with the intricacies of malpractice than you, my dear," Vincent said drily. "Dr. Dibbins is merely exercising his freedom of speech. What's more, there are plenty of quacks within the medical profession and some of its associated fields."

"What's that supposed to mean?" Brenda

stood up, her fingers curled. "Are you implying that I —"

"I meant nothing by it, nothing whatsoever. Now sit down and control yourself. I still have some unpacking to do." He waited until she obeyed, then went on. "It seems Dr. Dibbins does not adhere to his own or any other diet plan. He currently weighs over four hundred pounds, and has difficulty walking. Although he has not yet been diagnosed with diabetes or heart disease, he is a perfect candidate. He drinks to excess, smokes, and obviously overeats. He has a new book coming out in the fall, but his publishing company has threatened to cancel it if he can't go on tour and make the talk-show circuit. His literary agent has promised us a bonus of twenty-five thousand dollars if Dibbins loses a hundred pounds in ninety days, and a thousand for each pound after that. He'll need a series of surgical skin tightenings, as well as liposuctions, an abdominoplasty, and eventually a rhytidectomy. A severely limited caloric intake, as much physical activity as he can handle, and therapy."

"He's agreed to this?" said Randall.

"To some extent. According to the agent, Dibbins is tyrannical, egotistical, and verbally abusive. He's been divorced three times. No children, which is good, since he probably would have eaten them before their first birthdays. He is coming here only because of the pressure being applied by his agent and editor."

"I'll make sure he has a very *special* diet," said Brenda.

Randall nodded. "We can enhance his metabolism and disrupt the absorption of calories with medication. That ought to speed up his weight loss."

"All right, then," Vincent said as he closed the folder, "I believe that covers it. Randall and I need to inspect the surgical suite. Brenda, I'll see you in an hour to review the drug inventory lists and tidy up any details you've overlooked. Did you arrange for local motel rooms for the employees?"

"Of course. The van has already delivered them, so they can unpack and get settled in." She handed a typed page to each of her colleagues. "I've scheduled all four maids from seven in the morning until two, and then split shifts until after dinner. The number of orderlies on duty at any given time throughout will vary, depending on need. Guard duty at night will rotate. The chef and his assistants will arrive in the morning in time to prepare breakfast, and leave in the late afternoon. They'll have their meals with the employees in the break room behind the kitchen."

Randall raised his eyebrows. "Are you sure he's a chef?"

Brenda folded her arms and sat back, staring at him. "Let's not get into semantics. He may not have had any formal training, but I've instructed him on garnishes and presentation. We're not competing for stars in the Michelin guide. The food served here will be healthy, with an emphasis on raw fruits, whole grains, and vegetables. Portions will be rigorously controlled."

"Sprigs of parsley and artfully sculpted radishes can cover a multitude of sins," added Vincent.

She nodded. "That's everyone except Miss Foss. Did she find you?"

"Oh, yes," he said blandly. "I think she'll make a splendid addition to the staff. We wouldn't want our new patients to be greeted by a sullen, unattractive receptionist, would we? I suggest we have a celebratory dinner this evening, with the steaks and champagne I brought specifically for the occasion. There's no need to dress."

"You don't look all that dead," I said as I

slid onto a stool and lifted the glass dome to gaze longingly at a cherry pie.

Ruby Bee glowered at me. "It's about time you showed up, Miss Chief of Police. I must have left the message more than two hours ago. It's a miracle you didn't find me hacked to death on the kitchen floor — or worse. There I was, all by my lonesome, when that homicidal maniac came right up to the bar and ordered a hamburger."

"Was he packing a machete?"

"He could have been, for all you care!"

I replaced the dome and leaned over the bar to pour myself a mug of beer, since the proprietress wasn't at her most hospitable. "Tell me exactly what he said."

"For one thing, he said he was a personal trainer. I found that mighty suspicious."

I was definitely paddling upstream after a heavy rain. "All that means is he puts together exercise programs. What else did he say?"

"He asked for directions to that lunatic asylum. I figure he's one of the patients who escaped."

"Or he has a job there," I said. "And nobody said it was a lunatic asylum. It's more likely to be a genteel retreat for very rich women who want to lose a few pounds. A spa, or something similar."

"With a psychiatrist and a trainer," Ruby Bee said, unwilling to relent. "All you have to do is drive up to the front door and find out for sure. Put on some lipstick before you go. Your cheeks are so rosy these days, your lips are almost invisible."

"As I've said several hundred times, it's not in my jurisdiction. Furthermore, the guard has been replaced with an electric gate and a speaker box. I couldn't drive up to the front door if I wanted to — which I don't." I looked down the row of empty stools. "Where's Estelle?"

Ruby Bee sniffed. "I don't know, and I don't care one whit."

"You and she had a disagreement?" I said carefully.

"A sight more than that, but I don't want to talk about it. What if this crazy man kidnapped Eileen and has her tied up in a shack up on Cotter's Ridge?"

"I went over to Earl's earlier today and talked to him. It's pretty obvious Eileen got fed up with him, or with Dahlia, and took off of her own free will. She'll come back when she's ready to, although it may be a while."

"That ain't like her," said Ruby Bee, shaking her head.

"You've never seen Earl in an undershirt."

"I'd like to think not. So is that where you were all day? I was beginning to think you'd run off to Springfield."

I politely overlooked her remark. "No, I had to see a man in Belle Star about a fish, and that took half the afternoon. When I got back to town, Perkin came in to complain about something or other involving Raz. I never did quite figure it out. Just another exciting day in Maggody."

"Well, maybe tomorrow that maniac will come back and slice my throat, just so you'll have something to do," Ruby Bee said snippily. "If you'll excuse me, I need to see to some customers out back in the motel, then get ready for happy hour. Feel free to sit there, but keep your fingers out of the cherry pie."

She flounced into the kitchen, mumbling under her breath. I finished my beer, and after some thought, went back to my apartment to open a can of soup, watch the news, and perhaps call a certain telephone number in Springfield.

Saturday morning should have been sunny, with birds singing from the treetops and butterflies flitting over the flower beds in front of the Stonebridge Foundation. The scent of honeysuckle should have welcomed the new arrivals with a redolent embrace. However, this sky was low and dingy, and the steady drizzle had driven away the birds and butterflies. The flowers, lacking incentive, remained closed.

Dawn Dartmouth's lawyer, dressed in a dark suit, muted tie, and pricey Italian shoes, stepped into a puddle as he got out on one side of the limo. The driver opened the passenger door on the other side and waited.

Sid Rookman, a junior partner in the firm and therefore resigned to being stuck with the least appealing assignments, waited alongside the driver for several minutes while rain slithered down his back. Finally, he leaned over and said, "Dawn, we're here. You have to get out of the car sooner or later. Let's get it over with, okay? You either do the program here, or you do prison time — and it won't be in any minimum-risk facility with private rooms and tennis courts. You've got felony charges pending. What's it going to be?"

"Fuck you."

"Whatever," he said wearily. He'd been up since five o'clock to make the seven o'clock flight on the corporate jet. Dawn had refused to speak the entire trip, which suited him fine. She'd snapped once at the limo driver, but other than that, she'd been sullen, her lower lip extended in a pout, her eyelids puffy and red. "We can go back to the airport, if that's what you want. In a couple of days, we can try for a plea bargain so you won't have to do more than ten years."

"It wasn't my fault. If that scumbag hadn't been such a lying bastard, none of this would have happened."

"That may be, but the reality is that you committed a lot of felonies, including the attempted murder of a police officer."

"He was in my way."

"Then tell it to the judge," said Sid, shrugging.

Dawn emerged from the car. Her few remaining fans, most of them from her sitcom days, would have been aghast. She was bloated and pasty, as though she'd been living in an underground bomb shelter. Her once curly hair was limp and had faded to a dull oatmeal hue. She stopped to stare at the front of the building. "My God. Shouldn't there be hillbillies on the porch playing fiddles and drinking moonshine? Where are the mules?"

Sid forced himself to take her arm. "Dr. Stonebridge has assured me that it's very nice inside. You remember him, don't you?

Didn't he work magic on your face after you rear-ended that school bus a few years ago?"

"How was I supposed to know the damn bus was going to stop like that?" She looked at the limo driver. "Be careful with my luggage this time, you clumsy asshole. If anything is broken, I'll make sure you end up on unemployment."

Sid hustled her across the porch and into the reception room. A stunning blonde in a white lab coat came across the room, beaming at them. "You must be Dawn Dartmouth. Welcome to the Stonebridge Foundation."

Dawn stepped back. "Who're you?"

"Molly Foss. I'm so pleased to meet you, Miss Dartmouth. I hope you had a pleasant trip."

"Where did they get this bimbo?" Dawn asked Sid. "Central casting?"

He sensed a tantrum developing. It would not be pretty. "Perhaps you could show Miss Dartmouth to her room?"

"Yes, of course," said Molly, her smile slipping. "One of the maids will be along shortly to help you unpack."

"And search my luggage? Want to pat me down now and paw through my purse?"

Sid tightened his grip on her arm. "It

beats a cavity search and a hosing for lice," he said to Dawn.

She jerked free of his hand and followed Molly down a corridor. Sid held open the front door for the limo driver, who was struggling with three heavy suitcases and a cosmetics case. Once the suitcases were deposited in a corner, Sid followed the driver back out to the car and told him to head for the airport. To hell with Dawn Dartmouth, he thought as he lit a cigarette and opened his briefcase to retrieve a flask of gin.

"Is there any ice?" he asked the driver.

"This is ridiculous, Lloyd," Alexandra Swayze said as they drove by mile after mile of bleak forests and overgrown fields. The few houses they passed were mean little hovels with rusted cars and scrawny chickens in the yards. Toddlers in baggy diapers waddled through the weeds, their faces streaked with dirt. Faded work shirts and torn jeans hung on clotheslines. "All I need is a vacation on some island. As I've said many times on the floor of the Senate, rehabilitation programs are a waste of the taxpayers' money. They're nothing but a sham to mollycoddle drug addicts. I am not an addict, Lloyd. I am capable of dealing with this myself."

"By overdosing?" said her son. "By sitting in the car with the engine running and the garage door closed?"

"I was not myself," Alexandra said coldly.

"And you won't be until you're off these medications. Several of your colleagues have asked me privately if you've been having health problems. Have you forgotten the luncheon last month when you stormed out after someone asked you a question? It was a blind item in all the gossip columns."

"An impertinent question. I was invited to speak, not to be heckled."

"You can't continue to behave like that. The polls look good now, but they'll start slipping if you get a reputation for irrational outbursts. You have a heavy campaign schedule in the fall. You're going to have to be able to control yourself and play by the rules. Your opponent is already clamoring for a series of debates."

"He can go to hell — which is likely to be just around the next curve." Alexandra snatched up the map and peered at it. "What's the name of the town?"

"Maggody. You might as well put away the map, since it's not on it. That's why your doctor recommended this place." Lloyd slowed down as they came upon a tractor chugging along at ten miles an hour.

He tried to hide his impatience until at last he had a chance to pass. His mother had been bitching the entire trip, from the moment he'd carried her bag and briefcase out to the taxi double-parked on the narrow Georgetown street until they'd arrived at the dinky airport. Although the Stonebridge Foundation had offered to provide a limo, she'd insisted that he rent a car. He wouldn't have been surprised if she'd also demanded that they disguise themselves with wigs and sunglasses. Senators, he'd long since concluded, were burdened with a peculiar mix of egotism and paranoia. But if his mother hadn't been a senator, he would not have been a lobbyist with a high six-figure salary.

Alexandra tossed down the map. "I do hope these people understand that under no circumstances will I be coerced into sitting on a metal chair and spilling my soul to a group of strangers. These group therapy sessions are for chronic losers like alcoholics and battered women. I have always believed that we are responsible for our own choices, Lloyd, and must live with them. That is exactly why I allowed you to marry Patricia, even though she's quite stupid."

He ground his teeth and concentrated on the road. His heart began to thump with elation as he spotted the sign for County 104. When they arrived at the gate, he pushed the button on the box and identified himself and his passenger. He glanced at Alexandra. Her hands were shaking, despite the fact he'd seen her surreptitiously gulping down pills on the airplane. "It will be fine, Mother," he said gently. "They'll ease you off the medications and encourage you to gain back some of the weight you've lost. You'll be full of energy for the campaign in the fall. And soon after that, perhaps Patricia, the children, and I will be dining with you at Grosvenor Square in London."

He parked in front of the door and took her suitcase and briefcase out of the trunk. He was prepared to open her door and drag her out if necessary, but she eventually emerged. Her expression was leery, but her voice was as strident as usual as she said, "This is a very bad idea, Lloyd. If so much as one word gets out, my career will be ruined. The political pundits and cartoonists will have a wonderful romp at my expense."

"You have no choice," he said. "Either you get off the medications or lose the election. The media will never find out about this place. Officially, you're on a low-profile fact-finding mission in Asia. The press will be fed tidbits to confirm the story."

"Then let's get it over with," she said. "Stop gawking and pick up my luggage, Lloyd. All I can say is that there had better not be twelve steps up to the porch."

"You stupid motherfucker!" yelled Toby Mann at the car that shot out in front of him as he started to turn onto County 104.

"Cool it," said Myron Bollix, his agent.

"Yeah, sure." Toby took a hand off the steering wheel to gulp down a beer. "Easy for you to say, buddy boy. You're not about to be locked up for ninety days with a bunch of loons. We'll probably sit in a circle and hold hands while some asshole talks about how he's always wanted to bang his mother." He squeezed the beer can in his left hand until it crumpled, then tossed it out the window. "Look, Myron, there's a dinosaur."

"I believe it's more commonly called a cow."

Toby laughed. "What the hell do you know about cows?"

"Not much, but apparently more than you. You're gonna have to straighten up, Toby. Do your time and pray that your lawyers can settle this out of court. If it goes to trial, the league commissioners are going to come down on you like" — he hesitated — "a pack of feral cows."

"But why here?" Toby said, resorting to a whine. "There are a helluva lot of rehabs near the city. I don't like nature, Myron. I don't like cows and pigs and bugs. I don't even like playing ball on grass. Give me a domed stadium and artificial turf any time."

"Here, because the night after the charges were filed, the photographers found you at a club with half a dozen beautiful women. Here, because you skipped a court appearance to take off to a Caribbean island. Your lawyers want you to stay off the tabloid covers while they try to negotiate a deal. The judge was kind enough to allow you to undergo a psych evaluation before he makes a decision. Luckily for you, he happens to be a fan."

"It's all that bitch's fault," said Toby. "She was all over me in the bar, nibbling my ear and telling me what a bad girl she was. Once we got upstairs, she was naked on the bed before I could open the champagne. Guess I should have noticed the dollar signs in her eyes, but I was too busy admiring her tits." He stopped at a gate. "This it?"

"Yes," Myron said, trying to hide his delight. Toby had insisted on driving to Arkansas, which meant Myron had been

135

obliged to listen to griping and cursing for an intolerable number of hours. But Toby's lucrative deals provided much of Myron's income, and putting up with an inflated ego was part of the job, along with being awakened at ungodly hours of the night to go to police stations with bail money.

After they parked, Toby grabbed a duffel bag from the backseat. "This psych evaluation thing doesn't mean they're going to attach metal gizmos to my head or something, does it? I saw this movie once with Jack Nicholson where they strapped him down and —"

"Nothing like that," Myron said, slapping him on the back and secretly hoping the so-called metal gizmos were attached to Toby's testicles, which were the cause of the problem. "You'll just meet with a psychiatrist, relax, and get clean. You didn't bring along anything that you shouldn't have, did you? They'll search your bag, so you might as well hand it over to me now."

"What do you take me for — some kind of idiot?"

That was precisely what Myron took him for, but it didn't seem wise to agree. "Do you want me to go inside with you?"

"Yeah, why not?" said Toby, gripping the strap of the duffel bag.

They went through the front door and stopped in the reception room. An attractive young woman stood up behind a desk.

"Toby Mann?" she said breathlessly. "Like, wow, I must be like your biggest fan. I've never been to a game, but I watch every single time there's one on TV. I just love it when you pull off your helmet after a touchdown and the sun shines on your hair. My husband's so jealous, I have to go to my sister's house to watch your games. That game against the Vikings last year was so exciting I almost had an orgasm when you threw the touchdown pass with less than a minute left. My sister threatened to pour ice water on me." She clamped her hand over her mouth. "Ooh, I'm supposed to pretend I don't know who you are. You won't tell on me, will you? I'd absolutely die if I got fired on my first day."

"You work here?" Toby rewarded her with his famous boyish grin. "You gonna give me sponge baths in bed?"

"Don't I wish?" she said with a giggle. "I'm just the receptionist and secretary, but if there's ever anything I can do to make your stay more pleasant, all you have to do is ask. My name's Molly."

"A lovely name," Myron said politely, although he had a real bad feeling about the situation. He would have felt a lot more confident if they'd been met by a scowling gorilla in dirty green scrubs. He jabbed Toby in the back. "Let's find your room so that you can unpack."

"You're right down here," said Molly. "And it's not a room, it's a really nice suite. I wish I could afford to furnish my whole house like it."

Toby took her arm. "Well, why don't we go have a look at it? The key's in the car, Myron."

Shrugging, Myron went back to the car. He adjusted the seat and the mirrors, since he was eight inches shorter than his client. As he drove away, he decided not to mention his misgivings to the team of lawyers.

"I feel as if I should welcome Dr. Dibbins to Fantasy Island," Vincent said as he and Brenda stood at the edge of the pasture, partially protected by umbrellas.

"That's where he'll be wishing he was," she said grimly. "I can hardly wait to see his expression when I explain his dietary regime for the next three months."

"Tread gently, my dear. We can't have him storming off and then publicly spouting outrageously false claims about the foundation. Our biggest assets are our obscurity and pledge of privacy."

"You think someone like Dibbins would admit he was ever at a place like this? His book sales would plummet. Have you ever seen him on TV?"

Vincent's smile held a trace of condescension. "I don't own a TV. My practice and my social life keep me very busy. Whenever I have a few free minutes, I utilize them to read medical journals to keep myself informed of the latest innovations."

"Your practice and your social life? What about the time you spend in court battling malpractice claims? That must be time-consuming, too. I heard that your license was revoked after some woman died from an infection caused by an error on your part."

"That is a simplification of the facts," he said stiffly. "The patient was clearly negligent in not informing me as her condition worsened. My lawyers are appealing the decision. What's important is that I am licensed in this state."

Brenda looked up as she heard a whirring noise. "That must be the helicopter."

Vincent snapped his fingers at the two orderlies waiting nearby with a gurney. "Look alert, *muchachos.*"

The two men, one in his thirties and the other almost fifty, glanced at each other as they wheeled the gurney closer. Neither had a clue why they were out in the rain, but *el jefe* seemed to think it was a good idea. They stared as a *helicoptero* came through the clouds, circled, and then landed in the weedy expanse.

Vincent and Brenda ducked as they went under the rotors, their eyes stinging from the dust and bits of debris swirling around them. The pilot, a weathered man of indeterminate years, leaned out a window and said, "It may be a while. He says he's changed his mind."

From inside the helicopter, they could hear voices arguing. It was impossible to decipher what was being said, but clearly there was a great deal of acrimony.

"What should we do?" whispered Brenda. "Maybe you ought to intervene with your jovial banalities."

"Or you could assure him that he'll have all the alfalfa sprouts he wants for the next ninety days," Vincent replied with a cool smile.

A distraught woman slid open a side door and looked at them. "Is one of you Dr. Stonebridge?"

Vincent stood up despite his innate fear of decapitation. "I am he. And you are . . . ?"

"Deb Ables, Dr. Dibbins's literary agent.

We have a small problem."

"I understand Dr. Dibbins has some reservations," Vincent said tactfully.

A voice from inside roared, "No, no, no! I will not subject myself to this! Close that door and get this contraption back in the air! Do you hear me, you sniveling succubus! How many times must I say it?"

The agent glanced back, then stepped out into the weeds. "He indeed has some reservations, but he also has a five-million-dollar contract for his new book. It specifies that he must participate in the promotion or return the advance. In his current condition, he cannot handle a twenty-seven-city book tour and national media appearances."

"If you don't tell this lummox of a pilot to take off, you're fired!" Dibbins howled. "To hell with the book, and to hell with you!"

"Sedation?" suggested Brenda.

Deb thought for a moment. "A bottle of bourbon might work. I don't suppose you have one on the premises, this being a rehab facility, but it would calm him down."

Vincent pulled Brenda aside. "Get a fifth from the cabinet in my apartment. Crush twenty-five milligrams of Valium and mix it in."

"A curse on you and your children and

their children!" continued Dibbins. "May they be born with green scales and slitted tongues! May they grow up to be perfidious, scheming ingrates!"

"Make that fifty milligrams," Vincent murmured. "We'll get him inside, one way or another."

The Mexicans grinned as Brenda hurried by them. As soon as she'd gone inside, they lit brown cigarettes and sat down on the gurney to watch.

"Los doctores americanos son locos," one of them said.

The other nodded. *"Muy locos."*

6

Saturday morning was dreary, but pretty much every day in Maggody is, so this wasn't remarkable. I'd stopped by Ruby Bee's for breakfast. She was still giving me the cold shoulder, but this time it was accompanied by cold hash browns and burned toast. I didn't know if she was peeved because I hadn't rammed my car through the formidable gates of the Stonebridge Foundation, or just cranky because of her spat with Estelle. I knew better than to get into the middle of that one.

I walked across the road to Jim Bob's SuperSaver Buy 4 Less to buy a package of cookies to sustain me until she simmered down. The store was bustling with people doing their weekly shopping. Joyce Lambertino was trying to stop her older children from playing touch football with a cantaloupe, while the baby in the cart bawled. Eula Lemoy was wandering about with a shopping list held three inches from her nose. Darla Jean and Heather eyed me nervously while they skittered by with a bag of chips; the dip was probably in one of their purses. Raz was reading the labels on cans of smoked oysters and anchovies; whatever he selected would find its way into his coat pocket. At this time of year, shoplifting was more popular than baseball.

I was trying to decide between Oreos and Fig Newtons when a hand timidly touched my shoulder. I turned around and snapped, "What?"

Kevin shuffled his feet for a moment before he looked up. "Have you found my ma?" he asked plaintively.

He looked bad, which is saying a lot, since even at his best he doesn't look especially good. His eyes were bloodshot, the dark circles under them purple. Bits of toilet paper were stuck on his jaw and chin, and his shirt was smeared with grape jelly. He had a sour odor about him, like milk that had gone bad.

"No, I'm afraid not," I said. "But there's nothing much I can do, Kevin. She's a grown woman, and she left of her own free will. Things rough at home?"

His shoulders drooped. "You could say that. I invited Pa over to supper yesterday, thinking it might do him some good. He didn't appreciate Dahlia's cooking, and said so. All of a sudden the two of them was goin' after each other like mud wrasslers, and —" He broke off and wiped his eyes with his frayed cuff. "I don't know how much more I can take."

"I guess your pa hasn't heard from her, then?"

"I reckon not. All he does is sit at the kitchen table and mumble. When I git home, Dahlia's usually sobbing in the bedroom. The twins ain't bathed and fed, so I do that, while her granny hides behind the furniture. I used to try to wheedle her out, but now I just let her be."

"Sounds bad," I said, trying not to visualize the scene. "Do you know if your pa called the bank yesterday to check the balance in the account?"

Kevin shrugged. "Not likely, being that he's been drunker'n Cooter Brown since the morning she left. You got to get her back, Arly. Dahlia's darn near going out of her mind, now that she cain't even drop Rose Marie and Kevvie Junior off for an hour so she can have a break."

"There is something you can do to help. Today or tomorrow, go over to your pa's and get the information about his bank account. Also, find out if your ma has a credit card, and if she does, write down the information. If she's using the card, we might be able to find out which way she went."

"And that's gonna help?"

"Well, if she's staying in a motel, you could call her and try to persuade her to come back."

Kevin gave me a doleful look. "If you was her, would you come back?"

"I don't know," I said evasively, "but you might as well give it a shot. Call me as soon as you can." I hurried to the checkout counter. Idalupino was too busy smacking her gum to do more than count out my change and stick the cookies into a sack. I walked back to the PD, made a pot of coffee, and resumed my contemplation of South American geography.

Mrs. Jim Bob went into the Assembly Hall and made sure there were enough paper plates and plastic forks for the Wednesday-evening potluck supper, wrote a note to buy coffee filters, then went outside and across the lawn to the rectory.

She rapped on the door, waited a moment, and opened it. "Brother Verber? Are you here?"

"Why, Sister Barbara, what a pleasant surprise," he said as he stumbled into the living room, tugging up his trousers. "I was just thinking about you."

She averted her eyes as he fumbled with his zipper. "This is not a social call, Brother Verber. I have something to discuss with you."

"Can I offer you a glass of freshly brewed ice tea before we get started?"

She suspected from the purple dribbles on his shirt that he'd been sipping something other than tea, but let it pass without comment. She sat down on the edge of a chair and took a notebook out of her purse. "I happened to be across the road from that insane asylum this morning when I saw several unsettling things."

"You did?" Brother Verber's eyes were wide as he sank down on the couch.

"I do believe that's what I just said. At eleven-fourteen, a limousine pulled up to the gate and was admitted. There were two people in the back. One was dressed in a suit and tie. The other was a young woman, and from the unhealthy look about her, a patient. What's more, the driver carried in three large suitcases and a smaller bag, implying that she'll be there for a long while. After no more than five minutes, the man in the suit got back in the limousine, and it left."

"You could see all this from where you were parked?"

Mrs. Jim Bob bristled. "I did not say I was sitting in my car, Brother Verber. I'd gone out there to pick some persimmons to make a pudding, and I realized I might have better luck if I climbed up in the tree. I happened to have my binoculars with me."

Brother Verber was overwhelmed with admiration for her mettle. He wished he'd been there to boost her up to the lowest branch, his hands on her firm buttocks to steady her till she could cling to the branch with her thighs. He realized she was still talking and pulled himself away from the image.

"— a rather plain young man escorted her up the stairs like she was made of china," Mrs. Jim Bob was saying. "She had white hair pinned up in a bun, and was wearing an expensive suit. It was hard to imagine her as a patient, but she stayed inside when the man left. I think it's likely she's one of those black widows."

"You mean a spider?"

"No, I do not mean a spider in the literal sense, Brother Verber. If she had eight legs, I would have mentioned it. I am speaking of women who kill their husbands, usually for money. She had a very hard, calculating look about her. I could tell she wasn't a Christian."

Brother Verber slipped to his knees and clutched his hands together. "Then our souls are in peril, Sister Barbara. Who knows what will happen to us with this satanic killer in our quiet little community?"

Mrs. Jim Bob flipped to the next page. "At a quarter past twelve, two men arrived in an expensive foreign car. One was tall and muscular, the other short and scrawny. I wasn't at all sure which was the patient, but within a minute, the little weasel came out to the car and drove away."

"My goodness." Brother Verber got back on the couch and took out his handkerchief to wipe his neck. "How many more of them came? Are we to be infested with lunatics and killers?"

"It's hard to know for sure. I was climbing out of the tree 'long about one o'clock when a helicopter landed in the pasture out behind the building. I drove down the road a piece, but I still couldn't see what was going on. I would have stayed, but I'd invited Lottie and Elsie for dessert and coffee, so I had to go home."

"This is very disturbing," said Brother Verber. "I'm sorry to have to say that my seminary did not provide any guidance in how to deal with a crisis like this. We can pray for the Good Lord's protection, of course, but He may be occupied elsewhere."

"You'll have to warn folks tomorrow at church. Tell them to keep their doors and windows locked, report any strangers wandering around town, keep a loaded gun handy in case of intruders. This is not the time for a sermon about being a Good Samaritan, Brother Verber. If the law won't protect us, then we'll have to do it ourselves. I'm going to take it upon myself to organize a citizens' committee so we can monitor what's going on out there. I'm assuming that you in your role as spiritual leader will want to participate."

"You mean sit in a tree with binoculars?" When she merely stared at him, he cleared his throat and added, "But it's real important that I make myself available for lost souls in need of counseling and prayer. You wouldn't believe the number of times I've been called out in the darkest hours of night to rush to the side of a widow woman hovering on the brink of death. Why, only last week Maybelline Buchanon's boy got snockered and threatened to kill hisself. I was there most of the night, telling him how he'd be facing eternal torment in the fiery furnace of damnation if he went through with it. Just as the sun came up, he relented and asked me to pray with him. Maybelline was so grateful that she fixed a mighty fine breakfast for me. I could tell you many such stories, but I can see you're busy. Rushing to the aid of sinners — that's my sacred mission, Sister Barbara, and I can't shirk it."

"Then I'll put you down for the morning shift, say six to ten." She scribbled a note, then put away her pad and stood up. "I'm glad you share my feelings about the importance of protecting ourselves." She nodded gravely at him as she left.

He'd already poured himself a glass of sacramental wine before her car pulled back onto the road.

From the journal of Dawn Dartmouth:

dear diary . . . isn't that cute? i haven't kept one of these dumbshit things since i was eleven and i got tired of it in a week but dr zit says we like have to write in this every day as part of our therapy LOL!!! he swore we could keep it private but i know damn well he'll read it while I'm off sweating and getting needles stuck in my ass this is my first day of what's going to be ninety days of hell the room's not bad — better than a cell anyway i spent the night in county once waiting for mommy dearest to sign me out she said it was for my own good but i knew damn well she was too busy giving blow jobs to her current bimboy when i took some money out of his wallet i looked at his driver's license he was nineteen — four years older than me he used to come to my bedroom when the bitch was passed out but i won't get you all hot and bothered with the details

lunch today was a bowl of clear green soup guess what it tasted like? then, yum yum yum, a sliver of fish, a couple of baby carrots and a pile of alfalfa sprouts i guess you guys are saving a ton of money on food you couldn't pay me to eat this crap at home i can stand to lose some pounds — but at this rate, it's only gonna take a week it's a good thing there's this doctor here who can give me some boobs this time last time he had to do my nose and cheekbone maybe he should have sucked out my brains while he was doing it

From the journal of Toby Mann:

When I get out of this plaice, I'm going to track down my agent and ring his neck for dumping me off like this is nowhereville. It sure as hell ain't margaritaville.

I was way bummed out yesterday when we got here. I mean, little Miss Molly looks like an angle, but along comes this way ugly woman built like a tackle and she asks me so many questions I wanted to slap the smirk off her face. How the hell would I know when my grandparents died? There like dead, so what does it matter? That was like the stupidest question I ever heard.

Then I get to meet the shrink, and he says I need anger management classes. Me, fer chrissake! You gotta get angry to win.

The food stinks. I need a lot to eat to keep my waite up. I can just imagine what coach'll say if I show up carrying 140 pounds of flab. But that nazi said grass and berries and vitamins and pills to keep me mellow. Soon as I get out of this hell hole I'm going have a two pound steak, even if I have to kill the cow with my bare hands.

This morning at least I got to work out. Just because I have to sit out for ninty days doesn't mean I'm gonna lose my edge. That's why the reporters call me The Man. This one asshole sportswriter called me the Man-Child on account of me getting kicked out of a game. Funny thing — somebody torches his car the next week. We're playing Green Bay when it happens, so I have like ten milion witnesses for an alibi. Son of a bitch complained to the leage officials, but of course they aren't interested since they know damn well who the fans come to watch. Nobody's gonna touch The Man!

From the journal of Alexandra Swayze:

Lloyd, if you ever read this, I want you to know that I hold you alone responsible for the degradation and humiliation I shall suffer in the next several months. Should I survive, I will have a new will drawn up that gives my entire estate to a pro-life organization. I hope you and Patricia will be satisfied with the painting your Aunt Bess did of the sunset over the Potomac. I believe it's in the attic somewhere.

This has been the third day of my "voluntary" incarceration. Breakfast is brought to my suite each morning by what I presume is an illegal alien. I then go to a private session with Dr. Zumi, who is the son of immigrants from India. Frankly, these third world types should never have been admitted into the country. When the day comes that I am officially in the minority, I'll move to a remote South Seas island. Dr. Zumi has thus far been very mild, merely encouraging me to talk. After that, I meet with the personal trainer, whom I can only describe as an aged hippie. I smelled marijuana smoke on his clothing, and this morning his eyes were oddly bright. Dr. Skiller has tried to convince me to try acupuncture, but the very idea of someone inserting needles in my body makes me queasy. I did agree to instruction in yoga, although I find the concept ludicrous. Why would I want to cross my legs and chant gibberish? A total waste of time, but then again, I don't have much else to do.

Yesterday while I was having lunch in my suite, Dr. Stonebridge dropped by. He mentioned his long friendship with the Reagan family, so I was inclined to like him. After he left, I rested, then had a second exercise session and swam a few laps in the pool. Later, I shall have dinner here and read until I fall asleep.

I have not yet been introduced to my fellow inmates. The maids refer to them as Miss D, Mr. M, and Dr. D. I caught glimpses of the first two. Neither was familiar. I suppose they're pop stars or TV actors. We are not, by the way, allowed to have newspapers or watch any of the cable news programs. Yesterday evening I declined to watch some frivolous movie in what is called the day room. I may well be able to recite the entirety of Henry James before I am released.

As for this ridiculous business of my addiction, I am now being obliged to swallow more pills than ever. I am somewhat shaky and nauseous as my intake of Percocet and Vicodin has already begun to be decreased, but Dr. Zumi has promised that the process will be very gradual and relatively pain-free. I can sense that Dr. Skiller does not agree with his plan; she positively glowers at him at times. Then again, she glowers at me all the time, and has made it clear that she objects to my philosophical positions on social programs. These bleeding heart liberals are incapable of rational intercourse, and would much rather sniffle about the plight of the downtrodden and spend tax dollars to make amends, as if the rest of us should accept responsibility for these people's laziness. Some of America's greatest leaders came from humble backgrounds yet made something of themselves by hard work, sacrifice, and dedication.

Late last night I felt the need for fresh air, so I slipped out of my room and started in the direction of the door to the pool and garden area. I was surprised to see a light on in the office in the reception area, and I heard voices. I hesitated, but before I could decide how to proceed an orderly swept down on me and escorted me back to my suite. I must mention it to Dr. Stonebridge when next I see him. If one of these illegal aliens has been bribed to allow a member of the media access to the private files, I shall leave immediately.

From the journal of Dr. Shelby Dibbins:

Allow me to point out once again that I am paid in gold ducats to write my books. Why in hell's name should I waste my time writing in this cheap little notebook as if I were a school child?

Although presumably this is confidential, I have no doubt that one of those subservient spies will be sent to fetch this should I ever leave the room. Which I will not do for the next eighty-odd days. I have made it perfectly clear that I am at this despicable gulag under protest, and cannot be held should I decide to leave. That would be my agent's worst nightmare. I do hope that she is so fearful of losing her commission that she cannot sleep. Perhaps she'll develop ulcers and migraines, along with anxiety attacks in the middle of a meeting. Warts and pimples. An uncontrollable compulsion to burst into tears while negotiating contracts. Revenge by any other name would smell as rancid.

Gulag Maggody. After all, there is a chainlink fence topped with barbed wire, and a guard with a dog who prowls the perimeter after dark. Padded footsteps in the hall at night, and on two occasions, hushed arguments and muted sobbing. Perhaps the other inmates are plotting to escape.

Dr. Gandhi was not pleased when I made it clear that I refuse to go to his office for daily head-shrinking. Let the mountain come to Mohammed. Walter, the physical trainer, was less than pleased, but does he really think I'd put on shorts and a tank top in order to sweat? He comes here each morning and afternoon with his barbells and other peculiar devices, and pleads with me. I stare at him until he slinks away like a mangy cur.

Dr. Stonebridge is another matter. He is suave, almost obsequious, but with the intensity of a megalomaniac. He described various medical procedures to assist in my weight loss. I objected, having always had an aversion to scalpels and needles, but he merely nodded thoughtfully. It will make for an entertaining battle.

The food merits nothing more than contempt. I expend more calories swallowing various pills and tablets *than I consume from the twigs and leaves that comprise my meals.*

So I am doomed to stay in this suite for three months. A far cry from my home, with its lush gardens and views of the ocean from all the rooms. My golf cart to putter around the grounds. My king-size bed with black satin sheets. My kitchen, where Pietro strives to add the perfect pinches of herbs to enliven leg of lamb, veal scallopini, osso buco, fettuccine with alfredo sauce and a medley of freshly picked vegetables, the rum torte, the silky chocolate mousse, the tangy lemon sorbets and —

I am torturing myself. I will acknowledge that my weight has gotten a bit out of hand, although I am still more than capable of promoting the new book. I am, after all, a professional. What's more, should the bastards in New York renege on the contract, I shall sue their Yankee asses until they're reduced to bloodied piles of diarrhea.

Ruby Bee replaced the receiver and tried to think what to do. It might have helped to talk it over with Estelle, but she hadn't shown her face for five days. She wasn't dead or anything like that; Roy Stiver had mentioned only yesterday that she'd stopped by to browse. Ruby Bee knew darn well that the only reason Estelle would do such a thing was to spy on the bar & grill. And the day before that, Eula and Lottie had come by for lunch and mentioned seeing her at a flea market in Hasty that very morning. They'd sort of raised their eyebrows and waited for Ruby Bee to say something, but she hadn't obliged them with anything more than a grunt.

And Arly wasn't exactly dropping by to chat these days. She'd come in to eat every now and then, but always when it was crowded and it was all Ruby Bee could do to keep dishing up blue plate specials and filling pitchers of beer. Probably on purpose, she thought with a sniff.

That meant she was going to have to decide for herself. She'd been uneasy about what might be going on at the Stonebridge Foundation, but after listening to Mrs. Jim Bob, she was downright worried that something truly wicked was going on out there. According to Mrs. Jim Bob, everybody in town had a gun handy in case some crazy man came crashing into their home. Children weren't being allowed to walk to school alone or ride their bicycles. Women were making their husbands put extra locks on their doors and windows, and stay home at night.

Ruby Bee had never owned a gun, and she disremembered the last time she'd fired one. She had a baseball bat behind the bar, and another one under her bed out back. As for locks, well, folks didn't break into houses in Maggody. They didn't have to, since most everybody kept a spare key under a flowerpot or on the sill above the door.

It was a darn shame the New Age hardware store had gone out of business, she thought. She could have at least bought a couple of sliding bolts or a chain. And where in tarnation was she supposed to buy a gun, especially since she didn't know one blasted thing about them? She sure couldn't go asking Arly.

The rest of what Mrs. Jim Bob had said was equally troubling. She'd gotten it into her head that the Mexicans living in the Flamingo Motel knew what was going on at the foundation — and were even participants in satanic rituals, she'd whispered darkly. The reason they were there was to spy on the community, to see who might be easy to drug and carry off to be mutilated and eventually sacrificed on an altar.

Ruby Bee hadn't seen any suspicious behavior since the staff from the foundation moved in. They kept to themselves, never venturing into the bar for a beer or something to eat. They had a grill at the end of one of the buildings, and sometimes she'd see a few of them cooking on it and gabbing at each other. Part of the deal was that Ruby Bee didn't have to clean their rooms. She'd shown one of them, a stout woman with a grim face, how to use the washer and dryer in the back room. Every day one of them would run a load of sheets and towels, or skirts and trousers, then hang them on a makeshift clothesline by their little grill. None of them ever smiled or spoke, and Ruby Bee'd given up on trying to be friendly.

But the idea of sneaking into their rooms when they were gone didn't seem neighborly, and there was no telling when the van might show up. There were always two or three of them hanging around outside or in their rooms with the curtains drawn.

She could make an effort to try to talk to them, she supposed. Take them a pie or a plate of cookies, and see what they said. The lady doctor had said none of them spoke English, but Ruby Bee found that hard to swallow. Everybody could speak English, even the Buchanons that lived out in the booger woods. It might not be educated English, but Ruby Bee had learned over the years how to communicate with truck drivers so drunk their tongues hung down to their knees. And that Mexican who owned the Dairee Dee-Lishus had an accent, but she could understand him just fine.

It was too bad she'd have to do it by herself, but she couldn't hardly ask Estelle, who'd proved herself to be a mean-spirited, narrow-minded bigot. Why, if they gave out ribbons at the county fair for such things, Estelle would come strutting away with the blue. Until she came to her senses, she could just skulk around town and go off to flea markets by her lonesome. Ruby Bee knew for a fact it wasn't much fun without someone along to discuss the value of a chipped vase or a stained teacup. Estelle could stew in her own juices, for all Ruby Bee cared.

In the meantime, though, she figured she might ought to look into buying a gun. Roy was sitting out front of his shop, waiting for a tourist with more money than sense. She decided to take him a piece of chocolate cake and find out what all he knew about guns and how to go about buying one.

★ ★ ★

"What the hell are you doing?" demanded Jim Bob as he came in through the back door.

Mrs. Jim Bob was seated at the table in the sunroom. "I do not care for foul language in my own home. That sort of crudeness is best left at the trailer park or the pool hall."

He took a deep breath. "Why do you have that gun on the table?"

"I'm cleaning it," she said. "I found it in the garage, and it was covered with dust and oily grime."

"So you're cleaning it with Windex?"

She began to buff it with a rag. "I'm certainly not going to have it inside in this filthy condition. It's looking quite shiny now, don't you think?"

Jim Bob nearly tripped in his haste to duck behind a chair. "Don't point that thing. It could be loaded."

"Really? How would I be able to tell?"

"When you pull the trigger and my brains splatter out of the back of my head. Put it down — okay?"

Mrs. Jim Bob reluctantly placed it on the newspaper she'd spread on the tabletop. "There's really no reason to have it if it's not loaded. Bring home some bullets this evening."

"Who are you aimin' to shoot?" he asked nervously.

She crossed her arms and gazed at him, her eyes narrowed in speculation. "I haven't decided just yet. Do you have any suggestions?"

Jim Bob wondered if she'd been nipping on the bottle of whiskey he'd hidden in a toolbox in the garage. Dearly hoping she wouldn't shoot him in the back, he went into the kitchen and opened the refrigerator. "Where's that chicken we had last night?"

"On the top shelf," she said, "and the broccoli casserole is next to it. Does it ever occur to you to look for something before you ask me? I rarely go to the trouble of hiding food in cabinets or under the sink, you know. I put your socks and underwear in the same drawers, and hang your shirts in your closet. Clean towels, soap, and spare rolls of toilet paper are in the linen cabinet. Your fishing gear is in the garage. Your boots are in the hall closet. It seems to me that after thirty years you might have begun to figure this out."

"Yeah, right." He set the bowls on the counter and got out a plate and fork. "If you don't know who you're going to shoot, why'd you bring the gun in here? What if

Perkin's eldest finds it and shoots herself in the foot? We could get sued."

"I'd rather be sued than murdered. Since you won't do anything about the homicidal maniacs running wild here in Maggody, I have taken it upon myself to take action. Members of the Missionary Society are arming themselves and encouraging others to do the same. We will not allow ourselves to become victims."

Jim Bob stopped gnawing on a chicken leg and stared at her. "I ain't heard about any homicidal maniacs running wild. As far as I know, the only time there's any activity is when that van takes the employees over to the Flamingo Motel."

"If you paid more attention, you'd have heard that one of them escaped last week and nearly murdered Ruby Bee — and in broad daylight, too."

"Nearly murdered her? Seems like some-body would have mentioned it to me."

Mrs. Jim Bob shrugged. "She's so terri-fied that she can hardly stand to talk about it. If she hadn't broken down and told Lottie, none of us would have known." She picked up the gun and gave it another spritz of Windex. "You just remember to bring home some bullets. After dinner, you can teach me how to fire it."

"I was, uh, planning to stay late and work on the quarterly tax estimates."

She gave him a beady look. "Were you? And then stagger home after midnight, stinking of whiskey and perfume? Don't think for a minute that I don't know what you do when you say you're working late. Now rinse off the plate and put it in the sink. I have better things to do than clean up after you."

7

Vincent beamed at his staff, who were seated around the large table in the day room. He felt very kindly toward them, since their energy and dedication were vital to his economic well-being. Someday, he thought, the name Stonebridge would be synonymous with medical breakthroughs in the field of rehabilitation, rather than tummy tucks, breast enhancements, and malpractice suits. "Well, I think our first six days have gone splendidly, don't you? Our patients are relatively content, and we've established a functional routine. We should be proud of ourselves. Shall we have a toast to our initial success?" He moved around the table, filling each fluted glass with champagne. "To the Stonebridge Foundation," he said grandly, holding up his glass.

They all dutifully repeated the sentiment, but with varied levels of enthusiasm. He took an appreciative sip, then went on. "I'd like to thank Molly for agreeing to stay late for the meeting. I know you have obligations at home, dear, and I hope this isn't too much of an inconvenience."

"Oh, no," she said. "This is Ashton's bowling night, so he usually has a burger with the boys."

Brenda put down her glass. "Let's just get to it, Vincent. I have a pile of paperwork to do."

"Me, too," said Randall, although less convincingly so.

Walter rocked back in his chair and grinned at Molly. "What time does Ashton get home? Maybe you and I could check out a couple of clubs, see what all's going on in the big city of Farberville."

Molly ignored him. "This is my very first staff meeting, Dr. Stonebridge. I hope I do okay."

"I'm sure you will." He leaned across the table to refill her glass. "We need to review our case files, and then move on to mundane matters of fine-tuning the schedule for maximum efficiency. Brenda, I believe you have Dr. Dibbins's file. Why don't you begin?"

"He is not an easy case. After his suitcase was unpacked, I had the maid bring it to the storage room, where I inspected it. It has a false bottom. The space contained three pounds of Godiva chocolates, water crackers, candied dates and figs, a package of butter cookies, a box of cigars, eighteen airplane-sized bottles of gin, four ten-ounce bottles of red wine, a jar of caviar, and cans of smoked oysters. When I confronted him, he gazed at the ceiling and pretended not to hear me."

"How gauche," murmured Walter.

Brenda shot him a look, then said, "I have him on psyllium husks for fiber, chromium picolinate to reduce sugar cravings, dimethylamino-ethanol, flaxseed oil, a high dosage of vitamin C to increase metabolism, lecithin capsules, and fifteen hundred milligrams of kelp. Despite his vocal objections, he receives a coffee enema once a day to cleanse his liver and colon. He is allowed six hundred calories daily, most of them from protein. Randall has him on Prozac and a mild amphetamine, and ten milligrams of Ambien to help him sleep. As of this morning, he has lost nine and one-fourth pounds, although much of this can be attributed to water loss."

"Very good," said Vincent. "Comments, Randall?"

"I've had five sessions with him, and there's been no discernible lessening of hostility. He now calls me 'Gunga Din.' Although he will acknowledge that he's overweight, he refuses to admit he needs to alter his lifestyle. He views life as a series of meals, and he associates everything, from his failed marriages to his success as a diet guru, with food." He glanced at his notes. "His first wife was as flighty as meringue, his second as tart as hollandaise sauce, et cetera. His successes are not *coups de grâce,* but *coups de foie gras.* We need to station an armed guard outside the kitchen."

Vincent nodded. "He's rather recalcitrant about the necessity for surgical procedures as well, but he'll have to have skin tightening treatments unless he wants to end up looking like a used condom. Walter?"

Walter propped his feet on the table. "If I badger him, he'll do a few stretching exercises. It's a beginning."

"Do you have anything to add, Molly?" Vincent asked.

She shifted uncomfortably, then said, "When I took him some insurance papers to sign, he offered me a hundred dollars to smuggle in a bottle of some particular sort of brandy. When I refused, he called me . . . well, something not very nice."

"Son of a bitch!" said Randall.

"Oh, it wasn't that," Molly protested,

blinking at him. "In fact, I didn't even know what it meant, but I could tell it was rude."

Brenda rumbled under her breath, then said, "Let's move on, Vince."

"Indeed," he said. "Mrs. Swayze is somewhat more agreeable. She has voiced interest in a rhytidectomy and laser resurfacing, each of which costs several thousand dollars. I gather she's been exercising, Walt."

"Yeah, she said she used to work out before her accident. We're starting slowly, focusing on muscle tone and flexibility. She's too zoned out to do much."

"Because Randall insists on giving her all manner of antidepressants and antiseizure medications," said Brenda, "as well as the very medications she's addicted to. She would do better to rely on her inner resources to overcome the addiction." She opened a file. "I currently have her on a regimen of vitamin B complex injections, with extra pantothenic acid and niacinamide, and fifteen hundred milligrams of calcium and magnesium. Burdock root and red clover to cleanse the toxins from her system, milk thistle, Saint-John's-wort, and valerian root. When her blood pressure is under control, I'll add Siberian ginseng. She has high-protein soy-based drinks three times a day to put her intake at fifteen hundred calories."

"Wow," said Molly. "It sounds like all these patients do all day is gobble pills."

Brenda crossed her arms and stared at her. "This is a rehabilitation facility, Miss Foss, not a resort on a beach. If that concept is too complicated for you to grasp, you might be better off working elsewhere. Your performance here is only marginally adequate. I was up until midnight last night trying to make sense of your whimsical filing system. You are familiar with the alphabet, aren't you?"

"That's enough," Vincent said coldly. "Molly is working hard to learn the system. Randall, your sessions with Mrs. Swayze?"

"She's in textbook denial," he said. "Claims she's not really addicted and can stop any time she chooses. She reluctantly admitted to frequent mood swings, restlessness, loss of appetite, and emotional outbursts. The only reason she's here, she says, is that she was sick and tired of her inner circle harassing her. I've already started her withdrawal, and am monitoring her for depression, irritability, insomnia, and disorientation. She's experienced some hot and cold flashes, excessive sweating, and diarrhea."

"I'll add raspberry leaf tea and cayenne capsules," said Brenda, writing a note in the file.

Vincent nodded. "Let's move on to our star quarterback. Walter, would you like to go first?"

Walter refilled his glass. "Toby's all gung-ho to work out. I literally have to drag him off the machines and out the door, and then he heads for the pool and does a hundred laps. The other night at eleven, I caught him in the exercise room, lifting weights. When I told him he was supposed to be in his room, he took a swing at me. He scares me, to be frank."

"He's not that bad," said Molly. "He comes down to my desk when he doesn't have anything else to do, and we talk. He's real sweet when he talks about his mother. His father was a high school coach, and that's why Toby —"

"Leave the psychiatric evaluations to Dr. Zumi," Brenda said. "You have no business chatting with the patients. If you have free time, spend it mastering the computer."

Molly sank back in the chair, her eyes welling with tears. "I was just trying to participate, Dr. Skiller."

" 'I was just trying to participate, Dr. Skiller,' " Brenda echoed in a honeyed voice.

There was a long moment of silence in the day room. All three of the men looked annoyed, but none of them ventured a rebuke. Molly sniffled.

"As for the psych evaluation," said Randall, "Toby Mann has been taking both anabolic steroids and androgens since he was fifteen years old. Some were given to him by the team doctors, others he bought online. As with all addictive drugs, he needed to increase the dosage, which then forced him to rely on opioids to counteract insomnia and depression. No one knows if these steroids are dangerous in the short term, but they create serious health concerns over a longer period of time. Toby simply refuses to acknowledge the possibility of liver disease, decreased sperm count, testicular degeneration, and psychotic episodes. Either because of his exalted status or the drugs, he's convinced he is invincible, the epitome of the supreme macho athlete. Anyone who begs to differ may be in real danger of physical retribution. So, Walter, if I were you, I'd let him work out. He is highly resistant to the idea of reducing his daily steroid regime, but since his stash was confiscated, he has grudgingly agreed to use less destructive supplements."

"Did he rape that woman?" demanded Brenda. "We have female employees, as well as patients. Their safety is our responsibility."

Randall shrugged. "We haven't gotten into it very far. In his mind, he did not because he cannot conceive that any female would object to his sexual advances. He's been praised and fawned over since he was in high school. He claims to have slept with more than a thousand women in the last eight years."

There was another moment of silence as each of them did the arithmetic.

"Not bad," said Walter, smirking.

"You're disgusting," said Brenda. "He is allowed two thousand calories a day from lean protein, soy, grains rich in fiber, fruits, dairy products, eggs, and fresh vegetables. No processed foods or sugar, of course. He's also taking lemon balm and ephedra for depression, as well as ginkgo biloba, oat straw, and kava kava. To counteract these episodes of rage, I've added an amino acid complex, vitamin B compounds, zinc, and copper."

"No wonder he clinks when he walks," commented Walter. "All that metal."

Vincent rubbed his temples with his fingertips. "There is one thing I need to bring up. One of the maids found a bottle of bourbon hidden in a cabinet in his bathroom. He has denied any knowledge of it, but I'd like to know how he got it."

"I did a thorough search of his bag when he arrived," said Brenda, "and confiscated some pills and a plastic baggie of marijuana. There was no bottle of bourbon." Her gaze traveled around the table, then settled on Molly. "Someone must have smuggled it in for him."

"One of the orderlies?" said Randall.

"Highly unlikely," Vincent said, shaking his head. "Even if Toby could get around the language barrier, none of them has access to a liquor store. The only alcohol for sale in this place is moonshine. I checked, and the bourbon did not come from my personal supply."

Brenda smiled smugly. "Well, I don't have a personal supply. As far as I'm concerned, alcohol is a poison only slightly less lethal than cyanide."

"I brought nothing like that," Randall said.

Walter flashed his palms. "I stick to wine. I've got a couple of jugs in my van, but nobody's messed with them."

Molly stood up. "I can see just where this is going — and I don't like it one bit! Sure,

I'm friendly with the patients. That's my nature. If you don't believe me, just call the girls at the office where I used to work, and they'll tell how nice I was to everyone. That doesn't mean I'd break the rules, Dr. Stonebridge. Didn't I already tell you all how Dr. Dibbins tried to bribe me, and I told him under no uncertain terms that I —"

"I'll have a word with the chef," interrupted Brenda. "I don't see how he or his helpers could be guilty, though. They come in through the back gate at seven every morning, go directly to the kitchen, and leave at five. They have no contact whatsoever with the patients. Even if Toby hid a note on his tray, I don't see how it would be possible for any of them to get the bottle to him."

Vincent sighed. "All of the patients' suites will be searched tomorrow. I will personally oversee it, since our reputation is at stake, and I've invested too much to allow even a hint of failure. Should I determine that one of you is responsible, you will be dismissed immediately. I can assure you this is not a threat, but a statement of fact. Now, shall we move on to Miss Dartmouth?"

Brenda flipped open a file. "Didn't I say she was a typical Hollywood brat? Not only did she bring cocaine concealed in a baby powder container, she brought excessive quantities of makeup, hair products, and jewelry. There are enough clothes crammed in her closet to dress all the residents in town, although this would require some sort of charitable impulse on her part."

"She looks like a zombie," said Molly. "Poor thing stumbles around all day in her bedroom slippers like some kind of bag lady. She offered me a real pretty bracelet if I'd let her check her e-mail on my computer, but I told her she couldn't. She asked all kinds of questions about the other patients, too. Do you know her boyfriend was the drummer for the Sick Suck Six? I've got two of their CDs."

"How fascinating," drawled Brenda. "Perhaps you can share your insights into popular culture at a later time."

Vincent held up his hand before Molly was again reduced to tears. "Randall?"

"She's an alcoholic, probably since she was fourteen or so. She's done a lot of cocaine and Ecstasy, and has experimented with heroin and crack. A classic addictive personality, due in part to the pressure of her earlier years as an actress and her clashes with her mother, who's also an alcoholic. Dawn claims she was molested at the age of eight by the producer of the TV series. She was sexually active by twelve, and already drinking and taking tranquilizers. She says she was also raped by various therapists and psychiatrists, her stepfathers, male employees in the household, and a long list of boyfriends. It's too early to determine the veracity of these claims. She does, however, have a very fragile and unstable self-image, and is capable of violent outbursts. Currently, she's on heavy antidepressants, stimulants so she can function, and sleeping pills. She takes pain pills at night because she claims to have sore muscles from exercising."

"That doesn't mean she's not a brat," said Brenda. "I have her on a free-form amino acid complex, L-cysteine, three thousand milligrams of glutathione to reduce the cravings, pantothenic acid for detox, gamma-aminobutyric acid to prevent anxiety, alfalfa, burdock root, dandelion root and milk thistle extract, and valerian root at bedtime. She's lost six pounds this week."

"She'll work out for a while," said Walter, "but then she insists on soaking in the hot tub. This morning she . . . uh, tried to get personal. She kept rubbing her breasts against me and making suggestions about what we could do in the sauna. I didn't know what to do."

Randall shrugged. "You can't bluntly reject her. She's already stressed about being here. As she entered adolescence, she realized that she was no longer considered darling and adorable. She's very conflicted."

"So I'm supposed to screw her in the sauna to boost her self-esteem?"

"No, none of that," Vincent said, clearly alarmed. "No one on the staff should have anything more than a strictly professional relationship with the patients." He paused to think. "Walter, arrange for a maid or orderly to be in the exercise room whenever Dawn is there. I'll make a point of stopping by to encourage Dawn in her efforts. That should suffice."

Walter gave him a limp salute. "Yes, sir."

Vincent glared at him, then said, "Are there any other issues to be discussed? Any complaints about the maids and orderlies? No? Well, then, I'll see all of you in the morning." He picked up the champagne bottle and left.

Molly stood up. "I guess I'll run along home. Y'all have a nice night."

Walter winked at Randall, then followed Molly out of the room.

"Why did you hire him?" Randall demanded, his lip curled. "He smokes pot every night in his room; I can smell it next door. He probably does other drugs, too."

Brenda carefully closed the files and made a neat pile of them. "I owed him a favor. Besides, he's very good at what he does. I know I couldn't persuade Dibbins to lift a pinkie, much less do any exercises."

"What's his background?" Randall persisted. "Is he really a licensed physical trainer? Where was he certified?"

"You'll have to read his résumé. I'm sure Miss Foss will be happy to find it for you. She seems to be an obliging young woman with a heart of gold. It's unfortunate that her office skills are less glittery. I told Vincent months ago that I knew someone who could fill the position, but he hired her without consulting me. I suppose she must have done something to impress him, although not behind a desk. Under it is more likely."

"You're not implying they've had sex, are you? She's married, for pity's sake."

"Your naïveté underwhelms me, Randall." Brenda gathered up the files and went to the door. "I'll be in my office should you care to discuss this further. Good night."

Randall remained in the room for a long while, thinking about what Brenda had said.

She was plainly jealous of Molly's attractiveness and innocent charm. Randall was certainly not oblivious to them. Molly deserved to be admired, and even cherished. The idea of Brenda belittling her made Randall very, very angry.

He was not the only inhabitant of the Stonebridge Foundation who was harboring dark thoughts that night.

When the phone rang on Friday morning, I stared at it as if it were a coiled rattlesnake. It could have been Ruby Bee, demanding that I hustle over to the bar & grill so she could lecture me about my failings as a daughter, a police officer, or a potential breeder whose biological clock was beginning to hiccup. Or Jack, calling to say that we'd have to cancel our plans for the weekend, or even Mrs. Jim Bob, squawking about speeders in front of her house or kids playing in the creek at the back of her yard. Or Sheriff Harvey Dorfer, with some icky assignment that none of his deputies would touch with a twenty-foot pole.

I finally picked up the receiver. "Yeah?"

Alas, it was Harve, perpetual purveyor of ill tidings. "I reckon we got us a problem, Arly," he began genially.

"What do you mean 'we,' kemo sabe?"

"You gettin' your jokes out of old issues of *Reader's Digest*? This is serious stuff. A woman was killed last night out at that Stonebridge place."

"That's a damn shame, Harve," I said, "but it's not my jurisdiction. I hope this won't spoil your weekend."

"It ain't gonna spoil *my* weekend. Do you want to do this over the telephone, or here in my office? The coffee's worse than pond water, but the doughnuts are fresh — or at least they were on Wednesday."

I put my feet on the corner of my desk, rocked back, and in a less than amiable voice said, "What happened?"

"Hard to say. We got a call shortly after four this morning. The night guard, a Mexican fellow, found the woman's body on the grounds — in a fountain, to be precise. McBeen said it looked like she drowned, but won't swear to it until he does a preliminary autopsy. He also said there weren't any obvious signs she'd been sexually assaulted. Dr. Stonebridge was more agitated than a rabid 'coon, said we couldn't disturb the patients or question anybody until this morning. I couldn't see much point in it, either, so I left a couple of deputies to keep the scene secured. Now I've got a fistful of messages from the head of the county commission to keep this out of the media until we figure out what-all happened. Seems he has connections with everybody from the district prosecutor to the state attorney general. There's a lot of money in play. Pity none of it's coming my way. I'm thinking it'd be nice to buy a little cabin on one of the lakes for when I retire."

"Anytime soon?" I asked optimistically.

"Don't start planning to redecorate my office, missy. Raz Buchanon would get more votes than a girl in khaki britches, especially one who used to live in New York City. You want to wager on your chances or hear about this case?"

"Was the victim one of the patients?"

"I wish it was that easy." Harve paused long enough to light a cigar, then went on. "A young gal from Starley City, name of Molly Foss. She was the receptionist. We notified her husband this morning. As soon as he identified the body at the morgue, he was all set to go out there with a shotgun. We talked him out it for the time being. That ain't to say he's gonna sit home with a hankie, at least not for long."

"I don't suppose she committed suicide," I said.

"It's darn near impossible to drown yourself in four inches of water. McBean said there was some bruising on the back of her neck. Most likely she was held down."

I had a foreboding about my weekend plans with Jack. His children were leaving that afternoon for a church trip to a theme park, and wouldn't be home until Sunday. We'd already agreed on the menu, rental movies, CDs, and wine list. Scrabble was definitely on the schedule. "It's not my jurisdiction," I repeated (or bleated, to be more accurate). "I hope Mrs. Dorfer's not too disappointed when you can't take her to the arts and crafts fair in Mount Ida."

Harve harrumphed. "She's going with her sister. I'm going fishing with my brother-in-law. Afterward, we're going to grill T-bone steaks and watch baseball. You, on the other hand, are going to look into this. If we don't figure it out by Monday morning, the county commissioner is gonna serve my balls on a platter at the next meeting. I hear the patients out there are crazier than loons. It may not take you more than a hour or two to get a confession."

"I have an hour or two, Harve, but 'long about three o'clock this afternoon, I'm putting away my badge and heading for the state line."

"Then it's settled. Dr. Stonebridge doesn't want his patients and staff to get all upset, so wear civilian clothes. Les will be there in about ten minutes to drive you over. Go through the main gate and around to a parking lot in the back. The doctor's waiting for you there."

"Ten minutes? Sounds as though you've got this all figured out, you conniving bastard. What were you going to do if I was over in Belle Star, stalking lowly fish-nappers?"

"I would have tracked you down, sooner or later."

He hung up before I could respond. I replaced the receiver, took off my badge and tossed it into a drawer, and went into the back room to unplug the coffeemaker. At least I'd find out what was going on inside the Stonebridge Foundation, I thought as I headed outside to wait for Les. And I had every intention of keeping my date in Springfield, even if it meant the victim had to spend a few extra days in the morgue.

When Les arrived, I got into his car and said, "Tell me what you know."

He shrugged. "Not much. Sheriff Dorfer called me at four-fifteen and told me to pick him up at his house. I don't think he was real happy about being dragged out of bed, but neither was I. When we got to the place, a guard was waiting at the gate. We followed him around to the back, where there's a big garden with benches and paths and that kind of shit. Some guy named Stonebridge was waiting for us."

"Anybody else?"

"A woman, kinda bulky and with a scowl that could turn a freight train up a dirt road. Stonebridge was skittery, but she was cool, considering there was a dead body lying on the grass. McBeen and his boys showed up, made the official call, and had the body removed. Woman, early twenties, blond, not more than five-four, hundred and twenty pounds max, big boobs, probably a cheerleader in high school. You know the kind."

"I wasn't a cheerleader," I said.

"Neither was I," Les said with a smirk. "Anyway, I mostly stood around while the sheriff, Stonebridge, and the woman conferred out of earshot. Eventually they came to some kind of agreement, and Sheriff Dorfer told me and Palsy to stay there the rest of the night. He called me on my cell a few minutes ago and told me to come pick you up. That's about it."

"So the body had been pulled out of the fountain before you got there?" I asked. "Was anybody else around? Lights on inside the place?"

"Just a few in the part of the building

where the doctors have their bedrooms and offices. The patients' rooms are in the front, so I'd be surprised if they knew anything had happened." He paused. "Except for maybe one of them."

"Maybe," I agreed. "Any idea why they're there?"

"Nobody told me much of anything, Arly." He stopped at the gate and pushed the button on the box. After he'd identified himself, the gate swung open and we drove around back to a small parking lot. There were a couple of nondescript cars, an aged Volkswagen camper adorned with bumper stickers and dents, and two dusty vans. At the far side was a fenced pen restraining the dog I'd met earlier. "Dr. Stonebridge said he'll be waiting for you by the fountain. I'm going home to get some sleep."

"You're just going to drop me off and leave?"

"Sheriff's orders. You got a problem with that, call him at your own risk."

I watched Les drive away, then went though a small gate. The new additions matched the exterior of the old building. What had been neglected pasture a month earlier was now an elaborate green space, with manicured grass, pines and flowering trees, brick paths, and beds of bright flowers. Although I was sadly ignorant of the cost of landscaping, I could see that big bucks had been spent. I wondered if the birds and butterflies had been purchased, or just leased for the summer.

The only person I could see was a man skimming the pool with a long-handled net. Doubting that the exalted doctor stooped to such pedestrian chores, I went down a path. After a bit of meandering, I spotted a silver-haired man sitting on a bench near a fountain. I couldn't tell if he was mourning, thinking, or napping, so I approached quietly and waited until he looked up.

"Dr. Stonebridge? I'm Arly Hanks," I said, "the chief of police in Maggody."

"Ah, yes," he murmured. "Sheriff Dorfer said you were coming. A dreadful business, this. Miss Foss was a charming young woman. We are all deeply distressed by her unfortunate death."

"I understand it was a bit more than unfortunate."

He stood up and came over to me. His complexion was almost gray, either from grief or exhaustion, but I noted that he had found time to shave and put on a freshly pressed white medical coat. He studied my face as he clasped my hand and squeezed it with avuncular tenderness. "I do hope you were told about the necessity of protecting our patients from undue alarm. They are all quite sensitive at this stage in their rehabilitation, and I cannot allow them to be upset by any sort of unnecessary intrusion."

I forced myself to respond calmly. "There's been a murder on the grounds, Dr. Stonebridge. We can't ignore it for the sake of their therapy." I gestured at the fountain, where a marble cherub clutched a vase of dribbling water. "Is this where Miss Foss's body was found?"

"Yes," he said, gazing at it with a bleak smile. "The orderly on the night shift came out here to have a cigarette. None of the employees are supposed to smoke on the premises, but I find it best to be tolerant. As soon as he saw the body, he roused me. Once I saw what had happened, I called Sheriff Dorfer."

"I'll need to speak to the orderly," I said.

"Of course, but you may find it a challenge unless you speak Spanish."

I didn't care for the smugness with which he said this, and I didn't much care for him, either. Presumably he had the required education and credentials, but the capped teeth, perfect hair, and condescending manner were a bit too much for me to swallow. "Is he Mexican?"

"All of the employees are, with the exception of the chef and his crew. It's a matter of economics. Very few people are willing to work for minimum wage these days. We supply free living arrangements and an allowance for food. That way, most of them are able to send money home to their families."

"How magnanimous of you," I said drily. "I'll need some information about Miss Foss, as well as everyone who works here and your patients."

Dr. Stonebridge shook his head. "Miss Foss, the employees, and the staff, certainly, but doctor-patient confidentiality must be protected. In any case, there's no way any of the patients could have knowledge of what took place. They are sedated in the evening to ensure they get proper rest. The culprit is most likely to be someone local who breached security."

"What kind of security?"

"Two orderlies are on duty at night from eight o'clock until six in the morning. One is armed and uses a trained guard dog to patrol the grounds. The front gates are locked, and no one on the night shift is allowed to open them without consulting Dr. Skiller or me. No matter how carefully one prepares for every contingency, however, there is always a possibility that someone found a way inside."

"I'll get a translator out here as soon as possible. Why don't you tell me what happened last night? Did Miss Foss usually work late?"

"Her hours were eight to five, with Saturday afternoons and Sundays off. Last night we had a staff meeting to evaluate our progress thus far, and I asked Molly — Miss Foss — to stay late in case she had anything to contribute. She and I had a light supper in my apartment before the meeting; I believe the others —"

"The others being?" I interrupted, mainly to annoy him.

"Dr. Zumi, our resident psychiatrist, and Dr. Skiller, who is a psychologist who specializes in nutrition and herbal remedies. I believe you've met them. Walter Kaiser is a personal trainer."

"And your specialty?"

"I am a dermatological and plastic surgeon. I had a very lucrative practice in the Los Angeles area before coming here to open the Stonebridge Foundation."

I'd met a few of his ilk in Manhattan, and I hadn't liked any of them. Dr. Stonebridge was no exception. "So why did you come here?"

He began to pace slowly around the fountain, his fingers templed and his expression thoughtful. "This is the culmination of my dreams, Miss Hanks — or may I call you Arly?" When I shrugged, he smiled and continued. "Sadly, there are some well-known people who fall victim to various addictions. Because of their notoriety, they are fearful of seeking help. Here in this primitive backwoods, they know they are safe from unwanted media exposure. We offer a variety of therapies to suit each individual so that they can battle their inner demons and return to the public sphere."

"This is a charitable institution? Non-profit?"

He looked at me. "Not precisely. As you can see, we've invested a great deal of capital in the structure and grounds. Our staff-to-patient ratio is better than three to one, which you cannot find in a large, impersonal setting. Every patient has an exquisitely decorated suite and a therapy program based on their individual needs. This level of care is not inexpensive."

I would have bet the farm on that. "Please continue with last night. What happened after the staff meeting?"

"I wish I knew. Miss Foss said she was leaving, but it's possible she decided to stay and catch up on paperwork. I myself retired to make phone calls, leaving the others in the day room. Later I put on a Bach CD, had a glass or two of brandy, and caught up on some medical journals. I believe it was about midnight when I went to bed."

"You didn't see anyone after the meeting?"

"Regrettably, I did not. As for the others, you'll have to ask them. Dr. Skiller is waiting for you at the reception desk to show you what to do. You'll have to question the others when you have a break."

"A break?" I said.

"Didn't Sheriff Dorfer explain? In order to avoid upsetting the patients, you will assume Miss Foss's responsibilities. You can file, can't you?"

"I can file my nails, if that's what you mean."

"Hardly," he said with an amused look. "Have you never gone undercover before?"

"No, and I never intend to." This was not strictly true. I certainly intended to spend a good deal of the weekend under the covers.

"My dear Arly," he murmured. "It's all been arranged with the good sheriff."

"The good sheriff can take his arrangements and put them where the sun don't shine," I said, lapsing into the local vernacular. "You just tell the other doctors and the personal trainer to meet me in this day room. After I've interviewed them, I'll send for a translator and tackle the Mexican employees."

"We cannot disrupt the routine. Dr. Zumi has private counseling sessions throughout the day; in fact, he's in one now. Dr. Skiller oversees the dietary concerns, orders, and deliveries, and does yoga and other alternative treatments. Walter is already in the gym with one of the patients. Physical fitness is a necessity to relieve stress and channel our patients' energy in a more productive manner. If all of them were pulled away at one time, our patients would realize that something is going on and become quite agitated. Nor can the maids and orderlies fail to carry out their daily tasks. Bed linens must be changed, suites cleaned, hallways kept gleaming."

"What exactly do you do all day?"

"I am in the process of determining what surgical procedures will best benefit our patients at various stages of their gradual progress. A positive self-image is vital to complete recovery."

He was annoying the hell out of me, and I knew I was doing a poor job of hiding it. Somehow, I didn't much care. "You mean nose jobs? Face lifts?"

He winced. "I prefer to use the approved medical terminology, but in essence, yes. Now why don't you run along and find Dr. Skiller? I need to call my attorney to discuss potential liability."

I stood up. "I'll use the opportunity to question her about what took place after the meeting. I am under no circumstances going undercover, Dr. Stonebridge. If you need a replacement for Miss Foss, I suggest you try a temp agency."

Fuming, I left him by the fountain and headed for the pool area to find an entrance. The man who'd been cleaning the pool had vanished. Now a muscular young man with gleaming blond hair was swimming laps as if he were training for the Olympics. A patient, I surmised, but if he was all that famous, it escaped me. Then again, I don't have cable and I rarely make it to the movies in Farberville. Maybe he'd won an Oscar or an Emmy or whatever people won these days. Probably not the Kentucky Derby.

I opened French doors and went down a corridor in the direction of the front of the building. A uniformed maid carrying an armload of towels hurried by without acknowledging me. I recognized the man who'd been guarding the gate during construction. He was now clad in neat white pants and a shirt, and when he saw me, disappeared around a corner. No one was crying or howling in a distant room. No bedpans clattered to the floor; no querulous voices complained. It was all very civilized for a loony bin, if that's what it was.

When I arrived in the reception room, the desk was unattended. More maids were moving about in one of the wings, presumably where the patients were battling demons in their exquisitely decorated suites. I drummed my fingers on the desk while I tried to decide what to do — which would not include filing or busywork. I already had a job, and more importantly, a date later in the day. What's more, I suspected that if I called Harve to squawk, I'd be told that he'd gone fishing for the weekend.

I was considering giving it a shot when Dr. Skiller appeared from an office behind the desk.

"So it's you," she said flatly.

Nothing like a warm greeting to liven up my day.

8

Ruby Bee was keeping an eye on Tekeella Buchanon, who was draped all over a potbellied truck driver in one of the booths. As long as they didn't start fooling around with buttons and zippers, she had no call to interfere. 'Course it might get interesting if Tekeella's boyfriend showed up, but last she'd heard, he was doing thirty days at the county jail for assault. She couldn't remember when she'd heard it, though.

She felt a flicker of alarm as the door opened and sunlight splashed onto the dance floor. Her alarm turned to disdain as Estelle wobbled in on four-inch heels, all gussied up like she was going to church. However, she held her tongue as Estelle sat down on her customary stool and took a Tupperware container out of a plastic bag.

They looked at each other for an uncomfortable minute, then Rudy Bee broke down and said, "You want something?"

"I made a batch of guacamole dip for your

guests out back," said Estelle. "I just happened to have some avocados that were getting mushy."

Ruby Bee sniffed. "Oh, really? Last time I looked, the SuperSaver didn't have any avocados."

"I was shopping in Farberville, if you must know. Kmart was having a sale on purses, and I've been looking for a new one to go with my navy dress. Afterward, I stopped at a grocery store to pick up a few things."

"Like avocados," Ruby Bee said, nodding sagely.

Estelle chewed on her lip. "That's right. I found a recipe in a magazine for a chicken dish that called for avocados and black olives and salsa. The SuperSaver doesn't carry fancy things like that."

"So how did this chicken dish turn out?"

"I changed my mind about making it. I couldn't think of anything else to do with the avocados, so I made some guacamole. Do I need your permission to take it out back?"

Ruby Bee moved down the bar and began to wash mugs in the sink. "Doesn't matter to me, but I'm kinda surprised that you'd want to have anything to do with those foreigners. You want to leave your purse behind the bar in case they're pickpockets and thieves?"

"I don't know why you'd say such a thing, Rubella Belinda Hanks!"

"I'm sure they'll be forever beholden to you for your Christian generosity. The pope'll be impressed, too."

"If you'd druther, I can just leave," Estelle said, heating up.

"Pay no attention to me. Most likely they'll be thrilled out of their skins to get a bowl of mushy avocados. I'm surprised you didn't bring along a box of old underwear and rusty cans of tomato soup and pinto beans."

Estelle quivered, then composed herself. "I don't know what you want from me, Ruby Bee. I came here to make amends, but I ain't gonna grovel."

"Well, I ain't gonna grovel, neither," retorted Ruby Bee.

"It's just that . . . well, it's complicated. If you don't mind, I'll pour myself a glass of sherry." When Ruby Bee shrugged, she reached behind the bar and found her bottle. "The thing is, back when I was living in Little Rock and singing at the lounge, there was this Italian fellow. I don't want to bore you with the details, so all I'm gonna say is that it didn't work out. I ended up mistrusting foreigners. I know those folks out back ain't Italians, but it's hard for me to feel comfortable about them."

Ruby Bee tossed the dishrag into the sink and went down to the end of the bar. "So tell me about him. Was he good-looking?"

"He had this really thick hair that was blacker than a mule skinner's molar," Estelle said dreamily. "He always brought me flowers on Saturday night. Not daisies, but big bouquets of roses tied with ribbons. I have to admit I was smitten with him, in spite of his annoying habit of sucking on his teeth. One night we drove out to a bluff overlooking the river and he told me all about his house in Italy and his wife, who'd died of some kind of mysterious ailment when she was only twenty-two."

"And then . . . ?" Ruby Bee prompted her.

The ensuing conversation managed to undo a week's worth of animosity.

"I am not here as a replacement receptionist," I said to Brenda Skiller. "This is a murder investigation. My understanding is that Molly Foss was drowned in a fountain out back. Would you please tell me what you did after the staff meeting was over?"

"Sheriff Dorfer, if that's his name, agreed that you would ask your questions without causing undue alarm," she said coolly. "You cannot do so if you insist on attempting to bully everyone. I suggest you take several deep, cleansing breaths before you continue."

I couldn't quite bring myself to drop into a lotus position and focus on my navel. "I don't like this any more than you do, but we need to get it resolved quickly. What did you do after the staff meeting?"

She assessed me with no visible signs of warmth. "I agree with you that this must be dealt with expeditiously. After the meeting adjourned, I needed to pick up some invoices in the office. Miss Foss was here. I found what I needed and retired to my room. She and I did not speak."

"Didn't she announce at the end of the staff meeting that she was going home?"

"She did, but she lingered at her desk."

"Do you have any idea why?" I asked.

"Why would I? She was vapid, silly, and keenly aware of the effect she had on all the males in a quarter-mile radius. She couldn't master the computer or put files in the appropriate slots, but she could wiggle her ass and wink like a local beauty pageant queen. I found her behavior disgusting."

It didn't sound as if Brenda Skiller and Molly Foss shared tuna sandwiches and fashion tips at lunch. I tried again. "What time was this?"

"Eight-thirty or so. As I said, I took the invoices and left her here. I went to my office, did some work, and finished up at eleven. Dr. Stonebridge knocked on my door shortly after four o'clock this morning to tell me what happened. I dressed and waited with him in the garden for the authorities."

I perched on the edge of the desk. "Could Molly have been meeting someone?"

"I have no idea. When I last saw her, she wasn't really doing anything, just fiddling with the pens and paper clips. She seemed a little bit nervous. I did wonder briefly if she was waiting for Walter. He must have seemed exotic in comparison to her husband."

"You're quite sure it couldn't have been a patient?" I asked, thinking of the blond hulk I'd seen swimming laps.

"Absolutely not. They are all sedated by nine each night. We cannot have them wandering around the facility. We would be liable if something happened to one of them. Randall — Dr. Zumi — will be happy to provide you with the details of their medication."

I tossed this around for a moment. "Then

you agree that either someone from outside managed to get over or under the fence, despite the guard and the dog, or that one of the employees is responsible?"

"I see no reason to speculate," Brenda said. "My only concern is for our patients, who will be following their schedules for individual and small group therapy, physical activity, meditation, and meals. Although I suspect you're no more competent than Miss Foss, you must assume her duties in order not to alarm them."

"Your cash cows," I said.

"In a manner of speaking, yes. You'll find a white coat in the office. Please wear it while you're here." She picked up a clipboard and thrust it at me. "Here is a list of those expected to require admittance during the day. They must identify themselves before you push the button to open the gate. Do not attempt to file anything or use the computer. Miss Foss left a muddle that will take me days to undo. If any of the patients ask about her, tell them she was called away for a family crisis."

"Wait a minute," I said as she headed down the hall. She did not look back as she disappeared. I was not pleased with her assumption that I would put on a white coat and guard the gate, but I realized I might have an opportunity to find out something about what was happening inside the compound. Thus far it was creepy, to put it mildly. The two doctors I'd encountered were more worried about maintaining a tranquil setting than they were about the brutal death of Molly Foss. Dr. Stonebridge was on the phone to his lawyer to discuss liability. Dr. Skiller was no doubt making sure the latest delivery of fresh vegetables was one hundred percent organic. Clearly, I needed to talk to Dr. Zumi and the personal trainer before I tackled the patients and the terrified staff of Mexicans — none of whom spoke English. I wasn't fond of the current proprietor of the Dairee Dee-Lishus, but I was very sorry he was not available to translate. Presuming he would.

And if Sheriff Harvey Dorfer had been anywhere in the vicinity, I would have kicked his butt into kingdom come, and then some.

I was still sitting on the edge of the desk when a tall, thin woman with striking white hair and a grim expression came into the area. She wore a blue velour tracksuit and had a towel draped over one shoulder. She was striding with such intensity that she nearly crashed into me.

"Where's Molly?" she demanded.

"She couldn't work today," I said truthfully.

"Who are you?"

"Arly Hanks," I said. I studied her more carefully. She looked vaguely familiar, but I couldn't quite place her. "And you?"

"That is none of your concern. I need to make a telephone call. This is utterly ridiculous, this coerced isolation! Ridiculous! All this whispering and creeping about at night. People coming into my room without my permission. It's a disgrace. I must call Lloyd right now!"

I frowned, trying to remember when and where I'd seen her. "Help yourself. There's bound to be a phone around here somewhere."

"Do stop staring at me like that. I am not a specimen under a microscope." She went into the office behind me and slammed the door.

But she was a patient, I decided, and teetering on a very tall ladder. I had no idea what she would have done if I'd refused to give her access to a phone. And I was certain I'd seen her somewhere.

"Who are you?" asked a man who'd managed to come up silently behind me.

I turned around. As soon as I'd taken a good look at him, I realized he was Ruby

Bee's would-be psychotic killer. I could understand why she'd been alarmed by his long hair, now in a tidy ponytail, and dark eyes. He'd put on a white coat over a tie-dyed T-shirt, but it failed to give him a professional aura, since he was also wearing sandals and baggy shorts. His hairy legs were scarred as if he'd spent years tromping through sagebrush.

"You're Walter Kaiser, the trainer?" I said, although it seemed equally possible he'd murdered Walter Kaiser and donned his coat. We were about the same height, but he loomed over me all the same.

Okay, so maybe I was sitting down.

His lips twitched. "My fame precedes me. Does yours?"

"I'm here because of Molly."

"Yeah, what a bummer. Brenda told me what happened. Molly was one sweet chick. Clueless as the day she was born, which was probably in a log cabin with a midwife in attendance. She told me that the only time she's ever been out of Arkansas was when her family went to Pensacola for a week. She thought the ocean was 'really, really big.' I didn't have the heart to tell her she was looking at the friggin' Gulf of Mexico." He pushed aside a pile of papers and sat next to me. "So you're investigating the murder?"

"For the moment," I said. "Did you see Molly after the staff meeting last night?"

Walter grinned at me. "You'd make a fine lady cop on a TV show. You got any handcuffs in your back pocket?"

"After the staff meeting . . . ?"

"I followed Molly here and tried to talk her into going out to a bar. She claimed she couldn't because she was married. I told her that was a load of bullshit." He hesitated for a moment, then continued. "Things sort of went downhill from there, and she ended up slapping me so hard that my eardrums damn near burst. I told her to save her piety for church and went back to my room. I fell asleep about midnight. Guess I missed all the excitement."

"You were pretty pissed off at her, weren't you?" I asked.

"Not really." Walter stood up and peered down the hallway. "You seen a lady in a blue tracksuit? She was supposed to be in the gym ten minutes ago."

I gestured at the office. "She said she needed to make a call. Who is she, Walter? I know I've seen her before."

"You let her make a call? You'd better hope the top guns don't find out. They have a very strict policy that forbids patients from communicating with the outside world."

"Is she a journalist?"

"Something like that," he said. "I'd better hustle her off to the gym before she gets caught. She's a tough old bird, but I kinda like her. Be a shame if she got into trouble."

I stared at him. "This isn't exactly a boarding school for rambunctious adolescents. Aren't the patients free to leave?"

"One of 'em is here under court order for a ninety-day psych evaluation, and another at a judge's discretion. Technically, they could leave, although the repercussions would be nasty. The other two are here voluntarily, but under duress. And they know their addictions are life-threatening, even if they won't admit it."

"The woman in the office . . . ?"

Walter shook his head. "I've said too much already. The last thing I want to do is get canned. Easy job, good pay, free room and board. The food's lousy, since Brenda's got this vegan mindset. Last night we had broiled falafel patties and a salad of free-range endive with toasted sesame seed dressing." He gave me a mischievous smile. "You want to go to a steak house tonight, then take a long, lazy drive back here? We can stop somewhere and act out fantasies with your handcuffs."

"Sorry, I've got plans. Who offered you this job?"

His smile faded. "I don't remember. I probably just heard about it on the grapevine or something. Mrs. S. and I need to head for the gym before Brenda shows up. See you later, I hope."

He opened the office door and went inside. Seconds later, he and the woman emerged. She looked exasperated, but whatever he was saying to her in a low voice seemed to be effective. They went down the hall toward the rear of the building.

I was positively itching with curiosity to figure out who the woman was, as well as the swimmer. Not, mind you, that I had some sort of tingle of suspicion about either — or anyone else I'd met thus far. I still didn't have a clear picture of what had happened after the staff meeting, although it seemed that either Walter or Brenda might have been the last person to see Molly alive. I needed some idea of how long she'd been dead before her body was discovered, and that would have to wait for McBeen's report. I decided to give him until noon, then call the morgue and wheedle an estimate out of him.

Telling myself I would play out the charade until then, I put on a white coat and picked up the clipboard with the list of those authorized to enter the premises through the not-so-pearly gates. Nobody was expected until early afternoon. If I'd had bifocals, I would have been the perfect medical receptionist: grim, efficient, unsympathetic. I walked briskly into the wing, my mouth drawn in faint disapproval as though some hapless patient had failed to present a valid insurance card. The maids kept their faces lowered. An orderly wheeling a cart with the remains of breakfast glanced up, then looked away as if he might be turned to stone.

A card on the door of the first suite identified its occupant rather tersely as "Dr. D." I rapped once, then went inside. Music was playing, and some anguished soul was warbling in Italian. On the bed was a mountainous bulge that appeared to be breathing. Two slitted blue eyes peered at me over the edge of a blanket.

"How are we today?" I chirped.

"Good Lord, is it conceivable that there is yet another of you nattering ninnies? Let me guess — you've brought my midmorning snack. What can it be today? A sunflower seed? A bean sprout? I can hardly restrain my salivary glands."

"Nothing that exciting, I'm afraid. I'm

213

filling in for Miss Foss for a few hours. She was called away for an emergency."

"Balderdash! She was murdered in the garden."

I set down the clipboard and moved closer to him, hoping he wasn't the sort to spit — or at least that his range was limited. "How do you know that?"

He pulled the blanket over his head, but after a moment, pulled it down a few inches. "Why should I tell you? What's in it for me? Are you too dim-witted to grasp the essence of capitalism? Supply and demand, based on the fair market exchange of valuable consideration. I have information. What have you to offer?"

"You want money?" I asked, mystified.

"Please, Lord, save me from dunces and buffoons. I swear I'll give all my book advances to an organization that provides free lobotomies to the terminally ignorant. I'll give up caviar for Lent, or at least the beluga variety. Anything to rid myself of you meddlesome medical prevaricators!"

"You're a writer?"

"I am Dr. Shelby Dibbins."

I thought for a moment, but nothing clicked. "Should I have heard of you?"

"Yes, unless you live in a shack and read nothing more challenging than tabloids heralding the latest Elvis sighting. I feel as though I've been stranded on an island populated by sadistic scientists and their subnormal subordinates. I'm waiting to be measured for thumbscrews."

"If you're suffering, why are you here? Court order?"

He sat up, giving me a view of black satin pajamas. "I will not be insulted like this! Bring me my dressing gown and slippers. I shall march down the hall and lodge a complaint with Dr. Stonebridge, who shares many qualities with his mentor, Dr. Mengele."

"Get over it." I tossed him the dressing gown. "If you're not here involuntarily, who is?"

Although he was puffing, Dibbins made it to the sofa in the sitting room with surprising agility for such a large man. "I'm quite sure the washed-up actress down the hall does not have the option of leaving. She complains incessantly about the food, the size of her suite, and her obligatory therapy sessions. Tantrums are unattractive in children, but repulsive in adults. In an effort to gain extra privileges, she's attempted to seduce every man in this establishment. I've got my money on the orderly with the scar on his chin. He drives the van, so I suspect that she believes he'll smuggle her out with the trash some evening. All she can hope to get from me is an evening of Puccini. Are you fond of opera?"

"How do you know so much?" I asked, ignoring his question, since I'd never developed a taste for melodramatics. "I was told the maids and orderlies don't speak any English."

His eyes glittered with amusement. "Bring me a twelve-ounce white chocolate bar with hazelnuts and raisins, and I shall spill my heart. Do be quick about it, since Dr. Skiller no doubt has me scheduled for leeches in hopes they can suck up a pound of flesh along with my sickly corpuscles."

"I'll be back later," I said. I picked up the clipboard and returned to the hall. Apparently Dr. Dibbins had a pretty good idea of what was going on inside the Stonebridge Foundation, although I couldn't see him being included in any staff meetings. Either some of the maids and orderlies spoke more English than they'd admitted, or he spoke Spanish. Or he had access to the personal files, improbable as it seemed.

I was considering my next move when Randall Zumi hurried down the hall and caught my arm. He looked no more in command of the situation than he had more than a week ago when he and Brenda had wandered into Ruby Bee's Bar & Grill.

"Brenda told me you were here," he said in a low voice. He glanced over his shoulder, then added, "I need to speak to you somewhere more private than this. Can you come to my office?"

I followed him back through the reception room to the back of the building. As we went down the sidewalk, I said, "What are these rooms?"

Randall was clearly not in the mood to give me a guided tour. "The surgical suite and recovery area, followed by Brenda's rooms, Walter's, mine, and Vince's at the end. The living areas are behind each office. They're basically efficiency apartments, with limited cooking facilities. Not as posh as the patients' suites, but pleasant enough."

I suspected my roach-infested apartment with its stained linoleum floor and peeling walls would not compare well. Then again, the only way I'd ever have a six-figure income would be to erase the decimal point on my paycheck. "And on the other side of the pool?" I asked as he stopped to unlock a door.

"Uh, the day room, which nobody much uses during the day. The patients eat in their sitting rooms, and the employees in a room behind the kitchen. The rest of us eat in our apartments. Next is the gym, and beyond that, the kitchen, pantry, laundry, and furnace room." He opened the door and gestured for me to precede him. "I only have twenty minutes until my next session. If the schedule is disrupted, the patients become uneasy. They're like small children; they do better with a consistent routine."

"All right, but after we're done, I need to have a look at the day room and the gym," I said.

He nudged me into his office and closed the door. "I'll give you a key. Please, sit down and let me tell you what happened. Would you like water or a glass of Brenda's chilled herbal tea?"

"No, thank you." I sat down in a leather chair in front of his desk. The office was large, and decorated with the same thick gray carpet and elegant touches I'd seen in Dr. Dibbins's suite. "Is this about Molly Foss's death?"

He sank down in a chair across from me. "I wish I knew. It might be, or I could just be going crazy. Funny, isn't it? I'm the one who's trained to diagnose delusions, not have them. Luckily, I don't have much time to indulge myself, since I'm on call seven nights a week."

"In case someone freaks out?"

"We prefer to use more precise terminology," he said, wincing. "There have been moments when one of the patients has become unduly agitated and potentially violent. Only Dr. Stonebridge and I are licensed to administer narcotics."

"Not Brenda Skiller?" I asked.

Randall shook his head. "She's a psychologist. Once we add an RN to the staff, it'll make things easier." He picked up a pen and began to roll it in his hands. "It's imperative that you do not repeat what I'm about to tell you. Can you agree to this?"

"Of course." I didn't bother to add that I could also agree to invite Raz and Marjorie over for cocktails, run marathons, and buy beachfront property behind Perkin's barn. Didn't mean I would, though — especially if what he had to say involved the murder.

"Someone broke in here yesterday or the day before," he said. "I don't mean with a chisel or pry bar. Whoever it was must have had a key."

"Was there damage? Is something missing?"

He dropped the pen and stared at it as it rolled off the desk. "Nothing so obvious.

Someone went through my personal papers. I might not have noticed for a long time, but this morning I needed to find my lawyer's telephone number. I knew precisely where I'd put it. The papers in that particular folder had been taken out and then put back in the wrong order. Whoever it was searched everything, including my desk drawers and the books on the shelf over there. My apartment was also searched."

"You're sure?" I asked. "Isn't it possible that you might have unpacked hastily when you arrived last week?"

"I am quite sure," he said firmly. "I'm obsessive about keeping everything neat and in the proper place. My coworkers at the hospital used to tease me about it. They thought it was a big joke."

"Who has a key or access to one?"

He put his elbows on the desk and rested his head in his hands. "Vincent, Brenda, and I have master keys to all the rooms. There's also one in the reception office for the maids. I have sessions here during the day, so my office and apartment are cleaned between six and seven each evening. I use that time to walk in the garden, work out, or visit patients in their suites. I wish I could say that I never leave the door unlocked when I'm not here, but I probably do when I'm preoccupied."

That narrowed down the suspects to everybody within the facility, patients and staff alike. "Why do you think someone would risk being caught to look through your personal papers?" I asked. "Is there something significant?"

"No, nothing. I'm going through a divorce, but my wife's lawyer is aware of all my assets. I don't have an offshore account or a lockbox crammed with money. Hell, I don't have more than a hundred dollars of ready cash. I invested every spare penny I had in the foundation. I don't have anything left to hide."

"Somebody must think you do," I pointed out.

"If I did, don't you think I would have destroyed it before I came here?" he said bitterly.

I was startled by the change in his voice. "Tell me about yesterday. Could you have left the door unlocked?"

He opened a notebook. "It was fairly normal. I had a nine o'clock session with . . . well, one of the patients, and then —"

"Listen up," I said, "I'm going to have to know the names of everybody on the premises. A young woman was murdered here last night. I don't need to know the patients' specific problems — I just need to know who they are. This coyness isn't going to cut it. If I have to get a court order, I will." I was proud of this final threat, which always worked in TV shows but was quite a bit dicier in reality. The judges in Stump County were a bunch of old white farts who spent their weekends fishing, playing golf, or fooling around with their nubile clerks in motels across the state line. And when the weather was nice, these weekends began at noon on Friday and continued until the inevitable Monday-morning hangover had abated. I couldn't count on Harve for help unless the lake had dried up. However, I bared my teeth at Randall and waited silently.

"I should run this by Vincent," he said at last.

I leaned back and crossed my arms. "Whatever you think is best. Just keep in mind there are reporters hanging around the courtrooms, hoping for something more sensational than rote arraignments for spousal abuse and hot checks."

Randall looked as though he wished he could swallow a handful of whatever he prescribed for his patients' late-night anxiety attacks. "Has anyone ever told you that you have a passive-aggressive syndrome? It's probably due to conflicts with your mother. Did you feel manipulated as an adolescent?"

"Do you mind if I use your phone? I need to start the process for the warrant before noon."

"Oh, all right. Dr. Shelby Dibbins is an author from West Palm Beach. Dawn Dartmouth is a young actress from the L.A. area. Toby Mann is a professional athlete, and Alexandra Swayze is from D.C. and is involved in politics. Is that adequate?"

I suddenly realized why I'd almost recognized the woman in the blue tracksuit, having seen her face in the newspaper (and hoped she'd be struck by lightning). None of the others were familiar, but that was my fault, not theirs. "Adequate for the time being," I said as I wrote down the names. "Please continue with what you did yesterday, but use their names this time."

"Dawn came here at nine. At ten I saw Ms. Swayze, who then went to the gym for a session there. Toby came here a few minutes later from acupuncture therapy with Brenda. At noon I went to Dr. Dibbins's suite, since he refuses to leave it. Afterward, I took an apple and ate it by the pool. Vince joined me, and we discussed potential surgical procedures. That seems to be his solution to every problem, while Brenda argues that cures can be found only in the bowels." He paused to give me a wry smile. "That leaves me with the brains and Walter with the biceps. We're very thorough here at the Stonebridge Foundation. Our motto should be: Leave no tummy untucked and no feces unflushed."

I really didn't want to hear any more. "After lunch?"

"Dawn and Toby returned here for anger management. I'd hoped we were ready for role-playing, but both of them were, shall we say, too intense for objective analysis of their emotional reactions to minimal confrontation. I had to call an orderly to separate them. Toby went to work out with Walter. Dawn said she was returning to her suite. The orderly helped me put the furniture back in place and pick up the books and other projectiles. I took a few minutes to regain my composure, then went to Brenda's office to review her dietary supplements to make sure the two weren't receiving excessive stimulants. None of these herbal remedies has been properly studied, and their purported potencies aren't regulated by the FDA. I prefer to know exactly what my patients are ingesting. Brenda would much rather don a robe and collect her roots and berries under a full moon."

"It sounds as though you were in and out all day," I said to get him back on track.

"It does, doesn't it? I met with Vince in the surgical suite to make sure everything was ready for the tumescent liposuction he was planning to perform on Dr. Dibbins this afternoon. That, of course, has been put off because of what happened to Molly." He took a deep breath, then exhaled slowly. "A truly terrible thing. She was so . . . so vibrant and happy. I can't believe someone would do something like that to her."

I'd finally found someone who was plainly distressed by her death. "You liked her, I gather."

"If I'd met her fifteen years ago, I would have dropped out of medical school and dedicated myself to making her happy. We would have lived in a simple house, raised a few adorable children, and spent our evenings sipping cocoa in front of a cozy fire." He closed the notebook and went to the window. His back to me, he added, "Brenda was very cruel to Molly. Envy is a dangerous emotion that can simmer beneath the surface like molten lava. Molly tried to ignore it, but I could see how deeply it wounded her. She wasn't like the rest of us, especially these damned bloody patients who all believe that they deserve public adoration. She was pure."

"Do you think Brenda might have told Molly to meet her in the garden after the staff meeting?" I asked delicately, already imagining myself driving toward Springfield in time for a cold beer and a tantalizing greeting. And, of course, a warm-up game of Scrabble.

He turned around. "Molly wouldn't have agreed to that. She wasn't quite the doormat everybody assumed she was, nor was she stupid. She married out of high school to escape her parents, but she chose a boy whose family owned a successful business. She was squirreling away money in a separate checking account and planning to get away as soon as she could."

"She told you this?"

"People seem to think they can confide in a psychiatrist." He attempted to smile. "We're not supposed to have irrational emotions."

I would have sympathized with him had the clock not been ticking. "Do you think Brenda might have followed Molly outside?"

"Don't be ridiculous."

"You're the one who brought up the simmering lava."

226

"That's hardly a motive for murder. Killing Molly wasn't going to make Brenda twenty years younger, forty pounds lighter, and a foot shorter." He sat down behind his desk and stared at me. "Yesterday at five or so, I returned here to have a cup of tea, wrote some notes for the case file, and went to the meeting. Afterward, I came back to read, then went to bed. Vince woke me up to tell me about Molly."

"You weren't in the garden when the sheriff and medical examiner arrived?"

"I was too upset. Vince and Brenda were talking about her death as if it were nothing more than a nuisance. With Vince's permission, I got a glass of brandy from his room and took a sleeping pill. I was oblivious to everything until a maid came in this morning at seven-thirty with my breakfast tray."

"When did you notice someone had been through your personal papers?"

"While I was reading through the mail that came yesterday, I realized I needed to make the call. That's when I took out the folder."

"Is everybody's schedule as hectic as yours?" I asked.

"Brenda, Walter, and I stay busy. Vince will be once he starts doing surgery. He is intensely interested in the success of the program, since he invested as much capital as I did. I think he was stretched to his limit, too. He's had some problems with malpractice suits. His license in California has been suspended by the state board — or maybe even revoked. I don't know the details."

"But he can practice here in Arkansas?"

Randall shrugged. "When a physician from another state applies for a license, it's issued almost automatically as a courtesy. The petty bureaucrats don't bother to check, and there's no national registry to indicate a physician's record of malpractice suits. Most of them are settled out of court, anyway, with nondisclosure clauses."

"So the AMA looks out for its members, I suppose. Too bad for the consumers."

"The AMA has a very powerful lobby in D.C.," Randall said. The telephone on his desk rang before he could continue. He picked up the receiver, listened for a few seconds, said, "Yes, she's here," then handed it to me. "It's Brenda. You have an outside call."

I assumed it was Harve, since he and Les were the only ones who knew where to find me. "Hello?"

"Arly?" squawked Estelle. "It's a good thing I knew where to find you. You have to get over here to your office right this minute. Ruby Bee's gone and shot someone!"

"Who?" I demanded.

"Me, if you must know. Ruby Bee should be pulling up to the gate any second now. Get yourself out there so she can bring you back here right away!"

"And what are you doing?"

"Bleeding, of course. What else would I be doing?"

9

I tossed the receiver to Randall and told him we'd finish our conversation later. When I got to the reception room, Brenda Skiller was waiting, her hands on her hips like a belligerent coach.

"I thought I made myself clear earlier," she began, making no effort to hide her exasperation. "I may not have specified that answering the telephone was among your simple-minded duties, but —"

"It's an emergency," I said. "Someone's picking me up at the gate."

I scrambled down the porch steps and out to the brick driveway, my thoughts too muddled to come up with any kind of rational explanation. The idea of Ruby Bee shooting Estelle was too absurd to imagine. What's more, Estelle was a helluva lot more nonchalant than I would have been. What was she doing? Bleeding, of course.

Silly me.

When Ruby Bee pulled up, I almost dove

into the front seat. "What on earth is going on? You shot Estelle?"

"Don't get your pigtails in a poke, missy," Ruby Bee said darkly as she turned the car around and drove back toward Maggody. "It's not like I shot her on purpose. The gun just went off."

"What gun?"

She gave me one of her snootier looks. "The gun I bought the other day to protect myself. I took it out to show Estelle, not realizing it was loaded. The man who sold it to me warned me to be real careful about that, but then he rambled on for so long, I just plunked down my money and left."

"Okay, so you didn't know it was loaded when you shot Estelle. How badly is she hurt?" I said, resisting the urge to whack her with her own handbag (which was definitely loaded).

"How many times do I have to tell you that I didn't shoot her? Her foot happened to be in the way, that's all. She's carryin' on something fierce over what most folks would dismiss as a piddly accident." She braked at the stop sign and took her sweet time peering both ways before turning onto the highway. "The bullet grazed her big toe. From the way she shrieked, you'd have thought it hit her smack dab in the heart and she only had a few seconds before she keeled over dead. Nobody dies from gettin' shot in the big toe, for pity's sake. I offered to put a Band-Aid on it, but she insisted on me taking her to your office in case she passed out. She figured the ambulance would have an easier time finding her there."

I untangled my legs and sank back in relief, then jerked up as I grasped the grimmer implications of what she'd said. "Where did you buy this gun? Didn't you have to wait twenty-four hours while the seller requested a background check on you?"

"If you must know, I bought it at a little gun show over in Oklahoma. I swear, I've never seen so many guns, knives, and tattoos in one room. I got out of there as fast as I could."

"Please explain why you felt the need to buy a gun," I said.

"Ever'body in Maggody has one these days on account of the crazy folks locked up at that foundation place. Mrs. Jim Bob organized a committee to keep watch and report suspicious activity. I told her I wasn't about to sit in a persimmon tree all night with a pair of binoculars. I'm not the only one. Even Elsie and Lottie are beginning to complain, and I heard there was a squabble at the last meeting of the Missionary Society." She parked in front of the PD and got out of the car. "Don't pay Estelle any mind if she starts in about all this terrible pain she's in and how much blood she's lost."

"I'll do my best," I said, wondering how many other local residents were keeping handguns in their bedside table drawers. Most of the men hunted deer or bunnies or other hapless furry critters, but they knew enough, at least when they were sober, to keep their rifles locked up where their kids couldn't get to them. The thought of the members of the Missionary Society sipping tea while they compared calibers and admired each other's inlaid pearl handles was chilling. And if they'd bought them at backwater gun shows, they'd have no clue how to handle them safely.

Estelle was sitting behind my desk, her foot propped up and wrapped in a dish towel. The evidence, a lime green high heel with a rhinestone buckle and slight rip near the pointed toe, was centered on the desk. She waggled limp fingers in our direction. "Thank gawd you're here. I keep having these dizzy spells, like the room is closing in on me. My heart's still racing faster than a two-headed toad fallin' down a well, and I'm having a hard time catching my breath. I reckon I'm in shock."

"Shall I throw you in the backseat and race to the emergency room in Farberville?" I asked. "Better yet, I could take you with me back to the Stonebridge Foundation. There are two medical doctors who'd be delighted to sew up your toe and keep you overnight for observation. You'll be safe, since there are bars on all the cell doors to keep the drooling psychopaths from sneaking up on you while you're asleep."

"Good grief, Arly," said Ruby Bee, "I told you the bullet barely grazed it."

I smiled at Estelle, who was turning paler by the second. "But we can't be too careful, can we? Sometimes these minor wounds can cause blood poisoning, or even gangrene. You don't want to end up painting the toenails on a prosthetic foot, do you?"

Estelle pulled off the dish towel and dropped it in the trashcan. "All the same, you ought to take Ruby Bee's gun away from her afore she shoots somebody else."

"I did not shoot you," protested the accused gunslinger. "Besides, you're the one who insisted that I take the gun out of the drawer and show it to you. You should have seen ol' Hubbubba Buchanon when it went off. He liked to piss in his britches in his hurry to get out the front door. And of course there was Estelle, hopping around on one foot and gobbling like a wild turkey."

Estelle rolled her eyes. "I seem to recollect you were a mite upset yourself, Rubella Belinda Hanks. As well you should have been, considering you'd just shot me." She handed me a piece of paper from my scratch pad. "Some prickly man from somewhere up north called while I was waiting. He had me write all this down, but he wouldn't so much as give me a hint of why you'd care about these places. You aiming to take a road trip?"

I looked at the note, which was nothing more than a list of cities: Wichita, Denver, Laramie, Casper. They were, I realized glumly, locations where Eileen's credit card had been used in the last eight days. She was traveling northwest at a good clip. Earl, Kevin, and Dahlia would not take the news well, even though it implied Eileen was alive and kicking.

"Well?" demanded Ruby Bee. "*Are* you aiming to take a road trip? Being your mother, I have a right to know."

I stuffed the note in my pocket. "The only place I'm going is back to the Stonebridge

Foundation. How'd y'all know where to find me?"

"Brother Verber told Mrs. Jim Bob," Estelle said. "She called Ruby Bee, wanting to know what you were doing there. I'd like to know, myself."

"So would I," added Ruby Bee, giving me a baleful stare.

I sat down on the visitor's chair. "Was Brother Verber in the persimmon tree? Jesus H. Christ, if I'd known, I would have gone over there and shaken the tree until he and every last persimmon came tumbling down. This surveillance nonsense has to stop right now! What's more, I want one of you to call Mrs. Jim Bob and get a list of everyone in town who purchased a gun in the last week. I'll bet not one of you has a license. Harve can haul the lot of you to the county jail and let you cool your heels for a couple of weeks. Maybe the Missionary Society can save the souls of prostitutes, junkies, biker chicks, and sloppy drunks who'll be sharing the cells with you. I wouldn't count on it, though."

"Well, I never!" said Estelle. She stood up and came around the corner of the desk, apparently having survived the mortal toe wound, and poked Ruby Bee. "You tell her that's the rudest thing anyone's said to me in all my born days!"

Ruby Bee wasn't taking it much better. "Now you listen up, young lady. We had no choice but to buy the guns to protect ourselves, since you sure ain't gonna do it. That serial killer already knows where to find me. I wouldn't be a bit surprised if he told all the other inmates, too."

"They are not inmates," I said in a steely voice, "nor are they there because they've committed violent crimes. They're" — I tried to find an innocuous phrase — "people in need of help to restore their health. And before you jump on that bandwagon, they do not have contagious diseases. You are not in danger of contracting the plague, yellow fever, malaria, or smallpox."

"Then what are they doing in a place like Maggody?" Estelle asked suspiciously. "Seems to me there are plenty of hospitals all over the country. Are they hiding out from the law?"

I was on thin ice, and the temperature was rising. Anything I said would be spread all over town within an hour. On the other hand, allowing this increasingly hysterical speculation wasn't going to help. Mrs. Jim Bob might already be on the trail of discount Howitzers and grenade launchers.

"Okay, I'll tell you this much. There are only four patients, and they're relatively famous in their fields. They don't want any publicity."

"Famous?" said Ruby Bee. "Like who?"

"I can't tell you," I said, "but you've probably never heard of any of them. Instead of fretting about their identity, you'd better spend your time warning the local ladies' militia that if they don't turn in their guns to me by no later than noon Monday, there'll be hell to pay. I'm serious about this."

Ruby Bee and Estelle glanced at each other, then looked meekly at me.

I didn't have a chance of staring them down, so I shrugged and said, "Take me back to the foundation, please. I have some unfinished business there."

"Like a case of murder?" said Estelle.

Ruby Bee sniffed. "It ain't like you have to go back to give them manicures. Besides, the man who took you over there is a deputy sheriff. Has he taken to moonlighting as a cabdriver?"

"Never mind, I'll drive myself." I went out and got into Ruby Bee's car, adjusted the seat, and made my escape. Not a great escape, to be sure, but a satisfying one. I wondered how long it would take Ruby Bee to notice that I'd stolen her car.

★ ★ ★

Mrs. Jim Bob was on the phone when Jim Bob came home for lunch. Ignoring her, he made himself a ham sandwich and started toward the living room to see if he could catch a ball game on TV while he ate. He'd almost made it when his wife said, "Where do you think you're going? Perkin's eldest vacuumed in there, and I don't want crumbs on the carpet. Brother Verber's coming by later this afternoon for tea."

Jim Bob returned to the kitchen doorway. "So I'm not supposed to sit in my own living room on account of Brother Verber? Maybe he should be paying the bills every time you decide to decorate it."

"Maybe you should spend more time praying for forgiveness and less time with your harlots at the trailer park," she replied automatically.

He poured himself a glass of buttermilk and leaned against the edge of the counter while he ate. "Who were you talking to when I came in?"

"Joyce Lambertino. She reported that half an hour ago Ruby Bee drove right up to the gate in front of the Stonebridge Foundation. A minute later, the gate opened and Arly came racing out and threw herself in the car. Ruby Bee drove away so fast Joyce liked to have choked on the dust."

Jim Bob washed down the last of his sandwich with a gulp of buttermilk. "What was Arly doing there? Gettin' electric shock therapy?"

"Nobody knows for sure. When I called Ruby Bee earlier this morning, she claimed she didn't even know Arly was there. It's hard to believe they invited her to drop by for coffee and cinnamon rolls. Except for the foreigners living at the Flamingo Motel, no one's seen any of them. I'm beginning to think this is a matter for the FBI."

"Have you been making fruitcakes all morning?"

"Don't be absurd," she said, drumming her fingers on the dinette table. "You have to admit that it's suspicious the way they keep to themselves. For all we know, it could be a terrorist cell."

"Plotting to blow up the silo at the co-op?" Jim Bob couldn't help himself from smirking. "Maybe you should call the Pentagon so they can send in the Marines."

"You are the mayor of Maggody, Jim Bob Buchanon, not the village idiot. You have the responsibility to keep this town safe from outsiders. If you can't live up to your duty, then the citizens ought to elect someone who can." Mrs. Jim Bob licked her lips as she considered this. "It's a sad day when women have to protect themselves while men sit around and play poker. There's no law that says a woman can't be elected mayor."

"You'd run against me?" he said incredulously.

"Someone needs to, and it sure isn't Roy or Larry Joe. They'd make just as much of a mess as you have. No, it's going to take a woman's hand to get this town organized and on the map. If I was the mayor, we'd have a city hall, civic clubs, mandatory summer programs to stop the teenagers from engaging in sinfulness and debauchery at Boone Creek, and committees to plan festivals and put up Christmas lights every year. We could have one of those living nativity scenes in front of the Assembly Hall, bringing in tourists from all over the county."

"You can't run against me!" he sputtered. "You're my wife, fercrissake! How would it look? Who's putting these ideas in your head? Just give me a name and I'll — I'll go knock the snot out of 'em! No wife of mine is running for office."

"Then I suggest that you put your glass in the sink and go running back to the SuperSaver. I need to get started on a poppyseed cake for tea." She opened a recipe book and began to thumb through it. "No, I'll make date bars instead. Brother Verber couldn't get enough of them at the last potluck supper."

I pushed the button on the squawk box by the gate and dutifully identified myself. I wouldn't have minded if the gate remained closed, but it swung open. I parked in the back and went into the grassy expanse between the garden and the pool. A young woman with stringy blond hair was seated at one of the tables next to the pool. She was wearing sunglasses and a bikini. The latter was an unfortunate choice. She glanced up, then looked back down at an open notebook in her lap.

She was probably the actress Randall Zumi had mentioned, but I'd already forgotten her name. I said, "Hi, there. You look awfully familiar. Haven't I seen you on TV or in a movie?"

"Don't bother with the bullshit."

"No, I'm sure I've seen you somewhere," I gushed as I sat down across from her. "Give me a hint."

"Okay, here's a hint — get lost." She picked up a pen and began to scribble in the notebook. "And while you're at it, have someone bring me a bottle of water. The service around here's lousy."

"Yes, miss. You want me to massage your feet, too?"

She pulled off her sunglasses and stared at me. "Who the fuck are you?"

"I'm filling in for Molly Foss."

"I heard about that. Seems somebody tried to teach her to swim last night, but she was too stupid. If you're taking over her job, shouldn't you be in the office filing or something?"

"Shouldn't you be in therapy, getting your ego deflated?"

She slammed down the notebook and pen on the table. "I don't think I like you very much."

I leaned back and crossed my legs. "And I wouldn't spit on you if you were on fire. Now that we've found common ground, why don't you take a deep breath and relax? How's it going with the withdrawal? Nightmares, nausea, tantrums?"

"All of the above," she said warily. "I'm Dawn Dartmouth. I was in a TV series a long time ago. If you've seen me since, you must have very poor taste in trashy cable movies. And you are . . . ?"

"Arly Hanks. I'd tell you more, but I'm not supposed to disrupt the patients' fragile psyches or cause setbacks in their therapy. Is sunbathing on your schedule?"

"I refused to suffer through another boring yoga session, so I skipped it and came out here. The doctors at this hellhole have to be careful. The last thing they want is a reputation for running a prison camp. They want to be known as the poshest, most discreet rehab hospital in the country, where the rich and famous are trampling all over each other to pay fifty grand a month."

I couldn't help myself. "Fifty grand a month?"

"That's just for starters," Dawn said drily. "Additional services provided by the world-renowned cosmetic surgeon Dr. Vincent Stonebridge aren't part of the package. He's already got me down for a thermage tissue tightening, lipo, and a laser peel. That's another fifteen grand, and he'll probably have more bright ideas later."

"Sheesh," I said. "Are the others destined for cosmetic surgery, too?"

"How would I know? It's not like we all sit in a circle and share secrets. If you believed all the shit you hear at parties in L.A., you'd think no one has ever so much as had a tooth capped. Some of the women have had Botox so many times that they can barely move their lips. And those washed-up actresses who sell exercise videos and tacky jewelry on cable have had so many face-lifts that their eyebrows have disappeared under their hairlines."

"Really?" I said, leaning forward. "Was Dr. Stonebridge their doctor?"

"A lot of them, but if I name names, I might as well buy a cabin in Idaho." She paused, then made a face that reminded me of the gargoyles at Notre Dame. "Not that I wouldn't kill for a baked potato with sour cream, chives, and caviar right now. You would not believe the crap they serve here. For lunch today, I get a bean sprout, three peas, and a rice cake. One night I woke up and realized I'd been chewing on my pillow. I don't suppose you have a candy bar in your pocket or anything? I don't have any cash, but I brought credit cards."

"Sorry, Dawn. As soon as Dr. Skiller caught a whiff of chocolate on your breath, I'd be standing in front of a firing squad. Is that why you're here — to lose weight?"

She put on her sunglasses. "I had a little legal problem back home, kind of a misunderstanding. From the way everybody jumped all over me, you'd have thought I'd actually run over the cop instead of just bruising him. If I'm a good girl and get straight, I'll get off with probation and com-

munity service. I was thinking I could volunteer to raise money for art galleries in
homeless shelters. I mean, just because
someone's homeless doesn't mean he
shouldn't have anything to look at except
graffiti."

"Very commendable. Who told you about
what happened to Molly?"

"That repulsive diet guru in the first suite.
He wants me to be a spokeswoman for his
next publicity push. I told him to talk to my
agent." Dawn picked up her notebook. "If
you're quite finished, why don't you run
along and bother somebody else. I'd like to
work on my tan in peace and quiet."

I wasn't quite finished, not by a long shot.
"Did you like Molly?"

"Did you mean to ask if I murdered her?
There's a difference, you know. I thought
she was a scheming little bitch who'd dig up
her grandmother's grave to get the gold fill-
ings. She would have made a good Hollywood agent, she was always so eager to
negotiate. I might not have braked for her if
she ran out in front of my Jaguar X-L, but I
didn't kill her. Like I'd chip a nail over some
tractor-pull princess? I don't think so. You
might have better luck with Toby. He's so
horny that he'd screw anybody who wasn't
technically dead. One of the maids had to

fight him off with a mop a couple of days ago. They leave his trays outside his door. He hung around the reception room a lot, dimpling and winking like he had a facial tic. It was too pathetic."

"How did Molly respond?"

"She giggled and wiggled her tits and did everything else short of giving him a blow job on her desk. As soon as she spotted someone coming, she'd pretend to be all stern and remind him where he was supposed to be. She was such a lousy actress that she couldn't have sold water in the middle of the desert. Shit, she probably couldn't have given it away. Water, that is. She was probably spreading her legs in elementary school. Stupid little slut."

Dawn's opinion of Molly did not exactly coincide with Randall's, and although it was likely to be motivated by jealousy, I wasn't ready to dismiss it quite yet. I told her I'd see her later, then went into the garden and found the marble fountain. If I dropped to my knees and crawled around the fountain, all I'd end up with would be grass stains on my knees (and a red face if someone caught me in the act). Les was not a graduate of the Sherlockian School of Detection, but he would have done a thorough search.

The cherub smiled benignly as I approached him. There were scuff marks in the sod where presumably the killer had grappled with Molly — unless they'd been left by Harve, deputies, or the coroner and his flunkies when they removed the body. I examined the edge of the basin and the base below it for blood, but found nothing. Molly could have been easily overpowered. One hand on the back of her neck, holding her face under the water until she went limp. A few minutes longer to make sure she was dead. And then the killer had found a way to clamber back over the fence, or had simply gone inside the building and climbed into bed.

I wanted to talk to the orderly who'd discovered the body, as well as the guard. There was the language problem, however, and I wasn't skilled enough in charades to get anywhere. I sat down on the bench and glared at the cherub, who'd seen it all. Odds were not good that he would enlighten me anytime soon. And if he did, it would be time to check myself into the Stonebridge Foundation. Maybe they'd let me wax floors and wash windows to pay for my Prozac.

It would have been nice to sit there until the middle of the afternoon, then call Harve and tell him that I'd get right back on the case first thing Monday morning. I'd dump off Ruby Bee's car, toss a bag into my own backseat, and hightail it to Springfield. Jack would be waiting at the curb and insist on carrying my bag inside. Once the front door was closed, we'd be out of our clothes in no time flat. Much fooling around would take place until we reluctantly got dressed and went out to the backyard to grill steaks and drink wine. I could get used to it, I thought. And to him.

"Arly!" called Dr. Stonebridge, advancing briskly. "We've been worried about you. Brenda said you had some sort of emergency that required you to leave suddenly. I do hope the situation was not dire. If I can be of help . . . ?"

"No, everything's under control," I said, presuming he wasn't referring to my libido, which was working overtime at the moment. "A family situation, that's all."

"Have you made any progress in determining who did this dreadful thing?"

I wasn't inclined to keep him up to date unless he wanted to hire me and triple my salary, which still wouldn't have paid for a month's stay at his fancy rehab. "I need to speak to the orderly and to the guard on duty last night. Are you sure none of the Mexicans speak English?"

"Not a word," he said complacently. "I personally hired each one of them. They follow instructions when they're here, and stay together when they're off duty. I think of them as my burros — passive, uncomplaining, grateful for the opportunity to earn money for their families. And they've been warned that if they become ill or refuse to work, they will be fired and left to make their way home."

"It's a relief to know you're not exploiting them. I'm still going to have to talk to the two that I mentioned."

"Do your best, my dear, although you'll find out quickly that they're likely not to cooperate." He went to the fountain and let his fingers dangle in the water. "I understand you've spoken to several of our patients."

"I call it interviewing potential witnesses," I said coldly. "Have you noticed anything odd in the last day or two? Someone prowling around in unauthorized places or even searching the offices and apartments?"

"Absolutely not. We are all very conscious of the need for security. We have a large quantity of drugs on the premises, including narcotics. Randall, Brenda, and I are always careful to keep cabinets and doors locked to prevent theft. Several of our patients are heavy drug users who would love to get hold of medications like Pondimin, Adipex, Seconal, and Nembutal. If one of them were to overdose, we'd be liable."

"Don't the maids have access to a master key so they can clean?" I asked.

Dr. Stonebridge peered down at me. "The medications are kept in a storage room in the surgical suite that cannot be unlocked with the master room key. We keep a very tight inventory list so that we can account for every milligram that's dispensed."

If someone had searched his rooms, he obviously wasn't going to tell me. I decided not to push it any further for the moment. "I'll contact the sheriff's office to get a translator, but I doubt they can find anyone until Monday. It might be best if I put the investigation on hold until then. I suggest that you double your security measures for the next two nights, maybe have someone patrol the inside of the building as well as the grounds."

"Then you don't believe that someone from outside found a way to breach security? I know Randall and Brenda, and I can vouch for both of them. I met Walter for the first time a week ago, but he seems harmless. As you've been told, the patients are sedated for the night, so none of them could be responsible." He paused. "That leaves the Mexicans, but Brenda handles them. I would be very surprised if Molly knew their names, or if they knew hers. The coroner ruled out sexual assault."

"Just because she wasn't molested doesn't mean someone didn't attempt it," I pointed out. "And I don't know where she was between nine o'clock last night and four this morning, when her body was found."

"Hmm." He leaned against the edge of the fountain and regarded me with the same blank stare as the cherub behind him. "A very intriguing point, Arly. Do you think she might have hidden herself until the rest of us retired, then attempted to steal drugs? I've been told that the narcotics like OxyContin and Percocet sell for upwards of five dollars per tablet on the street."

"Would Molly have done something like that?"

"It's impossible to say. I certainly would never have hired her if I suspected she might. She seemed like a reasonably bright girl, personable and eager to learn. I had hopes that we might be able to increase her responsibilities. As we expand, we'll have to hire more office staff. She could have ended up in a supervisory position."

Not if Brenda Skiller had any voice in the matter, I thought. "You're probably right," I said cautiously, "but we need to dispel the possibility that she was a little bit too interested in the drugs. I'm going to arrange for a deputy to come out here later today and take everybody's fingerprints. That way we can determine if anyone has been in an unauthorized area like the surgical suite."

"Including mine?"

"Just for purposes of elimination." I knew this seemed like a glib explanation, but I didn't want to tell him about Randall's claim that his personal papers had been pawed through. Dr. Stonebridge was as likely a suspect as any of his colleagues, patients, and employees. I prefer to characterize myself as an equal opportunity investigator.

Dr. Stonebridge cleared his throat. "I thought I made it clear that the patients cannot be subjected to stress. The whole point of having you here undercover is to keep them unaware of this unfortunate incident. How am I supposed to ask them to submit to being fingerprinted?"

"They all know what happened," I said, "but if you'd like to maintain the pretense, the deputy can get prints off their drinking glasses. Tell the kitchen aides to label the trays with names and set them aside."

"Is this really necessary?"

"The reasonably bright girl you hoped to promote to supervisor one of these days is dead. I'm going to do everything I can to find her killer. If you have a problem with this, call the state attorney general or whomever and complain. I doubt you can get me kicked off the case until Monday, though. The sheriff's spending the weekend in a boat in the middle of some lake, drinking whiskey and cussing at the bass for not taking his bait." I stood up and headed toward the parking lot. "Come Monday morning, you'll see either me or someone else. Don't count on my replacement being a real sensitive guy. It's not part of the job description."

If he had a reply, I didn't hear it. I drove back to the PD and called LaBelle, who was too busy giving herself a manicure to run me through the wringer. I gave her a detailed request for a fingerprint technician and a translator, then reluctantly included a certain telephone number in Springfield. The only message on the answering machine was from Ruby Bee, who had a few choice remarks about grand theft auto. I didn't bother to call her back, since I'd left the keys in the ignition and she could fetch her car when she got around to it.

There remained only one thing to do before I packed a bag and hit the road. I unfolded the note I'd stuck in my pocket and reread it. It was hard to imagine Eileen running away to become a cowboy — or running away *with* a cowboy, for that matter. Unless she changed course, she would bump into the Canadian border within a week. And then what?

I called the SuperSaver and asked to speak to Kevin. Idalupino agreed to chase him down, but warned me it might take a while, since he'd left a case of ice cream on the loading dock all morning and was still hiding out from Jim Bob. When he finally came to the phone, I told him about the credit card and the list of cities.

"Oh, my gawd," he gurgled. "So where is she now?"

"My best guess is still in Wyoming," I said. "It's a big state."

"What's she doing there?"

"Beats me. You'd better tell your pa."

"He's been drunk so long he won't hear a word I say, except the part about Wyoming. You should be the one to tell him, Arly. You're the chief of police."

"If you're too scared to tell him, then don't."

Fifteen minutes later I was on the road — and not to Wyoming.

10

"I can't believe Arly left town without so much as a word," said Estelle, having heard about it from Bordella Buchanon, who'd been picking up beer cans along the side of the road. "Especially after the way she spoke to you earlier this afternoon. If I was you, I wouldn't give her the time of day after she comes skulking back from wherever she went."

Ruby Bee finished washing a couple of mugs and set them on the draining board. "She doesn't have to account to me, as she's so fond of claiming. After all, I'm just her mother. It's not like I worked my fingers to the bone to buy her new shoes for school and ruffled dresses for Easter. One year I stayed up all night sewing feathers on her costume for a school play. She was a blue-bird, or maybe a blue jay — I disremember which. I nearly sneezed my head off."

Estelle toyed with her sherry glass. "You know, I find it real interesting that these so-called patients are famous. I wonder who they are."

"I don't see how we can find out, short of climbing over the fence and peeking in windows. Arly said we wouldn't have heard of them, anyway."

"I don't see how she can be so sure," Estelle continued, her eyes narrowed. "Just because she doesn't read *People* magazine doesn't mean the rest of us don't. Britney Spears and Brad Pitt could be there, and Arly wouldn't recognize them."

Ruby Bee couldn't help but agree. "Movie stars are all the time going to expensive private hospitals on account of alcohol or drug problems. It's amazing any of them ever actually finds time to make a movie, what with the way they keep getting engaged, married, divorced — sometimes all on the same day. Wouldn't it be something if a really famous celebrity was hiding out not even a mile away from here?"

"I can think of a way we might find out."

"I'm not about to sit in that persimmon tree, if that's what you're thinking," said Ruby Bee. "I got better things to do, and so do you."

"What about the Mexicans in the motel out back? They must know who the patients are."

"Are you forgetting they don't speak English?"

Estelle pulled out her ace in the hole, which in this case turned out to be a book in her handbag. "I dropped by the high school yesterday to ask Lottie for her lemon pound cake recipe. While she was hunting it down for me, I went across the hall to the library and found this Spanish book for beginners."

"You stole it? I am shocked, Estelle Oppers. Stealing books from a library is worse than — than filching money from the collection plate!"

"I did no such thing. I simply borrowed it, and I'll make sure it's back on the shelf before school starts at the end of the summer. No one will even notice it's missing."

"Let me see it." Ruby Bee opened the book and flipped through a couple of pages. "This might come in handy if you want to find the train station or order ham 'n eggs for breakfast, but I don't see where it says how to ask about celebrities' names."

"We can patch together some questions from the vocabulary list at the back," Estelle said. "All we need are Spanish words for name, patient, movie star, and so on."

"Why on God's green earth would they tell us? If you recollect, we ate the guacamole while we were talking about your old flame in Little Rock. You gonna go all the way to Farberville and buy some more avocados — or are you planning to bribe 'em with pretzels?"

"I was thinking more along the lines of a fresh apple pie. They eat more than tacos and tamales in Mexico." She pulled the book back across the bar. "You fetch a pencil and a piece of paper, and we'll make a list of words they'll understand. It may not be easy, but that ain't never stopped us yet."

Ruby Bee could think of a lot of things that *should* have stopped them, and Arly could probably reel off a lot more. But asking the maids a few questions wasn't near the same as getting arrested for trespassing at the Stonebridge Foundation. All she and Estelle were gonna do was satisfy their curiosity, for pity's sake.

On that note, she opened a drawer and found a stubby pencil. "See if you can find out how to say 'Brad Pitt' in Spanish," she suggested while she tore off a page from the order pad and turned it over.

Kevin sat on the loading dock behind the SuperSaver, so slumped over he was in danger of tumbling off. He felt like he was strapped to two mules, each of them determined to go in a different direction. If he went to his pa's house and told him that his ma was in Wyoming, he'd get his ass whupped something awful. If he went home and told Dahlia, he'd spend the rest of the night listening to her bawl him out like it was his fault. Little Kevvie Junior and Rose Marie would get all scared and start screaming, and he didn't even want to think what Dahlia's granny might do. The last time she'd gotten spooked, she'd spent half the day on the roof, gnawin' shingles.

He darn near jumped out of his skin when a hand clamped down on his shoulder. Before he could turn around, Jim Bob sat down next to him and said, "Shouldn't you be at home, boy?"

"I was just sittin' here for a minute," he said, hoping he wasn't gonna get chewed out again about the ice cream. There were sticky patches at the end of the dock, although it was hard to see 'em under the swarm of yellow jackets and flies. "You want me to hose it down before I leave? I could get a scrub brush and —"

"Naw, it can wait till tomorrow." Jim Bob took a pint bottle of whiskey out of his pocket. "Wanna snort?"

Kevin gaped at him. "No, sir. I mean, it's right kindly of you to offer, but if I go home and Dahlia smells it, she'll smack me across the room. She's got a nose like a blood-hound."

"Women," Jim Bob muttered. "Sometimes they get too big for their britches. You got to remind 'em of their place before they get so uppity that ain't no one can tell them what to do. Am I right, boy?"

"Oh, yeah, Jim Bob, right as rain. Jest this morning Dahlia —"

"The only thing we can do is stop 'em before they start screeching about how they're better than us men. The minute they start bossing us around, we might as well put on their pantyhose and start scrubbing toilets." He took a gulp of whiskey and offered the bottle to Kevin. "Don't sit there like you're already pussy-whipped. If you want to have a snort after work, it ain't none of Dahlia's business. You ain't no little sissy in short pants. Go on, take it."

Kevin's hand was shaking so fierce he could barely hold the bottle. There was something so peculiar about him passing a bottle with Jim Bob that he couldn't begin to sort it out. "I sure as hell ain't no sissy," he said as he took a sip. He had to clamp his lips together so's not to spit it out. "Might fine whiskey, Jim Bob."

"Damn straight, considering it cost more

than two dollars." Jim Bob slapped him on the back. "Kevin, I was thinkin' you might want to play a little poker with Roy, Larry Joe, and me tomorrow night. Go on, boy, have some more — unless you're scared of your own wife."

"Me?" Kevin hooted, then took a swallow. Tears came to his eyes, but he blinked them away. Not once he could remember when Jim Bob had ever talked to him, unless it was to cuss him out for being stupid or lazy. He was so bewildered that he took another swallow. "You got a point, Jim Bob," he said as he wiped his chin with his wrist. "Once a man lets hisself be pussy-whipped, he's a goner."

"How's your pa doin' these days?"

"Been drunk as a skunk for a week now," Kevin said proudly. "He hasn't changed his underwear once, and he stinks to high heaven. The whole house smells like an auction barn in August."

Jim Bob belched. "On account of his wife running off. I'd never have thought Earl would stand for that kind of shit." He took the bottle from Kevin and allowed himself a sip before passing it back. "Women got no business running off whenever it suits their fancy. Us men are the ones who bring home the bacon."

Kevin was beginning to develop a taste for the whiskey. "Amen to that. Ain't a woman alive that could put meat on the table. All they're good for is cookin', cleanin', and having babies."

Jim Bob whacked Kevin on the back, then stood up. "I knew I could count on you, boy. After all, you got Buchanon blood running through your veins."

"Damn right," Kevin managed to say before he threw up on his shoes.

"Well?" Jack said as he handed me a glass of wine. "Do we have an issue?"

I leaned my head on his chest. "I don't have any issues. No, I take that back. I have a stack of issues of *Better Homes & Gardens* dating back to my birth. Ruby Bee's a real optimist."

"You've been distracted from the moment you arrived. While I was cooking the steaks, you paced around like an inmate in a prison exercise yard."

"Did I really?"

"You really did," he said, stroking my cheek. "I may not be the most perceptive guy on the planet, but I know when something's wrong. Are you sorry you came?"

"I can't think of any place I'd rather be than right here with you. It's just that I left a real mess back in Maggody. I can't forget about poor Molly Foss. She might have been an angel, or she might have been an unscrupulous bitch, but now she's just a body in the morgue."

Jack had heard a brief synopsis of the case earlier, but had not pressed me for details. "Is there something you think you should be doing right now?"

"No," I admitted grumpily. "The doctors are as slippery as greased piglets, and the patients aren't any better. The senator wouldn't have bothered to glance down if she tripped over my body. I've already offended two of the others by not recognizing them, or at least their names. The fourth one is a pro athlete. All I know about athletes is that they get paid enormous salaries for playing a game a few months every year."

"You don't know the patients' names?"

I frowned as I tried to think. "One of the doctors told me their names, but the only one I recognized was the senator. Have you heard of a writer named Dibbins?"

"He's at this clinic? No wonder he needs anonymity. He writes best-selling diet books that recommend pasta drenched in olive oil and served with garlic bread. One of the reviewers called Dibbins's first book 'Dr.

Death's Diet of Doom.' What's he in for?"

"Can you keep a secret?"

"Anything that happens on this sofa will stay strictly between the two of us," he murmured, then proceeded to engage me in some private maneuvers that I certainly wouldn't share with a reporter. Or my mother, who'd rather eat live lizards than admit she even knew folks did things like that.

After half an hour of convincing me of his sincerity, he sat up and took a drink of wine. "I'll assume Dibbins did too much research on the recipes in his books. What do you know about the athlete?"

"Nothing," I admitted as I buttoned my shirt. "I was told his name, but it didn't mean anything to me. I caught a glimpse of him in the pool. Young, blond hair, muscular, tight butt, maybe six-foot-four. I couldn't see his face."

Jack smiled. "Doesn't sound like you tried too hard."

I ignored his remark. "I can't imagine the diet guru or the senator being sent to rehab by a judge. That leaves this guy and the whiny actress."

"I can think of one athlete who might qualify. Could this guy's name be Toby Mann?"

"That's it," I said. "You've heard of him, I gather. What did he do?"

"He's accused of raping a woman in his hotel room. The trial was postponed at the request of his lawyers. 'The Man,' as he's called, is one of the highest-paid football players in the league. He drives expensive cars and dates models. He comes across as a jerk in interviews, but he's a fantastic quarterback."

"Did he rape her?" I asked.

Jack shrugged. "Nobody else was in the hotel room, so maybe, maybe not. 'The Man's Fans' don't care as long as he keeps throwing touchdown passes."

"From what I was told, Molly Foss was more than attractive. Toby must have been getting pretty bored at the clinic . . ."

"So bored that he raped her, and then drowned her to keep her quiet?"

"The coroner didn't find any evidence that she was sexually assaulted. Damn, it would have been nice to tidy this up with a phone call. On Monday, I could have been questioning this jock in a cell at the county jail. I'm really not excited about going back to the Stonebridge Foundation to face Brenda Skiller. We didn't exactly hit it off."

"What's she going to do — fire you?"

"Good point," I said. "I suppose she

could stir up some trouble for me at the sheriff's office, but Harve's not going to do anything more than nod and then hustle her out the door. And if the Maggody city council decides to get rid of me, so be it. I never planned to stay there forever."

Jack started to say something, then stopped and swirled the wine in the bottom of his glass. "So tell me about the actress."

"Her first name is Dawn. In her early twenties, looks like a cast member of *The Night of the Living Dead.* She said she'd been in a TV series a long time ago."

"Dawn Dartmouth," Jack said promptly. "She was in some sitcom when she was a kid. She had a twin sister who was also on the show, since there are stringent rules about how long a kid can be on camera on any day. Were you too busy drinking moonshine and tipping cows to watch TV?"

"We weren't what you'd call prosperous when I was growing up. Ruby Bee had a little black-and-white TV that someone gave her. The reception was so bad that watching it gave me headaches. Before you get too carried away imagining me barefoot and dressed in rags, let me assure you we had all the necessities and enough for a few extras. We weren't any better or worse off than most of the folks in town. I may have tipped a cow or two, but I spent most of my free time sitting on the banks of Boone Creek, drinking beer and plotting my escape."

"What about your father?"

I took a few minutes to consider my reply. "I don't have any memories of him. He took off when I was a baby and never looked back. I used to speculate about him. Had he gone to Europe to regain his lawful standing as the heir apparent? Was he running a hospital in some remote African outpost and working on a cure for malaria? Was he a Hollywood star living in a sprawling mansion with his new family? I finally acknowledged that he'd probably lost his footing while hopping a freight train and was buried in a pauper's grave in some obscure Midwest town." I held out my glass. "But as Ruby Bee used to say, it's no use cryin' over spilled chianti."

Jack filled my glass. "She said that?"

"Not in those exact words."

"Speaking of exact words," he said, "it's time for the preliminary round of the International Supreme Scrabble Player of the Millennium. This round will be played with a board, tiles, a dictionary, and a score pad, and be viewed via satellite by word aficionados on every continent, including

Antarctica. It will be played according to Hoyle."

"Meaning what?" I asked.

"You have to keep your clothes on."

"I don't know about the Hoyle business. What does the winner get?"

"Breakfast in bed. Maybe lunch, too."

I could never pass up a challenge.

11

Breakfast in bed was not to be, alas. Jack and I were debating the merits of muffins versus bagels when the telephone rang. He picked up the receiver, mumbled something, and handed it to me. Resisting the urge to dive under the covers, I accepted it and said, "Yeah?"

Harve Dorfer was not in his good ol' boy mode. "Listen up," he said in a most unfriendly fashion, "I ain't gonna say anything about you taking off in the middle of a murder investigation — at least not right now. How long will it take you to get your ass back to the Stonebridge Foundation?"

"Why? Is the paperwork getting out of hand?"

"It's too damn early for any of your smart-mouthed questions. Can you make it in two hours?"

I sat up and looked at the clock. "You're absolutely right, Harve. It's seven-thirty, and that's too damn early for much of anything. Call me back later, and we'll have a long chat about how you set me up to play the receptionist."

"We got us another body out there."

"Oh, shit." I covered the mouthpiece of the receiver and asked Jack to start a pot of coffee. After he left the room, I said, "Who? What happened?"

"One of the doctors, fellow by the name of Zumi. All I know is that a maid found him in his office a few minutes ago and told Dr. Stonebridge, who called me. I'm heading out there now, and McBeen should be along shortly. What about you?"

"I'll be there by ten." I hung up and headed for the shower, trying to process what he'd told me. The previous evening Jack had opened a second bottle of wine, which had seemed like an excellent idea at the time. Now I had a dull ache in the back of my head, and my tongue felt as fuzzy as a dandelion pod. There was a bottle of aspirin in the medicine cabinet, but after the few hours I'd spent at the foundation, the idea of taking any drug made me uneasy.

I told Jack what little I knew while we had coffee. Neither of us had any brilliant insights. We agreed to try for another weekend, preferably one without complications, and then I tossed my bag into the car and drove toward Maggody. I speculated about Randall Zumi's untimely demise for a few miles, but after I'd replayed our conversation several times, I'd bored myself silly and moved on to more entertaining thoughts (or fantasies, if you prefer).

When I arrived at the rehab facility, the gate was open. I continued around to the back and parked between Harve's official vehicle and McBean's death-mobile. Along with some civilian cars, there were two other cars with the Stump County Sheriff's Department logo and telltale blue bubble lights. At least, I thought optimistically, this time I wouldn't be cast adrift on my own.

There were no voices from the garden, or indications of activity. All the doors to the addition that housed the doctors were closed, as were the ones across from it. No one was visible though the French doors that led to the main part of the facility. A pair of ill-tempered blue jays strutted under a wrought-iron table in search of bread crumbs; if I'd been fluent in avian, I would have sent them across the road to a particular persimmon tree. A deputy with a conspicuous case of acne stood next to the pool. I joined him and said, "I'm Chief of Police Arly Hanks. Where's Sheriff Dorfer?"

The question seemed to perplex him, as if

I'd demanded that he explain a quadratic equation or summarize the causes of the Boer War. He was scratching his chin (not a pleasant sight) when McBeen came out of Randall's office, followed by two assistants in green scrubs wheeling a gurney.

"What happened?" I asked.

"Ya know something?" McBeen said, wheezing like an old coonhound. "Before you took over as chief of police, the only homicides out this way were either spouses going after each other with kitchen knives or damn fool hunters claiming they'd accidentally shot an in-law. The cause of death was plain as day. I'd tag 'em, bag 'em, and pack 'em off to the morgue for a quick look-see." He paused to catch his breath and shake his finger at me. "Then you showed up, and all of a sudden, it ain't safe to set foot in Maggody. Got any theories, missy?"

"Must be all those classified ads I put in newspapers inviting folks to come here to murder each other," I said, glaring at him. "I mentioned that the coroner was such a buffoon that they had a good chance of getting away with it. Are you planning to tell me what happened anytime soon?"

"Appears to be a suicide."

"Is that the extent of your preliminary report?"

"Narcotic mixed with booze most likely led to heart failure. Guy's been dead for ten to twelve hours, give or take. Unofficially, somewhere around midnight."

"What about the woman whose body was discovered early yesterday morning?"

"Within two hours of midnight, either side. Water in her lungs, consistent with her face being forced down. No alcohol in her blood. We ran tests for the drugs we usually encounter and didn't come up with any-thing. The lab in Little Rock will test for a broader spectrum. Now why don't you go badger the sheriff? He's waiting for you inside." McBeen caught up with the gurney and followed it out to the parking area.

My headache had receded, but I still wasn't at my best and confronting Harve wasn't going to help. I felt obscurely guilty, although I could hardly have identified the murderer the previous afternoon or stayed up all night with Randall, consoling him on the loss of his soul mate.

I went into Randall's office. Harve was sitting on the sofa with Stonebridge; neither of them bothered to greet me. Voices and noises from the apartment indicated that it was being searched. The surface of the dark walnut desk had been dusted for finger-prints. Plastic bags, dutifully labeled, held a small liquor bottle, a drinking glass, and a piece of paper ripped out of a notepad.

"Suicide?" I said as I sat down behind the desk.

Stonebridge sighed. "Looks like it. Randall knew the danger of mixing barbiturates with alcohol. God, I don't know what to do. First Molly, and now Randall. None of this should have happened. This was supposed to be a safe haven for the celebrities, not some kind of — of lethal madhouse. Randall and I invested more than two million dollars to ensure that it would be perfect. How could he do this to me?"

Harve kept a beady eye on me while he lit a cigar. "So what the hell happened yesterday that sent you hightailin' it up the highway?"

"You'd know if you hadn't gone fishing," I said. "I was dumped out here on my own, with nothing to go on. Nobody confessed. I couldn't interview the staff because of the language barrier. Supposedly yesterday afternoon a deputy came out and took fingerprints so we can run background checks. That takes a couple of days. I couldn't see any reason to sit around here all weekend and wait."

"Background checks?" Stonebridge stood up and went over to the bookshelf. After straightening a few volumes, he turned around and said, "Is that necessary? If you'd bothered to mention it to me, I would have gone through the personnel files and given you whatever information you needed."

"Presuming everyone was candid and forthcoming," I said. "Oddly enough, some people prefer to forget about prior convictions and outstanding warrants."

"Impossible." He looked at Harve with that man-to-man, condescending smile that infuriates women (or should, anyway). "Arly seems to have a volatile imagination, doesn't she, Sheriff? Molly was murdered, yes, but it's probable that security was breached. And as for poor Randall, well . . . I feel some sense of responsibility. He was in the middle of a nasty divorce, and the legal bills were suffocating him. He had to struggle to come up with his share of the investment. Initially he was eager to form our partnership, but as his financial problems worsened, he would call me at all hours of the night for reassurance. Had it been feasible, I would have bought him out. If only I'd known he was so depressed."

"He was upset about Molly," I said.

Stonebridge seemed bemused by my remark. "He'd only known her for a week or so. It's more likely he was worried that the news of her death would be leaked to the press and destroy our reputation. We'd have to take a big loss just to get out."

Harve cleared his throat. "So what's going to happen with his death?"

"I'm not sure. We both took out life insurance policies and signed the standard documents for this contingency. I don't think there's a clause excluding payment in the case of suicide. As long as there isn't, then I receive the benefit and will use it to buy out Mrs. Zumi's interest."

"So you'll be the sole owner?" I asked.

"That doesn't mean I'm pleased about the prospect. Randall was able to acquire our license because he was certified by the state and had some friendly contacts on the board. I have no idea what our legal status will be after his death is reported. Furthermore, it's vital that we have an experienced psychiatrist on the staff if we're to remain an acceptable option in court-mandated psych evaluations and treatment programs." He sat down in the chair across from me and crossed his legs. "I don't suppose I can convince you to go undercover as a shrink, can I?"

Harve was getting tired of being ignored. He came over to the desk and looked down at me. "Unless McBeen says otherwise, we'll assume this Zumi fellow committed suicide. Molly Foss did not, so you need to get that tidied up. I'm going back to my office to see if I can dig up a translator by this afternoon. I'll kick some butt and get the names and prints off to the FBI. Think you can manage to hang around for the rest of the day, or am I gonna have to put out an APB every time I got something to tell you?"

"I left the number with LaBelle, Harve. Just how hard was it for you to find me? But let me warn you — if you don't get off my back, next time you'll need Interpol to put out that APB."

I had hopes that I might spot steam coming out of his ears, but he clamped his lips together, then went to the doorway and began to bark at the deputies searching Randall's apartment. "What's with this baby booze bottle?" I asked Stonebridge.

"Randall isn't — wasn't — much of a drinker. I'm surprised he had it. There was an odor of grapefruit juice in the glass, so he must have mixed the vodka with it."

"And the note?"

"Sheriff Dorfer has assumed it's a suicide note, which seems likely. Illegible handwriting is a required course in med school. Randall must have received a high grade."

I picked up the plastic bag and squinted at the note. It could have been anything from a plea for forgiveness to hieroglyphic doodles. Shaking my head, I put it down and said, "So what's going on with the patients? Haven't any of them noticed they're not having their scheduled sessions?"

"I told them Randall was ill," Stonebridge said. "Brenda and Walter have agreed to stick to that story."

"Did either of them have anything to say?"

He thought about it for a moment. "Walter just shrugged and went off to the gym. Brenda was upset, but she swore she could pull herself together and carry through with her duties. I have to admit I'm worried about her. She needs to feel as though she's in control of a highly organized operation, and that she alone must take responsibility for even the most minute glitch. If I allowed it, she'd insist the patients arrive exactly five minutes prior to their sessions and wait in the hall like docile sheep. She suggested daily evaluations that we could discuss every evening. I told her we'd have one staff meeting a week, and that was all. I'm truly not interested in how many leg lifts someone did or if they bitched during acupuncture. If I let her have her way, we'd have been sitting around a campfire in the parking lot, holding hands and singing 'Kumbaya.' "

Harve came back into the office. "The boys didn't find anything except a couple of over-the-counter remedies for diarrhea and heartburn. Nothing I don't have at home. Guess he didn't have to go far to find the hard stuff."

"I'll do another inventory of the drug cabinet right away," Stonebridge said. "I refuse to believe Randall would steal anything."

"I doubt he was thinking too clearly," I said, then smiled at Harve. "So when do I get the translator? You going to wait until Mrs. Dorfer makes you a big breakfast before you start making calls?"

"You are trying my patience, young lady. One of these days you're gonna be real sorry."

"Gee whiz, you're not going to get me fired, are you? Whatever would I do without this high-salaried, glamorous, fascinating job? If you want to call Jim Bob, you can use this phone. I'll look up his number for you."

He rumbled under his breath. "Like I said, one of these days. Now you get your ass in gear and start trying to do some detective work. Soon as I get back to the office, I'll see if I can hunt up somebody of a bilingual persuasion. In the meantime, stay out of Missouri. Got that?"

"You bet your booties, boss," I said. I would have tugged on a forelock if I'd had one, but I had to settle for blowing him a kiss as he stomped out the door. Seconds later, Les and another deputy came out of the apartment.

Les gathered up the plastic bags. "You're in quite a snit."

"I'd rather be in Missouri. Did you find prints on the desk?"

"Oh, yeah, but everybody was in and out of here — patients, staff, maids, orderlies, maybe the guys who delivered the desk in the first place. I'll do what I can, but don't expect much. The deputy out by the pool, Quivers, is gonna hang around if you need him for something."

"Any relation to the catfish farmer in Belle Star?"

"His second cousin. Don't . . . uh, expect too much from him. I'll call you later."

"I bet you say that to all the girls," I said to Les as he left. I reluctantly abandoned the leather chair, which was a damn sight more elegant than my cane-bottom chair at the PD. "Shall we go count pink and purple pills, Dr. Stonebridge?"

"Yes, of course," he said, standing up.

"How does one go about farming catfish?"

"Once all this is resolved, I'll arrange for you to take your patients on a field trip."

Before we reached the door, Brenda came into the office. She gave me a furtive look, then shoved Stonebridge into a corner and began to whisper fiercely to him. His complexion became increasingly mottled as he listened to her. I wondered which of them had the higher blood pressure. At that point, I wouldn't have ventured a guess.

I waited politely for a few minutes, then said, "If there's another body, you'll have to tell me about it sooner or later."

"Nothing like that!" Brenda snapped at me, then sank down on the arm of the sofa. "Go ahead and tell her, Vince. We're going to need her help."

"I suppose we will. It seems that one of our patients has gone missing."

Brenda groaned. "It's my fault. With no one to help in the reception room, I was forced to leave the gate open when I went to the kitchen to review the day's menu with the chef. I knew the authorities would be coming and going, and I anticipated a delivery of produce. There was no way I could be in two places at the same time. You do understand, don't you, Vince?" Tears began to slide down her face as she gulped noisily. Sniveling did not become a woman of her age and physical proportions; I could see from Stonebridge's face that he agreed with me. "And I can't stop thinking about Randall," she went on. "I should have realized how depressed he was. I tried to talk to him, but he brushed me aside and came here to brood in solitude. Who can know how long he sat at that very desk in the dark, feeling overwhelmed and alone?" She rose unsteadily. "Have you notified his wife, Vince? Someone has to. I'd better look through his address book for her number."

He caught her arm and said, "The sheriff has that information, and he's going to call her. I'll also call her so we can discuss arrangements for the body when it's released. You need to go to your apartment and have a cup of tea. Once you're calmer, please return to the reception room in case . . . the patient calls."

"I hate to break it to you," I said, "but I already know the identities of all four of the patients. Who's missing?"

"Alexandra Swayze," Brenda admitted.

"When was she last seen?"

Vince nodded at Brenda, who took a breath and said, "She was in the gym with Walter until nine o'clock. She told him she was going to her suite to shower and change clothes. I went there about fifteen minutes ago to remind her that we were scheduled for yoga, and she wasn't there. Dr. Dibbins swore he hasn't seen her at all this morning, and Dawn said the same thing. Toby's suite was unoccupied, so I searched it and then found him and Walter in the gym. The day room is empty. I sent two of the orderlies down the wing that hasn't been remodeled. They returned and shook their heads, which I took to mean she wasn't there."

"What about the garden?" demanded Stonebridge. "Did you search there?"

"Very thoroughly. Vince, what are we going to do? Did she wander away in a drug-induced stupor, or did she escape because she was responsible for Molly's death? I don't know which would be worse for our reputation."

"Sit down, Brenda. Instead of tea, I think you'd better have a glass of brandy."

"No, I couldn't possibly. The employees are already snickering at me for enforcing the rules. If they suspect that I've had a drink, they'll retaliate with impertinence and defiance. And what about the patients? What would they think?"

Vincent propelled her to the sofa. "Sit down, shut up, and meditate or something while I get the brandy and a glass. Doctor's orders."

I left them to bemoan their fate and went out to the pool, where Deputy Quivers was . . . well, quivering. "Did you see a woman with white hair go into the garden?" When he shook his head, I continued. "Could she have slipped past you and left through that archway?"

"Nobody left that way but them that's supposed to. Sheriff Dorfer told me to keep a lookout in case somebody tried to sneak out." He gave me a pinched look. "I been here since eight o'clock this morning, sir. Do you think maybe I could step away for a minute and — er, take a break?"

"Go ahead, Quivers," I said. "I suggest you duck behind the kennel at the end of the parking lot."

"Thank you, sir." He scurried away, taking very small steps.

I sat down on one of the wrought-iron chairs to wait for him. Quivers was dim, but presumably capable of noticing Senator Swayze if she'd come this way. That pretty much left the front door, the brick driveway, and the open gate. She might have prearranged to have someone pick her up, but there was no way she could have anticipated the traffic and confusion that had followed the discovery of Randall's body.

So where the hell was she? Wading in Boone Creek, cutting through the pasture across the road, or hitching a ride with Raz and Marjorie?

From the journal of Shelby Dibbins:

> Tho' I've belted you and flayed you,
> By the livin' Gawd that made you,
> You're a better man than I am, Gunga Din!

This is by no means true, but it adds a literary touch to this puerile and pubescent piece of pontification. When Stonebridge came by to tell me my therapy session was canceled due to "unforeseen" events, I smiled enigmatically. The employees are in a complete dither. I heard them in the hall, whispering about "suicidio, narcoticos y whisky." *I shall be surprised if any of them proves capable of delivering lunch trays. How ever will I survive without a quarter of a cup of peanut, sunflower, and carrot salad adorned with a sprig of fresh mint leaves? A veritable feast to be topped off with a pe-*

culiar herbal tea and a mound of drugs and supplements. At least I shall be spared listening to that long-winded fascist politician lecturing the maids about their illegal immigration status. Too bad she doesn't know they spit in her food before they take the trays into her suite.

I was still sitting by the pool when Walter and Toby came out of the gym. Toby pulled off his T-shirt and dove into the pool. Walter watched him for a moment, then sat down near me.

"Our golden boy's compulsive these days," he said. "He's been lifting weights and running sprints on the treadmill for two hours. Most mortals might be worn out, but not Toby. If I could trust him to come back, I'd send him out to run twenty miles cross-country."

"You can't trust him?"

"Hell, no. Once the endorphins kicked in, he'd keep on going. I don't know what he was like before he came here, but the withdrawal regime has turned his brain to testosterone slush." Walter leaned back to expose his face to the sun. "Shame about Randall. Suicide, I was told."

"Dr. Stonebridge seems to think Randall

was overwhelmed by financial problems and afraid the foundation would fail. I'm not so sure that was the reason. Randall admitted to me that he was enamored of Molly. What do you think?"

"Randall kept to himself, and he sure as hell didn't confide in me. A couple of times I saw him and Molly in the office in the reception room. I just assumed he was waiting for her to get out a file for him. He could have had a crush on her, but we've only been here a week or so. Except for the night she was killed, she left around five to go make dinner for her beloved Ashton, master welder and bowling kingpin."

"Did he, or any of the rest of you, ever leave in the evenings?" I asked.

He lifted his face to look at me. "To do what? Hang out and have a beer with the locals? Now that would be exciting."

"I was thinking more like going into Farberville to watch a movie or go to the clubs on Thurber Street." Water splashed on my leg. I looked down as Toby executed a turn and took off for the far end of the pool.

"One of these nights, I might try it. But to get back to your question, as far as I know, nobody's gone anywhere. I watch TV or read. Brenda retreats to her office and does paperwork. Randall usually hangs out in the garden until it gets dark, then goes to his apartment to watch TV. I mean, that's what he usually *did.* Vince might swim a few laps. He said something about taking off next weekend for New Orleans. He told Randall to take off the weekend after that, but Randall didn't say anything."

"Did anything out of the ordinary happen yesterday afternoon or evening?"

He thought for a minute. "Not really. Brenda wigged out after you left, so I canceled my token session with Dibbins and hung around the reception room. Dawn and Toby had a brawl outside her room. Dibbins stood in his doorway and egged them on. Mrs. Swayze came out and screamed at both of them. It took two orderlies and a maid to separate them and mop up the blood."

"That's not out of the ordinary?" I asked, appalled.

"You've never been around people going through withdrawal. The replacement drugs and vitamin supplements are supposed to help, but these people are at the mercy of their brain chemistry. Some days everybody is at least superficially calm. Other days all hell breaks loose. The first two weeks are the worst, or that's what I keep telling myself, anyway." He looked at Toby. "Is it possible he has gills?"

"What happened after the fight was broken up? Did tranquillity ensue?"

"Yeah, I'd say so. Mrs. Swayze and Dawn sat out here until dinner. Toby demanded that I unlock the gym for him, and I wasn't about to argue with him. Dibbins went back to his opera. We had some sort of curdled bean paste soup for dinner, so I went out to my van and grabbed some provisions that would have given Brenda hives."

He was more forthcoming than the other remaining members of the staff, so I decided to see what else I could get out of him. "Randall told me someone searched his office and apartment."

"Why would anybody do that? All the drugs are locked up in the storage room off the surgical suite."

"You assuming it was a patient, then?" I asked.

"I suppose I am," he said, wincing as Toby made a sloppy turn that splattered both of us. "These people are addicts, and they always will be. They may be able to avoid certain substances, but they'll be tempted every waking minute. No matter what the voice of reason tells them about the dangers of whatever it is they crave, a second voice will be prompting them to try it 'just once' to prove they can take it or leave it. That second voice will never go away completely. It'll wake them up in the night, or catch them while they're reading a newspaper or driving home from work. Sometimes it's a scratchy little voice, whiny and filled with self-pity; other times it's loud and belligerent. 'Just once,' it says over and over."

"Sounds like you've been there."

He leaned back and crossed his legs. "A close encounter of the worst kind with smack. After I bottomed out in a dive in San Salvador and did some time in a rat-infested jail down there, I moved to Taos. I still smoke a little weed and munch on a magic mushroom when the moon's full, but I stay away from the hard-core stuff. That's why I sympathize with these poor bastards. It's harder for them than it was for me. Nobody ever told me I walked on water. That's not to imply that I'd trust any of them for fifteen seconds. They're all as devious as rattlesnakes pretending to bask in the sunshine."

"Is that why they're sedated at night?" I asked, resisting the urge to move my chair away from the edge of the pool before its occupant could rise from the water and lunge at me.

"In a pig's eye," Walter said, amused at my discomfort. "Let me brief you on how the meds are given, morning, noon, and night. Brenda labels each cup with the patient's name, then fills it with the various pills and places it on the appropriate meal tray. She has to administer the shots, of course, but it's up to the patients to take the pills. At eight each night, an orderly takes a cup to the patient with whatever sedative is prescribed and supposedly makes sure it's taken. Maybe it is, maybe it's not. There is a certain amount of late-night activity, both inside and out here."

"What about the guard and the dog?"

Walter snickered. "The guard spends most of the night nodding on a chair on the porch. Nocturnal prowling is a popular pastime."

I envisioned the garden at night. "Shouldn't you have mentioned this to Dr. Stonebridge and Brenda?"

"Why would I? I don't care if these people enjoy a little solitude. They're hounded all day long to go here and there, confess to compulsions, meditate, exercise, lie still while their backsides are stuck with needles, decide if they want their bodies tightened and trimmed, their noses tweaked, their wrinkles eradicated. Hell, I'd go crazy after a couple of days. I'm not going to rat them out for wanting an hour or two of freedom, even if it's inside a locked compound."

I looked up as Stonebridge escorted Brenda to her office door and waited until she'd gone inside. He did not seem pleased to see Walter sitting near me. "Aren't you supposed to be with a patient?" he asked him as he walked over.

Walter pointed at the pool. "I'm on lifeguard duty. We can't afford to lose another one, can we?"

Stonebridge struggled for a moment, then said, "Do you have any idea whatsoever about where Mrs. Swayze might have gone? Did she seem especially agitated when she was in the gym with you?"

"She was bouncing off the walls, if that's what you mean. She and the others are spooked by the murder and Randall's suicide. They all know, so you might as well stop deluding yourself."

"How do they know?" demanded Stonebridge, practically spitting out the words. "Did you tell them?"

"Good heavens, no," Walter said. "I have no idea where they're getting their information. If I had to pick a likely suspect, I'd put my money on Dibbins. He entertains visitors during the day, as long as they don't criticize his taste in music. Earlier in the week I had to interrupt a conversation he was having with Mrs. Swayze about Swiss table wines. Dawn despises him, but she keeps going back for more abuse. And poor dumb Toby can't figure out why Dibbins doesn't ask for his autograph."

"You didn't bring this up at the staff meeting," Stonebridge said as though accusing Walter of a serious crime.

Walter took a pair of sunglasses out of his coat pocket and slipped them on. "I didn't see any harm in it. It's not like they're in solitary confinement. They're all used to an adoring audience. We've taken that away, so now all they can do is try to impress each other."

Water splashed Stonebridge's face as Toby once again turned and took off. "What does he think he is — a damn otter? Come along, Arly. We need to check the drug cabinet and make sure nothing's missing."

I obediently stood up, nodded to Walter, and followed Stonebridge to what was referred to as the surgical suite. I'm not sure what I expected, but I wouldn't have been surprised if Igor was hovering in a dark corner. The suite proved to be more like an exam room in a doctor's office than an operating room with high-tech gadgets and gleaming stainless steel equipment. The fluorescent lights were no more intimidating than those at the supermarket. Everything was excruciatingly neat and undoubtedly sterile. The examination table had a paper cover, with towels and a pillow stack on one end.

"You do surgery in here?" I asked.

He smiled. "Obviously not triple bypasses or organ transplants. All of the procedures are done under local anesthesia, with a Demerol drip if indicated. Brenda has some training as an LPN, and will be able to assist me. Later, as we add more patients, I'll have an RN on the staff."

"You do face-lifts and tummy tucks with a *local* anesthesia? The patient is *awake?*"

"But in a pleasant haze. They can be quite gregarious. Ah, some of the shenanigans I hear about from the Hollywood set would curl your toes — and from the men as well as the ladies. If I weren't bound by ethics, I could make a fortune from blackmail."

I was still grappling with the idea of a patient blathering away as her facial skin was cut and stretched, or her nose was broken and reset, or a scalpel sliced across her abdomen. I stared up at the garish bright lights, then down at the table. Up and down, up and down.

And then the lights went out.

12

Dahlia sat on the top step of the porch. The twins was romping in the yard, chasing grasshoppers and whoopin' like wild Indians. She didn't know where her granny was, and she didn't care, neither. If she was lucky, the old bat had wandered up on Cotter's Ridge and was sitting in a tree while a hungry bear snuffled below her. The last time her granny had gone and gotten herself lost, she'd ended up at Petrol's shack, doin' things that weren't fit for a withered-up ol' woman of her age — or of anybody's age, for that matter. Kevin had gallantly offered to go thrash Petrol, but she knew darn well Petrol would skin him alive.

Raz's pickup truck rattled to a stop by the gate. The twins hightailed it under the porch. Dahlia sat, her fingers crossed that Raz hadn't caught her granny in his barn and brought her back home.

Raz climbed out of the truck but stayed on the opposite side of the gate. "You wanna buy a mess of catfish?" he called.

"I wouldn't buy a dollar for a nickel if it came from you, you ol' buzzard. Don't you be comin' in the yard."

He spat in her direction. "Suit yourself, but come suppertime, you may be wishin' you had some crunchy catfish and pipin' hot hushpuppies."

"More than likely I'll be wishing you was choppin' cotton at the state prison for making that godawful swill you peddle."

Raz bristled. "You got no call to say that, Dahlia O'Neill Buchanon. My 'shine is the best in three counties. I don't use no rusty radiators like those boys over in Cecil County. I've half a mind to come over there and tan your hide."

She held up a fist the size of a softball. "And I've half a mind to go out there and send you sprawlin' into a blackberry bush, you ornery coot."

"So you want some catfish or not?"

"You gonna gut 'em for me?"

Mrs. Jim Bob parked next to the rectory and rapped on the door. When Brother Verber didn't open the door, she opened it herself and called his name. She finally concluded he wasn't there and turned around. His car was parked in a patch of shade under a sycamore tree, so he couldn't have gone too far, she thought. Sometimes he went down to Boone Creek to try to catch the teenagers drinking beer and indulging in indecent carnal activities, but she figured it was too early in the day for that.

She decided to try the Assembly Hall on the off chance he was rehearsing his sermon for the following day. If he was, she would remind him that there were more pressing concerns, like sorting through the boxes of clothing and household goods that had been donated for their summer rummage sale.

The door to the vestibule was locked. Stunned, she yanked on the knob and then pounded her fist on the wood. The very idea of the Voice of the Almighty Lord Assembly Hall being locked was an insult to her, and an affront to the Lord. What was a sorry sinner who'd dragged his drug-ridden, crippled body to the door supposed to think when he was denied entrance to salvation? Would he crawl back into Satan's waiting arms and eternal damnation?

She returned to her pink Cadillac and sat for a long while, trying to remember when the door had last been locked. Years, maybe. Her forehead furrowed as she concentrated. There'd been rumors one summer that devil worshippers were planning to sneak inside and defile the church with their depraved midnight rituals. Brother Verber had been taking a refresher course at the seminary in Las Vegas (which had seemed curious to her, since it was a mail-order operation) and she'd taken it upon herself to lock the door every evening. But that had been a long while back, before Hiram's barn burned, and she couldn't remember what had happened with the key afterward.

She was still puzzling over it as she drove away.

Brother Verber watched her departure through a dusty window above the forsythia bushes alongside the building.

I cautiously opened my eyes and realized I was lying on the examination table. Dr. Stonebridge was looming over me, looking concerned. "I guess I fainted," I said with a weak smile.

"Would you like a glass of water?"

"No, thank you." I sat up but held on to the edge of the table. "That was pretty stupid of me. I got these horrible images of blood and exposed muscles and —"

Stonebridge squeezed my shoulder. "Stop thinking about it. Breathe in deeply and let the images fade as you exhale. I've

had plenty of patients who were equally surprised that most cosmetic procedures are
done under local anesthesia. It's really
much safer this way, since general anesthesia always poses a risk, however minor. I
can increase or decrease the pain medication as dictated by the patient's reaction."

I eased off of the table. "I apologize for my
lack of professionalism. I've seen bodies in
all stages of decomposition, and attended
autopsies. I've hooked floaters in the reservoir, and been the first on the scene of some
pretty damn gruesome car wrecks. I went
frog-gigging with some friends one night
when I was in high school, and sat on the
bank of the river until dawn, cleaning the
frogs. I had frog blood all over my —" I
stopped before I made an even greater fool
of myself, which at that point would have
been a challenge. "Shall we have a look at
the cabinet with the drugs?"

He led me into the second room. There
was a basin where I assumed the doctor
scrubbed his hands before surgery. One set
of open shelves held a boggling array of
Brenda's herbal remedies and vitamin supplements, all packaged in bottles with
labels. A second set of shelves held boxes of
supplies ranging from rubber gloves to rows
of antiseptic lotions, cotton bandages, dis-

posable hypodermic needles, tape, and rubber tubing. A tray with surgical instruments had been set on a cart, and a sterilizer on a stand in the corner.

The serious drugs were kept in a cabinet with a deadbolt that required a key. Stonebridge opened the doors and gestured at the tidy rows of bottles and vials. A clipboard hung from a hook and held a pad with columns for name of drug, date, quantity, patient's name, time administered, and by whom.

"As you can see," Stonebridge said, "we keep very concise records in accordance with state regulations for controlled substances."

"How can you tell if a bottle or a box is missing?" I asked.

He took a file from the top shelf. "This is the list of our original inventory. I can compare it to the list of what's been administered, and account for every pill and tablet."

"How often do you do that?"

"I was planning to update the inventory tomorrow. Later, when I expand the staff, I'll probably check it every three or four days. Health-care workers have been known to develop drug dependencies, too. Their jobs are stressful and their hours can be erratic. Constant switching from day to night shifts is fatiguing."

I wasn't interested in commiserating about anyone else's job description. "Please go ahead and make sure nothing's missing. I'd like to search the rest of the facility on my own. I'll need your key."

"What about Mrs. Swayze? We can't have patients wandering around the countryside, especially medicated. We have liability issues."

I almost told him we had a local resident wandering around Wyoming. "I don't think anybody will shoot her on sight. If she knocks on someone's kitchen door, she'll be served coffee and cinnamon rolls. After she's been obliged to listen to an hour of mind-numbing gossip, she'll probably head right back here. I'll call the sheriff's department if you want me to, but I'll have to give them a name along with a description. That may attract some unwanted attention from the media. We don't get a lot of newsworthy figures around here. The ordinary folks won't recognize her name, but the media will."

"Then what do you suggest?"

"Let's just sit on it until I've done a thorough search here and make sure she's not tucked in a laundry hamper or a closet. It shouldn't take me long."

He gave me the key. "Come to my office when you're done. You, Brenda, and I can have lunch by the pool while we discuss the situation."

I nodded and left, although I had no intention of dining on some concoction of tofu and bran when I could have a cheeseburger and fries at Ruby Bee's. And it wouldn't hurt to find out how the disarmament program was going. If I'd had the time, I would have hunted down Mrs. Jim Bob for a long lecture on the idiocy of encouraging the local women to buy handguns — and god knows what else. I suspected that for once I'd even have Jim Bob's support. At the moment Estelle was the only victim of the I-didn't-know-it-was-loaded club, but I was afraid she wouldn't be the last.

I started at the far end of the building on the other side of the pool. The kitchen was filled with all manner of stainless steel appliances, pots and pans hanging from hooks above the stove, open shelves of dishes, and unfamiliar (but undoubtedly utilitarian) utensils. The aroma was pungent with exotic spices. The so-called chef, a squat man in a stained apron, had greasy red hair and a cigarette clamped between crooked teeth. He looked as though he'd done his apprenticeship at a truck stop. He glanced at me, then resumed pulverizing vegetables with a heavy cleaver. His two subordinates careened around the central island, sliding on the wet floor and threatening to drop trays and serving bowls. A radio blared country music.

I waited for my chance, then hurried around the island to a door at the back. It led to a pantry that also served as a break room for the employees, a few of whom were seated at a table with bowls of some lumpy gray substance. We exchanged looks, but I couldn't bring myself to wish them *bon appétit.* Beyond that was another door that opened onto the outside. I picked my way through bits of rotting garbage and emerged by the archway. Deputy Quivers was back on duty. Walter had disappeared, but Toby was still swimming. I glanced at my watch and realized he'd been at it for more than an hour. Even Flipper would have taken a break.

I told Quivers to do a thorough search of the garden. After he trudged out of sight, I let myself into the gym. Unlike the exercise clubs I'd known in Manhattan, the room was sunny and free of the subtle stench of sweat. There was a faint smell of chlorine from the hot tub in a glass-enclosed area.

The closet-sized sauna was empty. A massage table held stacks of white towels and terry-cloth robes. The main room had all the customary equipment: stationary bicycles, weight machines, and a treadmill. The floor was covered with blue pads to lessen the impact of old-fashioned calisthenics.

I moved on to the day room. There were groupings of leather furniture at each end, and a gleaming conference table in the middle. Smaller tables supported brass lamps and fresh flowers. The walls were decorated with framed maps and prints of ducks. It reminded me of a gentlemen's club, although there was no discreet butler to raise his eyebrows at my feminist incursion. When the weather was less hospitable, it might be used, I thought, but it seemed rather pointless at the present. I ascertained that Senator Swayze was not hiding there, then went into the main building.

The reception desk was occupied by an orderly, who was reading a paperback with a lurid cover. He was older than some of the others, with a harsh, leathery complexion and irregular features. A puckered scar above one eye suggested he'd been in a few brawls and knife fights in his life. He hastily shoved the book into a drawer and stood up. *"¿Puedo ayudarle, señorita?"*

I managed a small smile and said, "No problem." I went past him and peered down the wing that had not yet been remodeled. It was as gloomy as an attic. Scraps of lumber and fragments of wallboard were scattered on the floor. A ladder was propped against the exposed insulation. Dust motes hung in the sunlight. There was no light at the end of the tunnel, although I knew there was an exterior door that had once provided Petrol Buchanon with a handy exit whenever he felt the need to spend some quality time with a quart jar of moonshine. To the previous director's chagrin, fire laws precluded locking the door from the inside.

The current crop of patients in the opposite wing had access to the door at the end of their corridor, too, but it would lead them no farther than the shrubs and trees along the interior side of the fence. I waggled my fingers at the orderly, then squared my shoulders and went into the unchartered territory, where I might encounter ferocious dragons and fire-breathing right-wing politicians. The latter was appropriate; since had I come through the front door, this would be the right wing. In my case, however, it would then be the wrong wing, and the left wing would, by default, be the right wing.

It occurred to me that I might have bumped my head when I'd keeled over in the surgical suite. I couldn't feel a lump, though, and the only twinges of pain came from my fanny. I still couldn't figure out why I'd reacted as I did. I was trained in emergency first aid. I'd made temporary splints, kept pressure on spurting arteries until paramedics arrived, cradled teenagers who'd been thrown from the backs of motorcycles. I may not have been the friggin' Florence Nightingale of Stump County, Arkansas, but I wasn't a weak-kneed wimp. Then again, I'd been out of whack lately, oddly off balance with myself, and admittedly on the testy side. I'd have to think about it when I had time. At the moment, I did not.

There were four doors on each side, some closed, some ajar. I crisscrossed the hall, checking each room. Most of the spartan furniture had been removed, but a few cast-iron bed frames and chairs were draped with tarps. Fixtures had been pulled from the small bathrooms, exposing rusty pipes and moldy plaster. Bluish-gray mildew was the predominate color scheme. I found nothing of interest until I reached the last room on the left. I'd been hoping for Senator Alexandra Swayze, hunched over and making guttural noises as she stared blindly at her toes, but my discovery was less rewarding. A few chairs had been salvaged and were arranged around a crude table made of a piece of wallboard, with paint cans serving as a base. On the table were half-eaten packages of crackers, dates, and figs; boxes of pricey chocolates and cookies; and empty tins of smoked oysters and caviar. Cigarettes and cigars had been stubbed out on a paint can lid. The magazines had Spanish words and depictions of dusky women in bikinis on the covers. I picked up one and flipped through it, noting with a grimace that the activities portrayed were not of windsurfing and beach volleyball.

At one end of the table was a collection of more than a dozen little liquor bottles, identical in size to the one that had been found on Randall's desk, along with a couple of undersized wine bottles. I couldn't imagine where the employees had gotten them, unless Stonebridge had flown his recruits to the Farberville airport. Bus tickets seemed more in keeping with his regard for their well-being and comfort — unless he'd had them smuggled into the country in the trunk of his limo.

I left the bottles where they were and went

309

back into the corridor. As I headed for the reception room, I tried to conceive of a scenario in which one or more of the orderlies or maids had doped a bottle and left it in Randall's apartment. It was not to their advantage to sabotage the Stonebridge Foundation and lose their jobs. Unlike Brenda, Randall did not strike me as the sort to bully and harangue them. From what I'd seen in the surgical suite, none of them could have taken drugs from the cabinet. And I wasn't about to get any of them fired for eating gourmet treats and nipping at the little bottles. If I'd had to deal with the celebrity patients all day, I would have done the same thing, although with a gallon of cheap wine.

The orderly looked panicky as I emerged from the dusty tunnel and paused to brush dust off my shirt. *"¿Es todo aceptable, señorita?"* he asked, his voice quavering.

No doubt visions of deportation were flashing before his eyes. I nodded and said, "Everything's okay, thank you." I continued across the room in the direction of the suites. Here the hallway was bright, well-lit, and squeaky clean. I tapped on Dr. Dibbins's door, then eased it open.

He was standing in front of the window, gazing at the driveway and the gate. Without turning, he said, "To what do I owe this honor, my lovely handmaiden of law and order? Are you here to read me my rights and haul me to your local jail? Does it have a cash bar, along with the iron ones? Or better yet, a piano bar?"

"How'd you know it was me?"

"Merely a process of elimination." Dibbins sat down on the sofa and gestured at the easy chair. Once I was seated, he continued with the pomposity of a professor at a lectern. "Shortly after ten o'clock this morning, Dr. Zumi left the premises in a body bag, and Dr. Stonebridge is in too much of a dither to come by for a visit. The boorish Brenda Skiller barges into the room without considering the possibility she might catch me in a moment of indiscretion. No, I retract that. She dearly hopes to catch me in such a moment, but I rarely comply. Walter's sandals flap when he walks. Whenever Dawn drops by, she doesn't hesitate to launch into a litany of her woes, as if she alone is subjected to injections of vitamins and a few green morsels for meals. She is very disturbed. If I were a compassionate man, which I am not, I might feel an occasional pang of sympathy for her."

"And your other fellow inmates?"

"Toby Mann has never knocked on a door in his life. Although I do not believe in the paranormal, the boy's ego seems to suck in all the oxygen wherever he goes. I find myself gasping whenever I'm in proximity to him. Furthermore, he continually curses under his breath." He arched his eyebrows and smirked unpleasantly. "Senator Swayze is no longer here, but I believe you already know that."

"Just how the hell do you know about Randall Zumi and the senator?" I demanded, exasperated. "Where are you getting the information? Why do you think I'm a cop, for that matter?"

"We've already had this conversation, if my memory serves me. It certainly should; I've been sober for eight days, which is an impressive feat in itself. When I had gallbladder surgery two years ago, I was sipping brandy in the recovery room." His lips puckered as he regarded me, clearly enjoying himself. He allowed me to fume for a minute, then said, "It's amazing what one can learn by judiciously analyzing human behavior. My diet books were not written without careful consideration. I observed the hostesses in West Palm Beach as they nibbled lettuce for lunch. Their bright smiles were forced and their eyes despairing with each measured dollop of fat-free dressing. I knew they were dreaming of lasagna and creamy risotto, of flaky croissants and pastries. I simply forbade them to eat the foods they'd grown to despise and gave them license to indulge in what they craved."

"Even at the risk of their health?"

"I feel their pain each time my broker parks in front of my seaside mansion to discuss mutual funds. I really do."

"And what means of judicious analysis led to your conclusion that I'm a cop?"

Dibbins chuckled. "You drove up the driveway this morning in a cop car. As for my other sources, I stand by my position of yesterday. If you make it worth my while, I'll reciprocate. Until then, you really should run along and pester someone else. I'm planning to listen to Antonio Salieri's *Europa Riconosciuta*, which I'm sure you know was performed at La Scala's opening night in 1778. You're welcome to join me, but I regret to say that champagne will not be served during intermission."

I was too pissed to be dismissed. "I'm surprised you didn't bring a three-month supply of forbidden fruit."

"Let me assure you that I did, and I was not alone. Brenda not only had a maid unpack my things, but she personally inspected each potential hiding place and confiscated the contraband. Our little Hollywood princess was livid, since she'd brought an expensive cache of cocaine. Alexandra hid her prescription pills in the toes of her shoes with wadded tissues to keep them in place. I'm not sure about Toby, but he's so profoundly stupid that he probably just tossed his drugs in the bottom of his bag. I shudder at the thought that he was accepted at any college. His SAT scores must have rivaled his IQ."

"He makes a lot more money than you do," I pointed out.

"Yes, I must admit he does, but only so long as he doesn't sustain an injury that ends his career. And even if he avoids injuries, he'll reach mandatory retirement within a decade. I invest prudently and diversify my portfolio with long-term, reliable investments. He has a reputation for spending his money in a reckless and carefree manner. By age thirty-five, if he's lucky to survive that long, he'll end up peddling time shares to retired couples from Iowa and Nebraska."

I vowed to diversify my portfolio as soon as I had one. At the moment, I had a few hundred dollars in a savings account and no foreseeable windfalls. I'd been so frantic to get the divorce over with that I'd literally packed my bags and walked away. Well, taken a cab to the airport, anyway.

"Listen, Dr. Dibbins," I began, making no effort to disguise my dislike of him, "this is not some little stage play performed for your enjoyment. Molly Foss was murdered two nights ago. I am not going to bribe you with chocolate. What I will do is have you transported to the county jail as a material witness. You will not be detained in a suite with a private bathroom and a CD player. The mattresses are an inch thick and reek of urine and vomit. You'll be fingerprinted and booked, and your mug shots won't be airbrushed. The media will pick up on it, so you'll be getting some unwanted publicity. The good news is that there are vending machines in the break room. How badly do you want a candy bar?"

His face turned red and he began to wheeze. "I shall sue you for false imprisonment."

"And you'll most likely win."

"Get out of my sight, you contemptible fascist! I must consider my options. You may return later if you wish, but do not allow yourself to be too confident that I'll meekly acquiesce because of these threats. You are not dealing with some illiterate redneck whose knowledge of the law is limited to DWIs and brawls."

"I'll be back," I said grimly, then returned to the hallway. Dibbins was worse than a meth addict going through cold-turkey withdrawal in a corner of his cell. The medications he was receiving seemed to prevent any overt physical symptoms, but I'd never encountered anyone quite so desperate for a sugar fix. If Molly had tucked a roll of hard candies in her purse, I could easily imagine Dibbins stalking her in the garden, his mouth salivating with anticipation.

Shuddering, I put aside the idea, at least for the moment. I went into the suite with a card on the door that read "Mrs. S." The sitting area and bedroom were immaculate. A biography of John Adams was on the table next to the bed, along with a pair of reading glasses and a box of tissues. The towels in the bathroom were dry, which meant she had not come back to her suite for a shower — unless a maid had already replaced them. Unfortunately, that minor question could not be resolved until the translator arrived. I opened all the drawers in the dresser and looked through the few clothes in the closet. Nothing caught my attention until I opened the bedside table drawer and found a spiral notebook.

I sat on the edge of the bed and opened it.

The first entry had been written on the day of her arrival at the Stonebridge Foundation. It had an undertone of bitterness, but a certain air of resignation. The next few entries described her sessions with the various doctors, her aversion to the food, her sense of isolation without access to a newspaper or cable news channels. She maintained in each entry that she was not addicted to the prescription pills and could stop whenever she chose. However, with each day, the entries seemed more disjointed and fragmented. She railed against Randall for his sly attempts to trick her into an admission of weakness. She loathed Brenda for installing hidden cameras in her suite. Molly was a spy for the ACLU. The employees were Marxists. The chef was poisoning her food. Dr. Stonebridge was determined to subject her to shock treatments. The last entry, written the previous night, was chilling:

Lloyd, should you ever read this, you must report to no one but the President himself. Not a joke — no! Clearly a plot to undermine the legitimate authority of the government. They think they're clever — the bastards — but I see them oh yes I see them clearly. They have only one goal — to use me as an agent of evil. After I've been brainwashed, they'll send me back to Washington. Inside my brain will be a microchip that has been programmed for only one mission — to assassinate the President of the United States of America! In the ensuing chaos, their troops will overpower the military, seize control of the media, and eventually subdue the entire nation.

My finger will be on the trigger. Bang, bang! Who has easier access to the Oval Office than I? Who attends more state functions? Who joins the President and First Lady for meals in their private living quarters? They want me to kill him!

My only hope is to escape before I'm whisked away during the night for the implantation. I've stopped taking their medications by pretending to swallow the pills then spitting them out. I'm not as stupid as they think. The murder of Molly Foss has caused confusion, which makes it all the easier. They're pretending she was drowned in a fountain for an unknown reason. But I know she had to be eliminated before she could inadvertently expose this vile conspiracy. She did so prattle on, much like Patricia — blah, blah, blah, until I thought I'd scream! She was a threat, and now she's dead. She used to come into my room when I was napping. I never let on I was watching her, but I was. A common little tramp who stole my money and jewelry. The maids did too. I hear them whispering in the hall outside my room. Plotting.

I shall escape at my first opportunity. If I am thwarted, you and you alone will have the burden on your shoulders to save this country from the godless liberals.

"Oh dear," I murmured to myself. I'd been telling myself Senator Swayze was currently attempting to buy a copy of the *Washington Post* at the supermarket. Idalupino would have a hard time trying to explain why they didn't sell such highfalutin newspapers and suggesting she might prefer the current edition of *TV Guide.*

Now it seemed I had a full-blown case of paranoia on the loose in a town that was ankle deep in illegal handguns. The ramblings in Senator Swayze's notebook made her seem more disturbed than the beady-eyed survivalists who live in remote compounds in the mountains. I replaced the notebook and went out to the hallway, unsure what to do. If I called Harve and clued him in, he might be able to send out a deputy with a dog to try to pick up her scent. I didn't know enough about abnormal psychology to predict her behavior. If her delusions came and went, she could be sitting on a gravel bar alongside Boone Creek, dangling her bare feet in the water. But if with each day that she failed to take the meds that Randall had prescribed, her paranoia deepened, she could be taking hostages by now. The entire membership of the Missionary Society could be in the back room of the Assembly Hall, bound with duct tape.

I finally decided to get Stonebridge's opinion, then call Harve. I'd taken a couple of steps when Toby Mann came around the corner from the reception room and blocked my way. Considering his height and bulk, this did not require any effort on his part. He had a towel draped around his neck, but water dripped on the floor and his hair hung in his eyes, partially hiding what I'm sure was a well-practiced twinkle on his part.

"You're the cop, right?" he said, scowling.

13

Harve bellowed for LaBelle, then realized she was off duty for the weekend. It was a mixed blessing. She annoyed the hell out of him every damn time he told her to do something, and more often than not she simply ignored him and went back to painting her nails or reading a magazine. On the other hand, her replacement was a mousy little woman whose name he never could recollect. She scurried around so quietly that he never knew where she was or what she was doing. Every once in a while, he'd look up and find her standing in his office, too timid to open her fool mouth. He was getting used to it, but it was still unnerving.

Cussing under his breath, he pushed his chair away from his desk, struggled to his feet, and lumbered down the hall to find her. Her desk was vacant. He frowned before remembering he'd sent her out to pick up sandwiches for lunch.

He snatched up the Rolodex and returned to his office. After some fumbling, he found the telephone number of the Maggody PD and dialed it. Nobody answered, which meant Arly was still out at the loony bin like she damn well was supposed to be — or on her way back to Missouri. He left a message that it was real urgent that she call him, then banged down the receiver and listened to his stomach growl.

As much as he would have liked to walk across the street to the café at the bus station for a bowl of chili, he figured he'd better wait by the phone. If Arly didn't call pretty damn soon, he was gonna have to drive out there to tell her what all the FBI had to say about the fingerprints they'd run through their fancy database.

She wasn't gonna like it one bit.

I looked up at Toby Mann, who was a good five or six inches taller than I was. I didn't even want to think about the number of pounds he had on me. "Yes," I said evenly, "I'm the chief of police." Just to annoy him, I added, "And you are?"

"You're kidding, right? Everybody knows The Man."

"I know a lot of men," I said, shrugging.

"I'm Toby Mann. I won the Heisman

when I was in college, and some sportswriters claim I'm the best quarterback in the history of football. You want to know how many touchdown passes I threw in the last Superbowl? I've been on the cover of *Sports Illustrated* four times." He thumped his chest. "I am *The Man*."

"I don't pay much attention to football, but if you say you're Toby Mann, I guess you ought to know. Do you want to speak to me?"

He gaped at me, still unable to believe I'd never heard of him. He finally pulled himself together and said, "Yeah, but not here. Let's go in my suite."

I trailed after him, since he was the only patient I hadn't interviewed. He continued into the bedroom and yanked off his swimsuit, no doubt thinking he could win my undying adoration with a stolen peek at his manhood (aka The Manhood). I averted my eyes and picked up a creased copy of a sports magazine that did indeed have his picture on the cover. His blond hair was tousled, his face streaked with sweat. The black smudges under his eyes made him look like a raccoon, but I decided not to point it out, since I was already pressing my luck.

When he joined me, he was wearing a

short robe and boxers. "There's something I got to ask you," he said as he sat down on the sofa.

"Have at it." I sat down on the easy chair and mentally measured the distance between us. My chances of making it to the door were not good.

"I saw you talking to Dawn yesterday. I want to know what she said about me."

I thought for a moment. "She said that you were horny and had a thing for Molly Foss."

"The fat cow's jealous. Yeah, Molly was pretty enough, and this stinking place is making me crazier than when I got here. There are a couple of maids I wouldn't mind banging, but they're terrified of getting caught with their apron strings untied. As for Brenda — you met her?" I nodded. "If there was an uglier, bossier woman, I sure as hell haven't met her. Brenda should go off to Africa and mate with a gorilla."

"I gather you're not fond of her."

He gave me a perplexed look, then relaxed. "That was a joke, right? So anyway, maybe I flirted with Molly out of boredom. I led her on, just for the hell of it." He paused. "Look, if Dawn said something about what happened the other night, she was lying through her teeth. She'd say anything to get back at me for not falling down and kissing her feet because she was in some stupid sitcom. She's all washed up, and she knows it. I'm the one with the screaming fans and the big bucks. Those women reporters who come into the locker room can't keep their hands off me. The talk show hosts all beg me to come on their shows. ESPN did a feature on me after I was named MVP at the Superbowl."

I couldn't help myself. "I remember now — I have seen you on TV. Don't you do commercials for Drippers or whatever those diapers are called?"

"That was my agent's bright idea. They pay me a lot of money," he said, flustered. "I've got a lot of expenses, you know. My fans expect me to drive expensive cars and be seen in the right clubs."

"Let's go back to what Dawn said about the other night," I suggested, as if she had said something. Which she hadn't.

"Yeah, well, whatever she said was a bunch of lies. She's made too many crappy cable movies about teenage girls who run away from home and become hookers. You ever seen any of them? One of the guys on the team had one on tape, so we watched it in the locker room after the coaches and trainers left. Turns out she was all fucked up because her sister got better grades and was a cheerleader. It should be a cult classic."

"Thank you very much!" snapped Dawn as she came into the suite. "I can't begin to tell you how happy I am that you and your teammates enjoyed the movie. I guess you know all about underage hookers, don't you? That woman you raped in the hotel — was she a pro or just a high school girl that you got drunk in the bar?"

I remembered what Randall had told me about the less than successful anger management role-playing session earlier in the week. "Dawn, if you want to talk to me, why don't I meet you out by the pool in a few minutes?"

She sat down on an arm of the sofa. "Oh, no, let's talk right here." She leaned over and flicked Toby's ear with a manicured fingernail. "You want to know what happened between Molly and Toby the night she was killed?"

Toby started to rise. "You stupid bitch, I ought to —"

"Wait just a minute!" I said loudly. I stood up and pointed at Toby. "Sit down and shut up, or I'll call for Brenda to bring a hypodermic and shoot you full of Demerol." I looked at Dawn. "And you either cut it out and sit over here, or I'll grab a handful of your bleached blond hair and drag you out to the hall. What's it going to be?"

She moved over to the chair where I'd been sitting, and in a sullen voice, said, "I don't know who the hell you think you are. If Dr. Stonebridge knew you'd spoken to me like that, he'd kick your ass out of here in no time flat."

"Why don't you trot down to his office and lodge a complaint?"

"Yeah," said Toby. "The cop doesn't want to listen to your lies."

Dawn glared at him. "She can decide for herself."

"An excellent idea," I said, finally daring to relax a little bit. "So tell me."

"Well," she began, still glaring at Toby, "I was in my suite at about nine, staring at the wall and counting the number of days I was stuck in this crappy place. I heard Molly giggling in the hall. I was kind of curious, since she usually leaves before dinner is served. Then I heard this conceited prick talking to her. They went into his suite and closed the door. I figured I could get them in big trouble, but I decided I didn't want to get Molly fired. She was pretty good about allowing me to make phone calls when Brenda wasn't around, as long as I paid her.

I didn't do anything for about an hour. That's when I heard Molly come out in the hall, whimpering and hiccuping."

"I hope you're not buying this shit," said Toby.

"At this point, I'm listening," I said.

Dawn was clearly having a fine time watching him squirm. "So I opened my door to see what was going on. Molly was leaning against the wall, her face all wet with tears and her hair tangled and ratty. I dragged her into my suite and asked what happened. She told me Toby tried to rape her."

"That is such a fuckin' lie!" he snarled.

"Why would she lie about something like that? She knew she'd get fired if she told any of the doctors. She was messed up so bad she could barely whisper. I tried to get her to stay until she calmed down, but she was afraid Toby would find her. I mean, she was really freaked out. I even offered her a Valium. She wouldn't take it because she had to drive home."

Toby leaned forward, his elbows on his bare knees, and gave me what was supposed to be a very earnest look. "Molly was freaked out, yeah, but it wasn't my fault. She told me earlier in the day that she was staying late for some kind of meeting, and would drop by for a visit when it was over. It was all her idea, not mine. She showed up, and we went into my room. I put on some music and we stayed on the sofa for a while. She was the one who suggested we go in the bedroom. I wasn't about to turn her down. We got to rolling around on the bed, and she got her hands all over me — and I mean all over me. I start to unbutton her blouse, and all of a sudden she panicked and told me to stop. I thought she was kidding. Maybe I tried a little harder to persuade her that she didn't really want me to stop, but she slapped the holy shit out of me, jumped up, and left. I sure as hell didn't force the little bitch into doing anything she didn't want to do. I wouldn't be surprised if she had been scheming all along so she could sue me for big bucks. For all I know, her husband put her up to it."

"Poor baby," cooed Dawn. "It's not your fault you're so rich and pretty that women are after your money. You must feel awfully insecure."

"Not nearly as insecure as you. At least I'm not a failure."

"Okay," I snapped, "enough of this. Dawn, what did Molly do after she left your suite?"

"She didn't want to risk running into

Brenda, so she went out the door at the far end of the hall. After that, I guess she decided to sit in the garden until she was calm enough to drive herself home."

"What about you?"

"Nothing," she said, blinking in surprise. "It wasn't like we were close friends or anything like that. I forgot about it and went to bed. Shouldn't you be asking Toby what he did?"

"What the hell do you think I did?" he said angrily. "Follow her and kill her? Give me a fuckin' break! So maybe I was annoyed with her on account of the way she pretended she was so hot for me and then left. I didn't try to stop her, fercrissake! When I get out of this place, I'll have more women than I can handle waiting outside the locker room. And a helluva lot classier ones than that little cock-teaser!"

"So what did you do?" I asked.

"I popped a pill and went to bed."

Dawn shook her head. "Oh, no, you didn't. I heard your door open about five minutes later. You went down the hall and out the same door that Molly left through." She looked at me. "You can ask Dibbins. He heard it all, too."

"I went outside," said Toby. "Big goddamn deal. I needed some fresh air, that's all. But I wasn't following Molly. I thought she'd gone straight to her car and left. I just walked around until I calmed down, then came back and went to bed."

I wasn't quite ready to buy his story. "Did your walk take you into the garden?"

"Hell, no," he muttered. "The last thing I wanted to do was run into her and have her start screeching."

"You said you assumed she left immediately," I pointed out. "How could she have been in the garden?"

"I don't know. You're getting me confused. Maybe I wasn't sure she wouldn't be in the garden. I sat by the pool for an hour or so, then came back here. That's when I popped the pill."

"Did you see anyone?" I asked.

"You mean, did anyone see me? How the fuck should I know? I was too busy kicking myself for letting her in my room in the first place. I should have known she was setting me up so I'd have to pay her to keep her big mouth shut. Another accusation of rape, and I might as well skip the trial and check into a cell."

"It sounds like a motive to me," Dawn said smugly.

Toby's face turned red. He started to stand up, then caught my stare and sank back down. "Okay, while I was by the pool, Walter came by and asked me if I wanted to smoke a little weed. We went out to his van and stayed there until about midnight, smoking and drinking wine. I don't want to get him in trouble, so don't ask him in front of Stonebridge or Brenda. They'd both shit in their pants if they knew."

That much I believed. "Was Molly's car still there?"

"I don't know. It was dark. There were some cars and vans, but I don't know what she drove. One of them could have been hers. Look, I can't afford to get booted out of here. The judge ordered a ninety-day psych evaluation, and I'll be in contempt if I don't cooperate. I'm already missing training camp on account of this stupid law-suit, and we've got exhibition games coming up at the end of the summer. I owe it to the team and my fans to get through this and back on the field."

Dawn wiggled a finger at him. "Don't forget your corporate sponsors."

"Them, too," he muttered.

I would have felt sorry for him if he hadn't been such a jerk. "All right," I said, "I'll have a private word with Walter and see if he confirms your story. In the meantime, I suggest the two of you keep a civilized distance. That means stay away from each other. I'll be back later this afternoon."

"You're not going to arrest The Man?" Dawn said, feigning disappointment.

"No, I'm not. Did either of you see Senator Swayze earlier today?"

They both said no. I ordered Dawn to go back to her suite and then went down the hall to the door that led outside, thinking about what I'd just heard. Toby was more of a dumb jock than I'd assumed if he believed Walter would lie for him. But if Toby's story was true, Walter might not be eager to admit it and risk losing his job. All I could do was ask Walter and hope I could tell if he was lying. He was glib, though, and probably had no qualms about saying whatever was in his best interest.

As I walked toward the back of the building, I glanced into the apartments that housed the doctors and Walter. I could see pearl gray walls and framed artwork, but no signs of the inhabitants. I wondered if there was any way to talk Roy into springing for a can of paint so I could add a little class to my own apartment, which was currently a sort of muddy beige. The only thing hanging on the wall was a calendar from the early 1990s that I'd left to cover a hole in the wallboard.

Deputy Quivers was seated by the pool.

When he saw me, he leapt to his feet and sucked in his gut. "I searched the garden, ma'am," he said. "I crawled under the bushes and examined the flower beds for footprints. I didn't find nothing."

Before I could congratulate him on his dedication, Brenda came out of her office and beckoned to me. "Could we have a word in private?"

She was already seated behind her desk when I got there. "Have you made any progress?" she demanded. "This needs to be cleared up immediately so that we can get our patients back on their schedules. They must have boundaries and structure. Right now we're shorthanded, as you know. Vincent is on the phone, trying to find another psychiatrist who can take over Randall's duties temporarily. The temp agencies are closed for the weekend, which means I had to assign one of the orderlies to the reception desk. I've coached him to say 'Stonebridge Foundation' and 'Please hold' if someone calls, but even that may be too much of a challenge for him."

"Aren't you going to ask about Senator Swayze?"

"Please tell me that she's back in her suite. I don't know how much more I can take. Vincent is so distraught he's already drinking, and it's not even noon."

"She's nowhere in the building or on the grounds," I said. "I found her journal and read a few entries. Are you aware she wasn't taking her medications?"

Brenda made a peculiar noise, something between a bleat and a gurgle of despair. "I've noticed she hasn't been as cooperative lately, but I assumed she was going through a transitional stage. How bad is she?"

"I'm not a shrink, but I'd say that she's delusional and paranoid as hell." I related the gist of Swayze's conspiracy theory. "I can't have her loose in Maggody. If she gets her hands on a weapon, we may end up with a bloodbath. The only thing I can think of to do is get a police officer with a dog out here as soon as possible."

"No! We cannot risk the media exposure. You have to go find her and bring her back with a minimum of fuss. I can promise you she'll take her medications, if I have to sit on her chest and pry open her jaws with my bare hands."

I could easily envision it, which was disturbing in itself. "I'll drive around town and ask people if they've seen her, but if I don't get lucky, I'm going to have to alert the sheriff. She could be anywhere in the county by now."

"Oh, god, what if she calls Lloyd?"

"Lloyd's of London?"

Brenda ran her fingers through her hair, leaving tufted rows that looked like withered stalks of wheat. "Her son, you idiot! Why are you sitting there? Go find her, and call me immediately. I need to talk to Vincent. Maybe we should call Lloyd first and warn him." She hurried out the door, mumbling to herself.

I sat for a minute in case she came storming back in, then left the office and went over to Deputy Quivers. "I've got to go into town for an hour or so. If you get hungry, ask one of the employees to bring you something to eat. The only people allowed to come and go are delivery men; they'll use the back door of the kitchen. Just keep everybody else here until I get back, okay?"

"You might should have told me that earlier," he said, his eyes darting like minnows. "That guy with the ponytail left about half an hour ago. That van of his really needs a transmission job. I was thinking I'd tell him about my brother-in-law's garage over in Hasty. He does good work and —"

"Did he say anything to you when he left?" I said.

"He told me I looked like Barney Fife. Is

that one of the deputies? I'm kinda new and haven't met all the other fellows yet."

"Yes, Quivers, and I'm sure you'll meet him soon. Don't let anyone else leave, and I mean it. Do you understand?" Without waiting for a reply, I went out to my car and drove around to the gate. It was locked. I honked the horn until it slowly swung open. As I drove past the persimmon tree, I noticed it was unoccupied by Mrs. Jim Bob's spies. Sighing, I headed for Ruby Bee's Bar & Grill to find out if the grapevine was humming.

Waiting for Old Faithful to erupt made Eileen think of Earl. He was regular as clockwork, too. Every single day he'd come in from the field or barn, grab the sports section of the newspaper, and lock himself in the bathroom for half an hour. He'd hardly ever missed a day except for the one time he had the flu and practically lived in the bathroom. She must have gone through a dozen cans of aerosol deodorizer, she thought fondly as she wiggled on the rock where she was sitting. Earl was her Old Faithful, dependable and predictable. She'd learned long ago not to expect any compliments when she'd made a special meal with all his favorites, or when she bought a new dress.

Did he think it was gonna kill him to say something nice ever once in a while? Or, heaven forbid, offer to help with the dishes?

Not once since they got married had he put his dirty underwear in the hamper or scraped the mud off his boots before he walked across the clean kitchen floor. Last Christmas he'd given her a vacuum cleaner attachment. On her birthday, he'd given her the same cologne he gave her every year. She had enough unopened bottles on the back shelf in the hall closet to open a shop, presuming anybody else'd be fool enough to buy the cheap stuff.

She felt a faint rumble and scrambled to her feet. Old Faithful was right on time.

Jim Bob spotted Jeremiah McIlhaney looking at cans of chaw by one of the checkout counters. He went over and slapped Jeremiah on the back. "How ya doin' these days?" he said genially.

"Same as always," Jeremiah said. "We could use some rain. The forecast don't look good, though. 'Course, it being June, we'll get some before too long."

Jim Bob nodded as if this were one of his major concerns. "You interested in playing a little poker?"

"Might be."

"Yeah, sometimes it's good to get out of the house, ain't it? If Mrs. Jim Bob had her way, I'd be wearing a frilly apron and washing up the dishes every night. Us men got to make it clear that we can do what we damn well please after a hard day's work."

Jeremiah gazed at him. "I hear tell you're spending a lot of your evenings out at the Pot O' Gold trailer park with some red-headed stripper."

"Hold it down, buddy. Those checkout girls have ears like elephants. Yeah, there's a divorcée living out there, name of Divine. Sometimes I go by and screw in her lightbulbs, if you know what I mean. So how about a poker game tonight? You reckon your wife will let you if you ask nicely?"

"I'll play if I've a mind to."

Jim Bob slapped him on the back again. "Us men got to stick together, don't we? No women are gonna tell us what we can and can't do."

He strutted away, feeling pleased with himself. Mrs. Jim Bob would be in for a surprise if she was still plotting to run for mayor.

When Estelle got home from the super-market, she could tell something was wrong. It wasn't like a burglar had been ransacking her house. As far as she could tell, nothing had been moved. The pink mohair sweater she'd left on the divan was right there. The magazines were in a tidy stack by the hair dryer, and the shampoo, conditioner, scissors, perm solutions, and manicure tools were in a tidy row on the shelf. Her living room smelled kinda funny, though it was hard to put her finger on it. Just kinda funny.

She went into the kitchen, still uneasy, and began to unload the bag of groceries. It was only when she opened the refrigerator that she knew for certain that someone had been there. Living alone, she kept an eye on her supplies and shopped only when she was down to a few slices of bread, a single egg, a little bit of bacon, and maybe a pork chop that she might cook for supper. Long about Saturday, she replenished what she needed for the week.

But the heel of the bread was missing, along with the last slice of cheese. The mustard was on a low shelf, instead of next to the mayonnaise. The dill pickle jar was empty. What's more, there was a butter knife in the sink.

Estelle went back to the living room and sat down to think about it. It could be the foreigners had been in her house. No matter what Ruby Bee said, she knew better than to trust them. Her house wasn't but half a mile from the Stonebridge Foundation, if you cut across the pasture in back of the Assembly Hall and crawled under a barbwire fence.

She finally forced herself to put away the groceries before the ice cream melted and the celery started wilting. It was hard, though, to keep herself from peering over her shoulder every time a bird peeped or a truck drove past. She figured that Arly had too much on her plate to deal with stolen food, so there was no point in calling her. And if she so much as said a word to Ruby Bee about the foreigners, accusations would start flying like a swarm of hornets and they'd end up not speaking for another week. At least she had a gun in her bedside table — not much of a gun, but better than nothing.

What's more, she wasn't absolutely sure she hadn't eaten that pickle herself.

14

I suppose I should have stopped at the PD to check messages, but I was more interested in finding out if Senator Swayze had been spotted roaming the back roads. Well, that and having a nutritionally incorrect lunch. Although I'd had breakfast only a few hours earlier, I felt as though I'd left Springfield days, if not weeks, ago. Jack was probably still in his robe, washing wineglasses and deciding what to do with the rest of the weekend. All I could do was hope that he was staring out a window, missing me as much as I missed him. I wasn't sure if it was the physical intimacy, the lazy cuddling, the conversation, or the increasingly comfortable companionship. Whatever it was, I was beginning to realize that for the last few years, I'd been content to do nothing more than watch spiders on the ceiling at the PD and sit alone in my apartment at night. Now I was feeling the urge to yank myself out of this self-imposed complacency, for better or worse.

However, being the conscientious cop that I was, I parked in front of Ruby Bee's Bar & Grill. The neon sign for the Flamingo Motel had lost another letter; it now read "V N Y." I wasn't sure, but it looked as though the flamingo had shed another feather, too. It must have been molting season in Maggody. I went inside and sat down on a stool. Ruby Bee came out of the kitchen, a dish towel in her hands, and immediately retreated. Although I knew she and Estelle were up to something, I kept a polite smile on my face as I picked up the menu to check the blue plate special for the day.

Ruby Bee reappeared with a pecan pie and set it under a glass dome. Acting as though she hadn't already seen me, she said, "Why, look who's decided to grace us with her presence. I hope you enjoyed using my car without permission. You recollect what happened last time you tried it?"

"I'd just gotten my driver's license and couldn't resist the temptation, even though I knew that I'd end up grounded for a month of Sundays. Which I was, but it was worth it. And you can't ground me now, because I commandeered your car in my capacity as a duly-appointed law enforcement agent." I caught myself before I stuck my tongue out at her. "If it's not too much trouble, I'd like a cheeseburger, fries, and a piece of that pie."

"You don't want fresh catfish? I just now put a batch in the skillet."

I shook my head. "I'm definitely not in the mood for catfish these days. Have there been any strangers in here today?"

"Beebop Buchanon was in here about an hour ago, and he's about as strange as they come. For some reason I didn't quite catch, he put a dozen boxes of Rit Dye in his bathwater and turned hisself green. He looks like a big ol' bullfrog, bug-eyed and all. What's worse, he was paying a mite too much interest in a fly on the window."

"What about an older woman with white hair?" I asked, trying to sound casual.

Ruby Bee gave me a suspicious look. "Someone I should know?"

"I don't think so," I said. "I'm in kind of a rush, so I'd appreciate it if you start the cheeseburger."

"In a rush to get back to that place? Did something else happen out there?"

I stood up. "Never mind, I'll get a sandwich at the deli at the SuperSaver."

"You just hold your horses, missy. I didn't say I wasn't going to fix your lunch.

Are you real sure you wouldn't rather have the catfish and hush puppies?"

"I'm very, very sure," I said. I sat back down and turned my stool around so I could see who all was wolfing down catfish. The usual suspects were there, along with a couple of truck drivers who were vaguely familiar. The only white hair belonged to Hepburn Hartbern, who lived in a cabin way back in the mountains on the far side of Boone Creek and only came to town twice a year to load up on beans, rice, and flour. He supposedly had a wife, but no one had seen her in a coon's age, as we say in Maggody. Jim Bob, Roy, and Larry Joe were in a booth, their heads together as if they were plotting to rob a bank. They'd have to go to Farberville to do it, though, because the local branch bank had burned to the ground a few years back. It didn't much matter, since no one in Maggody had any money except Raz, and he buried the profits from his moonshine operation in quart jars somewhere up on Cotter's Ridge.

I was idly speculating about the newest location of Raz's still when Estelle came in and slid onto her stool at the far end of the bar. We exchanged nods. She was somewhat disheveled, which was unlike her. A few tendrils had escaped her shellacked beehive of red hair. Her eyebrows had been drawn with an unsteady hand, and her firehouse red lipstick contrasted with the unnatural paleness of her complexion.

Concerned, I moved to a stool beside her. "Are you okay?" I asked.

"Why shouldn't I be okay? In fact, I'm feelin' perky as a petunia."

Ruby Bee honed in on us. "Good heavens, Estelle — you look like something the cat drug in. Are you coming down with a stomach virus?"

"I was just telling Arly here that I'm fine, thank you very much," Estelle replied, her nostrils quivering. "I had trouble sleeping last night, that's all. If you two don't mind, I'd prefer a little privacy so I can do some thinking."

"Well, excuse me," said Ruby Bee. She banged down my plate, then stomped back into the kitchen and began to rattle pots and pans so loudly we could hear the noise over the atonal angst coming from the jukebox.

I slid my plate down the bar and moved to another stool. Between bites, I watched Estelle in the mirror on the wall behind the bar. She was certainly doing some thinking, and the subject was disturbing her. She took a compact out of her purse and inspected her lipstick, then sighed so forcefully that the mirror was in danger of fogging up. Her hand was shaking so badly that she could barely take a sip of sherry. A dribble ran down her chin and landed on the bar.

When I couldn't stand it anymore, I abandoned my last few fries and went over to her. "You need to tell me what's wrong," I said softly.

"I think I must be going crazy, if you must know. I've been racking my brain for over an hour, trying to remember if I ate the pickle. I don't think I did, but I can't swear I didn't. Maybe I got up in the middle of the night and made myself a cheese and pickle sandwich. That'd account for the bread. I used to sleepwalk when I was a child. Once my mother found me out in the barn carrying on a lively conversation with the cows. She led me back to bed, and I didn't remember a thing about it. If I hadn't found straw in my hair the next morning, I wouldn't have believed her."

"And the pickle?"

"They ought to haul me off to that nursing home in Starley City. What if I was to forget how to mix a perm solution and cause one of my clients to end up balder than a walnut? I ain't fit to hang my diploma from the cosmetology school above the mantel." She hung her head and blinked back tears. "I'll be a disgrace to the profession."

"Because of the pickle?" I persisted, justifiably bewildered.

"And rightly so." She sighed again. "I might as well tell you and get it over with. I went to the SuperSaver this morning, same as I always do. When I got home, I had this eerie feeling that someone had been in my house. There wasn't anything I could put my finger on, but it didn't feel right. I went on into the kitchen to put away the groceries, and that's when I saw the pickle was gone."

"Did you lock your doors before you left?"

"I'm not sure. I had my hands full, since I was taking some chicken soup to Edwina Spitz, who's been ailing of late, and a bag of fabric scraps to Joyce for a quilt she's working on for the county fair. And of course I had my purse, and at the last minute I decided to take an umbrella just in case. You know how the weather can be in June. One minute the sun's shining, and the next minute black clouds are rolling in over Cotter's Ridge. The last time I got caught in a storm, I was drenched to the bone and came darn close to coming down with pneumonia."

Not all crimes committed in Maggody were of the magnitude of murder and mayhem, I reminded myself. Pickle theft was apt to be a misdemeanor. "Was anything else missing?" I asked.

Estelle began to fidget. "Well, two slices of bread — unless, like I said, I made myself a sandwich. I read in a magazine that sleepwalking can be caused by stress. It ain't easy knowing there's a loony bin across the pasture from my house."

"Was anything else missing?" I repeated.

"Last night I got to worrying on account of the murder over at the Stonebridge Foundation, so I —"

"How do you know about that?"

"LaBelle heard about it from one of the deputies. Yesterday afternoon she went to a Tupperware party at her first cousin's niece's house and happened to mention it. You probably don't remember Dilys Podd that lives in Hasty with her good-for-nuthin' husband, who must weigh six hundred pounds and had to buy a special-made wheelchair so he could —"

"So LaBelle told Dilys, who told you," I said wearily. "You got to worrying and then what?"

"Actually, Dilys didn't tell me. She called Edwina, who used to attend the Pentecostal church over there before her arthritis started acting up, and Edwina called me. That's why I knew Edwina was feeling poorly and took her chicken soup this morning."

"Ah, yes," I said, "now it's perfectly clear. As much as I'd like to stay here all afternoon and discuss purloined pickles and Edwina's arthritis, I've got other things to do. For the last time, was anything else missing?"

"My gun."

"Your what?" I gasped. "Please don't tell me you went out and bought a gun after what happened yesterday. I swear, I'm going to —"

"I didn't go buy a gun." Estelle plucked a napkin from a holder and dabbed her upper lip as if she fancied herself to be Scarlett O'Hara confronting the Yankees. "Back when I lived in Little Rock, a gentleman friend gave it to me on account of how I had to drive home so late at night. I thought he was being silly, but I accepted it as a token of his concern for my welfare. Yesterday afternoon I dug through my cedar chest, and there it was, along with some bullets. I didn't see any harm in putting it in a drawer next to my bed in case one of those lunatics escaped. After all, one of them murdered that sweet little girl from Starley City."

I sat down on the nearest stool and rubbed my face. "Let me get this straight. You found the gun and put it in a drawer in your bedroom, and now it's missing. Am I right?"

"Unless I put it someplace else. I have to admit I had some wine last night, more than I'm accustomed to. I'm not much of a drinker, as I'm sure you've noticed. But I was real worried about the murderer getting loose, and I kept staring out at the pasture, and before I knew it the wine bottle was empty and I was trying to make a long-distance call to Italy. Maybe I just imagined I got the gun out, and maybe I forgot about eating the pickle."

"Italy?"

"That is none of your business, and I don't appreciate you prying into my private affairs."

I gave up and left. One of these days I might be able to make some sense of the conversation, but I had my doubts. On the other hand, I had a pretty good idea who might have slipped into Estelle's house to eat the pickle — and taken the gun. It was time to talk to Harve. I drove to the PD and went inside. The evil red eye of the answering machine was blinking, so I hit the play button and sat down behind my desk.

The first few calls were from Ruby Bee and concerned her car and ungrateful daughters who behaved like they were raised in a barn. Mrs. Jim Bob, who apparently was on Edwina's call list, wanted details about "the cold-blooded murder that mocks the Christian values of our community." I presumed the reference was to the Old Testament commandment: "Thou shalt not mock Maggody." The manager of the Pot O' Gold trailer park reported that a woman named Divine had trashed a double-wide and left in the middle of the night, owing a month's rent. Elsie McMay was in a dither because two teenagers had trampled her pansies when they cut through her yard on their way to the high school. Kevin wanted to know if I'd had an update on his ma's whereabouts. Dahlia called to say her granny had run off and was armed and dangerous, so I should shoot her on sight.

I was hoping that someone would mention a trespasser with white hair when the door opened and Harve came in, huffing and puffing as though he'd scaled Mount Everest (as opposed to walking fifteen feet). He crossed his arms and stared at me until I turned off the tape, then said, "Were you planning to call me back any time soon?"

"You want some coffee?"

"No." He plopped down on the chair and took out a cigar. "What I want is to be fishing on this fine, sunny afternoon. Instead, I'm sitting here, wishing I was fishing. It ain't the same thing, is it?"

"Is that a trick question?" I asked. "Did you drive all the way out here to ask me that? You could have called, you know."

Harve kept an eye on me as he lit the cigar. "I came to tell you about those folks out at the Stonebridge Foundation. I'd have sent a deputy, but I can't trust any of them to keep their traps shut. This has to stay confidential. If the reporters get a whiff of it, I'm going to be collecting unemployment come the next election."

"What about them?"

"Maybe I will have some coffee." He flicked ashes on the floor, knowing it would irritate me, then said, "For starters, Dr. Stonebridge got caught prescribing way too many narcotics in Connecticut and lost his license. He moved to L.A., finagled a new license, and opened a practice. Seems some of his wealthy patients back in Connecticut were so grateful not to have their names mentioned in the investigation that they referred him to all their rich friends. He was doing real well for himself out there until he was accused of malpractice once too often. A lot of his patients developed complications, and one lady died after an infection set in. I couldn't follow all the jargon, but he used some drugs and techniques that aren't approved by the FDA. He ended up losing his license and coming here."

"With a track record like that, how did he lure in the current celebrities?"

"Beats me," said Harve. "I wouldn't let him clip my toenails. You gonna make coffee, or do I have to do it myself?"

I went into the back room and started a pot. "What else?"

"You'd better sit down before I tell you." He waited until I handed him a mug (black, heavy on the sugar) and returned to my chair. "We got a bigger problem with Brenda Skiller. For starters, she's dead."

I rocked back so hard I banged my head against the wall. "When? I left there less than an hour ago. What happened to her?"

"She died sixteen years ago, when she was eighty-two."

"Would you care to explain?"

"Miss Skiller was a retired piano teacher living in Phoenix. When she got so feeble she couldn't take care of herself, her niece put her in a private nursing home. There were only five other old folks, all retired and living on their Social Security checks. The home was run by a woman by the name of Alice Cutchens, who kept them fed and bathed and on their medications. Miss Skiller was the only one who had any relatives to keep track of her. Well, after not hearing from her aunt for several months, the niece went to visit and was told the old lady had been moved to a state-run nursing home. Only there weren't any records of which one. The niece finally got fed up dealing with the bureaucratic runaround and hired a private detective to locate her. Eventually, the private detective got a glimmer of what was going on and called in the police. Turned out that whenever this Alice Cutchens found herself with a dead resident, she was reluctant to notify the government and cut off the monthly Social Security checks. Instead, she just buried them in her backyard."

"And Brenda Skiller was under the roses?"

Harve took a slurp of coffee. "In a manner of speaking. The police found three more bodies. All of them were found to have died from heart attacks and other natural causes, so Alice Cutchens wasn't charged with murder. She was charged with illegal disposal of the bodies, failure to notify the authorities, polluting the environment, theft, and other pesky things. Luckily for her, the feds didn't get all fired up about the Social Security fraud. She did ten years at the Arizona women's prison and was released a few years back."

I couldn't think of a damn thing to say. My mind was overwhelmed with images of a woman dressed in black in her backyard at midnight, digging a hole, while the moon glinted on the blade of her shovel. Quietly, so that no one would hear. Methodically piling up the dirt nearby so that she could dump the shrouded body and cover it up. At dawn, planting the marigolds she'd purchased the previous day. Then going into the kitchen to wash her hands, turn on the radio, and make scrambled eggs and toast for her remaining residents.

Harve cleared his throat. "You want me to go on?"

"Yeah," I said, although I didn't.

"So Alice did her time, and used it wisely. She managed to get a bachelor's degree online in psychology, and then a master's degree. Not from accredited schools, of course, but the kind that give you credit for what they call 'life experience.' In her case, I don't reckon they asked for details. She knew she couldn't ever get past a background check if she applied for a job, so she used Brenda Skiller's name. All she needed was her Social Security number, and she had that. The day she walked out of the prison, she was Brenda Skiller."

"Jesus H. Christ," I muttered. "Does anyone else know this?"

"Might be. The private detective that the daughter hired was named Winchell."

"As in Walter . . . ?"

"No, as in Winchell Kaiser. His brother's name is Walter. Their parents must have had a real odd sense of humor."

My head, which had already had its fair share of abuse, began to pound. "Go ahead, Harve — tell me Walter's an alien from a distant planet who's collecting specimens for their zoo. Don't hold back on me."

"Nothing much on Walter. He was arrested a few times on drug charges, but weaseled out of them by claiming the drugs were part of a religious ceremony. It seems Taos is some kind of artist colony, which means it has more than its fair share of old hippies who get stoned and go wandering all over the desert. The police in Amarillo are kinda unhappy about how he slipped out the back door before he could be arraigned for speeding and possession of marijuana. Seems he managed to take the evidence with him, too. Slick as a whistle, they said."

"But he probably knows Brenda's little secret. Alice's. Whatever."

Harve nodded. "But I ain't sure how any of this has something to do with Molly Foss's murder. I just thought you might appreciate knowing who you're dealing with."

"I'll carry my gratitude to the grave, Harve. Any more dark secrets to share?"

"The Mexicans are all clean, far as the feds know. Randall Zumi was pretty much what we expected him to be. His degrees were all legitimate, and he was cleaner than a scrub bucket. I talked to his wife when I got back to the office. Lordy, after listening to her screech and wail for the best part of an hour, I could understand why he killed hisself. She was fit to be tied when she learned we had to order an autopsy, and she made some nasty remarks comparing me to a certain by-product of water buffaloes. I suggested she call her lawyer and hung up."

"What about Molly's husband?" I said.

"He was even more direct about expressing his displeasure. I finally got him calmed down, and he agreed to stay away from the foundation. Molly didn't tell him any details about her job, so it's not like he can try to sell the story to a tabloid. As for the night she was murdered, he was at the bowling alley until it closed at midnight, and then went to the Dew Drop Inn for a couple more hours. The boys on his bowling team all agree he was with them until they dropped him off at home."

I hated to ask, but I did. "Anything else I should know about Molly?"

"She had a bad reputation when she was in school, according to her friends, but she settled down after she got married. Went to a business school and learned all the crap she needed to work in a doctor's office doing the insurance and billing paperwork. One of the girls at the office where she used to work said she wasn't sorry when Molly quit. There were some rumors Molly was spending too much time in the doctor's office with the door closed. He denied any sort of romantic entanglement, but he's married with three kids and a big house overlooking a golf course. Also, the girl at the office said the rest of the staff suspected Molly was stealing money from their purses in the coat room. Just suspected, mind you. Nobody had any proof."

"Would you mind if I crawled under my desk for an hour or so?" I said. "I don't think I can take any more background information at the moment. All the circuits in my head have blown their itty-bitty fuses."

"Suit yourself, but that's about all. Two of the celebrities — the Dartmouth gal and Toby Mann — have been arrested on occasion for drugs and booze. The other two are upstanding citizens. Stonebridge most likely shouldn't be practicing medicine, but that's up to the state board. Alice Cutchens is doing something illegal, but I ain't sure what and I ain't gonna worry about it. I could tip off the police in Amarillo as to Walter's whereabouts, but it's not like they're going to extradite him." He pulled back his cuff and looked at his watch. "It's not all that late. I might just get in a couple of hours out at the lake."

"Don't bet your bass boat on it," I said darkly. "Let me tell you about that upstanding citizen, Senator Alexandra Swayze."

Harve listened, his face growing grimmer. When I finished, he took a final puff on his cigar and tossed it into the wastebasket. "You got any extra room under your desk?"

Brother Verber couldn't believe what-all he was hearing. In truth, he couldn't make much sense of it. Communists and aliens and a conspiracy to assassinate the president of the United States of America? Drugs that altered your mind? Innocent folks undergoing bizarre surgical procedures that turned them into killing machines?

He fell to his knees and said, "Let us pray."

The Honorable Senator Alexandra Swayze, who was sitting next to him on the pew, poked his shoulder. "Pray for what? Haven't you understood a word of what I've been telling you, you moron? There's no one we can trust. If I attempt to call Lloyd, the CIA will intercept the call and track me down. You'll be thrown into a cell and be left to rot, but only after you've been tortured. They're much more sophisticated than they used to be. These days they can attach electrodes to your genitals. I've been told the pain is excruciating."

"My what?" he squeaked. "You mean my . . . ?"

"I'll simply disappear, and a few weeks from now a story will be leaked to the press that I was killed by insurgents in one of those obscure Asian nations. You and I are the only ones who can defend democracy against this vile plot. We must take action."

Brother Verber was still pondering what she'd said about his genitals. He wasn't real sure what electrodes were, but they didn't sound like a good idea. He resumed his seat on the pew. "What do you aim we should do?"

"I wish I knew," Alexandra said. She stayed quiet for a moment, then grabbed his arm so fiercely that he yelped. "We must organize a resistance movement, as the French did during World War II. We'll infiltrate the core of the conspiracy and stop them. Can I trust you, Willard?"

"Oh, yes," he said, trying to pull free of her grip. "I can see that we're gonna have to infiltrate. Why, if the godless communists take control like you said, then what'll become of us righteous Christian folks?" He kept squirming, but it didn't do any good. She was a nice-looking lady, but she'd clamped on to him like a pit bull. "How do you think we should organize this resistance movement? Nobody here in Maggody knows how to speak French. Some of them can barely speak American."

She frowned, which alarmed him even more than the fact he couldn't hardly wiggle his fingers. "We need recruits we can trust. They must be armed and willing to sacrifice their lives for their nation." She released his arm and sprang to her feet. Slapping her hand across her chest, she bellowed, "One nation, under God, invisible, with liberty and justice for those who will stand beside us and guide us through the night with a light from the dove."

Brother Verber edged down the pew until he figured he was out of her reach.

"What's more," she continued, "they must be heavily armed. I cannot continue to take sanctuary here while those who are determined to destroy us rampage across the countryside, raping women and slaughtering innocent children."

"They're doing that?"

She swung around and pointed her finger at him. "Don't argue with me, Willard. How many times must I tell you that? Quit this blubbering and pay attention. The left-wing media would like you to think that everything is fine and dandy, but they know what's really going on. I've been a senator for" — she hesitated — "a long time. I don't know. Years. I've been on committees that deal with national security. Important committees. Some branches of the government don't want you to know the truth. Mail carriers read your postcards and report to the CIA. Garbage collectors sift through your discarded bank statements in search of suspicious donations to charities that are fronts for communist organizations. Grocery stores keep track of your purchases. Worst of all, teachers indoctrinate their students with liberal propaganda and fog their minds with sacrilegious theories. They even instruct them on how to have sex!"

Brother Verber's jaw dropped. "Teachers?"

"If citizens like you realized the enormity of the crisis that we as a nation are facing, you would rise up. Now is the time for all good men, not cowards and fools. Can I count on you, Willard Verber? Do you love your country? Will you sacrifice your life?"

"Yes, ma'am," he said hastily. "What say we go over to the rectory and have a glass of wine while we decide what-all to do? Sacramental wine, that is. The Good Lord might feel inclined to offer a suggestion or two, if he's not busy."

"Wine? Are you suggesting we indulge in alcohol when our very future is at stake? Don't you understand that they're already searching for me? Once they find us, you'll be praying for a quick and painless death."

She strode to the far end of the pew and back, her face contorted with concentration. He couldn't quite make out what she was saying to herself, but he could catch an obscenity every few words. Before he could point out that she was blaspheming, she turned and went out through the vestibule. The door banged shut. He sat for a long while, holding his breath and hoping she was gone for good. Although he'd always told himself he was a red-blooded patriot, he wasn't all that excited about the idea of sacrificing his life. Or having electrodes attached to his privates, if it was gonna come to that.

He took out his handkerchief and wiped the sweat off his neck. Her story might be true, her being a United States senator and all. She'd been mighty agitated, though, spewing spittle when she talked and waving her hands around like a band director. He'd never taken much interest in politics, but her name often appeared in quarterly newsletters from the seminary, citing her as a beacon in the fight against immorality. Immorality was something he knew well, having dedicated himself to helping his flock by learning all he could about the insidious forces of Satan. He subscribed to magazines that turned his stomach, just so he'd know what evils lurked between the covers. He prowled alleys and preached to loose women, trying to persuade them to abandon their wanton ways and seek redemption. He was a patriot, but his loyalties were to the Lord.

Which meant he didn't have to put on a beret and go crawling across some muddy pasture. Once again, he fell to his knees, but this time he was praying that he'd seen the last of Senator Swayze.

Harve and I had exchanged seats so he could call his office and try to get a dog to track Alexandra Swayze. He was scowling when he hung up. "I got good news and bad news. What do you want first?"

"What do I want first?" I said. "First, I want to get in my car and drive to a certain campsite by a lake. I want to listen to the birds. I want to watch the sunset. And the next morning, I want to drive toward Canada and never look back."

"By yourself?"

"That, Sheriff Dorfer, remains to be seen. So what's the bad news?"

"The K-9 corps is out for the afternoon, down by Hangnell searching for a little kid that strayed from the backyard. The best we can hope for is tomorrow morning, and that's assuming they find the kid today."

"Okay, then let's have the good news," I said.

"The translator is on her way, and should be here in the next fifteen or twenty minutes. Name's Norberta. You may have a problem with her. Her contract says she's on call whenever we need her, but she's supposed to be in a wedding tonight and she isn't happy about having to come all the way out here."

"I'm not exactly dancing on the desk, in case you haven't noticed. Based on what you told me, I doubt the employees will have much to say. She ought to be able to get home fairly soon."

Harve rocked back in my chair, but not so far as to hit the wall. "You've been acting real strange lately. Even Les noticed it. I know it's none of my business, but if there's something you need to tell me, I wish you'd spit it out."

"I don't allow spitting in my office," I muttered. "I'm just feeling edgy, that's all. Maybe I've been here too long. I was bitter when I got here, but I'm over the divorce and now I'm . . . I don't know, restless. Part of me wants to redecorate my apartment, and the other half wants to get out of Dodge once and for all." I stopped before I told him about my fainting spell in the surgical suite. He was in his avuncular mode, but he couldn't be trusted not to use the admission against me the next time he got pissed off.

"Up to you," he said tactfully, "but you might want to ease up on the second helpings. You're starting to look more like a

Maggody housewife than a former big city socialite."

My eyes narrowed. "What's that supposed to mean?"

"Nothing, nothing at all. Whatever's been going on at the Stonebridge Foundation will get cleared up before long. Hell, you may have a signed confession before that kid in Hangnell is found taking a nap under a bush." He hurriedly got up and put on his hat, which made him look like a stereotypic dumb southern cop in a bad movie. "Give me a call later, you hear?"

"Sure, Harve." I waited until he left, then took my rightful spot behind the desk and pulled out a legal pad to make notes about Vincent Stonebridge, the Connecticut drug pusher; Brenda Skiller (aka Alice Cutchens); and Walter Kaiser, wayward hippie in a time warp. This isn't to say I wasn't fuming inside.

"Yo, Earl," called Jim Bob as he went into the house. The stench stopped him in his tracks. It was an unappetizing hodgepodge of spoiled meat, urine, and stale sweat. It was a helluva lot worse than the Dumpster out back of the supermarket. Battling his instinct to get out of there damn fast before he puked, he forced himself to go on into the kitchen.

Earl was seated at the table, wearing a dirty undershirt and trousers smudged with everything but blood. It was obvious he hadn't taken a bath or shaved in a long while. Bread crumbs and half-eaten bananas and apples had been discarded on the floor. Flies hovered over the crusted remains of a casserole. What might have been a meatloaf was covered with blue fuzz. Gnats were feasting on an open can of chili with a fork stuck in it. It wasn't hard to see that Earl had been drinking. The counters were cluttered with empty whiskey bottles, crumpled beer cans, and quart jars that had once contained moonshine.

"Whattaya want?" said Earl, staring at the jar in his hand.

Jim Bob stayed in the doorway. "I just came by to see how you was doing. It don't look like Eileen's come back."

"Ain't you a clever sumbitch."

"Whatever you say, Earl. Some of the boys are getting together tonight to play poker. You interested?"

Earl's head swiveled so he could glare at Jim Bob. "Do I look like I wanna play poker?"

Jim Bob tried not to stare at Earl's mossy teeth and oily chin. "Hey, us men got to stick together. You want Eileen to show up and find you like this? She'll figure you're nothing but a big fat baby pining away for its mama. The next thing you know, you'll be mopping the floor and asking her permission to take a crap. You got to shape up, Earl. Clean up this gawdawful mess, then take a shower and put on some decent clothes. I'll tell Mrs. Jim Bob to fix us some thick sandwiches and apple pie. Then, tomorrow or whenever Eileen waltzes in, expecting you to be moping like a sickly hound, you'll be sitting in front of the TV watching a ball game, drinking beer, and eating chips. Maybe you'll notice she's back, or maybe not. And if you're gonna show her just who wears the pants in the family, you make damn sure the pants ain't soiled. I'll come by at seven and pick you up."

Earl grunted. Jim Bob took this as agreement and hurried outside to gulp down some fresh air. He sat in his truck and did some calculating. He'd lined up a total of six players, but there was room for one or two more. He was reluctant to invite doddery ol' Hirem, who'd fall asleep by eight o'clock, or Seldom Buchanon, who farted every time he got a decent hand. He finally decided to see if he could track down Big Dick McNamara over at the body shop in

Emmet. Big Dick could even bring his boy, who was gettin' old enough to act like a grown man.

Despite what he'd said to Earl, it might not be a real good idea to order Mrs. Jim Bob to fix food for the poker game. He took a swallow of whiskey from the pint bottle in his glove compartment, then drove toward the SuperSaver to tell the flabby sows at the deli to put together a fine spread. It'd be store-bought, but at least he wouldn't have to get into it with Mrs. Jim Bob.

15

I stuck a note on the PD door that said I'd be back shortly, then drove around town, looking for Alexandra Swayze. Nothing much seemed to be going on at the Pot O' Gold trailer park, except for a pack of grubby children running wild. Eula Lemoy's undergarments flapped on a clothesline. The manager was lugging trash bags out of one of the trailers, but didn't spot me. It was not Alexandra's kind of place. The picnic tables in front of the Dairee Dee-Lishus were occupied only by a few quarrelsome crows. The parking lot at Ruby Bee's was thinning out as the lunch crowd left. The SuperSaver was as busy as usual on a Saturday afternoon. I considered driving by Dahlia and Kevin's house, but I was afraid she'd come thundering out the door and throw herself in front of my car.

When I gave up and returned to the PD, a small woman with short dark hair was waiting beside a monstrous SUV. She wore jeans and a baggy sweatshirt, and was obviously not pleased to be called away from the prewedding festivities. Before I could get out of my car, she climbed into the passenger's side and said, "Let's get this over with; I've got a hair appointment at three. You're Arly Hanks, right? I'm Norberta Oseguerra. I don't want to hear what this is about. You tell me what to ask, I do it, and then translate. *¡Vamanos!*"

I didn't need her to translate the last word. We drove in silence to the Stonebridge Foundation. The gate was closed, but swung open after I identified myself on the squawk box. I parked in the back, and we came in by the pool. Deputy Quivers was sitting bolt upright in a chair, but he looked guilty, so I assumed he'd been napping. "Did they feed you lunch?" I asked him.

"Yes, ma'am, but I couldn't make out what it was and I was scared to eat it. Do you think I could go over to Ruby Bee's and grab a quick bite?"

"Try the catfish," I said. Norberta was at the edge of the garden, admiring some sort of flowering bush. I tapped her on the shoulder. "I'll have someone round up the Mexican employees, and we'll question them out here, if that's okay with you."

"I wish I could get my peonies to bloom like this."

I left her and went to Stonebridge's office. His door was open, and he was on the phone, extolling the virtues of the facility and the bucolic marvels of the Ozarks. There was desperation in his voice; he sounded as though he would have sold his soul to Mephistopheles in exchange for a licensed psychiatrist. A half-empty bottle of brandy and a glass were within easy reach.

Brenda Skiller's door was locked. I continued into the main building and found her in the office behind the reception desk. Except, of course, she wasn't Brenda Skiller, who was either in an urn on her niece's mantel or in a cemetery — both of which were preferable to a backyard. I decided to keep the information to myself for the time being.

I tapped on the door to get her attention, then said, "The translator is here. Please send the employees out to the pool area."

Brenda dropped the clipboard she'd been holding. "What about Alexandra Swayze? Have you found her? I read the entry in her journal. We can't have her out there in the mental state she's in. She could harm herself."

"Or worse," I said, thinking about

Estelle's missing gun. "I drove around, but I didn't see her. She may be holed up in somebody's storage shed, or hiding in the woods. The best we can do is get a police dog out here first thing in the morning. As soon as I question the employees, I'll go back to Maggody and keep searching for her."

"Three of the orderlies are here now, but only two of them were on duty that night. The fourth orderly drove some of the women back to the motel. He should be back in ten minutes." She picked up the clipboard and clutched it to her chest as if it were a life preserver. Stonebridge had sounded desperate, but she sounded perilously close to hysteria. "We have to keep functioning, you know. The patients are our responsibility. Toby was so upset that I told him he could work out in the gym for the rest of the afternoon, even though I couldn't find Walter to supervise. Dr. Dibbins was very uncooperative when I went in to administer his daily enema, and is refusing to do anything except listen to his opera CDs. The Hollywood brat has been prowling around like a stray cat. I had to shoo her back to her suite half a dozen times. She's currently watching videos in the day room. But I can promise you one thing — they're all back on their meds. I myself stood over them and made sure they swallowed every single tablet and capsule."

"It's good to know you finally decided to lock the barn door. I'll be by the pool." I looked at her for a moment, envisioning her digging graves in a backyard. It was not hard to cast her in that role. After I finished with Norberta's services and sent her back to have her hair done, I definitely was going to have a chat with Brenda about identity theft and prison food. And Walter, too, when he showed up. Although his whereabouts were not my first priority, I hadn't spotted his van in Maggody. I suspected he was eating ribs and drinking beer at one of Stump County's less savory taverns.

Deputy Quivers had wasted no time in heading off in pursuit of lunch. Norberta was not in sight, presumably having been lured into the garden by the prospect of more peonies, but I could call for her when an interviewee showed up. I sat down and tried to sort through what I knew — and didn't know. For one thing, sweet Molly Foss wasn't as saintly as Randall Zumi had claimed. She'd played the ingenue to the hilt, but her track record was spotty. It was obvious that she was open to bribery. She'd lingered after the staff meeting, then slipped into Toby's suite. He was probably right in claiming she'd led him on in hopes of forcing him to pay for her silence. He had a motive to kill her, but so did Brenda Skiller (as I'd decided to keep calling her) and Vincent Stonebridge if she'd made it clear to either one of them that she'd go public with a charge of attempted rape unless she was paid off. The Stonebridge Foundation would lose its precious anonymity, as well as its credibility as a rehab center. Maybe she'd threatened Randall, and the disillusionment had pushed him over the edge. I couldn't fit Walter Kaiser into the scenario, but he had disappeared and was therefore suspect.

Or, I thought, perhaps Alexandra Swayze had concluded that Molly was part of the conspiracy. Eliminating the gatekeeper would lead to confusion, and give Swayze a better chance to escape. That was based on the presumption she was capable of lucid thought. I dearly hoped she was.

The orderly who'd been minding the desk earlier approached me, his expression wary. Norberta emerged from the garden at the same time. I gestured at the chairs, and the two sat down. I asked Norberta to find out his name.

"*Guillermo, señorita,*" he said, looking at me.

377

"Ask him if he was on duty on Thursday, the night Molly was killed by the fountain," I said to Norberta. "And what, if anything, he knows about the patients and their treatment."

They had a lengthy, incomprehensible conversation, then she said, "Yes, he sits at the front desk every night until six the next morning. He responds if the patients press their buzzers for attention. A few times he's had to wake one of the doctors if a patient was unable to sleep and needed medication. He doesn't understand much of what goes on, and he's reluctant to offer many opinions. He thinks the fat man is amusing in a gruff way, like an uncle he has back in his village. The others are rude. He was at the desk when the girl was found dead."

I agreed with his assessment of the patients. "Did he see or hear anything in the hall that night around ten o'clock?"

Norberta asked him, then listened to his reply. "He heard doors open and close. Low voices, male and female. No one came into the reception room."

I hadn't expected to get that lucky. "Ask him about the little bottles in the room at the end of the unfinished wing."

An even lengthier conversation took place. This time Guillermo was alarmed, his eyes darting and his scarred hands trembling. Norberta kept pressure on him, sometimes shaking her head and leaning forward to hiss at him. Finally she sat back and said, "The little bottles, or *'las pequeñas botellas de whisky,'* as he calls them, were in a box outside the kitchen, where the garbage is set to be taken away by the cook and his helpers. He refuses to say who found them, but all of the men and a couple of the women have been enjoying them. The food they're served here is dreadful, he says. They do some cooking at the motel, but they have no access to liquor."

"Did they find any drugs in the box?"

"He says not, just the bottles and food. He's worried he'll be accused of theft."

"Please assure him that he won't, and ask him to send out whoever found the body in the garden," I said. After she'd done so and Guillermo had returned inside, we waited at the table. I'd expected her to be at least a little bit curious, but she seemed content to gaze at the garden. After a few minutes, another orderly appeared. He was short and wiry, with sharp features that reminded me of a fox. I'd seen him before, pushing a cart with stacks of clean towels. Like Guillermo, he was wary.

"Me llamo Rodolfo," he blurted out, having been briefed by his compatriot. *"Sí, encontré el cuerpo muerto por la fuente. Ella era una mujer joven, muy agradable."*

Norberta smiled. "Yes, he found the body by the fountain. She was a nice woman, very pretty." She asked him questions, listened to his responses, then added, "His job is to mop and wax the floors, sweep the sidewalks and areas around the pool, and wipe off the tables and chairs out here. The birds . . . ah, leave droppings. He's not sure of the time, but around four he decided to have a cigarette. He was afraid that Dr. Skiller — the *bruja,* or witch, as he calls her — might catch him if he stayed near the pool, so he went into the garden. As soon as he found the body, he went to Dr. Stonebridge's door and woke him up. That's all he knows."

"Ask him," I said slowly, "if he saw anyone between ten and midnight."

She turned to Rodolfo and quizzed him. At first, he shook his head, but after a moment he nodded and said something. Norberta was finally beginning to sound somewhat curious as she said, "He says the doctor with the long hair came out of his office about two hours after it got dark and wandered around for a while, then sat down at this table and stared at the pool. Eventually he went out to the parking lot, but didn't drive off. Rodolfo isn't positive, but he thinks he may have heard voices from that direction. They were whispering, so he isn't sure if they were male or female."

I thought about this for a moment. Maybe Toby Mann did have an alibi — unless the second person had been Molly. Walter had claimed to have little interest in her, but he'd admitted that the two of them had parted on hostile terms. He could have been a lot angrier than he'd implied. A woman scorned was purportedly a dangerous creature, but testosterone could be a potent drug. Ask Genghis Khan or Alexander the Great.

"What time did he hear this?" I asked.

Norberta relayed the question, but even I could translate Rodolfo's shrug.

I took a final shot. "Does he, or any of the others, know the names of the patients or why they're here?"

She asked him, but once again he shook his head and shrugged. She persisted, and after a long exchange, she sent him away and said, "He suspects one of the male patients is a professional athlete, but that's about all. Marisela, a maid, worked in a border town in Texas a few years ago and claimed that she'd seen one of the female

patients in a movie shown on TV one afternoon. They all agree the patients are here
because they're crazy."

"No argument from me," I murmured. "I
don't guess there's any reason to question
the others, since they weren't on duty that
night. I'll take you back to your car so you
can get ready for the wedding."

I dropped her off at the PD, then resumed
my search for Senator Swayze. I wasn't
about to go door-to-door and risk getting
shot between the eyes by one of Mrs. Jim
Bob's militia ladies. If the senator had gone
up on Cotter's Ridge and stumbled onto
Raz's still, no one would ever find her. The
best I could hope for was that she'd hitched
a ride out of town. If not, we were in for a
rough night.

"Just smile," whispered Ruby Bee as she
and Estelle walked down the motel parking
lot to the units at the end. She was carrying
an apple pie fresh from the oven; Estelle had
a pan of cornbread that had been liberally
laced with jalapeño peppers on account of
everybody knowing how Mexicans like
spicy food. Two women were sitting outside
on a bench made of concrete blocks and a
plank. One of them was wrinkled and
plump, with a few white hairs mixed in her

neat black bun. She looked like she might prove to be ornerier than Perkin's mule, given half a chance. The other was younger and had a flat sort of face, like someone had squashed her features when she was a baby. A gawky boy sat on the ground nearby, a guitar in his lap. All of them stared as Ruby Bee and Estelle joined them.

"This is for y'all," Ruby Bee said loudly, pausing between each word. She put the pie on one end of the bench and beamed broadly at them.

"And this, too," Estelle said as she set down the cornbread.

The older woman nodded, and the younger one smiled timidly. The boy did not respond, although he was watching them like they were some sort of wild animals.

Ruby Bee nudged Estelle and whispered, "Go ahead and say what we planned."

Estelle gulped, then managed to say, "Bonos dee-as."

"Buenas días," said the older woman, her expression stony. *"Muchas gracias por sus regalos."*

"That means thank you," Estelle said.

Ruby Bee snorted. "I figured that out by myself. Now go on."

Estelle opened the pad where they'd

383

written down significant words and phrases. *"¿Como está usted?"*

Apparently Estelle's accent was hard to decipher, but after the two women had a whispered consultation, the older one said, *"Muy bien, gracias. ¿Y usted?"*

"That means fine, thank you, and how are you doing," Estelle said, proud of her success. "This one's gonna be a mite trickier." She took a deep breath, squinted at her notes, and painstakingly read aloud each word. *"Me llamo Estellita. Esta es Ruby Bee."*

"Me llamo Marisela," said the younger one, looking pleased with herself. *"Su nombre es Ofelia, y su nombre es Miguel."*

"Pleased to meetcha," Ruby Bee said. "Okay, Estellita, we're making progress. Now ask them about the celebrities' names."

"Easy for you to say." She smiled at the three foreigners. *"Los* patients *en el* hospital. What are *sus nombres?"*

Indeed, it was more than a mite trickier for the women. They gestured for Miguel to join them. After a discussion, Ofelia said, *"¿Los pacientes en el hospital, si? ¿Sus nombres?"*

"That's right," Estellita said, getting into it. She figured if she kept this up, she'd be speaking like a foreigner in no time flat. *"Sus nombres, por favor."*

"No sabemos."

Ruby Bee peered at their notes. "I don't see that. What does it mean?"

"Right offhand, I'd say it means they don't know," said Estelle. "Lemme try a few names and see if they get the idea. She took a deep breath and said, "Sharon *Piedra?* Is she a *paciente?*"

"Sharon *Piedra?*" echoed Marisela. *"¿Quien es ella?"*

Estelle drew a line through Sharon Stone's name. "Okay, then, what about Russell *Cuervo?* Is he a *paciente?*"

Marisela glanced at the other two, then looked up with a puzzled frown. *"¿Un pájaro negro? No hay pájaros en el hospital, señoras."*

Ruby Bee stepped forward. "You know, a crow." She tucked her hands in her armpits and flapped her elbows. "Caw, caw!"

"You're spooking 'em," Estelle said, getting frustrated. "Hush up and let me try another one. "What about Jude *Ley?*"

Ofelia stood up and crossed her arms. *"No somos criminales, señoras. ¡No rompimos la ley!"*

"Good work," muttered Ruby Bee. "Now you've got them thinking they broke the law. This ain't gonna work, Estellita. I got better things to do than scare these poor folks half to death. They're just trying to make a living, same as the rest of us. Now you tell 'em to have a nice day and let's go."

"You can give up if you want, Rubella Belinda Hanks, but I ain't ready to turn tail as of yet." She gave Ofelia, Marisela, and Miguel her most congenial smile, like she was a contestant in the Miss Stump County Watermelon Pageant. Doing her level best to enunciate each syllable of the phrases in her notepad, she asked, "Are any of *los pacientes estrella de cine, celebridades de Hollywood?*"

"*¿Celebridades de Hollywood? Si, señora,*" Marisela replied happily. "*Uno de los pacientes es Dawn Dartmouth. La ví en una película hace varios años. Ella entonces era mucho mas bonita. Ella es gorda y fea ahora.*"

"My goodness gracious," said Ruby Bee, gasping. "I didn't catch all that jibber-jabber, but I heard the name Dawn Dartmouth clear as day. Can you imagine that? Dawn Dartmouth, right here in Maggody! Well, right near Maggody, anyway, not a mile away from where we're standing. Ain't that something?"

Estelle fanned her face with her notes.

"Never in my life could I have come up with that. Dawn was the cutest little ol' thing when she wasn't much more than a toddler, and she had that impish smile that made me want to give her a hug. Remember when she sang that lullaby to her doll on Christmas Eve? I liked to have bawled my eyes out."

Ruby Bee jabbed at the notes. "Ask 'em who else is there."

This time Estelle had to take out the book and thumb through it until she found a dictionary at the back. She licked her thumb as she turned to the page she wanted. "*¿Los otros? ¿Celebridades?*"

While Ruby Bee and Estelle had carried on about Dawn Dartmouth, Ofelia had pulled Marisela aside for a terse conversation. Marisela, now chastened, kept her eyes lowered as she said, "*No sé, señoras. Ahora iremos a nuestros cuartos. Debo escribir una carta a mi familia. Buenas tardes.*"

"What's that mean?" demanded Ruby Bee, who'd been hoping to hear that Charlton Heston or somebody like that was out at the Stonebridge Foundation, too.

"If I was to guess, I'd hazard to say the last thing meant good-bye," Estelle said drily as the three Mexicans went into their motel rooms and closed the doors. "I have a feeling that older woman wasn't real pleased with Marisela for talking out of school like she did. Should we leave the pie and cornbread sitting here?"

"It'll be gone afore too long. That Miguel fellow looked real interested in it." As they walked toward the back door of the kitchen, she said, "I know Dawn was born in Arkansas, but I disremember where. Somewhere down by Arkadelphia, wasn't it?"

"In that neck of the woods," agreed Estelle. "The newspaper made a big deal about how she was from Arkansas when 'Rock the Cradle' became a big hit. She and her twin sister, I mean. What was her name?"

"Sunny, I seem to think. There was some law saying that children could only spend so much time in front of the camera, so they was always on the lookout for identical twins. It didn't matter one whit to me, since I couldn't tell them apart. They took turns playing . . . what was the name?" She allowed Estelle to go into the kitchen first because of her hard work trying to talk Spanish. "Tinkerbell?"

"Twinkle, I think they called her. Her TV family, that is. Just imagine how hard it must have been on those little girls to have three names. They had their real names, their actress names, and their name on the show. I'd have been mighty confused."

Ruby Bee decided to get started on the braised ribs on the menu for that evening. She put on an apron, then began to gather up what-all she needed. "Dawn made some movies after the show was canceled. Whatever happened to Sunny?"

Estelle chewed on her lip while she tried to recall. "It's kinda hazy, but I think she died when she wasn't more than thirteen or fourteen. The family didn't want any publicity, so there was nothing but an announcement from their lawyer that Sunny had passed away. I remember hoping it wasn't from some disease that ran in the family, like that mysterious ailment that killed all four of Ambrosia Buchanon's daughters."

"Who all just happened to be pregnant by Ambrosia's seventeen- year-old boyfriend. I wouldn't go so far as to call rat poison a 'mysterious ailment,' " Ruby Bee said as she started browning ribs in a skillet. "Now something like heart disease is different. What with Dawn and Sunny being identical twins, they must have shared all the same traits. Do you think Dawn could be at the Stonebridge Foundation on account of being real sick?"

"I'd like to think you aren't planning to show up at the gate with a pot of chicken soup," said Estelle, "because that's as far as you'll get. The only way we're gonna find out about Dawn is if you ask Arly."

"And she's gonna tell us? I swear, Estelle, sometimes I wonder if you was sitting under a hair dryer when the Good Lord was passing out the brains."

"I do not appreciate that remark."

Holding in a grin, Ruby Bee started browning a second batch of ribs. "Then why don't you ask her yourself?"

"Maybe I will," Estelle said loftily. She went out to the barroom and across the dance floor to the front door. By the time she reached her car, however, she'd realized it might be wise to avoid Arly for the time being. After a moment of consideration, she drove home and began to search in earnest for the gun.

Brother Verber liked to have wet his pants when the phone rang in the rectory. It was the third time since the senator had left the Assembly Hall. There was no way she could be calling, he told himself as he crouched in the hall. There wasn't a local directory where she could look up his number. Surely she'd forgotten all about him by now. Still, he ducked under the window as he went into the kitchen and found another bottle of sacramental wine, and stayed low until he was back in his bedroom. The blinds were closed just in case she decided to peek in the window.

He sat down on the bed, refilled his glass with wine, and sank back to mull over possible topics for his sermon in the morning. Something about the sanctity of the body, he thought, reaching under the covers to make sure no electrodes had been attached while he'd been dozing. Jesus had brought Lazarus back from the dead. There ought to be a way to use that.

"I must say I'm disappointed in all of you," Mrs. Jim Bob began after calling the meeting to order. She, Elsie, Eula, and Lottie, being officers, were seated at the table in the sun room. Joyce and Millicent were sitting on wicker chairs, while Heloise Vermer, the newest member of the Missionary Society, stood by the window, admiring the flowers in pots on the patio. Heloise was aware that she'd been black-balled several times over the last few years on account of rumors that she drank alcohol, so she was being mindful of her manners.

Mrs. Jim Bob continued. "We are now in more danger than ever. A young woman was murdered at the Stonebridge Foundation only two days ago. Had our surveillance not slacked off, this would never have happened."

"I don't see how we could have done squat from the persimmon tree across the road," said Eula. "All we could see was the front porch and driveway."

"And you can't see anything in the dark," Joyce pointed out.

"Besides," added Lottie, "you already said the girl was killed in the garden behind the building."

Mrs. Jim Bob tightened her grip on the gavel. "That is beside the point. Had the men in Maggody agreed to cover the night shift, one of them might have seen the murderer escape and apprehended him. Instead, we allowed them to continue drinking whiskey, watching ball games on TV, and shirking their obligations to our community." She held up her free hand. "I will admit that Jim Bob is among the worst of them. You would think that as mayor, he'd be the first to step forward and volunteer. He did not, despite all my prayers and appeals to the Almighty Lord to encourage him to do his duty."

"I hear he was doing his duty elsewhere," Eula said, snickering. "Out at the Pot O' Gold."

"As well as getting up a poker game," said Millicent, who was still irked by the argument she'd had with Jeremiah at noon. "Gambling is illegal, as well as sinful. It doesn't reflect well on this town when the mayor himself is encouraging good Christian men to indulge in this sort of sacrilegious activity."

Mrs. Jim Bob ignored Eula. "I do agree with you, Millicent, and I'll put a stop to it when Jim Bob comes home for dinner. The mayor is supposed to set a good example, not lead others down that dangerous path to eternal damnation. Brother Verber has been off somewhere all afternoon. When he gets back, I'll make sure he addresses gambling in the sermon tomorrow morning."

"His car's parked by the rectory," Elsie volunteered. "I happened to notice when I was driving over here."

All of them knew that Elsie always "happened to notice" every last detail of what anybody was doing, who they talked to at the supermarket, what they bought, and how often they skipped church. She was particularly keen on taking notes about what the high school girls were wearing or which of the boys slipped out of the gym for a smoke. She devoted an hour each day to calling their parents, as well as anybody else who might be interested. She'd had twenty-seven years of practice and missed very little.

"I am aware of that," Mrs. Jim Bob said coolly. "I have also called him several times, but he must have gone out for a walk to appreciate the Lord's handiwork. Let us each take a moment to reflect on the beautiful spring we have been blessed with this year." She lowered her head and tried to think how to nudge the conversation into the possibility of a female mayor.

"Oh, my God!" said Heloise. She pointed out the window. "There's somebody down there at the edge of the woods."

Reflection was put on hold while the ladies stood up and peered in the direction Heloise was pointing.

"I don't see anybody," said Lottie. She moved her purse to her lap and patted it to make sure she had her handgun next to her reading glasses and wallet.

"Me, neither," Elsie said, disappointed that she hadn't seen one of the mental patients flapping around like a lame duck.

"I'm sure I saw somebody," Heloise insisted. "It was a woman, dressed in blue."

Mrs. Jim Bob elbowed Eula aside so she could get a better look. "I hope you haven't been drinking today, Heloise. It can affect your eyesight, along with your judgment. The only thing I see is a blue jay on the top of the fence. Are you quite sure you didn't catch a glimpse of it?"

Heloise's eyes filled with tears. "I know exactly what I saw, and I don't care to be insulted like that. If you think I can't tell the difference between a woman dressed in blue and a bird, then — then you're the one who's been drinking!"

"How dare you?" sputtered Mrs. Jim Bob. "I never touch alcohol! I am a good Christian woman. I read the Scriptures every single morning while I have my coffee, and I keep a Bible in every bedroom. Just who do you think organizes the rummage sale every summer? Who makes sure there are paper plates for the potluck suppers on Wednesday after the prayer meeting? What's more, I pray for the little heathen children in Africa almost every night before I go to bed."

"You never touch alcohol?" Heloise shot back. "My Marvin drove by your house the morning after those Civil War reenactors left, and he said there were so many bottles they were spilling out of your garbage can."

Mrs. Jim Bob cast around for a diversion. "Didn't I hear that Marvin was arrested last fall for hunting without a license? Maybe you should worry more about his sinfulness instead of making wild accusations." She picked up the gavel and banged it on the table. "This meeting is adjourned! We won't have another meeting until I've had time to take a hard look at the membership roster."

No one dared speak. They picked up their purses, filed out of the sun room, and went to their respective vehicles. Lottie was disappointed she hadn't had a chance to fire her gun. Elsie was real sorry Mrs. Jim Bob had ended the meeting so abruptly, since she'd have liked to hear more about the liquor bottles. Lottie decided to go back to the high school and make sure Darla Jean and Heather were still hard at work on the plans for the exhibit at the county fair. Heloise was so furious she could barely get the key in the ignition. Millicent and Eula were walking side by side, both thinking hard.

In the kitchen, Perkin's eldest was holding on to the mop handle. She looked as if she was thinking, too, but it was hard to tell with her. More than likely, it was just gas.

16

❦

I stopped by the PD to see if Jack had left a message on the answering machine. He hadn't. I debated calling him, voted against it, and grabbed my overnight bag to dump in my apartment. Roy Stiver was sitting in a bent willow rocking chair outside the antiques store, dressed in overalls, lying in wait for a couple of tourists to stop. Most of them figured they could outwit an ol' country boy. For the record, Roy winters in Florida and collects first editions of nineteenth-century British poets.

"Hey," I said as I stepped onto the porch.

"Back so soon?"

I stopped. "Back from where?"

Roy stuck an unlit corncob pipe in his mouth. "Springfield, of course. I used to know a gal up there, name of Peggy Sue Kawalski. She was a right pretty thing, with big violet eyes, dimples, and a heart-shaped mouth. We'd go to a tavern out by a lake and dance till the sun rose over the moun-

397

tains. When she died from a spider bite, it darn near broke my heart. To this day, I've never danced again."

"Save it for the tourists. You seen anything peculiar today?"

"Depends on what you mean by 'peculiar.' Raz drove by with water sloshing out of the back of his truck, most likely in case Marjorie got dust up her snout and wanted to take a dip. There's something kind of unnatural about that relationship, if you ask me. 'Course, you didn't." He took a pouch of tobacco out of his pocket and filled his pipe. It took him two or three matches before he got it smoldering to his satisfaction. "There must have been a meeting of the Missionary Society at Mrs. Jim Bob's house a while back; all of the fine Christian ladies drove by, headed in that direction. Jim Bob's getting up a poker game for tonight, but it's Saturday, so that ain't peculiar. Joyce Lambertino stopped long enough to ask me if I'd seen Larry Joe today. I told her I hadn't, which is the truth, so help me God. I may have heard he was goin' fishing this afternoon with Piglet Buchanon, but I didn't actually see him."

I was getting impatient with all his hillbilly blather. "Have you seen an older woman with white hair?"

Roy puffed contentedly on his pipe. "Reckon I did. I went inside mebbe an hour ago to take care of some personal business, and I saw her out back in the pasture. For a minute, I thought it was Dahlia's granny, but this lady was tall and moving faster than a snake slitherin' through a coon carcass."

"Which way was she headed?" I asked.

"There a reason why you're looking for her?"

"Yes, Roy, there's a reason. Which way was she headed?"

"Toward Earl's house, but that don't mean she didn't keep right on going. That place is such a sty I can smell it from here. If Eileen doesn't get back afore too long, I'm gonna rent a bulldozer and flatten it. And if Earl's inside, it'll be no great loss. There are already way too many Buchanons in this county, and they breed like fruit flies. If I were you, I'd pack my bags and head for Springfield."

I forced myself to smile. "Thank you ever so much for your advice, Roy. It warms my cockles to know you take such an interest in me."

"You ain't got any cockles, and I'm not all that interested." He put a battered straw hat on his head and rocked back. "Why don't you run along and find this white-haired woman? I feel a snooze comin' on."

I stalked past him and climbed the steps to my apartment. It looked even crappier, now that I'd seen the apartments at the Stonebridge Foundation. I tried not to think of the condo I'd lived in during the brief duration of my marriage. It had been decorated by a professional, and attention had been given to every square inch of it, from the volumes of books arranged by color on the built-in bookshelves to the tidy tassels of the window treatments. The throw pillows color-coordinated with the ashtrays. The sterile kitchen with marble countertops, Tuscan floor tiles, and bronze sink fixtures.

Too bad it had also been furnished with a first-class asshole.

I dropped my bag on the floor, intimidating the cockroaches into taking temporary cover, and studied myself in the mirror. Harve's remark about second helpings had not been missed, nor had it been welcomed. I decided I looked pretty darn good. My hair was shiny, my complexion a bit softer and rosier than usual. I replaced a few wobbly hairpins to secure my bun, touched up my lipstick, and then went to the PD to fetch my car and drove out to Earl's.

Bags of garbage were piled in the back of

his pickup truck, and all the windows were open. From inside the house I could hear a vacuum cleaner. It was very curious, I thought as I peered through the front screen, not sure if I'd see Alexandra Swayze, Eileen, or Perkin's eldest, for that matter. I did not expect to see Earl in an apron. He'd changed into clean clothes and shaved — an amazing improvement from when I'd last seen him.

"Everything okay?" I shouted.

Earl turned off the vacuum cleaner and glared at me. "Whatta ya want?"

"I just came by to see how you were doing," I said. "I haven't heard anything new about Eileen, but I'll let you know when I do."

"It don't matter to me. Do as you please."

"One other thing, Earl," I said as he reached down to turn on the vacuum cleaner. "Did you happen to see a woman with white hair out in the pasture or creeping around your house? About sixty years old, maybe wearing some kind of blue outfit?"

"Nope." He flipped a switch and the vacuum cleaner began to roar.

I decided I needed a glass of iced tea to erase the memory of Earl Buchanon in a floral-print apron with heart-shaped pockets and a ruffle along the bottom, so I headed for the nearest watering hole. Ruby Bee glanced up as I came across the empty barroom. "Back so soon? Guess nobody's been murdered out there today. You must be getting bored."

I sat down on a stool. "How's Estelle doing?"

"She left an hour ago." Ruby Bee filled a mug with milk and set it down in front of me, then stood there with an insufferably complacent smile on her face. A cat that had just annihilated a nest of field mice couldn't have looked more pleased with itself.

"Really?" I said lightly, willing to play her game. "What's for supper tonight? More catfish?"

She fussed around with a dishrag, taking great care to wipe the already spotless bar, and hummed while she rearranged the metal napkin holders and pretzel baskets. She finally cracked. "I guess you're not the only one who knows the names of the celebrities out at the Stonebridge Foundation."

"I guess not," I said. "The doctors and physical trainer know the names, and presumably whoever delivered each of them knows the names, too. Family members are good at keeping track of that kind of thing, too."

"Listen up, Miss Sassafras Mouth," snapped Ruby Bee, "you ain't so smart. I know for a fact that Dawn Dartmouth is staying out there, most likely dying of heart disease. You may not remember her from that series she was in, but I do. I must have watched it every single Thursday evening for more than ten years. She and her sister were four years old when the show started, and cute as buttons. As they got older, Twinkle was all the time gettin' into mischief, but she always fessed up in the end. One time she found a litter of puppies in an alley and took them home. Her parents were besides themselves on account of not knowing what to do with nine puppies. In the end, the owner came to the door and was so grateful that she insisted on giving one to Twinkle. Of course Dawn and Sunny were supposed to be one person, but everybody in Arkansas knew better."

I was baffled. "Dawn and Sunny were one person?"

"I wish you'd pay more attention," Ruby Bee said. "Dawn and Sunny were identical twins. They were from some little podunk down by Arkadelphia. It was in the newspaper when the show first started."

"How did you find out that Dawn is at the foundation?"

She arched her eyebrows. She wasn't nearly as good at it as Estelle, but her effort was more than enough to rankle me. "I have my ways. What I want to know is if she's dying of a heart disease like her sister. You must have seen her. Is she all sickly and pale and breathless?"

"You're going way too fast for me," I admitted, taking a sip of milk. "I'll give you a medical update after you tell me how you found out about Dawn."

Ruby Bee complied in detail.

I'd finished the milk during her recitation. "The Mexicans must think you and Estelle are crazier than bedbugs. I can assure you that Dawn does not appear to have any life-threatening diseases. Do you understand the importance of not telling anyone else about this? The same goes for Estelle. Deal?"

"What if I say no?" she asked.

"Then I'll solve this case, and as soon as I've handed it over to Harve, I'll throw all my worldly possessions in my trunk and go live in a more congenial place. Antarctica comes to mind."

"You wouldn't! Why, that's worse than blackmail! Imagine saying such a thing to your own mother. I ought to take you out back and paddle your bottom."

"Try it," I said coldly.

She spluttered and blustered for a few minutes, dredging up all the terrible things I'd done as a teenager (she didn't know the half of it), and then, when she realized I wasn't impressed, simmered down. "I wasn't aiming to tell anybody, and neither was Estelle, so you just go on about your business."

As I went out the door, I heard her yell something about an autograph, but I pretended not to hear it. I drove back to the Stonebridge Foundation, which I could do with my eyes closed by now, and jabbed the button of the box until the gate opened. I parked in back and came through the arch. Deputy Quivers had been replaced by yet another rookie, this one scrawnier than Kevin Buchanon and likely to be no brighter. I acknowledged him with a flip of my hand and knocked on Dr. Stonebridge's office door. When I received no response, I opened the door.

Vincent Stonebridge did not look any perkier than he had earlier, and the brandy bottle was empty. He gave me a bleary look. "Ah, Chief Hanks. Have you any good news to report?"

"Not yet," I said. "Were any drugs missing from the cabinet in the room off the surgical suite?"

"Not so much as an aspirin. Randall must have brought the pills with him."

"I need the key to the file cabinet with all the medical records."

"I can't do that. Doctor-patient confidentiality and all that bullshit. Would you like a drink? I think I have another bottle of this very fine brandy in my apartment. We can put on a CD and enjoy some music, get to know each other better. You're not a bad-looking woman, although you could use some work around your eyes. As the muscles age, they lose their elasticity. Maybe a couple of inches off your waist. Your boobs are nice and plump, though. I'll bet they're real firm."

I waited until I could trust myself, then said, "Give me the key."

"Oh, all right, if you insist." He battled with the top drawer and finally managed to open it. He tossed a key ring onto the desk and watched as it slid across the surface and over the edge. "Oops," he said with a giggle.

I picked up the key ring and left before he offered further assessment of my body. The reception desk was manned by a different orderly, one I hadn't spoken to. I veered behind him and unlocked the door to the office. I was worried that he might rush off to find Brenda, but if he was perturbed, he was doing a fine job of hiding it. I tried several keys until I found the one that opened the drawer marked "Records: Confidential." The printing was precise; I had no doubt Brenda had wielded the pen. I pulled out all four of the patients' files. Rather than risk having her catch me, I took them down the hall to Alexandra's suite and quietly closed the door behind me. I put the files on the coffee table and found Dawn's.

Ruby Bee's recollections were fairly accurate. Dawn (née Janine Louise Dartsmercher) was born in Stubbett, Arkansas, had become a child star in a popular sitcom, and later descended to Hollywood's B-list (or C-list, if there was one). The records that had been sent by her L.A. physician made no reference to any kind of potential health problems beyond dependency on alcohol and recreational drugs. I had no idea why Ruby Bee had come up with heart disease.

I read through the rest of the file. Dawn's sister Sunny had been diagnosed with depression and schizophrenia ten years ago, and died in a hospital. Randall saw this as a significant factor in Dawn's alcoholism, along with her hatred of her mother and fantasies of sexual abuse. One very screwed-up kid, I thought.

Somewhere in the hall a door opened. I held my breath as footsteps passed in front of Alexandra's suite, paused, and then continued. My reaction was ludicrous, since I had every right to be in the building until the murder was solved — but if it had been midnight and I'd been reading by flickering candlelight, I would have screeched like an owl.

Once I'd come to my senses, I read through the other three files. Randall was concerned about Toby's temperamental outbursts and was contemplating additional medications. Walter was worried that Toby was going to take a swing at him. Stonebridge had convinced Dr. Dibbins to sign consent forms for various surgeries that would suck, tuck, and tighten his torso as his weight dropped. Later, Stonebridge would get to work on the face. Unfortunately, none of the procedures would diminish his ego. Alexandra Swayze had been cooperative and seemingly willing to go along with her treatment. She'd signed a form for a face-lift and a chin job. Randall was still trying to persuade her to acknowledge her addiction to prescription pills. All of them were subjected to a myriad of medications, as well as Brenda's vitamins, supplements, and mysterious elixirs. Dibbins and Dawn were on restricted diets, while Alexandra and Toby were swilling protein shakes in addition to their meals.

I set aside the files and leaned back on the comfy cushions. The information about Dawn Dartmouth's roots was interesting, but not relevant. Stubbutt was at the bottom of the state, at least a seven-hour drive from Maggody. Arkansas's population was less than three million, and more often than not, the fabled six degrees of separation could be whittled down to three, sometimes two. Her lawyer had recommended the Stonebridge Foundation, perhaps pocketing a fee, so her return to Arkansas was liable to be a coincidence.

Another coincidence came to mind. I took the files back to the office and replaced them in the proper drawer. The orderly was hunched over a paperback book, the epitome of see no evil, hear no evil, tattle no evil. It would have been futile to ask him about Brenda's whereabouts, so I went down the hall to her office.

The door was not locked. As I entered, she looked up from her precious clipboard, which was meticulously centered on her desktop, and said, "You're back, I see. I don't suppose you found . . . ?"

"Still looking. She was seen two hours

ago, skulking across a pasture. How did all of you miss her increasing paranoia? She must have been terrified about this impending diabolical chip implant."

"She's a politician," Brenda retorted hotly, "so you can't blame us. They have coaches who teach them how to lie. If it was in her party's best interest, she'd look you straight in the eye and swear that Canadians are poised to invade this country. She'd claim that the *Challenger* was shot down by Chinese missiles and that earthquakes in California are caused by secular humanists opening vineyards in Napa Valley. Politicians have neither consciences nor souls, Chief Hanks. Most of them are borderline sociopaths."

I willed myself not to mention certain transgressions in her past. "Let me ask you something else. Did Randall bring those undersized bottles of gin with him from Little Rock? They're not exactly cost-efficient or convenient. On airplanes they're four or five dollars a pop. You can buy a fifth for the price of a handful of them."

"Randall told me that he rarely drank anything but wine. He was so tense once the patients arrived that I suggested he have a cocktail in the evening. He'd developed a taste for gin and grapefruit juice in his student days, he admitted after some prompting. I assured him that the additional vitamin C would cancel out the deleterious effects of the alcohol."

"So you gave him the gin?"

Brenda's face flushed. "Yes, it so happens that I did give him half a dozen bottles. He must have decided the gin and grapefruit juice would cover the bitter taste of whichever pills he chose to end his life. I should have sensed how stressed and despondent he was. I do not take responsibility for his suicide, however. He was a weak man who never once stood up to his wife and her family." She produced a tissue from a drawer and dabbed her eyes. "Vincent has his weaknesses, too. He could have made a fortune in L.A. if he'd practiced his craft more prudently, but he ran patients through his surgery as if they were body parts on an assembly line. The richer the patient, the higher his fee. It was no wonder he couldn't follow up on them." She stopped long enough to blow her nose. "Do you want to know the real reason why he lost his license to practice in California?"

"Sure," I said. She was sounding as though she'd dipped into one of the patient's paper pill cups. I sat down across from her and waited.

She licked her lips. "This has to stay between the two of us. Vincent did a few procedures on the trophy wife of one of the state board members — professional courtesy, as it's called. Well, not only did he enhance her lips and shoot her up with Botox, he also became sexually involved with her. I'm not saying it doesn't happen often, but in this case, Vincent underestimated his colleague's outrage and his appetite for revenge."

"How do you know all that?" I asked.

"I heard the gossip when I attended a seminar where Vincent spoke about psychological problems that could arise after cosmetic surgery. Not that he cared, of course, but he received a speaker's fee and the seminar was held in Las Vegas. Later I stopped him in the hall to ask a question about a topic in his lecture, and he ended up offering me this job. He met Molly in Las Vegas, too, at an AMA convention. I wonder how long it took for the two of them to end up in his penthouse. An hour?"

"They were sleeping together before the Stonebridge Foundation opened?"

Her laugh was harsh. "They celebrated the opening on the eve of the patients' arrival. I could hear them in his office, groaning like animals."

"He didn't seem very upset about her death," I said.

"Why would he? She was a plaything, a doll with all the anatomically correct equipment. Curly blond hair and big blue eyes, an innocent country girl who could keep him amused out here in the boonies. I'd be surprised if Vince has ever had any kind of relationship with a mature woman with original ideas. Molly Foss could barely offer her opinion about the weather. Oh, I'm sure she was an enthusiastic partner in bed, but what were they going to talk about afterward — bowling?"

"I couldn't say. You said you gave half a dozen bottles of gin to Randall. Why did you have them?"

Brenda's flush deepened into mottled red patches. "It was unprofessional of me, but I didn't think it would cause any problems. As each patient arrived, a maid came to the suite to unpack. I was there to supervise, and confiscate the contraband. I disposed of the drugs in the sink in the storage room of the surgical suite. Dr. Dibbins was craftier than the others, but no more successful. One of his suitcases had a false bottom where he'd hidden all manner of high-calorie foodstuffs. He'd also brought more than twenty small bottles of gin. Rather than waste my time emptying each of them, I set some aside for Randall and put the rest of Dibbins's treasure trove in a box. That evening, I set the box out with the garbage behind the kitchen."

"I guess the patients didn't appreciate your thoroughness," I said.

"They could hardly protest, could they? Each of them knew precisely why he or she was coming here. There was one thing that did not reflect well on me. A maid found a bottle of some kind of whiskey in Toby's bathroom. I was quite sure I hadn't missed so much as a pill or tablet."

"Molly Foss must have smuggled it in for him. She seemed to have been doing little favors for all the patients, as long as they had the means to reward her."

"That slut," Brenda growled. "I didn't trust her the moment I first found her in the reception room, simpering about how thrilled she was to have the job. Vincent must have given her some idea of what we were intending to do here. For all I know, he told her who the patients would be. The conniving bitch may have been dull-witted, but she could see the potential for making a small fortune by taking advantage of these pathetic addicts — all of whom are very rich."

"Are you sure you didn't see Molly after you left the reception room Thursday evening?" I asked delicately. "Perhaps she came here to talk to you before she went to the garden, or something like that?"

"She wouldn't have dared come crying to me with her problems," said Brenda, her voice dripping with venom. "It's a lot more likely she found a way to sneak into Vincent's bedroom. As I said, it wouldn't have been the first time."

"But he wouldn't have killed her, if she was just a plaything."

"Maybe the sex got too rough. Vincent wouldn't have intentionally suffocated her, but if he got too carried away. . . . Once he realized what he'd done, he took her body out to the garden and left it there."

I considered her scenario. "What about the orderly who was sweeping around the pool and cleaning the furniture? He would have noticed."

Brenda curled her mouth into a smile that was downright sinister. "All Vince had to do was wait until the orderly went inside for a minute. The garden's only twenty feet from his door. It wouldn't have taken him ten seconds to carry her across the grass and onto a path." Her smile disappeared as she realized what she'd said. "Not that I believe it for a second. Vince likes to think he's a roguish Don Juan with the ladies, but he's a realist. His profits are more important to him than his penis. All of his financial assets are tied up in this venture; if it fails, he may end up doing discount face-lifts in a grimy clinic in Tijuana. No, Chief Hanks, I'm quite sure Vincent had nothing to do with this recent unpleasantness. It would be best if you determine that one of the employees is guilty and have him deported. Let the authorities down there deal with him."

It would have made for a tidy resolution if it were true, I thought as I went outside. But if I couldn't buy it, I sure as hell couldn't sell it to Harve or the county prosecutor.

Kevin took his break out on the loading platform. It was peaceful, with nuthin' but sparrows hopping around the Dumpster. His head ached something awful, partly on account of the whiskey Jim Bob had forced on him, but mostly from the tongue-lashing Dahlia had given him when he got home and she smelled his breath. What was even more humiliating was the way she'd grabbed the broom and chased him all the way down the road past Raz's shack. His luck being so bad, Raz and Marjorie had been sitting on the glider on the porch. He could still hear Raz's cackles ringin' in his ears — unless it was from getting whacked upside the head with the broom.

He'd slept on the porch, and there'd been no hope of getting any breakfast, so he'd made do with a Twinkie and a soda pop when he got to the supermarket. Lunch had been a greasy tamale from the deli. Now his insides was bubbling away like a kettle of lye soap. On top of everything else, Jim Bob had hunted him down a while back to remind him about the poker game that evening. If he told Dahlia, he figured he might as well move his clothes and toothbrush down to his pa's barn for the rest of the summer.

He started sniffling as he thought about his ma. There she was gallivanting around Wyoming, of all places. He couldn't imagine what she could be doing. He knew that his pa, Dahlia, and hisself was responsible for her running away like she did, and when she came back, he'd see to it that all three of them got down on their knees and said they was sorry. But they couldn't till she came home, and he weren't all that sure she ever would.

He looked up as a car parked at the bottom of the steps. Mrs. Jim Bob lowered the window and said, "Where's Jim Bob?"

"I dunno. He was here this morning, but his truck ain't here now, so I reckon he's not neither."

"Do you think I'm blind?"

Kevin scratched his head. "No, ma'am, 'cause you shouldn't be driving if you are. It'd be real dangerous. You might run into a tree and mess up your pretty car."

Mrs. Jim Bob pinched her lips together for a few seconds. "Where is Jim Bob? I need to speak to him right away."

"He must have gone somewhere," Kevin said, always eager to be helpful to the boss's wife.

"Did he say anything about where he was going?"

"Not to me, Mrs. Jim Bob. He jest thumped me on the back and told me not to be late to the poker game tonight. I was sittin' here tryin' to decide if I ought to —"

"He didn't mention the Pot O' Gold or maybe Farberville?"

"No, he jest thumped me on the back and —"

"Tell him to call home the minute he drags his sorry self back here." Mrs. Jim Bob glared as the window rose, then backed up and drove away.

"You kin tell himself yourself at the poker game at the antiques shop," Kevin called as her brake lights flashed. He got up and went back inside, still wondering what to tell Dahlia so's not to set her off again.

Alexandra Swayze, who was crouched behind the Dumpster, resumed nibbling on a bruised apple. Many a poker game had been played in the Senate building late at night, but the participants were graduates of Ivy League schools. She'd seen enough of Maggody to suspect that only a fraction of the residents had made it through high school. That was the fundamental flaw of a democracy, allowing the uneducated and the ignorant to cast ballots beside those who were better equipped to make decisions about the complexities of the twentieth century. Or the twenty-first. It was so easy to lose track of time when one was heavily drugged. After the revolution, she would disenfranchise voters whom she deemed unworthy. If they objected, then off with their heads! *Vive le révolution! Tout est juste dans l'amour et la guerre!*

Alexandra had not gone to an Ivy League school, but she had done extremely well in a boarding school in Switzerland. Her accent was impeccable, or so she'd been told.

I decided to give Dr. Dibbins one more chance before I hog-tied him in his bed and tortured him with Barry Manilow songs. I could hear the pleas of a delirious diva long before I reached his room. He was seated on his sofa, his head back and his lips slack, as though he could taste the music. He did not greet me warmly as I came into the suite.

"Ah, the avenging angel with the hayseed in her hair," he muttered as he clicked the remote control to turn off the CD player. "Your encroachments on my privacy have begun to annoy me. Your only flair, my dear, is in your nostrils. Please go pester someone who is witless enough to enjoy your company. It may take a long while, but I'm sure you can do it long before hell is completely frozen over."

I picked up a plastic CD case and read the title. "*Cosi fan tutte*, by some fellow named Wolfgang Amadeus Mozart. Is it any good? Fiddles and banjos and a washboard? There's nothing I likes better than some good ol'-fashioned music. Lemme get it out of the case so's we can play it."

"Put that down, you infidel!" he thundered.

"Would you druther I borrowed it from you? I'll take real good care of it, unless'n my blue tick hounds get ahold of it."

Dr. Dibbins began to wheeze. "Just put down the CD and step away."

I dangled it in front of him. "I will — as soon as we've had a little chat. Otherwise, you can kiss your tutti-frutti CD good-bye." I hung on to it as I sat down on the easy chair. "So, do you speak Spanish?"

"Of course not. It is the language of dusty peons and petty dictators in ill-fitting uniforms adorned with medals stolen from corpses. I speak adequate French and exquisite Italian. Does that satisfy your curiosity? Would you like my shoe size or preference in toothpaste? No, wait, you want the name and address of my editor. All small minds aspire to write great novels. Luckily, very few of them can type. Are you a thwarted Anaïs Nin or Maya Angelou? Gertrude Stein? Or better yet, Mary Shelley?"

"Don't push your luck," I said. "I can make it all the way to my car before you can make it to your feet, Dr. Dibbins, and I'll be taking this" — I flapped the CD at him — "when I go. Will you swear on Wolfgang here that you don't speak Spanish?"

"I do not speak Spanish. However, it is very similar to Italian, so I do understand it to a limited extent. When the maids and orderlies jabber in the hall or come in here to clean, I can decipher the gist of their conversation. They are not happy campers. The pay is much better than they could ever make in their village, but they resent their shabby living quarters and erratic schedules. Any other questions?"

"Do you wander around at night?"

His lips puckered as he stared at me for a long moment. "Miss Foss was kind enough to bring me a box of cigars after I'd offered her a not insignificant amount of money. Since that blood-sucking harridan would notice even a lingering vestige of smoke and demand I submit to a full-body search, I go out to the garden after everyone's tucked in bed for the night. There is a bench in the farthest corner, away from the exterior lights."

"Isn't there a guard with a dog?" I asked. Brenda had told me that only two orderlies were on duty that night, and since her information came from her clipboard, it was more reliable than the June flashfloods and August droughts.

"Only for the first few nights. It seems the dog is prone to bark loudly at anything that dares to twitch. I complained, as did the others. Now Rodolfo, who sits at the desk all night, takes the dog from the kennel once every two hours and they walk around the building. The dog is then locked up until the next foray. Rodolfo lacks the initiative to vary the routine. If I were inclined, I could set my watch by him."

"Were you in the garden Thursday night?"

"Yes, but I was delayed by activity in the hall. I do not wish my nocturnal meanderings to become topics of speculation and gossip. It is not easy for a person of my circumference to be inconspicuous. I prefer to be dismissed as reclusive, but in a charmingly eccentric manner, naturally."

I doubted any of the others would describe him as charmingly anything. "Describe this activity, please," I said.

"Oh, just a bit of bother, as far as I could hear. Libidinous chitchat between Molly and Toby before they retreated to his room for what one suspects was a logical progression into carnal intimacy. Dawn came out into the hall, as did Alexandra. If I may digress briefly, I am concerned about Alexandra's state of mind. As the week progressed, she seemed increasingly irrational during our conversations, and hinted darkly of some sort of catastrophe. She really should not be out on her own."

"Did you overhear the maids talking about her departure?"

"Heavens, no. I watched her slip out the gate this morning. It reminded me of that movie with Steve McQueen riding a motorcycle into a barbed-wire fence while pursued by Nazis. One could hardly help rooting for her to escape."

"Even though you thought that she was irrational?" I asked. "Weren't you a tad worried about her?"

Dibbins gave me a contemptuous look. "Why in god's name would I care about anyone but myself? Here I am, confined to a claustrophobic cell, deprived of the essentials of a cultivated lifestyle, badgered and bullied incessantly, forced to undergo humiliating procedures. I would have been delighted if Alexandra had returned with an assault weapon and assassinated the sorry excuse for a chef, the butcher of Hollywood, the Freudian slip, and the Mistress of Evil."

"I assume you're kidding."

"Assume whatever pleases you. Are we finished now?"

"No, Dr. Dibbins, we are not," I said. "Let's go back to Thursday evening. You said you heard Dawn and Alexandra in the hall. Could you hear what was said?"

"Dawn told Alexandra what was going on in Toby's suite. Alexandra, who does not approve of premarital sex or quite possibly any sex at all, was outraged. She hissed for a long while, then went back into her suite. I was about to make my move when Molly came out into the hall, obliging me to again wait. I was most irate by this time. Eventually she went into Dawn's suite, again sabotaging my intentions. After that, there was a period in which doors were opened and closed, and I heard footsteps. The door at the end of the hall became very popular. After fifteen minutes of relative placidity, I myself took the opportunity to exit through the same door. And before you interrupt with another inane question, I saw no one. I stayed next to the fence until I reached my sanctuary, and remained there for half an hour. After that, I returned here, put in my earplugs, and went to bed."

What he'd described pretty well matched Dawn's version of the events, although she'd failed to mention Alexandra's inclusion in the scenario. I put the CD on the coffee table in front of him, nodded, and left before he could return to his dying divas, all of whom were considerate enough to do so in front of an audience.

I needed a libretto.

17

I wanted to call Harve and hash all this over with him. Instead of driving back to the PD or ousting Rodolfo from his post in the reception room, I went down the sidewalk to Randall's office. The door was locked, but I used the master key to let myself inside. The blinds were closed, and the room was dim. I continued into the apartment.

The deputies had disturbed very little, but they hadn't been looking for anything in particular, since Randall's death had been attributed to suicide. The bed was made, the cushions on the sofa aligned. A desk, much smaller than the one in the office, was set under a window. On it rested a computer, a printer, and a short stack of medical tomes. The single drawer contained only the expected collection of paper clips, pens, pencils, and unused notepads. A wastebasket nearby was empty.

I moved on to the kitchenette, which could be hidden by louvered doors. In the cabinet I found a few plates, cups, glasses, a box of crackers, and a jar filled with tea bags. The pint-sized refrigerator was no better stocked; it held a plastic bag of mushy grapes, a lemon, a container of yogurt, and a carton of grapefruit juice. Randall must have been at the mercy of Brenda's menus and the chef's incompetence.

Brenda had given Randall six bottles of gin on Sunday. On Friday night, he'd been down to his last one. He'd needed it in the aftermath of Molly's brutal murder. Maybe that had been the final impetus to compel him to commit suicide. Brenda had mentioned more than once that he'd been depressed and under stress from his divorce and financial crisis. He'd told me that someone had searched through his private papers. Although it didn't seem probable, he might have had a secret as unsavory as Brenda's. Could he have anticipated being blackmailed? But if that were the case, then why would he have mentioned it to me?

I was suddenly overwhelmed by exhaustion. Yawning, I sat down on the sofa and rested my head against the back cushion. Granted, I hadn't gotten much sleep the previous night, but I'd never faded like this before — especially in the middle of a murder investigation. And a suicide investigation. And a missing person investigation.

When I opened my eyes, sunlight was still filtering through the blinds. I looked at my watch. My nap had lasted only thirty minutes, which meant I still had time to catch Harve in his office. I went into Randall's office and sat down behind the desk.

I was surprised when Harve answered with a surly, "Yeah?"

"You demote yourself to dispatcher?"

"That damned woman, whatever her name is, has a hide no thicker than onion skin. She's bawling in the bathroom. As much as I hate to say this, LaBelle's a sight easier to work with. So what's going on? You found that loony senator?"

I sighed. "No, she's still on the loose in Maggody. Somebody will spot her before too long, and I'll go collect her with a butterfly net. Have you made any progress with the suicide note?"

"Unlike those dumbass shows on TV, we don't have a handwriting expert on hand, any more than we have a lab with microscopes and tests tubes and all that crap. I sent the note to McBeen over at the hospital and asked him to show it to some of the doctors. He called back, said the best they could tell, it was really bad poetry, comparing her to a rosebud on a spring morning. McBeen said if he'd written it himself, he would have committed suicide to save himself from humiliation."

"McBeen's such a kindhearted guy."

"Yeah, and by the way, Zumi took a heavy dose of some barbiturate. McBeen estimated in the range of two hundred milligrams. Taken with alcohol and on an empty stomach, it was more than enough to kill a scrawny fellow like Zumi. He was a doctor, so he'd have known what he was doing."

"What about fingerprints on the bottle and glass?"

"Only his on the bottle. They were on the glass as well, along with a couple that belonged to the maid who cleaned his quarters every evening. She must have washed the glass earlier and put it away. You need to stop stewin' about it, Arly, and find out if Zumi was in the garden with the girl."

"I suppose so," I muttered. I brought him up to date on what I'd learned, gave him a minute to chew on it, then added, "So Toby and Dibbins have admitted they were outside the building, and according to one of the orderlies, so was Walter. I wouldn't begin to guess what Alexandra Swayze was doing. For all I know, she might have been crawling around the air ducts in the ceiling, trying to overhear Stonebridge and Brenda discussing when best to implant the chip. Both of them could have gone outside, too."

"You're leaving out Dawn Dartmouth," Harve said. "Sounds like she might have gotten lonely in there by herself."

"I'll ask her. Did you ever see her in the sitcom?"

"I don't go in for that kind of syrupy nonsense, but —" He stopped abruptly, as if he'd had some great revelation. To my regret, he said, "That damned woman has gone and gotten herself locked in the bathroom. She's pounding on the door and carryin' on like the toilet backed up and she's gonna drown. I'd better go see to it. Keep me posted, ya hear." He banged down the receiver, but not before I heard him yell, "Lordy, woman, you're gonna set off a riot in the cell block!"

I sat and gazed at a watercolor on the wall next to the front door. It depicted a bending river flanked by trees with autumn leaves, no doubt chosen to soothe a restless patient. It made me want to pee. After I'd availed myself of Randall's bathroom facilities, I did a quick inventory of the contents of the medicine cabinet. The only incriminating evidence was a tube of hair gel guaranteed to cover gray. I could sympathize, since I'd sprouted a few of them during my divorce.

I returned to Randall's desk and opened drawers until I found his personal files. One held legal documents and copies of correspondence between his attorney and that of his wife, all in chronological order. At the back of the files were letters from his wife, shrill and acrimonious, describing in venomous detail his failure as a provider, a father, and a husband. I would have burned them.

Another file had legal documents concerning a second mortgage on his house, notes for personal loans adding up to more than a hundred thousand dollars from a Mr. Rajiv Singh (most likely his father-in-law), a statement from an insurance company establishing that he had withdrawn the maximum against his life insurance policy, and a receipt for a Mercedes-Benz he'd sold to a private individual. I would have burned those, too.

At the bottom, I found a file with his college and med school transcripts, evaluations from his internships and residency, a copy of his board certification in psychiatry, and a résumé. He'd worked at a hospital in Virginia for two years, then been in private practice in Little Rock for three years before joining the staff at the state hospital. He'd attended the requisite number of seminars each year to maintain his certification.

It was boring enough to send me back to the sofa for another nap, but I replaced the files, stretched, and stood up. I needed to ask Dawn about the senator, who'd been out in the hall while Molly was in Toby's suite. Brenda had mentioned earlier that Dawn was in the day room. It was as good as any place to look for her.

I went outside, locked the door behind me, and had taken a couple of steps when Brenda called my name from the French doors.

"Come quickly," she said, visibly shaking. "I don't know what to do! I'm not a doctor, or even a nurse. I know I should do something —" she sucked in a deep breath — "but Vincent's . . . well, indisposed in his apartment. Hurry, for pity's sake!"

I caught her arm before she lapsed into hysteria. "What's wrong?"

"It's Dr. Dibbins! I can't wake him up! Don't just stand there and gawk. You have to do something!"

I tried to keep up with her as she dashed through the reception room and turned toward the suites. "Are you sure he isn't playing possum to alarm you?" I said to her back. "He has a twisted sense of humor."

"Well, if that's the case, he's gone too

far." She turned and went into his suite. "Dr. Dibbins, this had better be some kind of sick joke!"

I looked over her shoulder at the supine figure on the bed. His face was gray; saliva bubbled at the corners of his mouth. He was breathing, but the sound was abrasive, as if his lungs were coated with sandpaper. "You need to call nine-one-one right now," I said.

Brenda sank down on the end of his bed. "But what about the notoriety, the publicity? Even if we use a false name, someone will recognize him from his photo on the back of his books. Can't you do something?"

I stared at her for a second, then said, "Okay, I'll call nine-one-one, but it'll take them at least half an hour. You need to wake up Dr. Stonebridge."

"I tried," she wailed, tears rolling down the furrows in her cheeks. "He's sound asleep, with a bottle tucked under his arm. I did everything but bounce up and down on his stomach to rouse him. Even if I could get him to his feet, he's too drunk to help."

I left her to drip tears on Dibbins's feet and went to the front desk. The orderly's eyes were wide with alarm, but there was no way to explain. I called 911, told the dispatcher who I was, described Dibbins's symptoms, then gave precise directions to the foundation. I pushed the button to open the gate and was poised to go back to Dibbins's suite when Toby and Dawn came up the hall.

"Is something going on?" demanded Toby. "I heard Brenda shrieking."

Dawn smirked. "Her only two modes of communication are shrieking and snarling. Well, I guess you could add glowering. She doesn't need to wear a mask at Halloween to frighten away children."

"Dr. Dibbins is ill," I said, unamused. "I've called for an ambulance. The two of you need to wait in the day room."

"What's the matter with him?" asked Toby.

"It might be a heart attack. Please, just stay out of the way."

"No way," said Dawn. "I want to see him in agony after all the rude things he's said to me since the minute he got here. So I didn't go to college, or appreciate his stupid operas. That doesn't make me an idiot."

"Something does," Toby said. "Maybe you inherited it from your parents."

I jumped in before she could come up with a retort. "Enough of this. Toby, you go back to the gym. Dawn, you stay in the day room. If I see either of you again, I'll have the deputy on duty transport you to the county jail."

"I am so sick of being treated like a child!" said Dawn.

"Then stop behaving like one. You're not the star of this show." I left them bickering and went back to Dibbins's suite. His condition did not appear to have improved, but he was still alive. Brenda was dabbing his forehead with a wet washcloth and moaning under her breath. I left her to it and looked around the room. On the coffee table was a glass and a wine bottle that had once held perhaps two servings. "Where could this have come from?" I asked Brenda.

She looked back. "I don't know. Dr. Dibbins is allowed a glass of wine with dinner, but Vincent uses his private stock. I feel like I've seen that bottle, though."

"Could it have come from the stash in his suitcase?"

"Yes, that must be it. There were two or three of them. I asked Vincent if he wanted them, but he said he never drank domestic wine. I put them with the other items in the box. How could Dr. Dibbins have gotten one? Oh, dear, this is very much like what happened to Randall, isn't it?"

Indeed it was. "Was Dibbins taking any

kind of barbiturate for pain or to help him sleep?"

She unconsciously swiped her forehead with the washcloth. "I don't think so. Randall had him on a metabolic accelerator and a very mild sedative. I didn't approve, of course. Herbal remedies are safer and more natural. They're the product of generations of simple folk seeking relief. Even today, many —"

"Right," I said. "Who wouldn't prefer to suck a berry than swallow an aspirin?" Before she could respond — and she clearly intended to — I returned to the reception desk and called Harve.

This time a squeaky female voice answered. When I politely asked her to put me through to the sheriff, she did so without any of LaBelle's typical chattiness. Harve was not pleased with my report.

"What the hell's going on out there?" he roared. "Jesus H. Christ, is everybody gonna be deader than a doornail before morning? And how am I supposed to keep this away from the reporters? My ass is grass, and it's all your fault! All you had to do was figure out who strangled that girl. You should have had this wrapped up and tied with a pink bow twenty-four hours ago. Then I'd have gone fishing all day, and be at home by now, grilling steaks and having a cold beer. Just the other day Mrs. Dorfer had the butcher cut T-bones two inches thick. They're in the refrigerator, begging to be charred."

"It's good to know I've got your support, Harve. I'm going to send the deputy in with the wine bottle. Have it tested for fingerprints and call me back." This time I had the pleasure of hanging up on him.

I gestured to the orderly, who was cowering in a corner, to come back and sit down. "Everything is okay," I said. "It's okay. Do you understand?"

"O-kay," he whispered.

Brenda had abandoned her pose as a nurse and was sitting on the chair, her face buried in her hands. Dibbins was still breathing, but his complexion seemed even grayer. I told Brenda to watch out the window for the ambulance, then went into the bathroom and found a dry washcloth. I wrapped the wine bottle in it as carefully as I could, hoping I hadn't smudged any fingerprints beyond identification. Brenda was still huddled on the chair as I left. The siren would startle her into action.

Deputy Whatever was seated by the pool, smoking a cigarette. He ground it out and stood up as I approached with my precious bundle. "Nuthin' to report, Chief Hanks. I mean, nuthin' strange. The gal and the fellow came outside and went in where you are, then came back. They was snapping at each other like mongrels."

"Thank you for the detailed report," I said soberly. "This is a piece of evidence. I want you to treat it with tenderness and respect. Do not unwrap it under any circumstances. Take it to the sheriff's office and see that it's labeled properly and handed to whoever can dust it for fingerprints. Sheriff Dorfer is expecting you."

"I'm 'sposed to stay here, ma'am."

"Are you married, Deputy?"

"Yeah, me and my wife just celebrated our first anniversary last week."

"Does she admire your prowess in bed?"

He shuffled his feet. "That's kinda personal, ain't it?"

I held out the towel-wrapped bottle. "If you would like to continue to please her, do as I say. Otherwise, I'll haul you into a little surgery room right over there and find a scalpel. You'll end up singing soprano in the church choir. Any questions?"

He took the bundle and headed for his car. I waited until I heard him drive away at a good clip, then went to the day room. Dawn was curled on one of the leather sofas. A muted movie played on the TV screen, but she did not appear to find it compelling.

"How's Dibbins doing?" she asked without looking at me.

"It's hard to say. Medicine's not my field." I sat down on one of the chairs next to the conference table.

"I didn't mean what I said. When I get scared, I say horrid things without thinking. I don't like him, but I don't hope he dies or anything. Is Dr. Stonebridge in there with him?"

I considered being tactful, but it didn't seem worth the effort. "No, he's drunk, passed out in his apartment. He's been trying all afternoon to find a replacement for Dr. Zumi. I guess he hasn't had much luck."

"Why would anybody want to come to this nasty, backward state? Bunch of rednecks and sluts, all using outhouses and wiping their asses with pages from a catalog." She glanced up. "Not you, of course. You're probably from a nice, ordinary family."

"Absolutely," I said. "What about your family? You're from Arkansas."

She frowned. "Yeah, but only until I was three years old. It's not like I grew up here and went to a one-room schoolhouse. My sister and I had a private tutor. Our first house was small, but once the money started rolling in, my mother bought a mansion up on the hill overlooking Rodeo Drive. We had a chauffeur, a real chef, maids, and a hairstylist who came to the house every week to trim our hair."

"It must have been hard on you when the sitcom was canceled."

"Duh," she said, rolling her eyes. "There was some talk of a spin-off, but then my sister got sick. Every time I see a picture of those smarmy Olsen twins, I want to barf. Sunny and I were so much prettier. Sunny was smarter than me; she could have gone to college at some fancy East Coast school and gotten a diploma and all that shit."

"But she died," I said.

Dawn looked away. "I don't want to talk about it. This place is way spooky, like in one of those teen slasher movies. Jason and Freddie are probably hiding in the garden. First Molly got strangled, and then Dr. Zumi committed suicide, and now Dibbins is dying. What if he has a deadly virus? I just want to get out of here. Can you call my lawyer and talk to him? Tell him he has to make the judge let me go someplace else for rehab. I swear I'll stay there."

"Dr. Dibbins most likely had a heart attack. The paramedics ought to be here any minute. And Freddie and Jason aren't responsible for Molly's death."

"Was Dr. Zumi?" she asked, perking up. "Is that why he killed himself? Unrequited love and all that crap? Maybe he was out in the garden when she went outside after Toby tried to rape her. She cried on his shoulder and told him what happened. Instead of being mad at Toby, he got all furious because she went to Toby's suite in the first place. He strangled her, and then got so guilty that he killed himself, too."

"It occurred to me."

"Ooh, maybe I could write a book about it. Not me, but my agent could get a ghostwriter and I'll put my name on it. I could get back on some of the talk shows, maybe even in New York. I'll have to admit I was in rehab, but that would be okay. I mean, everybody in Hollywood does drugs. It's no big deal these days. I'm old enough now that my mother can't get her hands on the money."

"You might want to put this project on hold until after you go to court," I said drily.

"Well, you'll have to prove my theory's right. How long will that take?"

"I can't promise I'll wrap it up before the

441

next commercial, but I'm doing my best." I gave her a few minutes to enjoy the vision of her reclamation of fame and fortune, then said, "When you told me what happened in the hall Thursday night, you didn't mention Alexandra Swayze. She came out of her suite, didn't she?"

"She's like one of those pop-up gophers in that arcade game. You take a stuffed mallet and try to bonk them, but they're fast. Yeah, she came out and wanted to know what was going on, like it was any of her business. She has a real thing about how my generation is nothing but sex fiends and drug addicts. She wants the government to outlaw condoms and the pill unless you're married, but then she wants unwed parents to be locked up in prison. Anyway, I told her to butt out and went into my room, just to get away from her. I'm glad she's gone, and I hope she never comes back."

"You don't know what she did after that?"

"Like I cared." Dawn caught a lock of hair and began to chew on it. "So are you gonna call my lawyer? I'm kind of low on cash, but I can write you a check."

I pushed back the chair and stood up. "Maybe tomorrow. You need to stay in your suite tonight."

"I can't lock the door."

"Then put a piece of furniture against it if it will make you feel safer. Just don't go for a stroll in the garden, okay?"

She nodded. I went back to the reception room to find out if the ambulance had arrived. The driveway was empty. Although I'd been careful with the directions, there were a lot of unmarked county roads, and it was possible the paramedics were lost. I called 911 and asked the dispatcher about the delay. She was testy because I'd failed to follow her instructions to stay on the line, although I wasn't sure what we would have talked about all this time. She put me on hold, then returned and told me they had taken a wrong turn but were back on route. I asked her to let them know to anticipate barbiturate poisoning. Naturally, she wanted details, but I had none, so I replaced the receiver, nodded at the orderly, and went to Dibbins's suite.

Brenda hadn't moved, and by now, looked incapable of it. I checked on the patient, who was still hanging on. He was three times the body weight of Randall, so whatever dosage he'd ingested might not be enough to kill him. Inadvertently ingested, I amended. Dibbins's wine bottle had been spiked, and I was convinced that Randall's gin bottle had received similar treatment.

I heard an approaching siren, and within seconds blue lights were flashing on the ceiling. I went to the main door and held it open for the paramedics. "Did you get the message about the barbiturate poisoning?" I asked as I led them to the suite.

"Yes, about two minutes ago," one of them said. "I called the doctor on duty at the ER, and he prescribed a stimulant. Hope you're right, lady." He stepped inside and froze. "Holy shit, look at the size of the guy! Is he even gonna fit on the gurney?"

"I can get a couple of men to help you move him," I said.

"They got a back hoe?" He barked orders at his partner, then opened his bag. "I don't know how much to give him." He took out a cell phone and punched numbers.

"Vitals are critical," his partner said, then looked at me. "How long ago did he take the drug?"

I tried to calculate the amount of time since I'd ended our unpleasant conversation. "I don't know. He was fine three hours ago. We found him like this almost an hour ago, so sometime in that two-hour period."

Brenda began to sob loudly. "I should have checked on him, but I was so upset, and I just couldn't stand the idea of listening to his beastly remarks."

The paramedic finished his call and filled a hypodermic to the hilt. "Get the gurney, Bernie. Lady, we're gonna need all the help you can round up. One of you is gonna have to ride back with us so the doctor on duty can get more information. This guy got insurance?"

"I'll fetch his records for you." I went to the reception desk and pointed at the orderly. "You, go there," I said, gesturing in the direction of Dibbins's suite. "Who else is here?" He stared blankly at me. "Just go, then." I grabbed his wrist to pull him up and shoved him toward the suite. I found Dibbins's file in the office. I took it back and stuck it in Brenda's limp hands. "You'll have to ride with them and explain things. Call me when you get to the hospital."

"I don't know if I can do this," she whimpered.

This, from a woman who'd buried bodies in her backyard. "Of course you can," I said sternly. Fernando grasped the problem and hurried off to find his fellow worker. Bernie wheeled in a squeaky gurney, and we all gazed dubiously at it.

The lead paramedic finished giving Dibbins the injection and straightened up. "Maybe he'll make it to the ER, anyway.

Bernie, you and me may be filing for workman's comp before this night is over."

Fernando reappeared with Guillermo. The four men positioned themselves on either side of the bed and placed the gurney next to it. I felt obliged to grab Dibbins's ankles and do the best I could to help. It took us more than ten minutes to make the transfer, but somehow we did.

Rotating the Statue of Liberty would have been easier.

The men rolled the gurney to the ambulance. With my encouragement, Brenda trailed after them. I put her in the front seat, buckled her seat belt for her, and reminded her to call me from the hospital. The paramedics and the orderlies were trying to heft the gurney high enough to slide it into the ambulance when Toby appeared. Very much the team captain, he reassigned their positions to his satisfaction, and took a deep breath. Seconds later the gurney was inside. The paramedics goggled at him as they realized who he was. Before they could ask for his autograph, I reminded them of their patient.

Toby and I watched the ambulance as it drove away, its siren blaring and blue lights flashing. "Thanks for helping," I said.

"Yeah, well, something to break up the

monotony. So what about dinner?"

"That's up to the staff."

"The chef and his boys split. The maids haven't shown up since they left a couple of hours ago."

We went up to the porch. "Maybe Rodolfo or Guillermo was scheduled to pick them up in the van, but all this delayed him." I stopped as I heard a vehicle coming around from the parking area. "See? One of them is on his way to get them."

Actually, two of them were on their way, and I had a sinking feeling they wouldn't be back anytime soon. And since there wouldn't be any trays to deliver, it didn't much matter if the maids came back. "I'd better call the motel and see what's going on."

"You'd better do something. I'm hungry."

"That's the least of my concerns," I said as I went to the desk and dialed the number of the pay phone at the bar & grill. After ten rings, a gravelly male voice answered, "What?"

The jukebox was blaring in the background, indicating that happy hour was under way. I raised my voice and said, "Let me speak to Ruby Bee."

"Don't see her right offhand."

"Then go find her."

"Might be in the ladies'. Last time I went in there, purely by mistake, I liked to git my head dunked in the toilet. Call back later." He hung up.

"Damnation," I muttered.

Toby scowled like a four-year-old. "I'm hungry. This place is costing me nearly two grand a day. I could be staying at the Ritz-Carlton for less than that."

I pushed the phone toward him. "Feel free to call and see if they have any rooms available."

"So I can get thrown in jail for contempt? You'd like that, wouldn't you? You're a real man-hater, with your prissy hair and baggy clothes and smart-ass mouth. What happened — boyfriend dump you at the prom?" He shoved the phone off the desk and took a step toward me. "Or maybe you're just frustrated, living out here in the middle of nowhere, surrounded by toothless jerks. When's the last time you got laid?"

I was not inclined to answer his question. "Cut out this crap," I said coldly.

"Ooh, did I strike a nerve?" he said with a sneer. Beneath his shirt, his muscles were rippling as he clenched and unclenched his hands.

"Hey, where is everybody?" Dawn called

as she came into the reception room. She stopped and took in the situation. "Fercrissake, Toby, when are you going to grow up? I hate to break it to you, pinup boy, but not every woman in the world wants to screw you. Why don't you go take a cold shower?" She looked at me. "What's going on? There's nobody out by the pool or in the kitchen. All the Mexicans have disappeared. I can't even find Brenda. This place is turning into a morgue."

"Brenda went with Dr. Dibbins in the ambulance, and the Mexicans . . . went. Walter's been gone all day. Dr. Stonebridge is here, as far as I know, so that makes four of us."

"Then what are we supposed to eat?" she asked. "The food's like really gross, but it's better than nothing."

"Yeah," Toby added, having lost his bluster.

I sat down behind the desk and leaned over to pick up the telephone off the floor. Aware they were both waiting for me to take charge, I finally said, "I don't know, but I can assure you that you're not in peril of starvation. If nobody shows up, I have a key to the kitchen. We can scrounge up sandwiches."

Dawn snickered. "Like you think there's

any bread in this place? Rice cakes, maybe. Blocks of tofu that look like paste. Sesame seeds. As long as Brenda's gone and Stonebridge is passed out, why don't we order a pizza?"

"The only dominoes in this town are played on a table in the pool hall," I said. "Go watch a movie or something. I need to think."

"C'mon, big boy," Dawn said to Toby. "I'll do my nails while I watch you swim laps. Don't count on me to save you if you sink to the bottom of the pool. I buy my nail polish on Rodeo Drive, and it's not cheap."

Toby stared at me, his eyes slitted, then followed her down the hall toward the pool. Once I heard the door close, I let out a sigh of relief. It was galling that Dawn had been the one to defuse the tension and save me from whatever might have happened. Maybe I'd slip her an extra rice cake for dinner.

Both wings were silent, and growing dark as the sun began to sink behind Cotter's Ridge. It occurred to me that I'd better check on Stonebridge. If I was correct in my assumptions, Molly and Randall had been murdered. Dibbins was likely to be added to the list. This was clearly a setback for the Stonebridge Foundation, conceived as a posh, peaceful, and most importantly, discreet haven for celebrities in need of rehabilitation. At the rate things were going, they'd soon all be in need of resuscitation as well.

I made sure I had the keys and went down the hall. Dawn was on a lounge, painting her fingernails. Toby was swimming with scarcely a ripple. I continued to Dr. Stonebridge's office and went inside. From his apartment I could hear snoring. I peeked inside. He was flopped across the bed, with the brandy bottle Brenda had mentioned still propped against him. To my malicious delight, I noticed that his silvery hair had slipped off his head, exposing a patch of shiny skin. Perhaps his perfect teeth went into a glass beside the bed each night.

In any case, he was merely drunk. I locked his office door behind me. Dawn glanced up, then resumed painting her nails. I returned to the office and dialed Harve's office. When I asked to speak to him, the dispatcher gasped.

"He's not here," she whispered as if she suspected the office was bugged.

"Where is he?"

"He left. He didn't tell me where he was going, but he never does. I don't think he went home, though. Someone called from a bar out toward Zellott and reported gunshots and some kind of hostage situation. Sheriff Dorfer likes to handle those himself."

"Especially when he can count on the TV vans to show up. Did he put on a clean shirt before he left?"

"I believe so," she admitted. "Would you like to leave a message, Chief Hanks?"

I knew hostage situations could last half the night. "I need a deputy out here immediately. Can you send someone?"

"I don't think so," she said slowly. "Sheriff Dorfer took Les and Wilton with him, leaving Palsy and me to mind the store. Not a minute after they left, I got a call about a real messy accident out past the reservoir. Two kids on motorcycles, a chicken truck, and a van with a lot of Mexicans. Palsy went to see about it. I'm all by my lonesome."

If I'd said what was going through my mind, she would have immediately hung up and dropped to her knees to pray for my salvation. "I need backup as soon as possible," I said. "If Palsy or anybody else gets back, send them to the Stonebridge Foundation. Do you have the directions?"

"I do indeed. Left on County 104, just before the Maggody city limits sign. Is there anything else, Chief Hanks?"

"No, we'll be all right," I said without conviction. She chirruped good-bye and went back to whatever she'd been doing. Since it was the foundation's nickel, not mine, I called information and got the telephone number of the hospital. I wended my way through a maze of options until I finally touched base with a human being, who forwarded my call to McBeen's office.

He answered with his customary charm. "You've got fifteen seconds, starting now."

I identified myself, then asked him if he'd learned anything more from the autopsies of Molly Foss and Randall Zumi.

"I didn't bother to do an autopsy on Zumi. The blood tests proved he took a handful of pills, and I don't have time to waste on suicides. His body was sent to the lab in Little Rock earlier this afternoon. As for the girl, there was one thing I missed at the crime scene. She was smacked on the back of her head before she died. It left a bruise, but it wasn't hard enough to cause any bleeding or kill her. She would have been feeling real woozy, though. Easier to hold facedown in the water. There was a trace of alcohol in her blood, no more than .02 or thereabouts. She'd had maybe one drink."

"Any idea what caused the bruise?"

"Your standard run-of-the-mill blunt object. Considering she was in a garden, I'd rule out a baseball bat or a hockey stick. Whatever it was, you ain't gonna find traces of blood on it. Hear tell you sent another one this way. Should I be expecting him?"

"I hope not." I thanked him and hung up before he could make any macabre jokes. He'd spent forty years in the morgue. I shuddered to think about what his home life might be like.

I pushed the button to close the gate, then went back to sit by the pool. Until a deputy arrived, Toby, Dawn, and I needed to stay together — at a civilized distance.

18

Ruby Bee delivered a pitcher of beer and a complimentary basket of cheese fries to a couple in one of the booths who had confided that they were celebrating their ninth wedding anniversary. She didn't reckon they'd make it to the tenth, but there wasn't any cause to say so.

She refilled a few mugs for the drinkers sitting at the bar, looked at the crowd to make sure everybody was doing okay, then went to talk to Estelle. "Guess what happened the middle of this afternoon?"

Estelle wound a stray curl around her little finger. "Roy Stiver proposed, and you and him are eloping as soon as you close for the night."

"I am serious, Estelle."

"Then give me a minute to think. Okay, Dahlia's granny came in with a shotgun and held you up. Am I gettin' closer?"

"About as close as Milwaukee. I went out back to take the Mexicans some biscuits left over from lunch, and every last one of them was gone. Their rooms are emptier than a dead man's eyes. They was considerate enough to strip the beds and pile the sheets by the door with the towels, which I thought was a real sweet thing to do. But they're gone, kit and caboodle, and most likely for good. They even took their grill."

Estelle frowned. "I have to admit that's strange. Does Arly know?"

"I suppose so," said Ruby Bee. "She's been out at the Stonebridge Foundation most of the day. Do you think they got fired?"

Before Estelle could answer, a group of fellows in matching plaid shirts and bolo ties came in and sat down at a table. Ruby Bee hustled over to get their orders. By the time she'd carried over a couple of pitchers, half a dozen mugs, and several bags of corn chips and pork rinds, she'd almost forgotten about the Mexicans.

"Do you know who they are?" she said excitedly to Estelle. "They're the Amarillo Armadillos. They sing at rodeos and tent revivals all across Arkansas, Oklahoma, and Texas. Ain't that something?"

"If you're such a big fan, why doncha get their autographs?"

Ruby Bee's grin faded. "I ain't exactly heard of them, if you must know, but they

456

said they were real famous. They met Willie Nelson once at a truck stop."

"If I felt any fainter, I'd topple off the stool and land on my head," Estelle said. "So what else about the Mexicans?"

"Nothing else," admitted Ruby Bee, peeved that Estelle didn't share her enthusiasm for the Amarillo Armadillos. They were kinda old, but they'd been real polite. In this day and age, that counted for something.

"You get paid in advance for their rooms?"

"I got one month, and since they weren't here much more than a week, I reckon I made out okay. You think maybe something happened out at that place to make them bolt like they did? Should I call Arly?"

Estelle sucked on a pretzel while she thought about it. "No, she'd just get all high and mighty about being bothered while she's in the middle of her 'official investigation.' She must know about the Mexicans leaving, and you don't have anything else to say."

"I suppose not," said Ruby Bee, then went back over to the Amarillo Armadillos to see if they wanted something to eat.

I sat down near Dawn and watched Toby.

"Maybe it'll burn off some testosterone," I said.

"Maybe it'll rain pennies from heaven." She held up her hand, her fingers splayed, and said, "Like it?"

"Love it," I lied. I didn't tell her that I'd seen the same puke pumpkin shade on Estelle's fingernails a week ago, and I was pretty sure the bottle of polish had cost less than a dollar. "I don't know what to do about dinner. You want to look around the kitchen with me?"

"Might as well. I was thinking we should sort of hang out together tonight. If I go back to my suite, I won't be able to sleep. Every time the damn dog barks, I'll break out in a sweat. Molly, Dr. Zumi, and now Dr. Dibbins. It's so damn creepy."

"No argument from me," I said. We went to the kitchen and I unlocked the door. The cook (I couldn't bear to call him a chef) and his helpers had had the decency to clean up before they galloped into the sunset. The cold storage room, however, had a padlock, and none of Stonebridge's keys would work.

Dawn grimaced. "What are we supposed to do now?"

I continued on to the pantry where the employees ate. Brenda, radical advocate of organic and unprocessed food, had made sure that no cans of beans or boxes of cereal would sully the premises with their poisonous chemicals and obscure polysyllabic additives. I spotted a bag of rice cakes. "Unless you want to pick field greens, we may have to make do with this."

"Lucky us," she said glumly, then brightened. "You know, I bet the doctors stashed some food in their apartments. You've got the keys, and we haven't got anything better to do. Let's see what we can find. Come on, it'll be fun."

It was as good an idea as any. We started in Brenda's apartment and found more rice cakes and a jar of what was billed as one hundred percent organic peanut butter. It looked vile, but I was getting hungry, so we took it. Dawn stopped in the office and giggled. "Look, she has her pencils arranged by size. Talk about anal-retentive. They ought to write her up in a textbook."

"I don't think she'd appreciate the publicity," I said.

"There's no such thing as bad publicity."

We did better in Walter's apartment. He had a bag of chips in a cabinet, along with a six-pack of beer and two avocados in the refrigerator. I was worried that the medications Dawn and Toby were taking might interact badly with the alcohol, but Dawn wasn't concerned.

"If we had salsa, we could make guacamole," she said as she gathered up the goodies. "Well, you could, anyway. I don't know how to make toast."

We went through Randall's office to his apartment, although I already knew the pickings were slim. Dawn turned up her nose at the grapes, but took the yogurt.

When we got to Stonebridge's door, I stopped. "I'm not sure we should go in. He might wake up."

"So what?" she said. "I mean, it's his place, and he's responsible for our health. Don't be such a wimp. You yourself said he was passed out. We could ride in on mules or cows or whatever they ride around here and not wake him up. He's probably got all kinds of food and booze."

I unlocked the door and we crept across the office like little elves. He was still on his bed, snoring. Dawn opened the refrigerator. "I told you so," she whispered as she grabbed a bottle of champagne. "Look in the cabinet."

The cabinet was well stocked with jars of caviar and pâté. Dawn greedily loaded up everything she could carry, then looked at me. "Get some more," she added urgently, as if we were headed into the hills to hide in a cave. "We need the crackers and a knife. Isn't this fun? Where do you think he keeps his booze?"

Stonebridge snuffled. We both froze until he flopped over and resumed snoring. I released my breath and did a quick search. The cabinet under the sink had enough bottles to stock a liquor store. Dawn could barely restrain herself from chortling as she took out a bottle of scotch.

We slipped outside and deposited our trove on the table by the pool. Dawn opened the scotch and took an unladylike swig. "Not bad at all," she said as she wiped her chin. "How about a cracker with a nice dollop of caviar? Too bad we don't have any capers or sour cream."

Toby must have smelled the food. He climbed out of the pool, shook himself, and joined us. "Jesus, where did all this come from?"

Dawn grinned. "Figure it out for yourself, Einstein — or should that be Frankeinstein? Get it? Frank-einstein?"

I leaned back and watched them scarfing down food and drink. I found myself staring at the champagne bottle. Bottles, bottles everywhere, but not a drop to drink. I waved off Dawn's attempt to share the scotch.

Two little bottles, both of which had been tainted with potentially lethal drugs.

"I'm going for a walk in the garden," I said as I stood up. "Yell if you need me."

"Are you sick or something?" asked Dawn.

"No, I'm just thinking about the bottles. Not these from Stonebridge's private stock, but the ones Dibbins attempted to smuggle inside. His fingerprints should have been on them."

Toby brayed. "That fat old goat? I'm not surprised. Did Dr. Skiller catch him red-handed? She's a damn bloodhound. I thought I'd get past her with a few pills, but she pawed through every inch of the stuff in my bag. And when she found them, I thought she'd box my ears like a Sunday school teacher."

"She got my coke," Dawn said sadly. "Over five hundred dollars' worth. I about cried, but I didn't want to give her the satis-faction."

I sighed, wondering if they were as clue-less as they seemed. "I'll leave you two to commiserate."

"We'll save some champagne for you," said Dawn, "but not forever." She picked up the bottle and read the label. "This is very pricey stuff."

Toby took it out of her hands. "Hell, when I was out at the clubs in L.A., we'd drink a case of it and eat caviar by the spoonful. There was this one chick who got sick all over the limo. It was a real hoot!"

I headed for the garden before I heard further details. I followed a path that I thought would take me to Dibbins's secluded bench. I could still hear Toby's and Dawn's voices as they vied to prove which one of them had behaved more badly in public, but at least I couldn't see them.

Brenda had confiscated Dibbins's cache, taken out the six bottles of gin for Randall, and then left the box outside the back door of the kitchen. The employees had found it, but not before someone else had removed at least one bottle of wine, and perhaps a bottle of gin. Whoever it was had not swilled the contents at the first opportunity, but instead had hidden them from Brenda's relentless scrutiny. This suggested some sort of premeditation. I bent down and peered under the bench. Dibbins had taped his precious cigars to the bottom, as I'd suspected. The garden offered innumerable hiding places.

A rather good theory was struggling to evolve, but Molly's murder kept throwing me off. It couldn't have been premeditated.

Instead of knocking on Toby's door, she could have gone home after the staff meeting. Her decision to stay had been serendipitous. Toby might have anticipated it, but none of the others could have. Surely no one could have counted on her to rush out of the building as she'd done. It wouldn't have occurred to Toby that she might not be susceptible to his charm and delighted to indulge in sex with "The Man." Humility was not among his virtues — if he had any.

Dawn came along the path and sat down beside me. She was carrying the bottle of scotch, and her words were less than carefully enunciated as she said, "Sure you don't want to try this? It's very yummy."

"What's Toby doing?"

"He decided to go lift weights. I hope he doesn't drop a barbell on his head, not that it could cause noticeable brain damage. He's beyond that." She took a drink, then put the bottle on the ground. "What are you doing back here?"

"Thinking."

"Good. I was afraid you were worrying about Dr. Dibbins. He's a menace to society with his diet plan. One of my best friends gained three pounds the first month she was on his diet. He spouts all this gibberish about how the gain is only temporary, but it's shit. Everybody knows you can't stuff yourself with bread and pasta. I mean, let's get real."

"Let's do that, Dawn," I said. "When I read your file, one thing went through my mind almost immediately: six degrees of separation. Funny, huh?"

"Hysterical," she said as she picked up the bottle and took another drink. "Don't quit your day job to become a standup comic."

I couldn't read her expression in the shadows, but I doubted she was smiling. "Well, you and Sunny were from Arkansas — and now you're back. Is Sunny buried in Stubbett?"

"My mother got all weepy and wanted her to spend eternity in the family plot out back of the Baptist church. The truth is that it was free. My mother's been scrimping ever since the show was canceled. She's done well enough to keep herself in gigolos, but she goes out every afternoon to look in the mailbox for residual checks. After I got my second DUI, she sold my MG and bought me a used Toyota. Can you imagine the humiliation? I dyed my hair black and ran away to Vegas, but the cops caught me."

"Tough life," I commented. "Let's talk some more about Sunny. After she was diagnosed, where was she sent?"

"Some hospital out of state. My mother was too embarrassed to tell anyone, so her story was that Sunny was studying in Paris. Like anybody believed it."

"Was the hospital here in Arkansas, in Little Rock? Don't bother to deny it, Dawn. I can make a phone call and find out in five minutes."

"Okay, so my mother packed her off to this gawdawful hospital with bars on the windows and padded rooms and straitjackets. My mother claimed it was the best place for her. It was for my mother, if not Sunny. Out of sight, and no need to visit because of the distance and bother. I went a couple of times, but I couldn't stand it. You can't begin to imagine how bad those places are. All these old men and women cruising up and down the halls with vacant eyes. A teenage boy playing checkers, except there weren't any checkers and he wasn't playing against anybody. Men masturbating in their rocking chairs. I would have done anything to get Sunny out of there, but by my second visit, her eyes had that same look. She barely knew me. She tried to pat my hand when I started crying, but it was like we were strangers." She stopped and stared into the shadows. "After a year, some administrator called to say that Sunny had managed to hang herself with the sheet off her bed. He told my mother all kinds of bullshit to avoid a lawsuit, but I knew better. These people were so damned drugged that they were like zombies. That's all the treatment they got. Sunny must have come to her senses long enough to realize that this was going to be the rest of her life."

I put my arm around Dawn's shoulders. "You must have been enraged. Did you track down the doctors' names on the Internet?"

She nodded, but I felt her muscles tighten. "It took me ten minutes. Sunny hung there all night. They found her in the morning."

"So how did you find out that Randall Zumi was going to be a partner in the Stonebridge Foundation?"

"I had to wait for almost ten years, and it wasn't easy. I wasn't about to get myself checked into that hospital. Finally, a friend of my mother's went to Dr. Stonebridge for a face-lift and all that crap. He let something slip about his hush-hush project in Arkansas. A psychiatric facility. It was a long shot, but I searched the Internet and found the stuff about the property sale. Zumi's name was included. After that, it was easy to find the application for the license for a re-habilitation facility. I may not have been as smart as Sunny, but I'm not as stupid as everyone thinks." She hiccuped. "Not as stupid as you think, either."

"Then you did what was necessary to get yourself in a position to be ripe for a few months of rehab. How did you convince your lawyer to choose this place?"

Dawn took another swallow of scotch. "He's such a little twit. He insisted that I go to this place in San Diego, but I walked out. I dropped a few hints about needing to get out of the state and suggested he call Stonebridge. Then I bitched like hell all the way here, just to make him feel as if the whole thing was his idea."

"Did Dr. Zumi recognize your name?" I asked. "You and Sunny were pretty famous back then."

"Don't talk about me like I'm sixty-five! I don't know if he figured out the connection, but if he did, what was he going to say? 'By the way, your sister was one of my patients. So sorry I gave her all that Thorazine and she killed herself.' Give me a break!"

I edged to the end of the bench. "It didn't take you long to find a way to get your revenge, did it? You were very clever."

"Of course I was. I searched his room,

just to make sure he was the one, and finally found his résumé. On the second day after I got here, I started bitching about how sore I was from the exercises, so Zumi agreed I could have Demerol at night. I pretended to swallow them, but as soon as the maid looked away, I spit them out and hid them. Yesterday I ground up four tabs and waited until Zumi left his office. I put it in the gin bottle. I didn't leave my fingerprints, did I?"

"No, the bottle had been wiped clean of any prints but Zumi's. That's what made me suspicious. There should have been all sorts of prints on the bottle. Somebody sold it to Dibbins, and either he or his valet packed the bottles in his bag. Brenda Skiller put the bottles in a box, but saved a few of them for her depressed colleague. But there were no other prints." I gave her a moment to mull that over, then said, "We won't find any prints on the wine bottle in Dibbins's room, either. You were very careful, Dawn. Almost too careful."

"I wasn't sure I'd have to do in Dr. Dibbins," she said, almost pensively. "I found the wine bottle down at the end of the other hall in this ghastly room, and I was going to drink it myself. But then I thought I might as well hang on to it in case I needed it. You never know."

"You must have overheard me talking to Dr. Dibbins this afternoon."

"I was afraid he could be bought for a Cadbury bar. That's pathetic, isn't it? He had millions of dollars, but he would have shot off his mouth for a dollar's worth of chocolate." She rose and went across the path to pick a flower. "Do you know what this is?"

It was dark by this time, and I was beginning to regret having chosen such an isolated spot. "No, sorry. I can identify dandelions and daisies, but that's about it. Molly's murder is the one that puzzles me. Why kill her?"

Dawn began to sway back and forth. "It was just one of those things. I knew Toby would look guilty as sin, so you might go after him. Even better, I'd seen Zumi mooning after her like a puppy, so I figured that could be the reason he committed suicide."

"You killed her just to muddy the water?" I said, appalled.

"Like I said, it was just one of those things. Once I realized she was in the garden, I found her and gave her a big hug. We sat and talked for at least an hour, girly talk. Then I hit her with a rock and held her facedown in the water until she stopped kicking. I never liked her, anyway. I know I've put on some pounds and let myself go, but once I'm clean and back to normal, I'll be a hell of a lot sexier than she'd ever been. It got so sickening to watch all the men, including those Mexicans, panting whenever she walked by. It was really annoying. She should have stayed home, had a couple of babies, and hung out with the other bovines, getting fatter and dowdier. You ought to see some of my cousins in Stubbett."

"I can understand why you did what you did, Dawn," I said, "but I can't just forget about it. Two people are dead, and another one may be joining them."

"Yeah, I know." She sat back down and picked up the bottle of scotch. "You sure you don't want to try this? I promise you'll like it."

What I didn't like was the way she seemed to be judging its potential as a weapon. There was no convenient fountain, but I doubted that would be a factor. Her identical twin sister had developed a serious mental illness, and their genes had come from the same pool.

"Maybe later," I said. "Why don't we go see what Toby's doing?"

"Does it matter?"

"Yes, I'm in charge until Brenda gets

back. I think we should clean up the table and decide where to sleep tonight. What do you think about the gym? It's got pads on the floor."

Dawn cocked her head as she looked at me. "Don't underestimate me, Chief Hanks. I've already told you I'm not stupid."

"Call me Arly," I said quickly. "We're friends, aren't we? Did I ever tell you about the five years I lived in Manhattan? The ethnic food was fantastic. Can you get good Thai in L.A.?"

She was puzzled enough to lower the bottle. "You're asking me about noodles and lemongrass?"

Before I could come up with a lame response, a bulky figure came stumbling down the path, grunting like a wounded animal. Both of us instinctively moved closer together, despite the fact she'd been on the verge of bashing me with the bottle. I clutched her hand as we both stared.

"There you are!" boomed Vincent Stonebridge, his hairless head glinting in the moonlight. "Where the hell is everybody else?" He lurched to a halt and pointed at the bottle in Dawn's hands. "How dare you steal that from me? You're in big trouble, little lady. I'm going to see you have high colonics for a month! What's more, I'm going to call your mother! What do you have to say to that?"

Nothing, obviously. Dawn shoved the bottle at me, then leapt up and ran down the path. I waited until I could no longer hear her, then stood up. "Take this," I said, putting the bottle in his hand. "Let's put you back to bed. You can make all the calls you want in the morning."

Stonebridge belched. "That might be prudent. Just who are you?"

I took his arm and steered him toward the pool. "Don't worry about it. Everything will be clear after you've had a nice long rest. Wouldn't you like to lie down?"

He moved obediently, although we had some tricky moments on the brick path. I draped his arm over my shoulders and persevered until we reached his apartment. His hairpiece was on a pillow as though it were snoozing. I gave Stonebridge a parting shove, and watched as he flopped across the bed. Had I been a better person, I would have removed his shoes and gone so far as to find a blanket to throw over him. I turned off the light and went into his office, locked the door, and picked up the phone to call Harve.

The dispatcher sounded choked up when

she told me that Sheriff Dorfer had not returned, nor had Palsy. I assured her that it wasn't her fault and hung up before she broke out in tears. I decided that I had two options: I could go around the pool to the gym, where Toby was likely to be pedaling the stationary bike hard enough to end up in Boone Creek, or I could stay where I was, which was safe. I had no idea where Dawn was. I did not want to step outside and find her waiting for me, when the most lethal weapon I had available was a framed photo of Stonebridge shaking hands with Governor Arnold.

I sat behind the desk for a long time, chastising myself for my foolish behavior. Before I'd set foot in the garden, I was certain that Dawn was guilty. I hadn't been able to determine how Molly's murder fit into the scheme, but I would have sooner or later. I hoped her family never found out that her death was merely "a distraction."

After half an hour, I couldn't stand it anymore. I tiptoed into Stonebridge's apartment and utilized the bathroom, but I had the decency not to look in his medicine cabinet for denture adhesive or makeup. He was doomed already. I wondered how long it would take him to learn how to speak Spanish. Maybe he could go back to the village where he'd hired his peons and take lessons. I didn't care.

I went to the window in the office and peeked through the blinds. Nothing, except the remains of the picnic on the table by the pool, was worthy of my attention. The sidewalk was reasonably dark, although the exterior lights were on. When I opened the door, the guard dog began to bark. That was a good sign. I darted to the door of the main building and went inside. There were too many places for Dawn to hide; I had no chance of finding her if she was still around. I looked out the front door at the gate. It was open, suggesting she'd fled. If Harve would just call me, I could tell him what had taken place and he could take over. I was not about to be a posse of one. I'd never quite grasped the reasoning behind the army's latest recruitment slogan: Be an army of one. Hell, I wanted a battalion, and then some.

Headlights flashed as a car turned into the driveway. Harve, I thought, allowing myself to relax. Or at least a deputy with a gun. The car stopped in front of the porch. My eyes widened as Jack opened the door and got out. He waved as he came trotting up the steps. I went out on the porch and flung myself at him. Eventually, he unwound my arms from around his neck and frowned at me.

"What's going on?"

I was still reeling, but I pulled myself together somehow and said, "You don't even want to know. What are you doing here?"

"I tried all afternoon to call you, just to make sure you made it back safely. I finally got worried enough to call your mother."

"Oh, god," I said as I sat down on one of the wicker chairs.

"I didn't know what else to do," he said defensively. "I am entitled to be worried about you, aren't I?"

I rather liked the idea. "I guess so. I hope you didn't go into detail about last night."

He sat down next to me. "I described everything we did, from lunch to our antics in bed. She was gratified to hear all about it. After I'd finished telling her about your amazing talents and that certain thing you do so well, I asked where you were. She was upset, to put it mildly. She said you'd been out here all afternoon. She tried to call at one point to tell you something about Mexicans — I never quite understood — and then started rambling on about people getting murdered. I didn't have anything better to do, so I thought I might as well come down and put her mind at ease."

"You'd better be lying about some of that," I said. "But, yeah, there was another attempted murder this afternoon, and I ended up babysitting the famous quarterback and the perp. I don't know where she is at the moment. The gate was open, so I'm assuming she's long gone."

"Maybe not," Jack said. "Ruby Bee told me how to find this place. When I came down the road, I saw this young woman whirling around and shouting. I pulled over and asked if she needed help."

"And then, being a good-hearted soul, you let her get in the car? Didn't your mother ever warn you about picking up hitchhikers?"

He leaned back and crossed his legs. "Shall I continue? It took me of all of ten seconds to realize I had a drunken psycho in my car. She was babbling about all the people she'd killed and how she'd have gotten away with it if you hadn't butted in. I didn't care for that, so I bundled her up and put her in my trunk. If you listen, you can hear her feet pounding."

"You can't leave her there. She'll suffocate."

"No, she'll be fine. How are you?"

"Relieved," I admitted. "It was pretty crazy there for a while. If you're sure she'll

477

be okay, let's just leave her there until the sheriff or one of his deputies shows up. Dr. Stonebridge is out for the duration, and Toby will probably pump iron all night."

"Then we can just sit here?" he murmured.

"Till sunrise, if need be." I settled into his arm, and we gazed at the sky. I don't know when Harve finally called, but I roused myself and went inside to answer the phone. That was the end of it, as far as I was concerned.

❦

19

Mrs. Jim Bob was fed up. She was sitting at the dinette, shredding paper napkins and brooding. Somehow, Jim Bob had managed to evade her all day. She'd left so many messages at the SuperSaver that she'd lost count. He was a weasel, she told herself as she took a gulp of chamomile tea to steady her nerves. Brother Verber was almost as bad. Here she was, needing his wisdom and guidance in her moment of need, but he was holed up somewhere. She vowed to never again volunteer to supervise the rummage sale, even if it meant the little heathens would have to get by without the donation.

And her so-called friends — well, they could just find out how taxing it was to run the Missionary Society, keep track of the hymnals, and make sure the Sunday school teachers were adhering to the Gospel. Let them eat somebody else's cinnamon rolls after the meetings. She'd wash her hands of the whole lot of them, and they'd be mighty sorry. Ingrates, every single one of them.

But Jim Bob was by far the most sinful, and she wasn't about to allow herself to be embarrassed by his behavior. Even if she was to resign her presidency, she was still going to hold her head up high as she drove through town. She'd heard the rumors that he was luring in otherwise upstanding citizens to gamble away their hard-earned money. Kevin was a prime victim, along with Jeremiah McIlhaney, not to mention Earl Buchanon, who should be at home fretting about his wife. She owed it to the community to stop the game and send these sinful men crawling home to pray for forgiveness.

She finished her tea. There was no choice. Jim Bob may have thought he was crafty, but she knew perfectly well that the game was going on in the back of Roy's antiques store. She picked up her purse and went out to the car. The idea of catching them gave her a glow of grim satisfaction.

There weren't any trucks parked in front of the store, but Mrs. Jim Bob figured they'd be parked around back where nobody would see them. She yanked at the rearview mirror and made sure her hair was tidy. Then, armed with the knowledge that the Almighty Lord was on her heels, she marched through the shop and threw open the door to the back room.

What she saw wasn't at all what she expected. The men were seated around a table, but instead of holding cards, they were holding up their hands. Their faces were all paler than a baby's bottom. Kevin, in particular, looked like he was liable to throw up all over the plastic chips scattered in front of him. Unattended cigars smoldered in ashtrays. Glasses of whiskey remained untouched. Nobody spoke, or even twitched. It was like she'd stepped into a grainy photograph.

Mrs. Jim Bob felt hot breath on her neck. Startled, she swung around. Standing behind the door was a woman with messy white hair, dressed in a stained blue sweatsuit. Her eyes looked peculiar. To make matters worse, she was holding a gun.

"Just who might you be?" Mrs. Jim Bob demanded.

"I am a United States senator."

"That's the most ridiculous thing I've heard in all my born days." She snatched the gun out of the woman's hands. "I don't even want to hear your excuses for being here. Now you just be on your way, whoever you are."

Mrs. Jim Bob nearly shrieked when Roy

and Jeremiah jumped up and grabbed hold of the woman. It was downright rude, she thought, and cast a bad light on Maggody. Once she was mayor, she'd organize a hospitality committee to make sure this sort of thing never happened again.

Dahlia was sitting on the stoop, heaving and sighing. Mebbe she'd been too hard on Kevvie, going after him with a broom and all. She didn't recollect anything about her pa, but she knew her cousins and uncles drank whiskey. Their wives groused about it, but they didn't seem to do anything to put a stop to it. It was all her granny's fault, she thought gloomily. If she hadn't had to put up with her, she might have let Kevvie off with a scolding.

She saw a scrawny figure coming down the road. Her granny, of course. She hadn't been eaten by a bear after all. Dahlia sat and waited, her brow lowering with each step the old lady took.

Her granny stopped at the gate. "I ain't comin' in, so don't get all het up. Jest put my belongings in a paper bag and bring 'em out to me. One of these days you'll be real sorry about the way you treated me. Get movin', lardbutt. I ain't got all night."

"Where are you goin'?" Dahlia asked.

"None of your beeswax. I don't aim to be a bother to you no more. I have found somewhere else to stay where someone will appreciate my cookin' and cleanin'. Why are you still sitting there, gal?"

Dahlia's chins rippled as she chewed on this. "You ain't shacking up with Petrol again, are you?"

"What if I am?" her granny replied hotly. "He's got the biggest pecker I ever seen — and I've seen a bushel and a peck of peckers in my life." She cackled. "I may be old, but I ain't dead yet. You want me to fetch my things, or are you gonna do it? Time's a-wastin'. Petrol picked me a nice mess of collard greens, and they're simmerin' on the stove."

Dahlia struggled to her feet. "I don't want the twins to hear your trashy talk. Don't you dare set foot in my yard ever again."

"Like I'd want to? Lemme know when you birth that bun in the warmer. It ain't that I care, but I might as well write it down in the family Bible."

"Yeah," Dahlia said, wondering why she felt so sad all of a sudden. "I'll be sure Kevvie goes by and tells you."

Jack spent what was left of the night in my apartment, but we were both too tired to do anything of prurient interest. He drank a cup of instant coffee, trying not to wrinkle his nose, and then headed home. I took a long shower, then reluctantly went to the PD to call Harve for the gazillionth time. I'd catch hell from Ruby Bee for not stopping at the bar & grill first, but I didn't care.

The evil eye was blinking, so I decided to listen to the messages while I made some decent coffee. There were the expected garbled messages from Ruby Bee, interspersed with increasingly distraught ones from Jack. This continued long enough for me to fill a mug and settle behind my desk. There was a bizarre message from Roy about someone who'd attempted to stick up the poker game, followed by a second sarcastic one saying he'd taken the interloper to the county jail. Elsie McMay left a message that she'd shot out a window at the high school but would have a word with the principal and handle the matter herself. Dahlia had called to say that I didn't have to worry about her granny anymore. Since I'd totally forgotten about it, I was pleased, although I would have to call her back at some point and make sure Dahlia hadn't carried through with her threat to dump her granny on a back road.

The message that rocked my socks was

from Eileen Buchanon, Maggody's very own missing person. She was calling, she claimed, from a motel near Mount Rushmore, and had maxed out her credit card buying souvenirs. If Earl didn't wire her money, she'd be obliged to hold up a liquor store to pay for enough gas to get home.

I pushed the replay button and listened to the message again. That was going to require my immediate attention, I realized. I made a note of the name of the motel and the town so I could call Earl with the details. It had the makings of a real interesting homecoming party.

I fixed myself another cup of coffee and called Harve. The dispatcher, who now seemed to consider me her best friend, warned me that he'd been even more churlish than usual when he came in. I thanked her politely.

"So what's going on?" I said as soon as he picked up the receiver.

"A day without you would be a day with sunshine. It'd include fishing, beer, a picnic basket filled with Mrs. Dorfer's ham salad sandwiches and fudge brownies." He stopped and scritched matches until his cigar was lit. "Dawn Dartmouth is not enjoying our hospitality, but the boys from the psych unit at the hospital are gonna pick her up any minute. It took four of my deputies to haul Toby Mann out of the gym. I couldn't think of anything to charge him with, but I was skittish about turning him loose. He's in the break room right now, signing autographs. We left Dr. Stonebridge to sleep it off. He's gonna be right bewildered when he wakes up and finds out he's the only one out there."

"What about Dr. Dibbins?" I asked. "Did he make it?"

"Oh, yeah, he most certainly did. The hospital administrator's already called this morning, demanding that we take him off their hands. I told him it wasn't any of our business. Brenda Skiller's staying with him, driving the nurses up the damn wall. I left a message for the prosecutor, but he's not likely to call me back until he gets to his office tomorrow morning." He paused for a moment, then added, "We found the Mexicans, in case you was worried about them. That accident last night that Palsy went out to see about — one of the vehicles was the van from the Stonebridge Foundation. None of them must have been injured, 'cause they were long gone when he arrived. Think I should inform the immigration boys?"

"Let 'em be," I said. "Maybe they'll find less stressful work and end up paying taxes like the rest of us."

"What the hell," Harve said magnanimously. "You don't have to spend the day hunting for that wacky senator, by the way. She's already over at the psych ward, trying to recruit the staff to join the revolution. I don't think she signed anybody up yet, but you never know. Guess I'll be calling all the patients' families today, telling them what-all's been going on."

"The media on it yet? Are you going to get some publicity for all your diligence and hard work?"

I could almost see the gloat on his face. "Might just happen 'long about noon," he said, puffing on his cigar. "Might see my face on the front page tomorrow, if I can keep the prosecutor from claiming all the credit."

"I guess the only person we're still missing is Walter Kaiser."

"Oh, we got him locked up, too. That dispatcher, whatever her name is, told you about there being a hostage situation, right? Well, it turned out to be the Kaiser fellow right in the thick of it."

"He took somebody hostage?" I said, astonished. "He seemed way too laid-back to bother."

Harve laughed. "He claims he was the hostage. Seems he went to the bar and picked up a pretty little thing, not knowing that her boyfriend was an ex-Marine. He lured her out to that hippie van of his. The boyfriend didn't much like this, so he started taking potshots in the parking lot. It gets kinda confusing after that, but the best I could tell, the girl skedaddled away. Her boyfriend and Walter ended up in the van, smoking pot and threatening to kill anybody who got within a hundred feet. We just waited until Walter came outside to piss, and grabbed him, then busted into the van and handcuffed one really messed-up ex-Marine."

"And that's why I was out at the Stonebridge without any backup? So you could sit in your car and wait half the night? I could have been killed, you know."

"But you weren't, so quit your yammering. I'll expect your reports in the morning, typed up real nice and neat."

I was tempted to throw my mug at the wall. "In the morning, you asshole? You'll be lucky to get them in three days."

"Nine o'clock, on my desk. Have a nice day."

I slammed down the receiver, then rocked back and willed myself to settle down. It

488

seemed like I was going off like a firecracker more often than was healthy. Maybe it was nothing more than PMS, I thought as I inspected the map of South America on the ceiling. The spider had disappeared into the rain forest, or more likely, the crack by the wall. He'd be back, and I supposed I would be, too. Unless I got a better offer.

Ruby Bee and Estelle were munching biscuits at the end of the bar. Ruby Bee looked over her shoulder at the clock. "Arly might be along shortly," she said.

"And?"

"I don't know. What do you think?"

Estelle dabbed her lip with a napkin. "You could tell her."

"I thought about it all last night, once she'd called to let me know she was okay. That fellow from Springfield stayed with her. I saw him driving off this morning."

"You're avoiding the issue."

Ruby Bee sighed. "Maybe it's best to let her figure it out herself. I don't want her to think I'm butting into her private affairs."

"Maybe so," said Estelle. "She must not have noticed she missed her period last month, but she's gonna miss another one before too long."

"It ain't gonna be easy," Ruby Bee said,

mostly to herself. "But it's not up to us to tell her what to do." She wiped her eyes. "You want some more coffee?"

"I'm thinking I might have a small glass of sherry."

"That's the best idea I reckon I've heard in a long while."

About the Author

Joan Hess is the author of thirty mysteries, including fifteen in the Maggody series. A former president of the American Crime Writers League and current president of the Arkansas Mystery Writers Alliance, she lives in Fayetteville, Arkansas.